"Johnnie Jones is a very creative writer. He is biblically sound in his research, yet very thought provoking in his presentation. I highly recommend his novel on Acts."

—Dr. Mike Smith, President
Jacksonville College, Jacksonville, Texas

"Two thousand years separate us from the disciples' paths and the hardships they endured. In Acts of the Spirit-Filled, *Johnnie Jones retells the acts of the first-century believers in a way that challenges us today to reconsider our mission as the body of Christ. This book will remind you of the power of God and His coming Kingdom. Around the world today, there is a tsunami of sexual immorality. Our need to make disciples and plant churches is vital. If read seriously, Johnnie's book will help us stem the tides of today's spiritual storms."*

—Derek Ross, National Director
True Love Waits Philippines
www.truelovewaitsphilippines.org/

"When I read this novel, I was taken back to a time and place that I'd always heard about, but had a hard time envisioning. Acts of the Spirit-Filled *takes you on the roads of Bible times and into dramatic events that keep you wanting to read more. You won't want to put this book down as you read the events that the apostles and others experienced in this time period. Straight from the Scriptures, this novel gives a unique behind-the-scenes look as only a novel could do. Johnnie Jones writes with an accurate knowledge of the Scriptures and history while telling a story worth sharing with everyone, Christian or not."*

—Jenny M.

Other books by the author:

Acts of the Spirit-Filled: Volume 1

Acts of the Spirit-Filled: Volume 2

50/50 Chance to Live – An Autobiography

Transformed! – The Power of God's Presence

Metamorphosis – Changes from Within

Metamorphosis 2 – The Transforming Power of Intimacy with God

Children's Guide to Discovering Jesus – Activity Pages

Diakonos – A Word Study and Service Guide for the Deacon Ministry

P.E.D.A.L. Plan for Evangelism

Hey! What's So Special About Christians?

Refer to "About the Author" in the back of this volume for information on his other books.

What others are saying about
Acts of the Spirit-Filled

"Johnnie Jones has a unique ability to take the narrative of the beginning time of our faith and packaging it into a compelling drama of how it played out in real life in the first century. One finds himself in the midst of the unfolding drama of the new church and its challenges. True to the New Testament revelation in the book of Acts, it reveals real people facing real challenges and experiencing triumph in the midst of a hostile world."

—Dr. Jimmy Draper, President Emeritus
LifeWay Christian Resources

"I've been through many [Bible studies] in my 85 years of church work . . . none of them made me realize the job that Christ left the Apostles to do . . . This truth even makes the survival of the Scriptures more of a miracle for me. Thank you for the joy of truths revealed to me by the Holy Spirit, as I read your books."

—Myra Z.

"As a young boy I attempted to read the Bible as a story. I failed because I could not get my imagination in gear, lacking the knowledge of the Ancient world. All through seminary and graduate school I studied Scripture as most preachers do. When I read the first two volumes of Johnnie Jones' books I found what I needed. His understanding of the ancient world has added clarity to the action of Acts.

"In Volume 3, we follow Paul from Felix to the Emperor of Rome through the waters of the Mediterranean Sea to the fertile mission field of Italy and beyond. The journey is exciting adding a different light to the book of Acts without taking anything away from the God-inspired text. This labor-of-love trilogy would be a welcomed addition to any library."

—Dr. Rickey Hargrave, Pastor
Chestnut Community Church, McKinney, TX

"Acts of the Spirit Filled, Volume 3, *is already on my 'must read' list. The few pages I have read have increased my anticipation. I am not normally a fiction reader, but these pages have put vivid pictures of the people, the scenes, and the attitudes of the characters in this reader's mind. It is surprising how quickly I began identifying with these men in the Scriptures and how clearly their passion for the Gospel is called out. Modern 'disciples' pale in comparison. If John-nie Jones intended to motivate his readers, he has certainly hit the target."*

—Jim S.

"I always enjoy biblical fiction, but this is the first time I've read any like this. I really like this concept of taking one book of the Bible and telling the story chapter by chapter. This brings the history of our faith to life. I'm looking forward to the next volume."

—Blogger Review

"Acts of the Spirit-Filled *is dramatically Christ-filled, projecting the life and times of the apostles—who were mere people, after all—and what they must have gone through as their faith was challenged in following the risen Christ during the establishment of His Church. Sure, this story projects personal stories to fill in the gaps left open by Scripture. But by filling in those gaps, we're motivated to think what our own stories might be like as well. It's a novel that makes us think: What if I were truly Spirit-filled? How would I act?"*

—Kat Christian, Author of *The Magic Flower*

"This book was exciting and spirit-filled. You could envision what was going on in every scene. What an interesting spin on the life and times of early Christians! Looking forward to the next vol-ume. Keep the books coming, Mr. Jones."

—JMart (Amazon Kindle eBook review, Vol. 2).

Johnnie R. Jones

Acts
of the
Spirit-Filled

Volume 3

a novel
of the
first century

CrossHouse Publishing
2844 S. FM 549
Suite A
Rockwall, TX 75032
www.crosshousebooks.com

The Arial Narrow font used in this volume designates quotations from the
Scriptures (paraphrased by the author) and dialogue by God, Jesus, and
the Holy Spirit.

ISBN: 978-1-61315-050-4
Library of Congress: 2014940973

Contents

* Some years not recorded

＆ ❧

Anno
Domini
59

Circa

❧ ＆

"Where is Cornelius?" The rippled lines across his stocky face revealed the impatience of Felix, governor of the Judean province.

A chamber guard snapped to attention. "My Lord, he has gone to the docks to receive replacement soldiers from Rome."

"Bring him to me as soon as he returns." Felix took several gulps of wine as he stared out the western window, allowing the sea breeze to cool his face. Caesarea was a busy seaport for bringing Roman supplies and soldiers into the region.

His wife, Drusilla walked into the room and joined him by the window. "Do you think he suspects anything?"

"Cornelius? By the gods, no! He would never hold any secrets from me. I've been much too tolerant of his kindness with our prisoners for him to plot anything against me."

She squeezed his hand. "He's still a Roman soldier."

"Enough with such silly talk. He has helped bring civil relations with the cities of Tyre and Sidon. Plus we have more peace with the Jews in our city here than with those in Jerusalem— thanks to him."

She pulled his cup to her mouth and sipped from it. "Then why hasn't he brought us money for the release of that deranged prophet?"

"Paul?" Felix stole his cup from her clutch, drank the remaining wine, and threw it to the floor. A servant ran over and snatched the container, wiping the floor before scurrying away. "We need more time."

"Time?" Drusilla turned away from the window. "My dear, it's been two years now and all we have received from this man are words—condemning words!"

Felix turned and looked out toward the sea. "I find his words intriguing."

"I hate his words! He is a crazed man, speaking of a dead Man he claims to be alive again!" She stepped in, close to his ear, and whispered: "Words will not buy us anything." Then she stepped back and got louder. "We have exhausted all our tactics on the local authorities and we must leave before the emperor gets word of the missing funds."

† † †

"Are you certain of these moves?" Emperor Nero gave General Septanius a chilling stare.

"Divine One, these reports come from the best sources of the region. And we've had several centurions from Samaria confirm it."

Nero picked up his lyre and began to strum a faint tune. "Then bring Felix and his wife before me . . . and place Festus in his stead."

"Yes, Divine One; right away!" The general turned to leave.

"Wait!" Nero stopped his strum. "Make sure Festus knows that I want an account of the affairs of Judea. Tell him to put the fear of our gods upon those superstitious rebels."

Six months later

"**G**uards! . . . Guards!" Two soldiers appeared at the doorway. Festus looked them over. "That was fast—and I expect it to stay that way. I want to travel to Jerusalem, so prepare me a chariot with several soldiers to accompany me."

"Your Excellency," one of the guards said, "traveling to Jerusalem requires at least fifty of our finest horsemen and one hundred foot soldiers."

"What?! And why is that?"

"Because Jews hate Romans, sir, and bandits live out along the trail. They have scouts and they watch for us."

Festus thought for a moment. "Have the necessary soldiers ready to travel at first daylight."

In Jerusalem, Festus was led to the regiment of soldiers that camped outside the city walls. Then, with a dozen fresh soldiers, he entered the city and proceeded to the temple grounds. As he made his way through the porch entryway, several temple guards appeared.

"You must stop here!" a temple guard commanded.

Festus was appalled at the guard's command. He made his way to the front of his soldiers. "And who commands you to halt your governor?" The dozen soldiers unsheathed their swords as Festus neared the guards.

The temple guards withdrew their spears and knelt on one knee. "Our deepest apologies, your Excellency. We are under orders by the high priest, who is appointed by the emperor and given local jurisdiction of this religious site."

Festus motioned to his soldiers who immediately sheathed their weapons. He stepped up closer to the guards. "You have responded well. Now do not hesitate to bring the high priest to me."

In a matter of minutes the guards returned with the high priest. "Greetings, Most Noble Festus. I am Ishmael. What gives us the honor of your visit?"

"Dispense with the accolades, Ishmael. As the new governor, I want to see what is worth defending and what is not."

"Then you will love seeing our great temple from the Gentile's porch."

He peered beyond the high priest. "Oh, so there's a place in the temple where I cannot visit?"

Ishmael tried to discern if this was a trick question. *I must try a diversion.* "Sir, might I ask a favor of you? There is a man in custody in Caesarea, named Paul. He was once called Saul of Tarsus and was about to become a member of our council.

"However, he turned against us and tried to incite civil unrest here in Jerusalem. We arrested him and were to try him, but he was taken into custody by one of your commanders." He pointed to other priests and scribes nearby. "Many of these men will confirm what I am saying.

"Now this man has been under house arrest, by Felix, for two years! We would like to clear this matter up, freeing you from having to bother with him."

The diversion worked. "And what do you propose we do?"

"Bring him to Jerusalem. Let us deal with the man."

"And would he have anything to do with all those bandits that I had to defend myself from on my way to Jerusalem?"

Ishmael kept a straight face. "My dear governor, I cannot control those who turn to violence, whether it's over the emperor's injustices or taxation. We are a peaceful people who only seek justice for those who violate our laws—like this Saul of Tarsus."

Festus felt one of the porch columns and then leaned against it, facing Ishmael. "There must be a reason for him being sent from Jerusalem to Caesarea. Usually men are tried in the city of their alleged crime. No, this man, Paul, will remain in Caesarea. You can gather a group of your men who are familiar with the incident and they may travel back with me, under my protection. There we will discover what crimes this man has committed."

"Agreed," Ishmael said. "And while my team of men are assembled for this trip, please allow me to show you some of the finer areas of Jerusalem."

"That's not necessary. I prefer to blend in with the locals to see if I really know their needs. You get your team together and I will let you know when we leave for Caesarea."

✝✝✝

"Time to go to court." Paul's usual smile turned into a frown when he saw chains in Cornelius's hands.

"Chains?"

"By order of the new governor."

Paul looked at the chains and then looked back at Cornelius. "I am bound by theses chains, but I am freer than those who have chains on their hearts."

"Then I pray our God will set some people free of their inner chains today."

Governor Festus and the high priest's entourage were seated before Paul was brought in. The governor raised his hand.

"Bring in the accused!" the captain of the guards cried out. Paul walked in with his traditional limp, making sure the clanging of his chains was heard. Some of the priests began hurling remarks at him. Ishmael, the high priest, raised his hand to silence his comrades.

"That's more like it," Festus said. Everyone was seated except Paul and Ishmael. "The records show that the Jews have a counselor—a Tertullus?"

Ishmael turned toward the governor. "We, the priests, feel it is better for us to speak for ourselves, Most Noble Festus."

"Then speak your accusations against this man."

For about thirty minutes, accusation after accusation was hurled at Paul by the priests, yet none of them displayed any proof to substantiate their accusations.

When they were finished, Festus gave Paul the floor. "Most Noble Festus, I have not offended our Jewish laws, I have not defiled the temple, and I have said nothing that is against the emperor. All their accusations are unfounded."

Once again, several priests began hurling accusations toward Paul. Festus stood up. "Silence in this court!" A hush fell over the crowd. "All I hear from you Jews are minor accusations contrary to your religious customs." He sat down again.

"He is a threat to our customs and traditions," Ishmael said. "In Jerusalem, we try our cases and we get a verdict."

Festus rubbed his chin as he thought this matter over. He turned to Paul. "Are you willing to return to Jerusalem so that I may get a better understanding of exactly what is going on here?"

Paul looked at the priests and then faced Festus. "I stand before you in Caesar's court and should be judged right here. It is clear that I have done no wrong against these men. If I was guilty and deserved punishment, I would not object. But if there is no substance in their accusations here, I would be mad to go back to Jerusalem. My legal rights as a Roman citizen allow no one to deliver me to these blood-thirsty men." Then Paul raised his voice: "I APPEAL TO CAESAR!"

For a moment, silence prevailed. One of the priests mumbled, "What does that mean?"

Festus turned and spoke briefly with his legal counselors. He then stood up and turned to Paul. "You are a Roman citizen; you have appealed to Caesar? Then to Caesar you will go!"

Ishmael cried out: "He can't do that!"

"Oh yes he can," Festus said. "This hearing is adjourned. Take the accused back to his quarters while I arrange for his deportation." Festus walked out of the judgment hall, while Cornelius and six guards led Paul away.

The priests appeared stunned. "We had him right here and now he's getting away again," one of them said.

"We may as well give up on this cause," another one said.

"Never!" Ishmael said. "We will follow him to Rome. There we will buy the emperor enough gifts that he will see how wise it is to show favor toward us."

"Where will we get the funds to travel to Rome?" another priest asked.

"And what gifts can we afford to appease Caesar?" another asked.

Ishmael looked angrily toward his fellow priests. "If necessary, we'll take every fund in the temple treasury to bring this man down!"

"What about the poor?" someone asked.

"This is more important than feeding the poor. We must save ourselves first!"

† † †

"She's a commoner, Mother—not a 'slave'." Nero continued to practice his dance moves, ignoring the ranting of his mother, Agrippina.

"You are married into the divine line of the Caesars. I made everything happen so that you would exalt this position and become the greatest of Caesars." Agrippina walked quickly up to his face, stopping his moves. "By the gods, I shall see you do not disgrace it!"

Nero moved in closer to her face. "Do I detect a threat from you, Mother?" In her eyes, he saw the woman who orchestrated the poisoning of Claudius.

"A threat? I do not make threats. But I can make life near impossible for others who would dare jeopardize the fate of the Caesars." She turned away from him and stormed out of the room. "I should have let Britannicus become the emperor!" she said, as she entered the hallway. "At least he would keep the royal line free of slaves!"

Nero stood there for a moment, his mind rehearsing the many disruptive encounters he had already experienced with his mother. The more he thought of her, the angrier he became. *Am I her puppet? She is not interested in me and what I desire. She wants to rule Rome and make life miserable for me . . . She is so stubborn! She wants Britannicus to be emperor, does she? I'll put a stop to that! . . .* "Guards!" Several soldiers entered the room. "Fetch me Seneca, Burrus, and Aniceteus. Tell them it is urgent."

Rome was not only noted as the melting pot of the civilized world's cultures, but also of the many varieties of foods from every corner of the world. It was always a delight to the taste buds when the emperor had an extravagant meal planned for the senate leaders. It could also be a dangerous gathering for anyone who was on Nero's "hit list."

About fifty people were enjoying the festive meal. Agrippina was there as well as Britannicus and his girlfriend. Nero was his usual loud and boisterous self. Near the end of the first course of the meal, a chef brought out a cup of steaming tea for Nero.

"And what is this?" Nero asked, as he sipped it.

"It is a special black tea from the Far East," the chef said.

Nero sipped it again. "Mmmm! It tastes very smooth—but very hot!" He stood up. "Do any of you care to join me in a drink to honor the Far East and their delightful teas?" No one moved. Finally Britannicus stood up, followed by his girlfriend. Next Agrippina stood as well. Before long about half the group had received the tea.

Britannicus sipped it before the toast. "By the gods! This *is* hot!"

Nero laughed. "My younger brother, do you have sensitive lips?" Nero looked around. "Where's Anicetus? There you are—come quickly!" Anicetus was soon at Nero's side. "Chef, give Anicetus some cool water to give to my brother for his hot tea." Several others requested cool water as well. Anicetus gave Britannicus a small cup of water. Servants throughout the room began pouring water into everyone's tea—just a small amount to cool the drink.

Nero held up his cup. "To the Far East; may they have a golden harvest of tea this year." Nero then began drinking his tea, everyone following his lead. "Mmmm, didn't I tell you how smooth it goes down?" Again, everyone took another drink of tea.

Suddenly the chatter around the tables was interrupted by a loud scream. Britannicus's girlfriend screamed as he gagged while grasping his throat. He fell to the floor while convulsing.

"Where's the doctor?!" Agrippina shouted.

In a matter of minutes, the palace doctor showed up. He loosened the collar around Britannicus. "Get him to a room with a bed!" the doctor said.

Several servants lifted Britannicus and took him away, his girlfriend and Agrippina following. Nero looked around the area that was now quiet. "We cannot allow this meal to waste. Please continue eating and be merry. Your emperor insists upon it." He smiled as he once again sipped his tea. Soon, everyone else began talking and eating as if nothing happened.

†††

"Make sure you wear your red gown for the visit," Agrippa said.

"How does this look?" Bernice spun around, as she displayed her toying tactics. "Do you think this will seduce him?" She spun her body again, allowing the shimmering red gown to swirl out from her body. Her fingernails and toenails were painted in matching red.

He walked up to her backside and wrapped his arms around her waist. "You will seduce only me," he said as he kissed her neck.

Bernice gently pulled away from him, turning to face him. "Now, now, you mustn't have feelings for me; I'm your sister." She smiled as she broke away from his arms. "And besides that, what if Festus is the rich ruler for whom we seek?"

Agrippa laughed. "He is definitely not rich. But the more of these men we get to know, the better our standing with Nero." A guard knocked on the door. "Yes?"

"Your Most Excellency, Governor Festus is here to greet you."

"Take him to the receiving chambers and seat him. We will be there momentarily." Agrippa watched Bernice as she sat down and adjusted her hair piece. "These people are always in such a hurry!"

"Maybe he's anxious to see you?"

"Maybe; but these visits always have some favor tied to it."

"King Agrippa, such an honor to be in your presence."

"And congratulations on your promotion, Festus."

Festus turned his gaze toward Bernice. "And who is this charming woman?"

"This is my sister and acting queen, Bernice."

Festus bowed and kissed her hand. "May you find your visit pleasurable, dear Queen Bernice. Your beauty far surpasses all reports of you." Bernice smiled and nodded her head. Festus then turned to Agrippa. "And what brings you to Caesarea?"

"Oh, I just wanted to check on the palace and to meet you."

"The grounds and quarters have been well kept."

"Yes, I noticed; but some guards were stationed at one of the guest quarters."

"Yes, Felix left me with a bit of a problem. I have a Jewish leader who has been accused of heresy, sacrilege, and treason. And his accusers are the high priest and his council."

"Really? And who is the accused?"

"His name is Paul of Tarsus. His accusation papers call him Saul and say he is a Pharisee and a member of the sect that follows that dead man, Jesus, who they say rose up from the dead."

"Oh?"

"Yes, and he's also a Roman citizen. This whole case is about their religious beliefs. Now that you're here, perhaps you could help me?"

"And how can I help you?" Agrippa was delighted that Festus asked for help because he knew that Festus would be indebted to him.

"Well, I asked Paul if we could move the trial back to Jerusalem where I might get some assistance in understanding all these religious procedures and customs; however, he refused and appealed his case to the emperor. So now I have to deport him with an order to Rome."

"I understand your frustration. Bernice and I are well versed in the ways of the Jews. Perhaps we could hear his story?"

"Great! I'll arrange a hearing in the morning. And I hope you will accept my dinner invitation for tonight?"

"We would be most honored; Bernice?"

"Lovely."

The next morning

Horns were blown as Agrippa and Bernice entered the stadium. He stopped their walk for a moment to take it all in. "This could be the day." She smiled but said nothing.

The local Roman officers were seated with the important men of the city. Roman soldiers formed two rows in a semi-circle around the backside of the stadium. Additional soldiers formed a pathway for all the delegates to walk through. Agrippa and Bernice marched down the pathway, dressed in their full official robes.

Festus was also dressed in his formal attire. He stood in front of the judgment seat as the king and queen were seated. When he raised his hand, the music ceased. "Everyone, be seated." There was a brief moment, as the people adjusted themselves in their seats. Festus motioned to the guards. "Bring in the prisoner."

A large door slowly opened from the side of the stadium, about fifty yards away. At first there was silence. Soon the rattling of chains broke the silence as several guards used the tips of their swords to push a short-statured man into the stadium. Paul slowly limped in, dressed in a simple garment, allowing the chains attached to him to produce as much sound as possible.

As Paul neared his assigned place, Festus quieted the crowd. "Friends, Romans, and fellow members of this fair city, I introduce to you our special guests: King Agrippa and Queen Bernice!" Once again the horns and the audience roared as if a conquering gladiator had just entered the arena.

Festus quieted the crowd again and faced his guests. "King Agrippa, all the Jews of Caesarea and of Jerusalem have complained about this man's teachings and activities. They say he should not live any longer. After questioning him and listening to his accusers, I have heard no accusation worthy of putting him to death. Since he has made an appeal to stand before the emperor, I need to know what to write about him. So that is why we meet this morning. Perhaps after he speaks you will find some reason for me to write on his order, because it would be a waste of time to send him to Rome without a legitimate charge."

grippa stood up and walked over to Paul to get a better look at him. Paul's receding hairline and unkempt beard caused the king look at him in disgust. "You may speak freely when I am seated."

As Paul watched the king sit down, he remembered the words of his Lord who said he would testify before rulers and kings. *My Lord, give me strength to speak. Weigh their heart chains down with conviction.* Paul bowed before Festus and the king and queen. "King Agrippa, I consider myself most fortunate to speak before someone such as you, for you know the customs of the Jews. From my childhood, I have lived an impeccable life as a Jew. I grew up in training as a Pharisee and was mentored by Rabban Gamaliel himself.

"Your Majesty, I am on trial because I believe our God keeps His promises. All our ancestors believed God and they worshipped Him day and night. They believed God could bring a dead person back to life—but my accusers do not!

"I was once a man who refused to believe in the one named Jesus of Nazareth. In Jerusalem, I was given the authority to lock up the followers of Jesus in prison. I went door-to-door dragging these followers out of their houses, forcing them to curse His name, and casting my vote to have many killed. I was so zealous that I hunted them down in other towns as well.

"I was on such an authorized trip to Damascus when, at noon, a brilliant light burst forth from the sky. We all fell off our horses, blinded by the light. Then I heard a voice speaking to me, in Hebrew, from within the light: 'Saul, Saul, who are you that persecutes Me? Your task is impossible, for you are resisting Me!' I asked, 'Who are you, Lord?' And the voice answered, 'I am Jesus—I am the one you persecute. But I have decided to use you as My servant and as a proclaimer of what you have seen and heard. I will protect you from the Jews and the Gentiles as you open their eyes to the light of the truth and turn them from the darkness of the evil one, wrestling them out of his control and placing them into the control of God. Then I will forgive them of their sins and allow them to share My blessings with others as they seek to become holy while believing in Me.'

"Oh King Agrippa, from then on I could not disobey this revelation from heaven. Instead of locking people up, I began setting people free with this message from God. I first told the Jews at Damascus. Later I returned to Jerusalem and into the regions of Judea. But the power of the message did not stop with the Jews. Soon Gentiles were receiving forgiveness of sins the same way as we Jews did. Now the message I proclaimed was not easy. I told them that they had to show evidence of change by repentance of the way they acted and to turn toward God.

"This is why the Jews at the temple tried to kill me. As God is my witness, I stand before all men today—poor and rich!—proclaiming what Moses and the prophets said would come to pass: that the Messiah would come as a humble Servant, suffering at the hands of the Jewish leaders. As the prophets said, the Messiah would be the first to come back to life and send out His messengers to spread the light of life to all peoples."

Festus was overwhelmed at such statements. He jumped up. "You are insane, Paul! This new understanding has driven you crazy!"

"No, Most Excellent Festus, I am not crazy. What I have testified is both true and sane. What I speak today before the king is something that he has already heard. None of these teachings have been kept secret, so I know that he has heard of these things. King Agrippa, you do believe the message of our prophets, don't you? I feel certain that you do."

Agrippa was silent for a moment. He did not want to reveal that Paul's message had troubled him. "Paul, you almost make me want to follow this Jesus, just like you."

"I pray to God that not only you, but that everyone listening to my testimony today would immediately and fully become as I am." Then, slowly raising his arms: "Except for these chains, of course."

Agrippa stood up. "I've heard enough."

"You are dismissed, Paul," Festus said. Once again, the spears prodded Paul out of the area. As he was being led out, Festus turned to his guests. "You see why this is difficult for me? This man has done nothing deserving death or imprisonment."

"I agree," Agrippa said. "This man could be set free today had he not appealed to the emperor."

Acts 27

"Luke, I don't know if they listened to me or not," Paul said, as Luke treated his eyes.

"Oh, from what I heard on the streets, you told them how the camel eats the straw. I doubt they will hear you any further."

Paul remained imprisoned for another week. While waiting for his orders, many Christians came to visit Paul and encouraged him. Finally Cornelius returned. "Paul, Luke, it's good to see you again. Have my men taken good care of you?"

"Superbly," Paul said.

"Well, I have your orders, from the governor. You are to set sail for Rome immediately. I am arranging for you to travel with a former officer of mine, Julius. He was recently transferred to the emperor's fleet and has a group of prisoners to take to Rome.

I spoke to him about the need for your personal physician and a personal body guard. So Luke, I want you to go with Paul. But before you do, find someone who is seaworthy and capable of helping him, should he need protecting."

Luke stood up. "I will see to it."

Cornelius moved toward Paul and embraced him. "My brother, God has His hand upon you. I will continue working on these folks here at Caesarea while you go and convert that emperor and his family to Jesus."

"If God allows, I will, my brother."

"Day after tomorrow, your ship lets out of its dock. Your orders will be delivered to Julius by the guards who escort you to the ship. May our Lord provide and protect you on your way."

"Thank you, Cornelius. You have been a God-send in my life." Cornelius left the room. Paul sat there momentarily. "Luke, I want you to go to the local fellowship here and have them send a runner to Antioch. I will jot a few lines asking the fellowship at Antioch to send other runners to all the Asian fellowships, letting them know where we are going. I want them to send runners into Macedonia to share the same news, asking everyone to pray for us daily."

"I will do that, Paul."

"A body guard? Do I need a body guard?"

"I think it would be a wise addition for our trip."

"But I don't know anyone here in this city."

"Let me handle that. I think I might have just the man in mind."

Several days later

"State your name."

"Paul of Tarsus." The Roman soldier checked his manifest and nodded to the soldier who accompanied him. Paul thanked the soldier and stepped past the other soldier checking in the prisoners for the voyage of the Adramyttium.

Two men followed Paul. "Stop!" the soldier said. "Who are you?"

Paul responded: "Officer, these men are my servants. They have been given clearance by the governor."

"A prisoner with servants?" He laughed as he scanned over the manifest. I see no documentation for these two. You shall not pass."

"What's the problem?" Julius walked up from behind the soldier.

"Sir, this prisoner claims to have permission for two servants of his to travel with him."

"Let me see his papers." Julius took the orders from the soldier. "Oh, so you're the special cargo that Cornelius told me about." He walked over to Paul. "These men may accompany you, but you must still be chained to one of my men. Register the servants' names and let them pass."

"Your name?"

"Luke of Cilicia."

"Aristarchus of Thessalonica."

Julius turned to Paul. "If these servants impede our mission in any way they will be cast off the ship."

Paul looked at him, momentarily, and then motioned for Luke and Aristarchus to follow him. As they neared the boarding rail, another soldier stepped up to Paul with a long chain. He smiled. "Well what do we have here? A rich prisoner?"

"No, officer," Paul said. "I have an appointment with the emperor. Governor Festus and King Agrippa wanted to make sure I get to Rome in one piece."

"With the fall equinox approaching, we'll be lucky to make it to Crete."

Within the hour, the ship set sail to follow the coastline north to Sidon. Julius allowed Paul (with Luke, Aristarchus, and his chained guard) to visit fellow followers in Sidon while the ship unloaded and uploaded some of its cargo. Next, the ship continued northward along the coastline. The captain navigated the ship to the north side of Cyprus, hoping for more favorable winds.

"The shoreline of Cilicia," Luke said.

Paul moved over to the ship's rail to look with him. "You and I may never see our hometowns again."

Luke smiled. "It looks like the rest of the Asian shoreline to me. Don't miss it a bit."

Several days later, the ship docked at Myra. Since it had a major unloading necessary, Julius looked for another ship by which he and his prisoners might continue their journey. A ship from Alexandria, on its way to Italy, was found and space was procured for the prisoners.

For several days the ship had difficulty sailing. Paul was allowed to stand on the deck and watch the captain and pilot navigate through the tumultuous waters. The captain seemed unsure about the route, so Paul offered his help. "I have sailed this route numerous times," he said to the captain. So Paul's advice was heeded, which produced a safe journey past the island of Cnidus.

However, the winds would not allow for any direction than toward the island of Crete. Soon, Salmone of Crete was straight ahead. After anchoring there for the evening, the ship resumed its journey along the south side of Crete. The winds constantly churned the waters, causing great difficulty for the ship. Finally, it docked at Fair Havens, near the city of Lasea.

The next day, while the food supplies were replenished on the ship, the captain and pilot met with several of the Roman officers and the commerce owner. Paul was allowed to join them. They were discussing where the ship should anchor down for the winter.

"I say we go to Phoenix," the commerce owner said. The captain studied the flag on the mast.

Paul interrupted their discussion. "Men, it is past The Day of Atonement—very dangerous to proceed farther. A nor'easter can attack our sails any day now and if it does we will face disaster, causing us to lose the cargo, perhaps damage the ship, and the possible loss of lives."

The commerce owner laughed. "What does this superstitious prisoner know?" He turned to Paul. "Have you ever piloted a large ship before?"

"No, I have not; but I've been in this area before when a strong nor'easter hit."

The captain looked at the flag again. "What do you think?" he asked the pilot.

The pilot studied the flag. "The winds are favorable right now, so I'm good to go."

The captain turned to the Roman officers. "Men, do you have an opinion?"

"We're not sailors," Julius said, "so it's your call."

He looked at the flag one more time. A south wind blew lightly. "Let's raise anchor and set our sails for Phoenix."

About thirty minutes later, the south wind picked up. "Oarsman," the captain said, "steer us farther out to sea." The command was obeyed and the ship began its usual trek westward. Soon, the shoreline became a light-blue, hazy silhouette.

Suddenly, the wind died down. For a moment, the ship's flag fell limp and the sails rolled and popped against the mast. Puffy clouds from the northeast began to thicken, growing darker by the minute. The flag fluttered around its rope as it turned in a southwestward direction.

"A nor'easter!" someone cried. "A nor'easter!"

"Drop the sails!" the captain ordered. "Steer into the wind!" As the ship turned into the wind, the sea's waves became choppier, tossing the ship like a piece of driftwood.

"Harder, men!" the oarsman cried. The more they tried to steer the ship, the worse it became. The darkened clouds opened up, creating a torrential rainstorm. Navigating against the wind became impossible. Soon the ship passed the small island of Clauda, a few miles southwest of Crete. The winds continued blowing from the northeast. In a matter of minutes, the waves crested above the ship's deck, tossing some of the deck's nomenclature overboard.

"Reel in the lifeboats!" the captain ordered. "Take the ropes and run them below the ship's deck! Quick! Lower all the sails!"

The next day continued to be a stormy day. The rain was heavy and cold. The captain thought of a worse-case scenario: *The sandbars of Lybia!*

"Throw the cargo overboard," the captain ordered.

"No!" the commerce owner cried. "You can't do that!"

The captain pointed at a Roman soldier. "Take him beneath the deck!"

The ship continued tossing violently for the next three days. Wave after wave of torrential rain pounded the ship's deck. The captain wiped his face. He wondered, *Is there any hope of survival?* He hurried to the oarsman. "Suggestions?!"

"Throw all our equipment overboard. Make the ship as light as possible. Our only hope is for the currents to push us in a northwestward direction when we near the Port of Spain!"

"That far?!"

"Maybe!"

The captain shouted to the rowers: "Men we must try to turn the ship toward the northwest!"

It was then when Paul showed up on deck. "You should have followed my advice!" Paul shouted to the captain. "But I'm here to tell you to be courageous! A messenger of my God came to me in the night and told me that the ship will not be spared—only our lives!"

"A messenger from your God?" the captain asked.

"Yes, an angel; he stood by me last night and told me, 'Paul! Don't be afraid! You must defend yourself before the emperor.' Therefore, God has granted safety to everyone on this ship." Paul then turned to the rest of the crew. "Take courage men, for I believe everything that my God has told me. But be reminded, this ship will run aground somewhere."

Fourteen days later and the ship still drifted in the Great Sea. The crew began plumbing the depths. The first measurement was 120 feet; then a little later, it was ninety feet. "We're going aground soon," the oarsman told the captain.

"Go to the back and drop all four anchors. Maybe we can slow her down until daybreak."

The oarsman went to the crew. He spoke softly to several lead crew members. "Go let down several anchors in the rear and begin lowering the lifeboat. I'll tell the captain that we need the lifeboat to manage the anchors in the front."

"What's your plan?" one of the lead men asked.

"This ship is too large to manage when it runs aground. The lifeboat is our only hope of survival."

Paul returned to the deck to check on the captain. He watched as the crew members let down two anchors and then began lowering the lifeboat. He went to the captain. "What's going on in the rear?"

"I've instructed the crew to lower all the anchors to slow us down until daybreak."

"I saw them drop only half the anchors and they are now lowering the lifeboat. If your crew abandons the ship, you have no hope of staying alive."

"What?!" The captain looked at the Roman soldier chained to Paul. "Soldier, get some of your comrades and cut the lifeboat loose. Make sure no one gets on that lifeboat!"

The soldier released himself from Paul and ran toward the back. By the time he and four other soldiers reached the lifeboat, some of the crew members were about to go down a ladder. "Stop!" a soldier ordered. The soldiers drew their swords as they approached the lifeboat and ladder ropes.

"Back away," a soldier ordered.

"What for?" a crew member asked. "We're just checking on a few anchors."

The soldier looked at the two large bags next to the ladder. "Then what is this?" He took his sword and ripped the side of the bag. Grain, bread, dried meat, and skins of water poured out the side of the bag.

The crew members backed away as the soldiers cut the ropes holding the lifeboat and the ladder.

"You're sealing our doom!" a crew member cried out.

"The captain's orders are for you to drop all anchors—do it now!" Several crew members mumbled a few complaints, but did as instructed.

Paul walked back to the group and stopped at the ripped bag. He picked up a piece of bread and a water sack. "Men, you've been starving yourselves for fourteen days now. You need your strength when the ship runs aground. My God has said that none of you will die." Then he took a piece of bread, thanked God for it, broke off a piece, and ate it in front of them all. This encouraged the rest and they all began eating—even the soldiers, prisoners, and others (about 276 people total) began eating as well.

"Did he say that the ship was going to run aground?" a soldier asked his comrade.

"That's what he said."

"Then we should lighten the load as much as possible," a crew member said. "If we're near land, the cargo should all come ashore anyhow." So the soldiers ordered all the wheat to be tossed overboard.

The morning sun was a welcomed sight for the ship's passengers. They saw land and a bay with a beach.

"Let's run the ship aground at the beach," the captain said. "Cut the anchors and set the sails for land!" The crew obliged and steered the ship toward the bay. But as they neared the bay, the ship's bow struck a sandbar separate from the beachhead. The waves continued beating the ship's stern, causing the bow to wedge deeper into the sandbar. Suddenly, the stern of the ship cracked open.

"It's going to break into pieces," a soldier told Julius. "Shall we kill the prisoners?"

"No! Do not slay any of them. We must trust this man's God to do what He said He would do." Julius began to shout orders. "Crew members, help people get off the ship and swim toward the beach. If any can't swim, find them a piece of the ship on which to float. Soldiers, unchain yourselves from the prisoners and help them make it to the shore."

Julius turned his attention toward another prisoner. "Where's Paul?"

"Right here, sir."

"You stick with me. I don't want you to get hurt."

"Do not concern yourself with me. I have my two servants right beside me."

"Then I'll help the others."

Acts 28

E ach sea breaker brought either people or supplies onto
the beach. The crew members remained busy collecting
as many supplies as possible. Barrels of wheat also washed
ashore. The soldiers began securing the prisoners, using ropes
that came ashore. Luke and Aristarchus helped Paul onto the
beach. They placed him on a large piece of driftwood. "You stay
here while we go help the others," Luke said.

Paul looked around. Beyond the beach he saw a group of natives walking slowly toward the beach. *Well, I suppose I could
tell them who we are.* He stood up and walked in their direction.
"Peace be yours, today." Paul spoke in a variation of the Aramaic
dialect, one he was taught for the island of Crete.

The chief of the natives looked at the beachhead. "It appears
you've not had a peaceful voyage."

Paul pointed toward the sandbar where a portion of the ship
remained. "Our ship was caught in a storm many days ago and
we have many people who need help."

The chief motioned to several men who began spreading out
across the beach. "We will collect wood for a large fire so that
your people may dry themselves and warm their bodies."

"Thank you for your gracious act of kindness." Paul helped
the locals gather more wood for the fire. He pulled a bunch of
branches out from underneath a large rock and brought them to
the fire. As he was putting the branches into the fire, a poisonous
snake came out from under a branch of his and bit him on the
hand! In fact, it would not let go.

When the locals saw it, they gasped. "This man must be a
murderer!" one of them said. "He was saved from the sea only
to be judged on land!"

Paul shook the snake into the fire and continued to place more wood in the fire. "He won't last much longer," a local remarked. They watched Paul, waiting any moment for the venom to take effect. They waited and waited, but nothing happened to Paul. Even his hand did not swell. The locals looked at each other. "He must be a god!"

The ship's passengers were relieved to be on land again. They lingered around the fire, getting to know each other and allowing Luke to check their cuts and bruises. Soon, the Roman magistrate of the island came to greet them.

"Greetings and welcome to the Isle of Malta. My name is Publius. I am happy to hear that there was no loss of lives. I have numerous barracks in the area that I think most of you can use as a shelter at night. I will speak to the soldier in charge and see that his men maintain the peace among you."

"Thank you, sir, for your kindness," Paul said. "And is there any way that we can return a favor on you or your people?"

Publius smiled. "Not unless you have a cure for dysentery. My family lives here with me, including my father, who is old and very ill."

"Wait just a moment." Paul turned to look for Luke. "Luke! Luke! Where are you?" Down the shoreline a bit, Paul saw him waving his hand. "Come quickly, my son!"

"Is he a holy man?" Publius asked.

"Actually, he's a doctor. Let us come with you and we will check on your father." When Luke came over, Paul explained the need and, with Julius's permission, they followed the magistrate to his house.

Publius showed them into his father's bedroom. Luke immediately began diagnosing him. He was running a very high fever and had a severe bout of dysentery. "He needs to stay hydrated," Luke said. "But other than that, there's nothing else I can do for him."

Paul saw that Publius was very close to his father. Paul also knew that they needed the support of him to get off the island later on. He walked over to the elder man and placed his hands on his feverish head. Then he prayed, "Father, in heaven, I pray that You would heal this man that this family may know who is the true God. In Jesus' name, amen."

Paul backed away from him. The elder man began moving in his bed. When Publius saw his movements, he quickly pushed his way between Paul and Luke. "Father?" His father opened his eyes and pulled his arms out from underneath the covers.

"Help me sit up," the father said.

Publius pulled him up on the side of the bed. He looked at his father in amazement. "Father, are you well?"

"Yes," he said. "My son, I'm healed."

"Father!" Publius embraced him.

Luke felt the man's forehead. "The fever has left him."

Publius began weeping, as he continued embracing his father. Then he looked at Paul and bowed his head. "You have come from the gods."

Paul smiled. "Not *the* gods—for there is only one true God—the God of heaven and earth. It was He who decided to visit your father with healing."

"Paul! There are many more on this island that need healing. Tell the magistrate to get the word out that I might heal others through your hands."

Paul obeyed the Spirit's beckoning and many others on the island were healed of their diseases as they heard the gospel proclaimed to them.

One day, Julius came to Paul. "We need to get the prisoners off this island. I'm fearful of what some of them are capable of doing."

"I'll ask the magistrate." Paul discussed the matter with Publius.

"We have a short supply route to Syracuse, from which most ships head toward Rome. As soon as the winds allow, I'll get you passage to Syracuse."

"Thank you very much."

Julius was satisfied with Paul's report and gave him unlimited freedom to move about on the island, preaching the gospel and healing the sick.

Three months later – AD 61

The captain of an Alexandrian ship, docked on Malta Island, decided to continue his journey to Syracuse. The magistrate and Julius met with him and came to terms on transporting the prisoners to Rome.

As they boarded, Luke smiled. "Well, it looks as if the sons of Zeus are helping us get to Rome."

"Oh don't bring that story up again." Paul said.

"No, look at the ship's figurehead: the *Dioskuroi*—Castor and Pollux—the twin sons of Zeus."

Paul took a glance at the figurehead. "Well if they turn this way, they're going to hear about Jesus!"

The ship remained at Syracuse for three days for some major unloading and loading of cargo.

On the third day, the winds remained favorable; so the captain set sail for the southern tip of Italy. Rhegium was reached within a day. The south winds continued, which allowed the ship better sailing, reaching Puteoli the next day.

During the transfer of cargo at Puteoli, Julius invited Paul, Luke, and Aristarchus to walk with him to the central market. "Paul, I never told, but Cornelius shared with me the story about this Jesus you serve. I must admit that I was a bit of a skeptic until this voyage. I found myself totally helpless in my destiny. Then you stood up and told everyone to take heart and eat food because an angel of God stood beside you. At first, I laughed. But then everything you said would happen did happen.

"Next, the locals treated us favorably—that's a first! Then you healed people in Jesus' name. Cornelius told me that placing my life into the hands of Jesus meant that I would have to live a life of faith to see Him work miracles such as I witnessed on this voyage." Tears welled up in his eyes as he stopped Paul and the others and looked at him. "Paul, I want to surrender my life to Jesus of Nazareth now."

Paul looked Julius in the eyes. "Aren't you afraid of what these onlookers may think or say when they see a Roman officer kneel down and pray with a chained prisoner?"

"I'm not interested in what they think—I want this Jesus in my life today." Paul then knelt on the ground. Luke and Aristarchus did likewise. Then Julius joined them—all four on their knees right in the middle of the market square. Paul shared the gospel, loud and clear. Julius prayed and was saved. He began weeping as he embraced the necks of his three new brothers in Christ.

About two dozen men and women watched the event. Four men walked up to Paul and the others. "We heard your words about Jesus and saw what this man just did. We are followers of Jesus as well."

Julius looked at Paul. "Another miracle?"

"Perhaps. You know, there are others who have surrendered to the call of proclaiming the gospel of Jesus." Paul turned to the men. "Tell me, how did you men come to know about Jesus as the Messiah?"

"We have a trade outlet in Rome. It was there that we met a Galilean named Peter. He preached this same message that we just heard from you. We saw him heal many people of their diseases. Our hearts burned inside of us to accept Jesus as the Son of God, the Savior for our sins."

So Peter has begun a great work! Thank You, my Lord and my God. "Then tell me where I might baptize this new brother?"

"We have a meeting scheduled tonight in an open field, near a small river; there's plenty of water flowing. And we'll set up a fire as well."

Paul looked at Julius. "You know, I think maybe we should invite all the prisoners and the soldiers to this meeting."

"Are you sure?" Luke asked.

Julius looked concerned at first, but then he smiled and said, "Why not? What a great way to start a new life!"

After receiving directions for the meeting place, the four headed back toward the ship. "I think we should travel by land the rest of the way to Rome," Paul said. "That is, after a few days here with our new brothers."

Julius laughed. "I think you're stalling, Paul."

Paul smiled. "No rush to meet the emperor."

Paul proclaimed the gospel to the prisoners, the soldiers, and many locals for six days. Most of the prisoners asked Jesus to save them. Many of the soldiers and locals did the same. The week ended with a large baptismal service.

After what had happened during the storms at sea, no one minded traveling by foot. As the group neared Appii Forum, a large group of people approached them. These turned out to be Christians, from nearby and Three Taverns, who heard about the meetings in Puteoli. "We want to escort you into Rome," one of them said.

When Paul saw their faces and heard them speak the wonderful words of God, he was encouraged about entering Rome. *Thank you, Lord, for this wonderful experience!*

Rome was large—larger than any city Paul had ever seen. It appeared to span endlessly through the valleys to the base of the eastern mountain range. As he looked around, Paul was overwhelmed by its size. Then he remembered something his father had taught him as a little boy: "Saul, when in a crowd—whether of men or words—concentrate on just a few main ones and deliver your speech, focused on the few."

Paul relaxed in his spirit as the soldiers neared the prison. Each prisoner was documented and taken through the iron gates. "Not this one!" Julius said. "He has an appointment with the emperor and I want him placed under house arrest in one of the emperor's guest housing—along with his two servants."

The guard looked at Paul's orders more carefully. "That's okay with me. I can hardly read these blurred documents anyhow! What did you do, bathe them in sea water?" The guard roared with laughter.

Julius smiled and motioned for the three to follow him. "I will see if I can get a couple of guards for you who I trust, and I will check on you while I am in Rome."

"You have been so kind to us," Paul said. "I wonder if I might ask one more favor?"

"Sure. What do you need?"

"I would like to meet with the Jewish elders of the city and announce my presence here."

"I think I can arrange that."

The guest house was very accommodating—enough room for all three and the guard attached to Paul. It had a large front room—enough space to gather several dozen people if necessary. "Let's go find some Jews!" Paul said.

"Why?" Luke asked. "Won't they just oppose you and then hassle you?"

"Maybe; but I want to find out how much they know about Jesus and me." Paul headed for the door. "Guard, sir, do you have a name?"

"Quintus—my name is Quintus."

"Quintus, I want to go walking to visit some Jews near a synagogue. Do you know your way around this city?"

"I have lived in this city for six years. I think I know it quite well."

"Good! How about finding me a Jewish synagogue?"

"Well, the Jewish merchants tend to hang around each other and if my memory serves me correctly, they do that on the west side."

"And where are we located?"

"Central—near the arena."

"Okay then, let's go for a walk on the west side."

"I have to alert my commanding officer."

"I understand."

After a brief discussion with the commanding officer, Luke, Aristarchus, Paul, and Quintus began walking the streets of Rome. The city was bustling with people—people of all ethnicities. The people groups were best identified by the clothing they wore. The farther west they ventured, the more recognizable the clothing became for Paul. "Ah, yes, this looks more like Judea!"

"I don't see it," Aristarchus replied.

"Look at the colors and cloth attached to the headbands and the outer garments. And look at the pattern by which the garments were sewn."

"Oh, I see it better now." Aristarchus looked as if he were in a palace for the first time, admiring the fixtures and furniture.

Paul walked over to a group of men. He spoke in the Judean native tongue. "Brethren, do tell me where I might find the elders of the synagogue?"

One of the men pointed to a street. "The synagogue is about three blocks farther."

"Thank you."

"Did they understand you?" Aristarchus asked.

"Sure did—just three more blocks." Paul pulled on his chain. "Come on, Quintus, this is not a shopping trip." Quintus put down a few items and began walking with the others. Soon they were at their destination. As usual, there were several men sitting around the synagogue discussing issues. "Peace be unto you, my brothers. I wish to speak with an elder."

"I am David, one of the elders. And you are?"

"Paul, Paul of Tarsus." The other men quickly stood up. "Please, I'm not contagious."

"We were just visited a half-hour ago by a Roman centurion. He demanded we meet you at the emperor's guest housing near the arena."

Paul turned to Quintus. "I suppose Julius has gotten the word out."

"It will take a few days to gather the leaders," David said. "Will day after tomorrow be soon enough?"

"That will be fine. Now tell me a little about the Jewish populace in Rome." Paul sat down and listened about the expulsion of the Jews six years prior and the current, slow return of many to pick up where they had left off.

On the third day of Paul's stay in Rome, about midmorning, Jewish leaders began arriving at Paul's house. After about an hour, forty men managed to get inside the front room. After observing the crowded room, Paul pointed toward the rear of the house. "Let's go outside by the shade tree. I think we will be a bit more comfortable." Paul picked up his chain and Quintus followed him.

When everyone was comfortable, Paul spoke. "Men and brethren, as you can see by this chain, I am under arrest. Although I have committed no crime against our people or our customs, I was accused by our brethren in Jerusalem and was placed under arrest and handed over as a prisoner to the Roman authorities.

"The Romans put me on trial twice and wanted to let me go because there was nothing I had done worthy of punishment. But our brethren spoke against my release and plotted my death.

Therefore, I appealed my case to the emperor. I am not here to accuse our brethren, but to clear my name. I called you together so that you may know of my burden: that I am in chains for proclaiming the hope of Israel."

Several of the men began talking to themselves. Then one spoke up. "Sir, we have received no documents from Judea concerning you, nor have there been any reports about you from those who have traveled from Judea. But this 'hope' of which you speak, we wish to know more about it. And if it is tied to this new sect of Jews concerning a new Way to God, we would like to hear your take on the matter. We have heard a lot of Jews speak against it."

"Tomorrow is a Sabbath," Paul said. "May I speak to the brethren tomorrow?"

"We will confer with our priest—he is equally interested in this sect. We see no reason why he would object to your testimony."

"You do not have permission to participate in this meeting tomorrow," Quintus said.

Paul turned to face him. "I'm sure Julius won't mind."

"Julius is not in charge now. You'll have to wait until permission is granted."

"Then let's meet you here on *Sol*-day," one of the elders replied.

"*Sol*-day?" Paul asked.

The elder smiled. "You're in Rome now. The Romans worship *Sol*, their god of the sun, the day after our Sabbath.

"Oh . . . is that a problem?"

"Not really. It is a slower work day for us, so we will come to your house to hear your message."

"Good. Come back on 'Sun-day' and I will tell you what I know of the Way and the group that is called Christians." The men nodded their heads in agreement and left the house.

As they were leaving, Quintus came closer to Paul. "Do I need some backup for this gathering?"

Paul looked at him curiously. "What do you mean?"

"You Jews have a reputation of arguing over your religion and even getting violent at times."

Paul smiled. "Sounds like my brethren . . . Do you think I am a violent man?"

Quintus backed up a bit and looked Paul over. "It appears that you have been in many battles, yet there is humility and right-eousness in you. You're not a violent man."

"I proclaim to my brethren a peace that comes from God that surpasses understanding."

"Which god?"

"Oh, I see I have a lot to teach you, Quintus."

On Sun-day, many Jews came to hear Paul speak at his house. Paul preached and taught concerning the kingdom of God, giving compelling evidence concerning Jesus as the fulfillment of the Law of Moses and the Prophets. He preached from morning until evening about Jesus being the Christ, the hope of Israel.

Many believed what he said, amazed that they had not heard this message from the elders. However, the local priest and chief elder did not accept this news of the Messiah having already come. "This cannot be true," the priest said, "or we would have heard from the high priest in Jerusalem. And it's common knowl-edge that the Messiah will come and free us from our oppres-sors—who are the Romans!" He made a glaring face at Quintus.

Paul intervened. "You must get your notification of God's Messiah from His Word—not Jerusalem!"

"We receive a word from God through His Sacred Writings and His prophets," another elder said.

"I am one of His prophets!" Paul was tired and getting irri-tated at the stubborn attitudes of the priest and elders.

"By what authority do you make such a claim?" the priest asked.

"By His Word! Isaiah spoke the truth through the Holy Spirit when he said to our fathers, 'Go to this people and say, "In hearing you will hear and never understand; and, in seeing you will see and never perceive. For callous have their hearts become and their hearing has become dull. And their eyes have scales, lest they should see, hear, and understand with their hearts and turn to Me that I should heal them."'

"Therefore, see if you can hear and perceive this: The salvation of God has been sent to the Gentiles and they will hear the gospel!"

Now when Paul said this, the priest and elders turned and walked out of the back yard. Others followed—some still arguing over whether this was the truth being taught them. Paul sat and hung his head down. There was a time of silence.

"Let's go inside, Paul," Luke said.

Paul began weeping. "My people have rejected their only hope of deliverance. Oh, my Lord, please open their ears and eyes. Please give them hearts to understand. Take my life as a sacrifice if it will save them from their sins!"

Luke and Aristarchus helped Paul to his feet and walked him into his house, Quintus following behind them. The rejection was breaking Paul's heart. *Lord, this burden is too heavy for me!* He sat down on his bed and put his head into his hands. His eyes were tired and hurting, plus the recent travels on land and sea had weakened him. He sat there wondering if there was any hope of him being a voice for his Master in Rome.

Then he heard something inside his hurting heart: "Paul! I came to our people and our people did not receive Me—even you rejected Me, remember? No one in My family understood My mission. But others did, Paul; and it will be through those others that your own heart will be healed over your brothers' rejection and rebellion. Believe Me, Paul, and walk in the Spirit."

Paul had pushed everyone out of his mind as the Lord spoke to him. He thought he was alone in his room. Suddenly, someone nudged him. "Paul?" Paul slowly removed his hands from his face and raised his head. It was Quintus.

"Quintus, I'm praying; please leave me alone."

Quintus slowly knelt beside Paul. He was trembling. "Paul, can a Roman soldier be forgiven of his sins and receive this Jesus of whom you proclaim?"

Paul lowered his hands and slowly turned to look into Quintus's eyes. For a moment he saw the eyes of his beloved Master. *Lord?* Paul remained silent momentarily. Then he understood what Jesus was doing for him right then and there. He sat up and placed his arm on Quintus's shoulder. "Yes, my dear friend, even a Roman soldier can be forgiven of his sins."

Acts 29 ~ Historical Tradition

James, half-brother of Jesus and elder of the Jerusalem fellowship, paced the floor in the secret villa outside Jerusalem. "Where's Matthew?"

Simon (the Zealot) stood nearby, gazing at Jerusalem through a window. "He remains in hiding."

James joined him at the window. "Still writing his story about our Lord?"

"Yes. He says the Spirit is giving him many examples from the Sacred Writings to prove Jesus is the Messiah."

"I wonder if our kinsmen will ever receive Him as our Messiah." James hung his head. "Oh Jerusalem, how long will you rebel from your God? You are more turbulent than ever!"

Simon breathed heavily. "Our Jewish leaders continue to taunt the empire . . . it's only a matter of time before a war breaks out." He turned and grabbed James by his shoulders. "You must consider relocating your family—our Lord's mother must be protected!"

"Where? . . . Where could we go?"

"Antioch," Simon said. "Antioch has become the hub for all the Gentile mission work—the Christians there have been our greatest supporters here in Judea; they will help us when we arrive."

"Abandon Jerusalem?" James backed away from him. "Simon, don't say that! I just can't bear to think of abandoning God's favored city."

"He has left the city! And so should we."

James began weeping. "No! . . . Not yet. The others depend on us remaining here. We must wait until we hear from Bartholomew, Judas, James (the Less), and the other apostles. They may report to us soon . . . We will stay here for now."

†††

"No, my precious child!" Mary, mother of Jesus, wept. "You can stay here with us—we will protect you!"

Mary of Magdala embraced her. She had stalled for months sharing what had been placed in her heart. But it was time to obey. "Mother . . ." That was all she could say at the moment. She ran her fingers through the smooth flowing silvery hair of her Lord's mother. They wept together.

"Mother," she said, trying again to speak. "I must obey our Lord . . . He's given me a vision. I must return to Magdala."

Mary managed a smile. "Listen to me, trying to keep you from following my Son—our Lord." She wiped her tears. "I will miss you so much. Our women's gatherings will not be the same without you."

"Perhaps I can return next Passover, but I must go now. My past has wronged many people in my community and I must set the record straight—I must testify of how Jesus changed my life."

"Will your family receive you as a Christian?"

"I pray so, for they are the first who will see me. But if not, my Lord will be with me and, together, our love will find a way."

✝✝✝

Paul's concentration in prayer and writing was interrupted by the roar of the arena participants as each group of horses galloped past the grandstands. "Quintus, is there any way we can drown out those terrible screams?"

He laughed. "It sounds like a lot of bettors sided with the emperor's choice." Quintus turned to Paul. "Would you like for me to take you to the emperor's sitting booth and you can register a complaint with him?"

"Oh you would try, wouldn't you?"

"Don't tempt me. You know I—" A noise outside Paul's house interrupted their conversation. "Quick, Paul, attach your chain to mine!" Since Quintus turned his life over to the Lord, he had allowed Paul freedom to roam the house and the back area without the two being coupled together. He pulled out his sword and walked toward the door. He swung it open and discovered two men standing at the threshold.

"Sir!" one of the men said. "We wish you no harm—we have no weapons!"

Quintus placed the tip of his sword on the chest of one of the men. "Then why are you sneaking around this house?"

"We're looking for an old friend—a Paul of Tarsus? We were told he was living here."

"And who is it that is looking for him?"

"I'm John ben Zebedee and this is Barnabas of Cyprus."

"Barnabas?" Paul raised his voice. "John? Quintus, please let them come in."

Quintus drew back his sword. "You may enter."

"Paul!" Barnabas said, as he embraced his old friend.

"Barnabas! Oh, how much I have prayed for this day." Paul and Barnabas both wept as they remained embraced for several minutes.

"Stop it," John said, "or you're going to make me cry as well. We're arriving—not leaving!"

Paul and Barnabas both laughed. "What has brought you to Rome? And how did you find me?"

"You and Peter," John said. Barnabas continued to wipe tears from his eyes. "We had to come to Rome and see for ourselves the ministry of which we heard bits and pieces about."

"An elder at the synagogue told us how to find you," Barnabas said. "Have you spoken before the emperor?"

"No, not yet. It seems he has more important duties to perform than listening to 'a raving madman,' such as I have been described."

"That's too bad," John said.

"No, my brother, it is good. I have had numerous meetings with the Jewish elders—all under the protection of the empire!" Paul pointed to Quintus. "And I have been granted freedom to go to the markets and, of course, speak to the many Gentiles in this enormous city."

"And?"

"And our blessed Master has produced much fruit in the city—mainly among the poor and slaves—and a few soldiers." He pointed at Quintus. Then he pointed to the other men in the room who were copying his words. "And look, I'm writing several letters to the assemblies."

"What a blessing to hear this!" Barnabas said.

Paul pointed to the men. "This is Onesphorus and this is Demas, fellow slaves in our Lord's work."

"Greetings to you both, my brothers," Barnabas said, as he went to both men to embrace them.

"Don't touch them," Paul warned Barnabas. "They mustn't lose their places in the copies." Barnabas stopped, smiled, and waved at the men.

"Where's Peter?" John asked.

"I haven't seen him, but I have met many of his converts. He's been very effective among the citizens of the region. Last I heard he was north of Rome."

"Oh," John said. "I do pray I shall see him soon."

"Then we'll pray for that to happen . . . Barnabas, where have you been? I heard once that you traveled to Egypt?"

"Alexandria," he said. "Paul, the Lord worked mightily among the people there. Six house fellowships were formed by the time I left—truly remarkable!" Things got quiet momentarily . . . "Paul, any word about John Mark?"

"I sent him with Peter to glean from him the words and works of Jesus."

"Oh," Barnabas said.

"I thought he should stay with me to write, but the Lord told me to send him off with Peter."

"So who is writing for you?" John asked.

"Doctor Luke, mainly; then men like these have come by to copy my letters or give Luke a break."

"That's great! Where is he?"

"He left for Asia last week. I sent him back with Tychicus— another follower—to return a runaway slave back to his owner."

"You did what?!"

"I know it sounds unusual, but the man had stolen money from his master and ran away to Rome. He was converted to Christianity and wanted to make things right with his owner."

"Why you?" Barnabas asked.

"I happen to know his owner—I led him to Christ years ago. I felt a letter from me to him would reduce the conflict between the two."

John walked over to a window and looked outside. "Barnabas and I have been roaming the streets looking for you. Are you ready to show us the city?"

Paul laughed. "Oh I'm afraid it will take more than me to show you this mammoth place. But I have been helped tremendously by Quintus here."

Quintus turned and bowed toward the three. "At your service, Master Paul," he replied.

"A Roman guard enslaved to a Jewish prisoner?" John asked. "Someone should write a book about this."

†††

Eliezer wiped the blood from his bleeding lips. The priest and keeper of the synagogue looked at him as if he was a scavenging dog.

"You dare say that name in our synagogue again," the priest said, "and you will feel each stone that makes your grave. Escort this blasphemer to the city gates."

The synagogue keeper picked Eliezer up from the ground and turned him toward Capernaum's southern gate. "This way, you troublemaker."

Eliezer responded to a push and began walking in front of him. *Why did I even think they would listen to me?* He was so full of joy, since he had surrendered to Jesus of Nazareth, that he thought anyone—everyone!—would respond to the gospel. This was a wake-up call for him.

As they neared the gates, the synagogue keeper gave him one final push. Eliezer tripped and fell to the ground. "Now when you come to your senses, you may come back and ask the priest for forgiveness and apologize for your disruptions. But until then, stay away from our synagogue!"

"I will pray for God to open your eyes to the truth."

"Ha! If I want to know truth, I know who to go to . . . and it's certainly not your Jesus!" He turned and walked away.

Eliezer picked himself up and brushed the dust off his garment. Several men nearby stared at him but made no attempt to inquire about the incident. He was in no mood to testify any further, so he walked out of the gates. *My Lord,* he prayed to himself, *what can I do to share Your message? If my people reject You, who else matters?* The walk back to Magdala was a quiet and lonely one for him.

The next day found Eliezer up early and scrubbing down his salt boards for the overnight catch of fish. Although he lacked the patience to fish, he was excellent at cleaning them and had a paring fillet knife second to none. He smiled as he thought about yesterday's encounter with the two leaders of the synagogue and how, several years earlier, he could have easily carved his name on their chests with his knife.

He stopped momentarily and rebuked himself for such a thought. *I mustn't think such thoughts. My Lord, forgive me . . . Please help me with my thoughts. May they always be pleasing to You . . . My Lord, how do I share Your message? This place is so small and I am so busy each day!* Eliezer remained subdued in his thoughts as he worked through nets full of fresh fish. Each fisherman appreciated his speed and assistance in preserving the daily catch for the larger markets in Capernaum.

It was not uncommon for certain women to come close, in the late afternoon, asking for the heads and extra pieces of discarded fish. These beggars would take them to a camp of outcasts and cook them. Eliezer was known to give a little extra since he had become a Christian.

But today he was *not* in a generous mood. The sweat and salt burned the wounds in his lips. Several women came close to him, expecting his usual smile—but not this time. "Get away from here! No extras for you!" One of the women quickly turned and walked away. The other, however, did not move. "I said go away!" He looked up, expecting to see a familiar face of a wretched female outcast. But instead he was looking at someone he had never seen before. And instead of a face of fear, he saw compassion. He looked back at his paring knives and his salt boards, thinking she might go away if he would only ignore her.

She came in closer—next to his stack of dirtied boards. Quietly, she got on her knees and began rubbing the fish scales off a board with her outer garment. Eliezer stopped for a moment and watched her. Although her skin did not appear to be sun-soaked, she seemed to know exactly how to clean a salt board. Now he felt guilty.

"Okay," he said, "you can stop now. I will give you my remaining fish heads." She didn't stop. "Woman, can you hear me? I said I would give you some fish."

"I can hear you very well," she said. "I did not come expecting anything from you, but to offer you a most precious gift." She stopped cleaning his boards, stood up, and walked over to his side.

He still did not recognize her. Then she reached for and grabbed one of his paring knives. He stepped back, wondering if maybe he was about to be cut. But she turned around and continued scraping his boards. *Who is this woman? My Lord, what is happening here?* Eliezer stopped momentarily and stared at her. "Thank you for this gift of yours." He tried to smile, but again his cracked lips started bleeding. "Ouch!"

She stopped again and stood up. She could see the blood forming on his lips. "Don't touch your lips with your dirty cloths—here, let me help you." She carefully pulled out a clean, soft cloth from her outer garment and slowly touched his lips, dabbing the blood. "Hold this to your lips while I get you some salve from my bag." She helped him position his hand to where he would not contaminate the clean part of the cloth. She then turned and walked toward a small tree nearby where a large canvas bag was leaning against it.

A few minutes later, she returned with a smaller, but equally clean, cloth—only this one had a white lotion on it. "Try this," she said, handing the cloth to him.

"Ouch!" he responded when the lotion burned in the cut. She laughed. "What?"

"Oh nothing," she said.

He thought through the earlier conversation with her. "Oh, so this is your 'precious' gift?"

She smiled again. "Neither." She said no more.

Eliezer continued to rub the salve on his lips. "I cannot imagine what your precious gift is then. Please tell me."

"It's not a 'what'—it's a Who. I have experienced a new life, with hope and peace, in the Man of Nazareth: Jesus. Because of Him, I can now share how you can experience this same kind of life."

"Stop!" He held out his hand as if he was ordering someone to halt. She obliged, as he once again stared at her. *My Lord, what have I done? I have ruined my witness for You!* He wept.

The woman looked bewildered. "Sir, have you heard of Jesus before?"

He wiped his eyes with her clean cloth. He looked at the once white cloth, now mixed with streaks of dirt and sweat. He saw himself now as that sullied cloth. He wept again as he got on his knees and looked upward. "My Master," he prayed aloud. "I have sinned in that I was not a witness for You today. Please, Jesus, forgive me." He began weeping again as he held the cloth to his face.

Moments later he heard the scraping of his boards again. He looked up and saw this woman cleaning his salt boards again. She was smiling and humming a tune that sounded like a psalm he once heard from a gathering of Christians in Samaria. He stood up. "Woman, will you—?"

"Only if you'll help me feed some poor people in the camp down the road."

Once again, he stared at her and wondered, *Is this an angel?* "Then let's finish the cleanup." Eliezer loaded the salt boards on a small cart tied to his donkey.

Within the hour, they were cooking fish on an open fire at the outcast camp. Many people gathered around the fire, enjoying the fresh-cooked fish.

While Eliezer continued the cooking, the woman stood up and spoke. "Men and women, this fish is a gift from God to us tonight. But our God has offered us an even greater gift through His Son, the Deliverer of whom our prophets have spoken. This fish will satisfy for only this one night; but our Deliverer from God will satisfy your spiritual hunger forever."

"And who is this Deliverer of whom you speak?" another woman asked.

"This man, who has supplied our fish for tonight, he will tell you." With that remark, she walked over to Eliezer and took the pronged stick from his hand. "I think you have a testimony to give?" She smiled as she bent down and turned the fish over.

Eliezer, stood up and faced about twenty onlookers. *My Master, what do I . . .?* He smiled as he remembered his prayer earlier in the day. Then the words of the transforming power of Jesus gushed from his mouth. As he testified, Eliezer realized that his Lord had answered his prayers.

About an hour later, Eliezer had finished his testimony. In response to it, six people prayed and received Jesus into their lives. He and the woman who helped him—still a stranger!—gave further instructions on living for Jesus. Finally, Eliezer began gathering his gear while loading his cart. As she started helping him, he grabbed her arm. "Not another minute's help from you until you've answered my questions."

"It's getting dark and you must hurry home to your family," she said.

"I have no family. My wife died five years ago and I live alone. Who are you? And where do you come from?"

"I am from Magdala. My name is Mary. I was healed by Jesus many years ago and have ministered to His followers in Jerusalem for many years. But my Lord told me to come home and witness to my family and friends." She looked at the ground. "But they all turned me away and my family would not allow me to live in their home. This camp is now my home." She then looked at the fire and smiled. "And this is my first meal in three days—and what a meal it was!"

Eliezer turned and mounted on his donkey. "Come early tomorrow and help me, and you can have as many fish as you need for you and your friends."

"Only if you will come and speak to *our* new friends about Jesus."

Eliezer saw that her smile came from her heart. "I think I can do that."

"And vegetables! We will need some vegetables from the market."

"Okay, some vegetables also."

"And some bread?" Her smile was too great to offend.

"Yes of course! But you're going to do the shopping and baking." This time he smiled as he kicked the side of his donkey and headed back into the small town of Magdala.

† † †

The two men were drunk and obnoxious toward those who came near them, laughing as each one tried to quiet the other.

"Anicetus, we mustn't waken the children."

"Pssst," he responded quietly. "What children?" Again, howling laughter filled the night air.

Two Roman soldiers remained hidden in the shadows not far from Anicetus and his friend.

"What a night," Anicetus spoke loudly. "The horses were great, the games were excellent, and there is not another word in my vocabulary for the wine."

"That was wine? I thought there was another word for strong drink . . . vinegar?" Again, laughter filled the air as the two stopped beside a house to relieve themselves.

About that time a door opened beside them and two men came out. A large dagger was in each man's hand as they pinned the two drunks to the wall.

"You have disturbed my family for the last time tonight," one of the dagger-toting men said.

The other man put his dagger to Anicetus's friend's neck. "Perhaps you would like to apologize before I slit your throat?"

"I wouldn't do that if I were you," Anicetus said.

"And what will you do to stop me?"

"Uh, I wouldn't do anything . . . but those two soldiers behind you *might* object to the way you're handling your emperor."

The man with the dagger against Nero's neck turned his head to see the two soldiers with their swords drawn, about two steps away from him. He dropped his dagger and fell to his knees. "Oh, my Lord! I did not know it was you!"

Nero tried to straighten out his vagabond garment. "Anicetus, you didn't have to tell them. I wanted to see their faces with swords in their backs."

The other man fell to his knees as well. "Please, my Lord, we did not know!"

Nero picked up a dagger and ran its blade across his finger, cutting it. "Ouch! . . . Your dagger has cut my finger." He stuck his bleeding finger in the face of one of the men, smearing some of his blood on the man's face. "Now I am sad; you've chased my laughter away." Nero pulled out a cloth and wiped his finger. "Anicetus, what should we do to these who have chased my laughter away?"

Anicetus circled around both men. "Dog meat?"

Nero laughed. "Anicetus, Anicetus, you have restored my laughter—a good idea, however . . . Guards, see that these two remain posted to their home. And do invite the dogs to come for a visit."

One of the men cried out, "Please, my Lord! Don't! We have wives and children!"

"Oh? And do you wish I should bring them out and post them as well?"

The man hung his head down. "No, please don't disturb them on account of my disrespect."

"That's what I thought. Guards, hurry up so that we may leave."

The soldiers placed their swords through the men's clothing, behind their necks, and raised them up, pinning them to the wall. Taking several spikes from their girdles, they nailed the two men against the wall. After tying their hands and feet together, securing them to the wall, they took the men's daggers and raised them up into their faces. "Shhh," one of the soldiers said. "You don't want to wake the family, do you?" Each soldier knelt and slowly cut the muscle behind each man's leg, allowing the blood to trickle down the men's ankles, and wiping the blood of the dagger blades across their bare feet.

Anicetus stared at the two men as the soldiers backed away from them. "Dog meat," he said as he turned to Nero.

"Arff, arff!" Nero barked. They laughed as they turned and walked away.

Anicetus helped Nero back into the palace. It was after midnight and everything was quiet—except for the mumbling from Nero. "I tell you, I have to do something soon."

Anicetus put his finger to his lips. "Shhh, my friend," he said. "These corridors have ears and they hear every word spoken."

Nero smiled—even let out a small laugh. "Glad they can't hear thoughts." They both laughed out loud, putting their fingers to their lips—"Shhh," they said together, still laughing. As they entered Nero's secondary bedroom, several servants met them and began undressing them both, preparing them for more leisure clothing.

"Leave us alone!" Nero commanded. The servants left the room immediately. Both men sat at a table, pouring a little more drink into the cups set before them. The flickering candles made for an eerie mood. "Anicetus, she is going to do something to Acte."

"How do you know?"

"I saw it in her eyes." Nero bent down toward a candle, creating a shadow on the table. Then he used his fingers to give the shadow some tantalizing legs. "She has a demon!"

Anicetus let out a quiet laugh, but lost his smile when he saw Nero was not laughing. "What do you plan to do?"

"I think it is time for an accident to occur in my mother's life . . ."

† † †

"Is he always chained to you?" John asked, watching Paul walk with a leg chain attached to Quintus.

"In public and when unexpected guests arrive at the house."

"Our tax coins are serving us well," Barnabas said, smiling at Paul and his guard. As they walked down the busy streets of Rome, room was always given for the man who was chained to a Roman soldier.

Paul stopped and tugged on his chain. "Quintus, gather me some people."

Quintus pulled out his sword and motioned for the people to gather around Paul. Sometimes ten would gather, or twenty-five—even fifty would be corralled by Quintus! Then Paul would preach the gospel to the crowd. With hardly an exception, after about an hour of preaching, numerous people would respond to the appeal for repentance from sin and to turn to the Lord Jesus for salvation.

John and Barnabas joined in the counseling of the new-born followers of Christ. Soon there were hundreds of new Christians, anxious to be baptized and discover how Jesus would have them serve. The expressions of joy and peace among the commoners and foreigners were ironic, compared to the faces of the senators and the fear embedded in the faces of the senators' and emperor's staff.

† † †

"Mother, I have a special gift waiting for you on the Baiae."

Agrippina eyed Nero with suspicion. "And what's the occasion?"

"Must I wait for a holiday to give my mother a gift?"

She continued to pry. "Well, it's unusual for you to be so generous."

He walked over to her. "Okay, you hate it when I go to the races; so I thought I would keep my land winnings a secret until I presented them to you at the Feast of Minerva on the Baiae."

"Land? On the Baiae?" Agrippina could hardly believe what she was hearing. "What a lovely gesture on your part . . . Thank you!"

He turned away from her attempt to embrace him. "But it's no special gift now since you know what it is."

"I'm sorry, my son. I'm just weary of your continual absence from your duties at the senate. We—they—ask for you every time they meet."

"Then speak for me—you seem to know me better than I know myself."

"It's because I have been among the emperors for more years than you, my son. I only want what's best for you."

Nero changed the subject. "I have prepared a special boat to take us to the Baiae. You remember that boat I had built for my last play?"

She thought for a moment. "Is it seaworthy?"

"Of course! I had it assembled at the docks. We will float leisurely through the night after dinner."

Agrippina arrived with her servants at an empty banquet hall . . . that is, except for Nero and his attendants. "Where is everyone?"

"I gave them permission to go before us to the Baiae to prepare for our arrival. Anicetus and a few others went to prepare the boat for our journey tonight."

She smiled at her son. "I am anxious to see this new parcel of land."

"And I believe you will find it breathtaking." Nero smiled as he sipped his wine.

When Agrippina arrived at the dock, the boat was being loaded with lumber. "And what's with this wood?" she asked the captain.

"Madam Agrippina, the emperor ordered this cargo for your safety. There is a weakness at the steps at the docks and he does not want you hindered in any way."

"Well, keep it away from my sight." She boarded onto the boat and made her way down the flight of stairs to the main chamber. Downstairs, she sat in a designer chair and allowed her servants to massage her feet as she munched on some fruit.

About fifteen minutes later, the captain came down to the cabin. "Madam, the emperor has had an interruption in his schedule and has requested you go ahead of him. He will meet you about midmorning tomorrow."

"Oh . . . okay."

The ship hoisted from the dock and steered toward the Baiae. The distance was only a couple nautical miles, so not much time to rest. Once out in the bay, however, the crew began moving the lumber over the cabin area. Agrippina's conversation to her servants continued to be interrupted as the lumber was dropped overhead.

"What's with all this noise?" Agrippina asked one of the servants.

"Do you wish for me to inquire, Madam?" a servant girl asked. About that time, a cracking sound was heard in the ceiling.

"Yes! Go up there immediately and tell the captain I said to stop moving the cargo!" She turned to another servant. "Just wait until I get my hands around that captain's neck!"

The servant climbed up the stairs to exit, but the door was locked from the outside. "Madam!" she shouted. "The door is locked!"

"It's what?!" At that moment, the ceiling joists of the cabin began to splinter and break loose above the cabin. Several of the servants screamed as the ceiling fell on top of where Agrippina sat. A piece of the ceiling hit her in the head and knocked her out. Fortunately, for her, the iron frame of the chair prevented her from being crushed. But the servants around her were killed—only the servant girl on the stairs survived.

"Help!" the servant girl screamed. "Help! Please, someone help!"

"Is the madam, okay?" someone from atop asked.

"I don't know. She's been hit, but she's not crushed—please help us!"

"Check on the madam first!" the voice from above said.

The servant girl ran down the steps, crawled over some of the lumber debris, and felt Agrippina. Then she ran back to the top of the stairs. "Sir, she's still alive, but is knocked out. Her head is bleeding. Please, open the door and help us now!"

The crewman above turned to the captain. "Sir, she has survived the cave-in."

"Then we have no other choice." The captain walked over to the side of the ship where there was another vessel of similar size. He motioned to the captain of the other ship. "Ram the side, quickly! We must sink her now." He then turned to his crew. "Abandon the ship!"

"What?!" the lead crewman shouted.

"I have my orders. She mustn't survive this trip."

The crew began lowering a small boat for their escape while the other ship positioned itself.

Below the deck, the servant girl went back to Agrippina and wiped the blood off her face. "Madam, you must awaken! Madam, please wake up!" She moved some of the lumber and ceiling joists away from Agrippina, clearing enough space to lay her down. "Madam, wake up! Please, you must wake up!"

She slapped Agrippina. "Huh? Ouch! Wha . . . What's happened?"

"Madam, we're locked in here and they won't let us out!" Agrippina moved her arms and felt her head. "You've been cut by the ceiling pieces and have been bleeding. Can you move your legs?"

Although groggy, Agrippina managed to move both legs. "Yes, I can move my arms and legs. Did you call for help?"

"I did, I did, Madam; but they will not open the door from above!"

"By the gods! My dear child, they mean to kill us!"

At that moment, the other ship rammed their boat. Several boards on the side of the lower cabin cracked open. The two women shrieked. The ramming ship was oared backwards as the captain of both ships looked at the damaged side. "Not enough—we must ram it again!"

Water began spilling onto the cabin floor from the cracks. "What are we going to do?!" the servant girl cried.

"They're going to ram us again! Quick, find me some cloth to wrap my head where it's bleeding. We must prepare to swim out of the hole before we sink."

The servant girl removed her head scarf and wrapped her madam's head. By now, Agrippina was fully alert. She stripped down to her undergarments. "You must remove your outer garment," she instructed her servant. "Now tear some strips to tie the rest of your clothing through your legs. You must give your legs plenty of freedom to paddle your body through the hole and up to the top of the water."

The servant girl began crying. "Oh Madam, I cannot swim!"

"Now stop crying! You can wiggle your legs back and forth, can't you?" Agrippina looked around at the rubble. "Over there—get that piece of lumber!" The servant girl obeyed. "Now listen to me very carefully. This piece of wood will float you to the top of the water. Whatever happens, do not let go of this piece of wood—do you understand?"

Still crying, "Yes, my Madam."

"Okay, the ship will hit us again on this same side; let's get as far from this side as possible. Once they see the hole is big enough to sink us, they will back their ship back up and watch it sink. We will let the cabin fill up with water. There should be an air pocket or two. We must wait and allow the ship to begin sinking and then we will make our escape through the hole."

"I don't think I can do this."

"Look at me! Yes, you can! See this long rope? I have tied it around me; now you tie the other end around you and hold on to your board. But listen, once we get to the surface we must not make any noise. We must keep ourselves hidden among the ship's cargo and rubble. It's dark outside and they will have a very hard time seeing us." Agrippina grabbed her servant's face. "Together, we can do this! We are tied together and we will survive! Do you understand? We will survive!"

They moved over to the far side of the cabin, awaiting the next crashing blow. Then it happened: "CRACK!" The ramming ship hit much harder this time. Five or six sideboards split open, leaving a gaping hole in the cabin's side. As the ramming ship backed out of the hole, water poured into the cabin at a much higher rate of speed.

"Scream, my dear. Let's give them something for their conscience!" They both began to scream and shout for help. When the cabin was nearly two-thirds full, Agrippina motioned for her servant to stop.

Agrippina spoke softly. "Now put some water in your mouth and cough it out. Make some gagging sounds." They both began coughing and gagging.

Several wooden barrels floated nearby. Agrippina grabbed two of them. "It's possible we can capture some air in these and take it with us. But we must act quickly. You must follow me and do what I do. We will put the barrels ahead of us and push them through the holes. Once outside the ship, put your head in your barrel and hold on to its rim. Hold your breath until you get your head inside the barrel where there's air. The barrel will float you to the top. Now be very quiet."

As the ship took on more water, objects appeared on the surface. The captains and their crews lit torches to look for any sign of Agrippina and her servants' bodies. "There's one!" cried a crewman, as he pointed to the right. Several escape boats rowed toward the body.

The sinking boat rolled on its side, with the hole at the top. As water continued pouring into the hole, all sorts of floating objects began popping up onto the surface. Lumber shot up into the dark night as if they were catapulted from beneath. One piece burst through the bottom of an escape boat.

"Back up!" cried the captain of the ramming ship.

"No!" the other captain said. "We must watch carefully!"

"I said we are backing up! We're not sinking my vessel just to see a couple more dead bodies. Their bodies will fill up with water and sink to the bottom, just like the rest of the garbage."

The ramming ship backed up while the crewmen abandoned one escape boat and boarded the other. The captain of the damaged boat looked as carefully as possible as it disappeared under the dark and turbulent waters. Lumber, all sorts and sizes of the ship's hardware, and barrels began spreading out from where the ship sank. Only a couple of servants' bodies floated to the top. There were no signs of Agrippina.

Agrippina and her servant girl floated to the surface undetected. They quietly kicked their legs, steering their bodies through the cold, dark waters in the direction of the Baiae. "Let go of your barrel," Agrippina said quietly to her servant. "Grab this piece of wood and float alongside of it." When her servant did so, Agrippina let go of her barrel as well and grabbed another piece of lumber. "Keep paddling, dear, but do so quietly."

"Yes, Madam." As they floated farther away from the ship's debris field, they heard the smashing of the floating barrels. The crew had orders to sink all signs of the ship and its cargo.

꧁ ꧂

Anno
Domini
62

Circa

꧁ ꧂

"**M**y Lord, how long must I stay in these chains? When can I leave for Spain?" Paul prayed, expecting a response from his Lord. He paced the floor atop his dwelling, waiting to hear from Jesus. *I must learn to be patient.* He then went back down to his room for some sleep.

Early the next morning, Paul resumed his supervision of the scribes copying several of his letters. John and Barnabas came to his quarters about midmorning.

"Still copying?" John asked.

"Yes; they are copying the letter I sent to Rome several years ago."

"What an awesome responsibility," John said. "Where will these letters go?

"Three will follow me to Macedonia and Spain. The other two will stay here in Rome."

Barnabas grinned. "So you already have plans to leave?"

"I must go to Spain; there are people there who have never heard gospel of Jesus. I keep asking the Lord to speed up my hearing before the emperor; but so far, I've not heard a word from our Lord."

"You are doing a great work here," Barnabas said, "writing and witnessing in the power of the Spirit."

"This is not my calling; others can oversee this copying while I return to the areas that have not heard the gospel message."

"Your writings are helping many fellowships," John said. "Barnabas and I heard your words spoken at several locations in Asia and Macedonia. So don't see your captivity as a waste of time."

Paul looked at the five men who were seated around the large front room. "I suppose you're right, but I will feel better once my day in court is over."

Paul finished proofing the five copies of his letter to the Romans. They were as close to the original as anyone could expect. Only a few corrections were noted in the margins by Paul. With the help of several men, the papyri were rolled up, sealed, and put in canvas bags. Three were placed in Paul's large bag that Jacob had made for him when he was in the Arabian Desert.

Quintus came into the house and relieved the other guard. After the exchange, Quintus unshackled Paul. "And how is my prisoner today?"

"Trying to make the most of this time, my friend."

"How would you like to take a little trip into the city?"

"Another vegetable run for the emperor?"

Quintus smiled. "How about an audience with the senate?"

Paul stood there and stared for a moment. "Really?"

"Yes; I was given orders to have you seated in a couple of hours."

"Where are we going?" John asked as he entered the house.

Quintus laughed. "Oh, I think there may be room for a couple of character witnesses, should the senate ask."

"Great!" Paul said. "Finally, I get my day in court."

"I hope they let me say a word or two about you," Barnabas said. "I'll tell them how easy-going you are with everyone you meet." They all laughed.

The Roman senate sometimes sprinkled in a hearing or two just to break the monotony of the day. Paul's hearing was picked at random. The chief senator read the letter from Governor Festus to the crowd. "Are there any accusers here for this hearing?" the chief asked. There was silence in the chamber. "Will the accused please stand?" Paul stood up, ready to give his defense. He looked at Paul. "I've read this letter twice and see no reason for us to waste our time on matters of your religion." He turned toward the senate. "I move we suspend this arrest on the basis of it being out of the senate's jurisdiction to settle matters pertaining to one of the many religions of our empire."

"So moved," another senator said.

"Any objections?" the chief asked. No one spoke. "Then, Paul of Tarsus, you are released of your arrest and are free to go. If you need travel arrangements back to Tarsus, you may find a complimentary seat on any of our ships heading in your direction. Please stop by our registration office for a certificate of passage. Dismissed."

Paul looked up in the visitor's balcony and saw the smiles of his comrades. He returned a smile as he was led out of the room. After about thirty minutes, Paul and Quintus joined John and Barnabas in the outer courtyard.

"Can you believe that?" John said.

"What a defense!" Barnabas said. "I've never heard you defend yourself better." The three laughed and embraced each other.

"For the first time in my life, I was at a loss of words when he said 'Dismissed.' I couldn't believe it."

"So, where do we go from here?" John asked.

Paul looked at Quintus. "Don't look at me, Master Paul, you're a free man."

Paul reached over and embraced the soldier he had come to love. "I must go back to the house and get my belongings."

"Oh, I wouldn't rush," Quintus said. "You may take a few days to relocate."

"And what about you?" Paul asked. "Can you go with us?"

"Me, leave Rome? Oh, it's much too dangerous for me to travel." He smiled. "I'll leave all that adventurous stuff for those with stamina—and a vision! Besides, I have a lot of people in this town who are waiting for me to slip up and lose my 'religion.' You seem to have our God's protection wherever you go, so I don't think you need a Roman guard around to slow you down."

Paul embraced him again. "You have been a God-send for me, Quintus, and I will never cease to lift you up in my prayers."

"Just be sure you look me up the next time you come to Rome."

"You can count on that. As the Lord allows, I will see you again." With that being said, Paul, John, and Barnabas turned away from Quintus and headed back to Paul's house.

† † †

Agrippina and her servant girl managed to get ashore at the Baiae. It was early morning and they were both shivering from the long stay in the water.

"We must find someone quickly," Agrippina said. She looked along the shoreline. "Let's hurry to that dock over there. Perhaps we will find some dry rags to put on." They walked as quickly as they could, but Agrippina had to slow down due to the loss of blood from her head wound.

"Madam, there's a small house atop the dock area. Allow me to run ahead and see if there is someone living there."

Agrippina stopped and sat down on a rock. "Yes, my dear, please run ahead and see if you can find help. I will try to make it to the dock." As the young woman ran off, Agrippina tried to think things through. *Nero, my son, you have a cruel heart— much like my own. I am so sorry I trained you to be this way . . . How will he react toward the news of my survival? Maybe he will respond to a kinder and gentler mother?*

As she sat there thinking, she heard a cry of delight. "Madam! Madam! I found help for us!" The servant girl ran ahead of two men and a woman who carried some dry clothing.

At the emperor's estate on the Baiae, both women were given hot baths and were clothed in fresh, dry clothing. The estate's chief servant, Agermus, came to them with food and drink while another servant cleaned Agrippina's wound.

"I will send word to the emperor that you have been hurt, but you are recovering at the estate," Agermus said.

"Tell him that I am well and not to rush. I will need a few days' rest." She had figured that Nero was not planning to arrive at midmorning. She needed some time to think through on how to outwit her son's future attempts to kill her.

† † †

"She what?!"

"Yes, Divine One," a servant said. "Her boat collided with a larger vessel in the night and it sank. But she survived and swam to the shore at Baiae."

"Where is she now?"

"She remains at the estate. Agermus sent me to gather her some fresh clothing."

"Do so and wait for me to go with you to see her."

"Yes, Divine One; as you wish." The servant excused himself and departed for Agrippina's quarters.

Now Nero was furious. "Get me Anicetus!

"Yes, my friend; did you wish to see me?" Anicetus tried to remain relaxed around Nero, but he had to always keep his guard up because of Nero's mood swings.

"I suppose you heard that my mother still lives? Our plan failed!"

He looked at Nero with a stoic look. "You mean *your* plan failed?"

"Listen, if word gets out on this assassination attempt, both you and I will pay for it."

"What do you suggest, Divine One?"

"Take twelve of our best soldiers, go to Baiae, and finish the job—and do so today! Get a dagger with her blood on it and hide it in the small bush on the left side of the east gate."

"As you wish, Divine One."

Nero stepped out into the hallway. "Guards, see that Anicetus has twelve soldiers to escort him to Baiae immediately and they are to follow his instructions."

Nero went to a nearby window and looked toward the Baiae. *You escaped this first attempt, but you will not live long enough to rise up against me.*

† † †

The servant girl prepared Agrippina for a rest. She busied herself making Agrippina as comfortable as possible.

"Stop," Agrippina said.

"Madam, I must soften your pillow and help you with your head—you're not well yet."

"No, sit beside me and do so now."

She obeyed her madam, but was afraid to speak. This command was very unusual from Agrippina.

"What is your name?"

"Oh Madam, my name is not important. You need not know."

"I said, what is your name?"

She lowered her head. "Nesuptia, Madam . . . my name is Nesuptia."

"Do you have family, Nesuptia?"

"Yes, Madam. My father works in the emperor's garden and my mother and older sister cooks for him. I have a younger brother who is a soldier in the far north country."

Agrippina smiled as she felt the face of her servant girl. "You are a brave young woman and I want to thank you for helping me escape last night."

"Oh, Madam, once you awakened, you did all the brave things. I was but your servant, doing as you commanded."

"Oh, but Nesuptia, you were brave as well. Together, we saved each other." Nesuptia smiled. "Listen, my dear child, I need you to deliver a message to your father."

"Yes, Madam, as soon as we return, I will do as you request."

"No, my dear, I want you to deliver it right away—tonight. Now go fetch me some writing utensils and I will arrange for your departure."

After the note was sealed for Nesuptia, Agrippina gave it to a servant. "Take her to the docks and see that she leaves as soon as possible. And see to it that no one knows of her whereabouts."

"Must I leave you now?" Nesuptia sobbed. "You need me now."

"No, my child, this message is more important than your personal service to me at this time. Now go with the chief and do not turn back—that is my command." Agrippina hugged her servant girl and turned her toward the door. Then she looked at the servant. "Make sure she gets off the Baiae—and do so quickly!"

"Yes, Madam; as you wish." He turned and exited the room with Nesuptia. Now Agrippina was all alone.

Approximately four hours later, Anicetus and the soldiers approached the emperor's estate on the Baiae. The estate guards recognized his insignia and bowed to recognize its authority. As they walked through the corridors of the house, a set of soldiers checked each room. Finally, they approached the guest bedroom.

Agrippina was seated in a chair, drinking a cup of wine. Anicetus and four soldiers entered the room. "I've been expecting you."

Anicetus drew out a dagger from his garment. "I'm only following the emperor's orders, Madam."

"And did the emperor give me the dignity of departure?"

"That he did," he said, as he turned the dagger around and handed it to her.

"Be sure and thank the emperor for his consideration." She then took the dagger and began the blood-letting process. The soldiers stood guard at the door to her room until her life was ended. Anicetus checked her pulse and then took the dagger to the east gate.

† † †

Nero sent the servant ahead of him. "See to it that my mother has an opportunity to change clothing before I arrive."

"Yes, Divine One."

Nero smiled. *Such a wizard am I! Soon, I will be set free of her hideous tricks.*

As Nero neared the east gate, he stopped his entourage to relieve himself by a small bush. He found the dagger and slipped it under his garment and was about to enter the estate.

Agermus met him at the palace entrance. "Divine One! She is dead!"

"What?!"

"Yes! I found her in her room—it was suicide!" Agermus hung his head in despair.

"Come here," Nero said.

Nero gave him a long embrace as though he were comforting him. But suddenly he backed away. "You have a dagger in your garment. Guards, search this man!"

Agermus was shaken. "No, Divine One, I am not allowed to carry a weapon!"

Several guards began to feel his garment. They found the dagger that Nero had just planted during the embrace.

"That's not mine! No! It's not mine!"

"Let me see it," Nero commanded. He took the dagger and examined its blade. He slid his finger slowly down the blade, causing a small trickle of blood to form on his finger. He smelled the blood and then tasted it. "This is the blood of my lineage! You dare to kill my mother and call it a suicide?!"

Agermus was speechless. He knew the emperor had planted the dagger on him. He also knew it would be useless to say more, so he hung his head down as two soldiers grabbed him.

"Take him to the barracks and allow him to let his blood flow." Nero watched as they dragged him away. "The rest of you will go and get my mother's body and prepare it for the ceremony."

✝✝✝

"We must go east to Macedonia or until I find Luke," Paul said. He looked at his imprisoned house of two years one last time.

"What about Peter and John Mark?" Barnabas asked.

"We will stop at one of the fellowships and tell them of our departure. Peter and John Mark will discover our whereabouts through them."

Paul, Barnabas, and John entered the small house of Judas of Ephraim, where one of the Roman fellowships gathered.

"Peace to you all in Jesus' blessed name," Judas said.

They each embraced the elder. "And peace to you and your household, Judas," Paul said.

"I hear that you have been dismissed of your charges and are now a free man."

"Yes, my brother. After two years, it is a blessing to be able to go back into the mission fields."

"Ah, but you have been in a field ripe for harvest these past two years. God be honored that He allowed you to stay in Rome and help us build our fellowships."

"Glory and honor to Him alone; but we must journey back to the east until we are refreshed in the fellowships, and then turn back west to Spain."

"Yes, Spain; now there is the frontier of the empire. Spain joins the sea with no boundaries."

"Have you been there?" John asked.

Judas smiled. "No, I've only heard stories of the call of the sea and the giant rock that guards it's entryway to the Great Sea."

Barnabas was anxious to enquire about his cousin, John Mark. "Have you any word from Peter or John Mark?"

"No, and that surprises me. We usually hear from them every two or three months, but it has been nearly six months since we received an update . . . perhaps soon."

At that moment, there was a commotion outside the house. A young child broke through the outer door. "Grandfather, there are people outside looking for you."

Judas stood up and made his way past his guests. "Excuse me while I investigate."

Moments later a familiar voice was heard as the door opened. "I hear some people are looking for me?"

"Peter!" John leaped toward him, grabbed his old friend, and embraced him tightly.

"Come now, my beloved friend . . . easy on this old body."

"We were just about to leave you a message—and now you're here!"

Perpetua entered next and exchanged greetings as well.

"Where's John Mark?" Barnabas asked.

Peter looked toward the door. "My guess is that he is wherever my Petronilla is." At that moment, both Petronilla and John Mark entered. "See?"

"John Mark!"

"Barnabas!" They both embraced.

"So good to see you again, my cousin! I have missed you so!"

John Mark held him at arm's length. "Oh Barnabas, how I have prayed for you for many years! And you're all safe!"

"Yes, all of me is safe!" They laughed and embraced again.

Judas headed for the kitchen. "We must have some drink and bread to celebrate this glorious occasion!"

Paul smiled. "Yes, but we must leave soon."

"What's the rush?" Peter asked. "You can't leave today." Several others walked in. "Here are Quartus and Gaius. They are true brothers in the faith."

"Grace and peace to you both," Paul said, as they exchanged embraces.

"And to you as well," Gaius responded. "And please know that I have several dwellings here in Rome that are available to you, should you be in the area."

"Thank you, dear brother; but look at me." Paul lifted an arm and then a leg. "No chains to keep me here any longer. That's why I will depart soon and find Doctor Luke to journey farther west."

"Paul, you're not going anywhere," Peter said. "I have a few stories to tell you. And what I have to show you will change your mind about leaving so hastily."

"Paul, we must stay awhile and listen to the report . . . can't we?" John was almost begging.

"Oh, I guess so." Paul had seen enough of this city and was anxious to leave. But now he looked around for a chair or mat on which to recline.

"Ahem." Peter cleared his throat. "I think most of you know my dear wife and daughter; but I would like to introduce you to my soon-to-be son-in-law, Master John Mark."

John Mark blushed as he grabbed Petronilla's hand.

"What?!" Barnabas nearly screamed. "John Mark and Pet are to be married?"

"Yes, it is true, my cousin."

"Well praise be to our Lord!" John shouted. "And when is the occasion to occur?"

"That's why we're back in Rome," Peter said. "I wanted some counsel on the matter, but I didn't know that our Lord would provide you three for the occasion!"

"Oh no," Paul said. "We cannot wait another year."

"The year's betrothal has come and gone," Peter said. "But none of us feel like we should settle down."

"That's correct," John Mark said. "Petronilla and I wish to continue in the mission work. We do not sense our Lord wanting us to settle into one community." He then turned to Barnabas and Paul. "We would be honored if the both of you would share the rites of our matrimony."

"I would be more than honored, my dear cousin," Barnabas said, as he embraced the young couple.

Paul smiled. "Well count me in also . . . when will the occasion occur?"

"As soon as we can get the dust off our clothes," Peter said.

"*And* secure a place for the newlyweds to stay," Perpetua said. "*And* a small area for the celebration; *and* some new wine ordered; *and* . . ."

Peter spoke to Paul while Perpetua continued her "to do" list. "Don't despair, brother. We'll have this over in two days or less."

John Mark looked at Petronilla. "I think this means we will marry soon."

She squeezed his hand. "I pray so, John Mark, I pray so."

He looked at his bride-to-be. "Let's go outside while they discuss all the plans for the wedding." He gently guided her out the door to a tree near the entrance, where they sat down.

"Wow, there was a lot of chatter in there," Petronilla said.

"Yes, but now it's just me and you." He smiled.

"What are you smiling about?"

"Oh, I just remembered when Paul asked me to go with your family to Rome, I objected."

"You did?"

"Yes. I wanted to be Paul's scribe and write for him. I was so disappointed when he said 'No'." He grabbed her hand. "But our Lord knew what was best for me—for us!"

"That He did." Now it was her time to smile.

"Okay, why are you smiling?"

"Oh, nothing."

"That's not fair. I told you mine, now you tell me yours."

She giggled. "I remember when Father said you were coming with us, I was afraid he would pay more attention to you than to me. I was jealous of my time with my family."

John Mark piped in. "Then to punish us for arguing, your Father made us sit together and write his stories about Jesus."

"But eventually you became the writer and Mother and I did the cooking and cleaning."

John Mark stood up. "Speaking of writing, I think now would be a great time to reveal my present to Barnabas and Paul."

"Why now? I'm enjoying our time alone."

"I suspect they will want to begin reading it before they leave Rome." He helped her stand up and they walked back into the house.

Peter was talking as they entered. ". . . but we eventually baptized the man that tried to run us out of the town."

"Oh, there you are," Perpetua said. "We were about to send some Roman guards after you."

"Mother, have you decided what we're eating at the celebration?"

"Anything but swine!" Peter said. "I want fresh fish."

"I thought you liked bacon," Paul said. "Remember Antioch?"

"Do I ever! I was just being polite."

Perpetua jumped back into the conversation. "Judas says there is a nice place near the Tiber River where many weddings are celebrated. There are stone tables and a small covering where the food can be served."

"Sounds great!" Petronilla said.

John Mark got the crowd's attention. "We have a gift to give to Barnabas and Paul."

"A gift for us?" Barnabas asked. "Can't it wait until after the ceremony?

"No, this gift is something that must be given now." John Mark looked around. "Uh, where is my canvas bag?" He continued looking around.

Peter rolled his eyes and smiled. "Probably still on the donkey out front."

"Oh . . . excuse me please." John Mark ran out the door while everyone else sat in silence, smiling at each other.

"I think he's been bitten by a love insect," Peter said.

When John Mark returned, he brought in a large bag filled with papyrus sheets. He placed it down in front of Barnabas and Paul. "Here is my calling—my gift—in ministry." He pulled out the first two pages and handed one each to Paul and Barnabas.

Paul looked at the Greek writing: The beginning of the great news of Jesus Christ, Son of God.

Barnabas began reading his page: And after John, being delivered up, Jesus came into Galilee proclaiming the great news of the kingdom of God . . . Barnabas and Paul looked at each other.

"Is this the story of the ministry of Jesus?" Paul asked.

John Mark beamed. "As told by the Apostle Peter . . . mostly."

Paul and Barnabas continued looking at their pages, moving their hands across each page. "This is wonderful, John Mark—and Peter!" Barnabas said.

"Yes," Peter said. "After a few weeks with John Mark, he began asking me stories of the things Jesus said and did. We both felt the Spirit leading us in writing this. It was a precious experience."

"Thank you—both of you!" Barnabas said.

"There's only one problem," John Mark said. "You must share your copy. My soon-to-be father-in-law has requested the original."

"Oh we will share," Paul said. "I promise!" He smiled as he looked at the pages in the canvas. "I must read this right away!"

"And so must I!" Barnabas said.

"And what about me?" John asked.

"Well of course, John," Paul said. "We will share with you."

Peter looked at John Mark. "I think, perhaps, they may stay long enough to get copies made—one copy for each of them." They smiled as the three men began reading portions of the pages to each other.

†††

"Is he sleeping?"

"Yes, my lady," the servant girl said.

Octavia peeked through the partially opened door. She had an eerie feeling about this day. She stepped back. *Will he dismiss me?* She could only think of the tragedy of being banished from the Rome she had learned to love. She looked again through the gap—but this time Nero was standing on the other side of the door looking at her.

"Find something interesting to gaze upon?" he asked.

She bowed her head. "You didn't come to bed. I was worried about you."

"Ha!" he laughed as he swung the door open. "And when did you begin being concerned about me?" She did not reply. "You have given me no heir! I have given you a life of royalty, yet what have you given me in return?"

"I have been faithful to you all these years. Do you not see love in my commitment?"

"I do not seek your love—I want a child! Do you understand?" She began crying. "Enough of the theatrics! And leave my quarters immediately. I will assign you to another facility until the divorce papers are complete . . . Now leave." Nero walked back to his bed and sat on its side. Octavia left the area with her servant girl.

"Guards!" Several guards came to Nero's room. "Send this woman to Campania . . . and find Acte and bring her to me." They turned around and left the room. *Perhaps she will bear me an heir.*

"Did they buy it?" Nero asked.

Anicetus laughed. "Hook, line, and sinker! She is an adulteress!"

"Great. Poppaea should be pleased." He turned toward the door. "Guards!" Several soldiers came into the room. "Take Octavia to the prison yard and have her beheaded immediately."

"Yes, Divine One." They then turned and left the room.

Nero smiled. "Now it's time for Marcus Salvius Otho and his charming wife to come for a visit."

"Poppaea Sabina," Anicetus said. "Now there's a woman of true beauty—designed by the gods for a god."

"My feelings exactly. My divinity and her beauty shall produce the finest of offspring."

"But what of Marcus?"

"He will give us his blessing," Nero said as he raised his wine cup and drank, "or he will lose the rest of his possessions."

† † †

The fish markets in Capernaum had a reputation of the finest fish from the Sea of Galilee. Eliezer had a good reputation as well—especially since his new wife, Mary, remained by his side every day, cleaning and filleting fish. But this was their secondary job. Every day after work, they managed to go to the camp for outcasts and feed the hungry. Other residents of Magdala were converted and helped them at the camp as well.

"Eliezer?" Mary asked. "Please come and share your testimony with this poor man." Mary always smiled at him, reminding him of his great gift of leading people to profess Jesus as Lord. He never thought of himself as a proclaimer or a prophet, but it never ceased amazing him how his testimony would cause others to want to turn to Jesus.

On the Sabbath, Eliezer and Mary tried to reason with the Jews near the synagogues, telling them about Jesus as the Messiah. Some listened—most did not. But early on the first day of each week, they held a worship service in honor of Jesus and His resurrection. Many Galileans listened and responded to the gospel.

One Sunday morning, after the early worship service, they were walking down to the fish preparation area. "Oh, what a morning this has been," Mary said.

"Yes, many responded to the testimonies of some of the former outcasts. It is effective."

"It always is when you have had an experience of the new birth with Jesus."

Eliezer grabbed Mary's hand. "And I thank God for bringing you into my life."

"And you are so sweet to me," she said.

"Well it is true. Life was becoming more and more difficult for me until you came along. I feel as if I've been born again a second time."

Mary stopped him. I would kiss you here and now, but it may cause a problem."

Eliezer smiled as he looked around. The market around them was swarming with people. "Don't want to jeopardize our witness?"

"Yes . . . but here's something to remind you of the power of our Lord through the love He has given us." Slowly she led them to the side of a vendor's tent. Then, carefully, she moved his hand across her tummy. "Right there! Do you feel it?"

At first, Eliezer didn't catch on. But then it hit him. "Oh my! Oh my! Are you having a baby?"

She laughed. "No, silly . . . *We* are having a baby."

"Oh my." He gently pressed on her tummy, feeling a tiny lump. "Don't you need to stop walking? Here, let me carry you!"

Mary laughed again. "Eliezer, becoming pregnant does not cripple me. I'll still fillet more fish than you for the next four months!" She laughed again, as she started running down the road to Magdala. "Come on! I bet I can beat you to the shop."

As she continued to trot, Eliezer could only stare in awe of God's wonderful gift. "My Lord," he prayed. "Thank you for this wonderful woman I now call my wife." Tears began to form in his eyes. "And now I thank you for this new gift of life You have given us. May we be careful to raise the child to honor You in all areas of living, in Your precious name, amen."

† † †

The Roman highway, from Rome to the east, was much easier to travel on than the roads around Judea. The smoothness of his horse allowed Paul to continue reading John Mark's life and ministry of Jesus. Peter had told him many of the events recorded in this writing, but reading them was like a breath of fresh spiritual air. This made him think of all the letters he had written to the various fellowships.

My Lord, he prayed to himself, *should I encourage Your fellowships to copy and distribute all my letters?* Paul was not expecting an immediate reply, but he received one.

Barnabas pulled up alongside Paul's horse. "I hope you don't mind, but as John and I traveled through Macedonia and Asia, we encouraged the fellowships to carefully copy all your writings so that they may keep several copies available for each fellowship and to pass other copies along to new fellowships."

John joined them. "And you know Matthew has written the story of Jesus for our people of Judea. How many letters and books does that make?"

Paul smiled. "Oh, I'll leave the counting up to you."

"Come on, Paul," John said. "What else do we have to do on this road trip?"

"Okay, let's see . . . there's the letter to the fellowships in Galatia; then I wrote twice to the Thessalonians; and two times, wasn't it, to the fellowship at Corinth? Then there was my large letter to the Roman fellowship—before I arrived. Next, let's see . . . yes, a letter to the fellowships in Ephesus, Philippi, and Colossae. I think that's it for me."

"I thought you said you sent Luke back with a runaway slave, with a letter of explanation?" Barnabas asked.

"Oh, that little letter—to Philemon, my friend . . . oh, and a letter to Timothy!"

"Wow," John said. "That's eleven letters, Paul. I think you win the prize for the most written."

As Paul pondered over all his writings, he thought of his Jewish kinsmen and their rejection of Jesus as the Christ, their Messiah. "Will there be more letters?"

"If everything could be written on what Jesus said and did," John said, "I bet the whole Roman fleet couldn't carry them!"

"So when are you going to write?" Barnabas asked John.

"I'm still collecting my thoughts on a project, but my Lord has not told me to start writing just yet."

"Wait on Him," Paul said. "The burden will come and His Spirit will guide you in the truth."

The three arrived at Three Taverns just before dark. They acquired a room and purchased tickets for a ship leaving the following day for Syracuse. Following that, they boarded another ship for Corinth. In Corinth, Paul spoke to the fellowship, strengthening them, as well as introducing them to the apostles John and Barnabas.

After a week's stay in Corinth, the three continued on land, heading north to Philippi, stopping at every fellowship along the way and speaking to the Christians.

"I pray Luke is in Philippi," Paul said. "I need some of his eye salve."

"I met Doctor Luke," John said. "He was in and out of Jerusalem while you were imprisoned in Caesarea."

"Yes, I remember those days. He was gathering information from Mary, the mother of Jesus. He's a very smart and useful brother in the Lord."

"I agree."

Several hours later, they arrived at Lydia's house in Philippi. Paul saw several men outside the house, one of whom he recognized. "Epaphroditus!"

Epaphroditus turned and stared momentarily. Then he smiled, waved back at Paul, and ran out to the street. "Paul! I can't believe my eyes! You're not chained!"

Paul dismounted from his horse and embraced him. "My brother, it's good to see you again."

Epaphroditus was nearly in tears. "We thought you were in serious trouble in Rome. Our people have prayed for you every day. Now look at you—here in person! Praise be unto our Savior for His merciful deliverance!"

Paul smiled. "It sounds as if you have been spending quality time with our Lord."

"Oh, Paul, you won't believe how our Lord has been working in Philippi since my return from Rome—and your letter . . . it has blessed us so! Our women have made peace among themselves and are meeting regularly for prayer and are ministering to the poor. We've had to make about a dozen copies of the letter for other fellowships and individuals."

"Really? Then God is truly working through the many letters . . . Have you received other letters written by me?"

"Of course! We would not give the Ephesian group ours until they gave us theirs—the same for the delegation from Thessalonica, Colossae, and Corinth!"

"Wow," John said. "That many?"

"Yes, my brother—John is your name, isn't it?"

John smiled. "Yes, you do remember me. And remember, this is Barnabas."

"Yes, Barnabas; grace and peace to you, my brother."

"And how is Lydia?" Paul asked.

"She is on a ship enroute to Ephesus right now with a delivery of her merchandise. That woman is a real hard worker . . . and she works even harder for our Lord!"

"Oh, I see."

"Stay for a while; she'll be back in a week or two."

Paul did not respond to Epaphroditus' invitation. "I am looking for Doctor Luke. Has he been in town lately?"

Epaphroditus smiled. "Yes, and even now he is at the prison giving medical help to some of the prisoners."

"Great!" John said. "Now maybe we can slow the pace down and rest a couple of days."

Paul gave a glancing smile at John and Barnabas. "I've been a little anxious to find my doctor."

"I can understand," Epaphroditus said. "He has a special gift of healing in his bag—and sometimes he doesn't even open it!"

† † †

"Doctor, what's wrong with me?" a prisoner asked.

Luke smiled. "I'd say you're pushing on these bars too much."

"Aw, doctor, it's worse than that."

"There is something else wrong with you—worse than this rash on your arms and shoulders." Luke looked at all the prisoners around him. There is a sin-rash that is inside you and only Jesus can heal you of this rash. Only Jesus can deliver you from sin."

"We've heard this from the jailer," another prisoner responded.

"And what have you done with what you've heard?"

"Nothing," another prisoner said.

Luke opened his bag and brought out a small flask. "It's like this ointment: I can tell you that it will heal you and you might believe it can heal you, but you won't benefit from it unless you apply it to your wound. You have seen the change Jesus has made on some of your fellow prisoners, but until you apply it to your own personal need it won't do you any good."

A large prisoner rose up from a stone bed. He snorted and reached for his walking stick. "All I hear are words of change— I will never believe until I see this faith in Jesus change someone."

Luke looked his way. "Tell me, what is your ailment?"

"I see men as trees—everything is a blur."

Luke walked over to him. "May I examine your eyes?"

The man bent down on his knees. Luke carefully raised one of his eyelids. "Hmm."

"Just what I thought," the large prisoner said. "More words."

"What if Jesus healed you? How would you respond?"

"If He healed me, I would devote my life to Him and let Him guide my every step."

"Do you believe He can heal you?"

"How can I believe unless I see?"

"Physical healing of a body part does nothing for your eternal needs. Your sin sickness is deeper than this flesh on you. Jesus wants to heal your soul."

The prisoner growled. "Just as I thought; your Jesus is a myth—a ghost!" He reared his cane to strike Luke—but he froze. He could not lower his arm. "Aughh!" he screamed and fell back onto the floor. Some of the prisoners backed away from Luke and the others. Several other prisoners moved over to help their large comrade. "Aughh!" he screamed again. "Don't touch me," he growled. He tried to rise up from the prison floor—but he couldn't. "What's happening to me?!"

There was silence. Luke moved over closer to him and spoke softly: "I once was like you. I said that I had to see a miracle before I believed. God, in His mercy, allowed me to witness a blind man get his sight back."

The big prisoner was still on the floor. "So what's the difference between me and him?"

"The only difference between him and you is that he said he would believe even if God did not heal him. He asked Jesus to save him regardless."

"But how can one believe without seeing?"

"It's called 'faith'. Faith believes something before you actually see its physical response. If you ask in faith, Jesus said that by believing you will receive it—you will have it. Again, I ask you, do you believe Jesus can heal you?"

The prisoner looked at his stiff arm and the hand that held the cane. He slowly removed the cane from his hand. Several of the other prisoners that had believed got on their knees beside Luke and began praying. He looked at the praying men. He remembered one of them as a murderer. Tears began welling up in the corner of his eyes. "I believe!" he cried out. "I believe! Lord Jesus, have mercy on my sickened body and soul!" He began sobbing as he pulled up his knees and arms toward his body. "I will follow You whether You heal me or not—just save me from myself!"

The believers joined Luke as they laid their hands on the man. "Lord Jesus," Luke prayed, "You have heard this man's plea for salvation. You promised to save those who truly repent and call on You for salvation. Heal him now, I pray, in Your powerful name, amen."

"Amen," the others said.

The three stood up and backed away from the large prisoner. For a moment he remained stiff on the floor. Then he stretched out his arms. Next, he moved his legs. He slowly maneuvered his body into a squatted position, grabbed his cane, and managed to stand on his feet. "I'm healed," he said.

"Can you see better now?" one of the believing prisoners asked.

"No, not with my physical eyes . . . but Jesus has healed me from the inside—I feel joy, peace, and forgiveness! Now I understand, doctor . . . Now I understand."

Luke came and embraced him. "There is always a new understanding of spiritual things when Jesus comes inside you to take over your life." Luke backed up. "But you must learn to walk by faith and not by sight."

"My Jesus," he said, "teach me how to walk through Your spiritual eyes."

The remaining prisoners in that section of the prison came up to Luke. "We want to follow Jesus as well."

Luke sat with them and told them what they must do in order to be saved.

†††

James looked out his window toward the temple in Jerusalem. "No! . . . Not yet." He turned to face Simon. "We must wait until we hear from the others: Bartholomew, Judas, James the Less, and the other apostles. They may report to us soon . . . We must remain in Jerusalem for now."

"Most of the believers have fled Jerusalem," Simon said. "James, it is no longer safe to remain here."

James acted as if Simon did not even speak. "Soon, the others will report. Perhaps then we will make a decision on whether to abandon the city."

†††

"He's where?" the high priest asked.

"Your Most Excellency, the new governor, Lucceius Albinus, is enroute from Alexandria."

Ananus rubbed his chin momentarily. *This is my chance to make a statement.* He turned to the chief priest. "Call the Sanhedrin council into session. I need to speak with them immediately."

Two hours later

"What is the meaning of this hastily called meeting?" a council member—a Pharisee—asked. "You know many of the Pharisee council members are in Caesarea this week.

"I need to speak with the council about an urgent matter concerning the Christians in Jerusalem," Ananus said. Now Ananus was a Sadducee.

"Oh, those rebels? Just leave them be."

"No, we can't 'just leave them be.' They are the source of our unrest in Jerusalem. Now I have one of their leaders in custody and must act quickly before the new governor arrives."

"You have arrested him?"

"One leader and several of his followers."

While the council members took their seats, Ananus stood before them. "Men of the council, please hear me out. Some of my guards heard about a private meeting of the Christians and raided a house this morning. After scourging them, we discovered one of them is the brother of that Nazarene whom we crucified during the reign of Pontius Pilate."

"He has a brother?" someone asked.

"Yes. And this brother continues to teach and train others in this heretical Way to our God, bypassing our priesthood completely."

"Blasphemy!" another Sadducee member cried out.

"Wait!" a Pharisee member said. "Shouldn't we have the full council here for such a decision?"

"Yes!" another Pharisee said.

Ananus could sense the disparity between the Sadducees and Pharisees. He knew he had to get a quick vote on this issue. "I say we act before the new governor arrives. We must not burden him with this problem at the very onset of his rule."

"Amen, amen!" the other Sadducees cried out. A vote was cast and the Sadducees won.

"Bring them to us," Ananus said.

James (the Elder) and two men were brought into the high chamber. James marveled at how few of the council were present. *Lord, should I object and appeal to the full council?*

Jesus spoke to him: "My child, do not fear man. Remain faithful to the end. They must see the hope of Israel in you."

"Which one of you is the brother of the Nazarene?" Ananus asked.

"I am," all three said together.

"What is the meaning of this? I ask a simple question and you try to confuse me?"

"I am James, half-brother of Jesus."

"I am Simon, half-brother of Jesus."

"And I am Joses, half-brother of Jesus."

"We're all related to our Messiah, Jesus," James said.

Ananus put his hands over his ears. "Speak no more of this name before us!" Ananus moved to the front of Elder James. "Do you deny that you continue teaching our brethren that they must now acknowledge this Nazarene in order to have their sins forgiven?"

"I do not deny this. Jesus became the sacrifice for all sin for all time. God, our Father, has given us equal access to Him through His Son, Jesus."

Ananus motioned to a guard nearby who came over and slapped the face of James. "I said, do not speak of His name before the council!" He then turned to the council. "This is the blasphemy that this 'Way' poisons our people's minds. I say we cast judgment on these blasphemers now."

"Yes!" many of the council members said in unison.

"No!" said some of the other members. "Something this serious needs the attention of the whole council."

The high priest ignored the Pharisees' negative response. "What is the punishment for blasphemy?"

"Stoning!" a Sadducee member said.

"Stoning?" a Pharisee asked. "Don't we need the governor's approval?"

"We have no governor at the present," Ananus said. "And this crime's punishment must not be delayed . . . Guards! Take these three out to the Hinnom!"

A dozen temple guards grabbed the three half-brothers of Jesus and led them out of the high chamber.

"Why is this happening to us?" Joses asked.

"The Lord has truly left this place," James said. "I just wouldn't believe it. I'm sorry, my brothers, but I am to blame for this tragedy."

"No, James," Simon said. "I'm afraid we can only blame ourselves for not listening to our Lord. I only hope word gets to Jude to take Mother into hiding."

✝✝✝

"Mary!"

"Yes, my Lord?"

"You must leave with Jude right away! Those who wish to harm My children are seeking you as well."

"Where are we to go?"

"Go north to Capernaum and seek Simon Peter's family. There you will find refuge and further instruction."

Mary went outside. She saw her son at the front gate with another man. "Jude! Jude!"

He bid the man goodbye and turned to her. "Yes, Mother?"

"We must leave Jerusalem immediately. Our Lord has spoken to me."

"Mother, I just received word that the high priest has arrested James, Simon, and Joses."

"That's what I feared. We will pray for them on our journey. Go, gather your things and meet me at the stable."

✝✝✝

The three half-brothers of Jesus were marched out to the Valley of Hinnom. There they were stripped of their outer garments and their hands and feet were tied together. Then they were brought to the precipice of a rubbish dump. Several wild dogs stood among the rubbish below, eyeing the men above them.

The council arrived shortly and assembled before the three. "This is your final opportunity to denounce this heretic you call the Messiah," Ananus said. "If you refuse, then you will be stoned to death."

James looked at his two brothers. "Be faithful to the end," he said to them. Then he looked at the high priest. "You do not understand that the Messiah's kingdom is not of this world. We are but ambassadors, telling our brethren that our Deliverer has come and how we must prepare for entrance into the heavenly kingdom."

"Denounce the Nazarene!" the high priest ordered.

"I cannot denounce the One who has set me free of my sinful nature and has promised me eternal life in His kingdom. I will always be a co-heir of my Savior, Jesus the Christ!"

"This, too, is my final answer," Simon said.

"And mine as well," Joses said. "Jesus is my Lord!"

"Enough!" Ananus cried out.

"Blasphemy!" some of the council members shouted, as they ran forward and pushed the three over the edge of the cliff. The fall was about fifty feet, causing some cuts and scratches on them as they fell. They were so tied together that neither of them could wipe the blood that poured from their noses and mouths.

"Lord, Jesus!" Joses cried out. "Receive us quickly!"

"Lord," James said, "do not let this sin keep them from ever receiving Your truth and Spirit."

"Yes, Lord," Simon said. "Forgive them this wrong!"

By this time, many of the council members had retrieved some large rocks and began casting them down upon the three men. Several dogs yelped as they ran from the area. Rock after rock was hurled down by the council until all three men were nearly covered with the stones. Ananus ordered the soldiers to go down and confirm the deaths of the half-brothers of Jesus. In a matter of minutes, they were confirmed dead.

"There," Ananus said. "It is finished."

✝✝✝

"My Son," Mary said, weeping as she rode on a donkey, guided by Jude. "Keep my boys close to You during their test."

"Woman," Jesus said, "they are now with Me in Paradise. They are more alive now than ever and are rejoicing in the presence of the Father. You and Jude will reside with Peter's family until John comes to find you. Then you will go with him to Ephesus."

Mary wept even more. "Stop, Jude, and help me down."

He stopped her donkey and helped her down. "What is it, Mother?" She told him the news as they wept together.

✝✝✝

John sat in the backyard area of Luke's uncle, Johannes's place in Philippi. He was burdened to know where he would go next. While the others were at the assembly hall of the fellowship, he decided to stay behind for prayer. That's when he heard from Jesus.

"John!"

"Yes, my Lord?"

"You must depart for Capernaum where you will find Jude and Mary. Jude will continue ministering in Judea and Samaria, but I want Mary to go with you to Ephesus."

Paul was resting from about an hour of teaching the followers about the priesthood from the Sacred Writings and how the Christ became the eternal High Priest. He listened to several testimonies before the voices of those speaking faded out and a new voice began speaking to him.

"Paul?"

He responded quietly. "Yes, my Master?"

"You must not go any farther east. I will send the others on to give your report to the assemblies throughout Asia and on to Antioch, Syria. They will gather support for your future journey."

"But where do I go?"

"You will journey west through Rome and then on to Spain."

Paul bent down to his knees and slowly lowered his head to the floor and worshipped. Barnabas saw this and he also lowered himself to the floor. Soon the entire fellowship had fallen to their knees—some even prostrated themselves!—to the floor and worshipped. No one spoke—only inaudible groanings were heard for about an hour.

"It is the Lord's wish," Paul said to the others at Johannes's villa. "Luke and I must go to Spain. The rest of you will continue east to visit the fellowships and encourage them to remain true to His words and to support our planting of new assemblies in the west."

John came over to Paul and embraced him. "You have encouraged me to press on."

"And you have blessed me with your loving response to the Gentiles."

"And what about me?" Timothy asked. "I want to go with you."

"Timothy, my son; you must continue to build up the fellowships in Asia and Macedonia. I want you to go to Ephesus, for the Lord has warned me that the Judaizers will continue teaching false doctrines. The fellowships of the regions must be fore-warned."

Timothy embraced Paul and then looked at him. "I'm not like you, Paul. I don't have your courage. Confrontation frightens me."

"Son, you have your testimony and you have the presence of our Master. If you stand with the Lord, you will have strength for each occasion. Do not be afraid, but proclaim His word! Be ready at all times to stand up to anyone who may try to contradict the simple truths of the gospel. Trust in our Lord to strengthen you."

Barnabas and Epaphroditus walked up to them. "Paul," Epaphroditus said, "I will be available to you and the others to transport any resources or messages that our Lord desires."

Paul embraced him. "My true partner in the faith, I know you will be ready when the time comes. Only listen for His bidding."

"The Lord wants me to head for Crete and then to Cyprus," Barnabas said. "I will go with John and Timothy to Ephesus and then sail from there."

"That is a good route. I know you will be an encouragement to the fellowships along the way."

"Paul," Barnabas said. "Please send word as to your journeys . . . and let us know of Peter and John Mark's whereabouts."

Paul embraced his old friend. "If I see them or hear about them, I shall forward that information back to Ephesus; and, perhaps, it will be passed on to Antioch.

"Perhaps so . . . perhaps so."

"You need to rest," Luke said to Paul. Paul smiled, but Luke could see the tiredness in his face. "Follow me—I need to check your eyes."

†††

"You need to rest," she said, as she kissed him.

Eliezer looked into her eyes. "Me? You're the one who is pregnant . . . I have to care for you."

Mary smiled. "My Master is caring for me; any day now, He will bring forth our baby."

Eliezer felt her tummy. "Wow! It better be soon or he'll hit the floor walking!"

She laughed. "'He'? And has the Lord told you something that He has not revealed to me?"

"Oh, it'll be a boy, I'm sure. And his name will be Elijah— 'the Lord, He is God'!"

"Fine; and *he* will learn to prepare fish for the market— speaking of that, we must clean up and head for Capernaum."

Eliezer grabbed her arm. "No, you will lay here and watch while *I* clean up."

She smiled as she watched her husband begin the cleaning. *Jesus, I see You in him . . . Thank You for such a gift.*

†††

Jacob bowed down before her. "You are most welcomed to my humble dwellings."

Mary reached out to him. "Please, sir, you do not bow down to me. I am just as you—a follower of our Lord Jesus, the Christ."

"You are more than that," he said. "You are the mother of our Lord."

She smiled. "I too am flesh and blood, just as He was while walking among us."

"And you are the brother of our Lord?" he asked Jude.

"Half-brother," Jude said. "And a follower of Jesus—such as you."

Elizabeth came from the kitchen area. "Then I bet you are hungry and weary from your travels. Please recline with us and allow me to prepare you a meal."

Jude obliged but Mary followed Elizabeth to the kitchen area. "I am not used to being served. Please allow me to help."

Jacob began speaking as he showed Jude where to recline. "Tell me, have you seen my son-in-law and daughter?"

"No sir, not lately. Our last report on him said that he was in Rome planting new fellowships."

Jacob smiled. "He was always the adventurous type."

"Yes, Peter has been through a lot for our Lord."

"And you say our Lord spoke to you to come here?"

"Yes—to find my mother."

"Why not stay in Jerusalem? I do not understand."

"Neither do I fully understand; but it appears as if God is going to allow the Jews and Romans to fight over our homeland . . . and the Romans will win."

"Oh . . . I see."

"The priests are becoming more corrupt and rebellious to the things of God. It's only a matter of time."

"And what will become of our people?"

Jude looked deep into the eyes of Jacob. "We will all be persecuted and hunted down like wild beasts until we surrender and bow down to the Romans and their gods."

Jacob looked away. "I was afraid you might say that." He stood up. "I am too feeble to run away—what will become of people like me?"

"You are a fisherman. I suspect you will be put into slavery and will supply fish for the soldiers and other slaves."

"And my wife?"

"I wouldn't worry too much about her. If she can cook, she will be in high demand."

Mary and Elizabeth brought some food to the table and re-clined by the others. Jacob stood up. "We must pray for our meal and thank our Lord for His provisions. And we must pray for our people, that they will see Jesus as the Messiah and turn from their rebellion."

It was now mid-afternoon and the men were outside. The Lord spoke to His mother, who was resting in a bedroom. "Mary, you must go to the fish market and find Mary of Magdala. She will need your help in delivering her child."

She smiled. "Mary has a child?"

"Yes; go now and find her and her husband, Eliezer of Magdala, for it is her time to deliver a son."

"Yes, my Lord." Mary arose and walked to the back entrance. "Jude? Jude, my son, where are you?"

Jude came running from the side of the house. "Yes, Mother?"

"Quickly; we must go to the fish market and find Mary of Magdala. She needs our help."

"Mary of Magdala? At the fish market? I'm not sure where to go."

"I do!" Jacob said, as he made his way to the back of the house. "Come and I will show you the way."

"Elizabeth?" Mary asked.

"I'm afraid she has gone to the market for supplies," Jacob said. "But she will return soon."

"Good," Mary said, "because we're going to need her help in delivering a baby."

"A baby?!" the men asked together.

Mary smiled. "Don't worry; you men will stay with her hus-band through the delivery."

†††

Eliezer carried the large basket of fish he was using to trade for other household supplies. Mary walked alongside of him, with the donkey in tow, telling him the things they needed for the house. The market was busy at this time of day, for many were preparing for the evening meal—and especially the Jews, for the next day was the Sabbath.

Suddenly Mary stopped. She grimaced as the pangs of birth hit her. "Eliezer!"

"Yes, my dear?—oh my!" he said, as he saw her bent over and holding her abdomen. "Mary!" He helped her sit on the ground.

She groaned again. Then she yelped out a cry as the birth pangs hit her again, stronger than before. "Eliezer! Please get me away from this crowd!"

Eliezer looked for a side path, but everyone's booth was tied to each other for support. *Lord, we need Your help! Please help us!*

At that moment, Eliezer heard a voice. "Mary! There you are!" It was Mary, the mother of Jesus. "Jude! Jacob! Help her up."

Mary of Magdala recognized the voice. "Oh Mary! Thank You Lord for hearing my cry!"

Jude and Jacob knelt beside Mary and Eliezer. "We are her friends," Jude said to Eliezer. "Let us carry her and you bring your basket and animal."

"Oh blessed be the Lord!" Eliezer said. "Thank You, Lord, for sending us a band of angels!"

A booth owner came to their aid. "Here's a gurney! Use it."

"Thank you," Jude said. "We'll get it back to you soon."

"No need to rush, young man," he said. "I know Jacob and he's always good for his word."

As they helped Mary onto the gurney, a woman nearby handed her a small damp cloth. "Put this in your mouth," she instructed. "It'll help you through the birth."

"Thank you!" Mary managed to say, as the men lifted her up and hurried up the street.

†††

John stood aside as the elders of Philippi and some of the women assisted Paul, Luke, and a few others for the journey west. He smiled as he reflected on the many times Jesus had assisted the Twelve prepare for numerous journeys from Jerusalem to Capernaum and many points in between. And now, here were followers of Jesus—those who had not seen Him in the flesh—acting in the same manner.

Master, I miss your physical presence. If I could only touch you one more time—or gaze into your face once more . . .

"John, My beloved, I am in you now. Close your eyes and by faith see Me—feel Me!—for I Am, My dear child . . . I Am."

John closed his eyes and slowly rested on his knees. *My Lord, You are here . . . thank You for Your presence and Your encouragement.*

"John, you must teach and show the little children that I am with you now and forever. Express your love for Me to them. Teach them to love Me the way you always have. This is how they will know and experience the equal access they all have with Me."

John opened his eyes and continued watching the activities these men and women were showing toward one another. *I do see You better now, my Lord.*

Everyone having said their goodbyes, Paul looked at John. "My brother, would you be so kind to lead us in a departing prayer?"

"It would be an honor to do so. 'Lord Jesus, I speak for us all, knowing that we believe that You are sending us to different places to share Your good news. May Your presence guide Paul, Luke, and the others as they depart for new areas to the west. Where there is no assembly of followers, give birth to a new one. Continue building Your church, our Lord, for Your glory and for the advancement of the Kingdom. In Your precious name I pray, amen.'"

"Amen," the others said.

Barnabas assisted Paul onto his horse. "Okay, Luke," Paul said, "you lead the way."

Many of the Philippian Christians waved their hands and looked on until Paul and Luke were out of sight.

Epaphroditus stood beside John as they watched the others disappear from sight. "Rabbi John, it would be our honor to have you stay a while in Philippi and teach us the words of Jesus."

John smiled. "Please, call me John; I'm no rabbi. I will stay for a season, but then I must also take leave of this place for Capernaum."

†††

Matthew and Andrew brushed off the desert sand from their garments as they and several Christian brothers approached the villa of Joseph of Arimathea.

"It will be great to get some home-cooked food this evening," Andrew said.

"That will be nice," Matthew replied. As they neared the gate of the villa, they noticed it was already ajar. "That's strange."

Andrew grabbed the handle and slowly opened the gate. He looked inside as Matthew and the others awaited instructions. "I don't see anyone, Matthew."

They all stepped inside the courtyard and experienced an eerie stillness in the villa. Andrew pointed to the dining area. "Let's check in there." Once there, they saw a man stirring a pot of food in a kettle over a small fire.

Matthew recognized him. "Joseph?"

Joseph turned and stared for a moment; then he smiled, dropped his ladle, and raced over to the men. "Matthew! Andrew!" He embraced the two as the others looked on. "What a blessing to see friendly faces again! Come, come!" He cleared off a few cluttered benches. "You look weary; sit with me and rest."

"Where is everyone?" Andrew asked. He could see a restrained look on the elder council member's face.

"Oh, here, there, everywhere, I suppose."

"Tell us about the others," Matthew said.

Joseph ignored Matthew's request. "And who are these two men?"

"This is Arsak and Bozan. They're followers of Jesus from Parthia," Andrew said. "We brought them here to help us give our report of the work we've accomplished in the east."

Joseph reached out to embrace them. "Greetings to you both." They stood upright, but didn't return Joseph's embrace.

"They bow to each other instead of embracing," Andrew explained.

"That's fine with me as long as they know that they are my guests while here in Jerusalem."

"Joseph?" Matthew asked. "What's wrong?"

Joseph's warm smile quickly gave way to sobs. He lowered his head. "Oh dear brothers, we've had some terrible, terrible losses since you've been away."

"Should we wait until James is here before you tell us?" Andrew asked.

Joseph looked at them both, wiping the tears from off his beard. "I'm afraid we can't. James and his two brothers, Simon and Joses, were killed recently."

"What?!" Matthew stood up. "Who would dare do such a thing?"

Joseph's face turned angry. "That high priest, Ananus! He saw a delay in the new Roman governor's arrival and decided the timing was right for a killing."

Matthew sat down, as a state of shock set in. "A new governor? What happened to Festus?"

"He died suddenly."

Andrew shook his head as he thought of the deaths of his friends. "Were you there for the trials?"

"No. It occurred while many of us council members were in Caesarea to see Festus off for his burial tomb. It was a devious, cowardly act and I plan to report it to the new governor when he arrives."

Matthew rubbed his beard for a moment. "Where are Mary and Jude?"

"The Lord sent them to Peter's family in Capernaum. Mary said she was going to meet John there and stay with him. Jude said he would return to Nazareth later on."

"Are there any other apostles in Jerusalem?" Andrew asked.

"I haven't heard, but if they do report, they will do so at Jonathan of Gischala's house." Joseph peered around his dining area. "I regret that this place is too dangerous for any further meetings."

Matthew stood up. "Then we must go to Jonathan's house and see if any others show up."

"No, please don't rush off. You're here now and the bath house is ready for some desert sand. Plus, I have prepared a large pot of stew—more than Hamath and I can eat. Please go and clean up that we may have a mid-day bowl of stew together."

"The big guy is still here?" Andrew asked. "Well I feel safer already! Let's clean up and eat!" He smiled as he led the way to the bath house, explaining to Arsak and Bozan the size of Hamath.

Matthew stared at his large canvas bag. It contained his copy of the life of Jesus. He had been hopeful to get copies made of it while in Jerusalem . . . but now? *I wonder if we still have a trustworthy scribe in town?*

† † †

A shriek filled the air in the small house . . . then the cry of a newborn was heard. Soon, Elizabeth came outside where some concerned men stood. "It's a boy!"

Eliezer smiled as Jude and the others around him embraced and congratulated him on the arrival of his son.

"What is his name?" Jude asked.

Without hesitation, he said, "Elijah—his name is Elijah."

Elizabeth stood at the doorway. "Well come see your Elijah."

Eliezer quietly led the way as he and the other men walked into the room. He got on his knees beside Mary, who was cradling the baby in her arms. He said not a word, but knelt there in awe and wonderment.

"Here's our Elijah," Mary said in a weak but grateful tone. She moved the baby toward Eliezer.

At first, Eliezer was afraid he may hurt the baby; but Mary gently slipped the child into his arms. He looked down into the newest pair of eyes he'd ever seen. Elijah made no sounds except an occasional smacking of his lips. "Elijah? Elijah, my son, this is your father speaking."

Mary smiled. "I think he may be as tired as I, after what we both went through."

Eliezer handed Elijah back to his mother. "I pray he loves fish when he gets older."

"In time," Mary said. "In time."

Mary, the mother of Jesus, came into the room. "Now you men need to go back outside while we clean up in here. It won't be long before Elijah will want something to eat."

Eliezer, Jude, and Jacob left the room and returned to a shaded area out front. Eliezer looked at the other two. "I have a son! I have a son!" He looked up with outstretched arms. "O praise be unto Jesus! O praise be unto our God! For God is the Almighty—Lord of all creation!" Then he ran out onto the street and began telling everyone who walked by about his new son, Elijah.

Jacob smiled as he watched Eliezer interrupt complete strangers as they walked by his house. Jude, however, stared at the ground, reflecting upon the irony of a new life replacing the lives of his brothers who had recently lost theirs. *Lord Jesus,* he prayed silently, *help me to understand why some live and some die.*

✝✝✝

In Gaza, the entourage of Lucceius Albinus was intercepted by a delegation of Judean citizens, formed by Joseph of Arimathea. Albinus was enroute to Caesarea to take over the governorship of Festus.

"What emergency has arisen that calls for such a drastic intervention of my travels to Caesarea?" Albinus asked. He eyed each traveler, taking note of whether they were serious about their cause.

"Most Honorable Albinus," one of them said, "we Jews have a high respect for the life of man—such as you! However, the high priest of our people chose to break our moral laws—and those of the empire—by stoning several men to death without due process of law and without your consent, which is according to Roman law. We fear he is about to do more of this illegal action before you arrive and have come to not only protest his past illegal proceedings, but to ask that you send word as fast as possible to the high priest, forbidding him to stone anyone else without your consent."

Albinus turned to one of his advisors. "Ruficius, is this true? Must the high priest have my consent on such matters?"

"Several events, such as this, have occurred in the past," he replied, "and Emperor Caligula wrote a new edict that the Jews may convict their own of wrongful doing and may punish them by flogging. But the high priest must inform the governor of any crime that calls for the death penalty."

Albinus turned back toward the spokesman of the citizens. "What is your high priest's name?"

"Ananus ben Ananus."

"Ruficius, write up a short notice to this Ananus that he will not punish anyone else until I have reviewed the alleged crime and approve the punishment. Tell him to obey Roman law or I will personally see to it that he himself will receive the same punishment that he is advocating illegally."

"As you have ordered, your Excellency."

"Maximus, find Agrippa and notify him of his high priest's actions in my absence."

"Yes, your Excellency."

Albinus turned to the delegation. "By the time you return to your homeland, my changes should have been put into action. Now be on your way."

The spokesman bowed his head as he backed away. "Yes, your Excellency. We are deeply grateful for your quick response." The delegation remained in their place until the governor's caravan left the area.

Albinus inspected the governor's palace as soon as he arrived in Caesarea. "A bit open-aired, I suppose; but nothing that a woman or two can't fix. What do you think, Ruficius?"

He remained focused on the window ahead of him. "I'm not a maker of walls, your Excellency. Perhaps I can find someone in town to come hear of your wishes?"

"An excellent idea! Go do your thing."

Ruficius left as Maximus came into the room. "Your Excellency, I have good news from Agrippa."

"Yes? Go ahead."

"He has deposed Ananus as high priest."

"Very well; that should settle things down in Jerusalem."

"There is another problem in Jerusalem."

Albinus threw his cup down. "By the gods! What sinister place is this Jerusalem?!"

"Sir, there is a group of rebels who terrorize our soldiers. They are called, Sicarii."

"Sicarii?"

"Yes, your Excellency. They conceal small daggers, called sicae, in their belts and attempt to slit the throats of our leaders and soldiers."

Albinus removed his formal outer garment. "How many centurions do we have in the region?"

Maximus thought for a moment. "Fifteen camped near Jerusalem—another twenty within a three-day's march."

"I want the fifteen—plus ten more—to prepare a thorough search in the city of Jerusalem. Every male and female will be stripped down and checked for these weapons. Every house, villa, and building will be searched." Albinus stared out of a window. "It is time these assassins experience the power and resilience of Rome."

"These Jews are a stubborn, obstinate people," Maximus said.

"Yes, but with the help of our gods, I will bring about the fulfillment of Tiberius's prophecy: 'Straighten them out!'"

Maximus laughed. "'Run them out'" would be a better response for these renegades."

†††

John woke up from the noise on the boat. The dense fog made him wonder if the overnight trip from Philippi to Troas was worth it. But the crew was getting familiar signals from the approaching dock, which was a good sign that they would navigate into the dock without trouble.

John shook his companion. "Barnabas, wake up!"

"Huh? Oh . . . Are we there already?" Barnabas yawned and rubbed his eyes. "I can't see a thing."

"Neither can I, but the crew seems to be operating by faith."

Barnabas laughed. "This will make for a good sermon illustration someday."

"Where are Timothy and the others?"

"In back somewhere; I'll go check on them."

Within a couple of hours, the group from Philippi neared the house of Rueben, a Christian whose house served as the fellowship's house of worship. Rueben was outside feeding a few yard animals when he saw Timothy and the others. "Timothy!"

"Rueben!" Timothy ran and embraced him. "How are you, my brother?"

"Blessed beyond measure, my friend . . . and you?"

"The same. Our Lord has done miraculous things from here to Rome."

"That's wonderful news." He looked at some of his chickens. "Now you'll have to help me chase down several of these yard birds for our evening meal."

"You just point the ones out and I'll have them cornered, necks wrung, and ready for cooking within minutes!"

"Ha! Those legs of yours are still the greatest."

Timothy rubbed one of his legs. "Yes, the Lord has been gracious to me." He turned toward the others. "You remember Barnabas . . . and the Apostle John?"

"Grace and peace to you both. I am honored to have you back in Troas. I trust you will stay for a season?"

John embraced him. "I'm afraid we are on a mission to go elsewhere this time . . . sorry."

Barnabas detected some concern from Reuben's voice. "Is everything well?"

"Okay, I suppose. We hear rumors of a constant stirring of trouble out of Ephesus. The silversmith, Demetrius, and his friends continue to harass our meetings from there clear up to Troas."

"That guy," Timothy said. "I remember Paul's trouble with him."

"Yes, he continues to try and get some of his business back."

"What about Aquila and Priscilla? How are they holding out?"

"They've had a few encounters with Hymenaeus and Alexander, but not much with Demetrius.

"And are they silversmiths also?" Barnabas asked.

"No, they are coppersmiths. They are in the same business as Demetrius, except their wares are less expensive."

"So what can we do to stop them from harassing the brethren?" Timothy asked.

"We pray," John said. "We must spend the evening in prayer to get the mind of our Lord concerning these attackers."

"Then let's get to it!" Timothy said.

"Now hold on to your camels, Timothy," Reuben said. "First we must discuss our meetings while you're in town. I want all three of you to speak to our fellowship. We need encouragement and instruction from the Sacred Writings and the letters from the other apostles."

John smiled at Barnabas. "Didn't I say we were on a mission to go elsewhere?"

"Looks like the 'mission' has come to us. Let's unload our gear and clean up before Reuben has us visiting the houses of the brethren."

Reuben smiled. "And don't forget the chickens, John."

John enjoyed the travels throughout the Gentile regions, but he missed those long days of solitude when he could meet with and worship His Master. As the fellowships grew, so did the time necessary to maintain them. This was heavy on his mind as he dismissed himself from the others to go find a place of solitude.

"My Master," he prayed, "I miss my time with You—I miss You! Why are we getting busier with keeping up all the fellowships? My Lord, I'm tired; I want to rest in You." John was lying on the ground, behind the chicken coop. "I need Your refreshing presence, Jesus . . . come quickly to me!"

"John!"

"Oh Jesus, yes, speak to me!"

"The time will come when you—My disciples—will all be gone. Those who believe in Me from your testimonies, will do so from what is written. My Spirit will guide them through My words. My words are truth! My Spirit will speak these words to you and to others."

"My Master, when will I find time to write? I travel as You have instructed me and the others."

"You must trust Me from a day-by-day fellowship. In its time, you will write; but for now, continue toward Ephesus. You will get established there and then you will go get our mother at Capernaum. You two will return to Ephesus for a long ministry."

"Master, what of these men who are harassing the fellowships? How do we oppose them?"

"The purest of metals must be put through the fire more than once. These metal workers will not understand their roles to purify My Bride until it is too late."

This shook John up. "Lord, are You saying that You have sent them?"

"I did not send them, but I will use their hardened hearts to serve Me for the sake of My Bride."

"I don't understand, my Lord."

"You've heard enough for now. Go back to the group and give them My peace that surpasses all knowledge . . . Go now."

"Lord, please don't leave."

But His voiced faded out, "Walk by faith . . . Go now . . ."

John remained on his face before the Lord in worship for another hour. When he returned to the others, they knew he had been with the Lord.

"What did He say?" Timothy asked.

"The Lord said that the metal workers who are harassing our fellowships are actually being used to purify us."

"Huh?"

"It sounds complicated, I know; but with Jesus, there is always a bigger picture—one that you and I can only understand in part. He says that we must walk by faith and not by sight."

"What do we say or do if they should return to our fellowship?" Reuben asked.

"We refute their heresy and commit them to the Lord for discipline. And at all times, we are to do so in the love of Jesus, just as He taught us many times."

"What is faith?" Reuben asked.

John smiled as he placed his arm on Reuben's shoulder. "Faith is seeing the hand of God working a solution through each encounter in our lives. It is seeing the substance of His presence; and when He is in our midst, we receive that for which we ask, because we ask according to His will."

John, Barnabas, Timothy, and Reuben continued their discussions until it was time to eat the evening meal prior to the services.

†††

Paul, Luke, and a few others left Philippi for Thessalonica, Berea, and Corinth. Although each fellowship wanted Paul to remain and teach the elders, he refused. His heart and vision were set for Spain via Rome.

One month later, in Corinth, Paul and his entourage boarded a ship for Rome. It was spring and the ship made good time for Rhegium. "At this speed," Luke said, "we should be in Rome in a couple of weeks."

"Luke, we must be careful in Rome. You must help me go through the city unnoticed."

"Where will we stay?"

"I know where Quintus lives; he will keep us."

Luke walked over in front of Paul. "Let me see your eyes . . . they're swollen." Luke pull Paul's eyelid back. "Too much sea salt in them. Come, let's go below deck and I will fix you a salve patch."

Rome looked better in the springtime. The occasional rains renewed the roadside plants and the atmosphere. People everywhere seemed to be nicer in the spring. Luke tried to keep Paul secluded as they walked, but Paul's heart wanted to speak to people about Jesus.

"Are you prepared for the coming Deliverer?" Paul would ask a passerby.

"What Deliverer?" someone asked. "Who are you talking about and who are you?"

"Oh, don't mind him," Luke said. "He's excited about springtime."

Paul looked at Luke. "I can't help it, Luke. Look at all these people who do not know about Jesus."

"Unless the Lord speaks directly to you to stop and proclaim, then I strongly suggest we keep to our plans." Paul walked on. "Are we near Quintus's house?"

Paul looked around. Then he pointed to a secondary street. "It's down this street—three houses on the left." They walked down the street to the house and Paul knocked on the door. No one answered, so he knocked again—louder this time.

Finally the door swung open—it was a Roman soldier—not Quintus! "What do want?"

Paul did not recognize him. "Sir, we are seeking Quintus, a soldier of your rank."

"He moved out months ago—now go away!"

"We are friends of his," Luke said, "and I am his doctor."

The soldier eyed the two of them. He then pointed farther down the street. "His place is the last house on the right; now be gone with you!" He slammed the door shut. Paul and Luke turned away and continued their walk down the long street.

"He wasn't very friendly," Luke said.

"He needs Jesus," Paul said.

The last house on the right was much larger than Quintus's older house. There was a front courtyard and it appeared that there was even a back area that nestled up to a grove of trees.

"Quintus must have gotten a promotion," Paul said. They entered the courtyard and went to the front door. Paul knocked several times.

A young maiden answered. "Yes, sir?"

"We're here to speak with Quintus," Paul said.

The girl disappeared behind the door. A woman soon appeared. "I am Carolina, Quintus's wife. May I—oh, forgive me Master Paul; I did not recognize you."

"Carolina, you're as lovely as ever. Is Quintus here?"

She blushed. "Master Paul, please, you and your guest come in and let us refresh you. Ashchara, go get these men something to drink."

"Yes, my lady." The maiden girl left the room.

"Thank you very much," Paul said. "I don't wish to trouble you."

"You, sir, are no trouble at all. You changed my husband; he's a different man now—a man who loves and cares for me like no other."

"I can assure you that any change made in your husband was not my doing; it was Jesus in me . . . is Quintus coming home soon?"

She looked on as Ashchara served them drinks. "I never know. A soldier's hours are not determined by time, but by duty. He said that he hoped to be home by sundown."

"Then perhaps we should go and return at a later hour."

At that moment, a young man came into the room, with the servant maiden. He knelt down, loosened their sandals, and began washing their feet.

"Thank you, kind one," Paul said.

"Thank you," Luke said.

"Oh, you cannot leave."

"We cannot?" Paul asked.

"You see, Quintus moved to this house because it has several guest rooms and a large dining area. He said this place would become a fellowship house for the Christians and that he wanted rooms for men like Paul—you, Master Paul. This house is God's residence!"

Paul stroked his dried-out beard and looked at Luke. Luke smiled. "I think this is just the place that Master Paul needs while we pass through Rome."

Carolina smiled. "And wait until the others hear that you have arrived!"

"Oh you mustn't tell the others!" Paul said. "We're only passing through. We haven't the time for meetings."

She frowned. "But Master Paul, we know so little about Jesus and we have been praying for you to return to teach us. Besides, there is a meeting scheduled here tonight for several dozen Christians." Paul looked at Luke. "Please, stay and speak to us."

Luke shook his head in silence. Then he looked at Carolina. "Paul needs to—"

"I need to spend some time resting and in prayer before this meeting," Paul said. "But no one must know that I am here, Carolina—no one."

"My lips are sealed," she responded. "Come now and I will show you your rooms. And our servants will bring you some food before the meeting."

"Oh bless you, dear sweet Carolina."

She turned to Paul. "You do want me to tell Quintus you're here, if he should arrive early?"

Yes, please send him to my room that I may see him and be refreshed in my spirit."

Paul had been in prayer for several hours before a knock was heard on his door. He opened the door. "Quintus!"

"Master Paul! What a pleasant surprise!" They embraced.

"Is it safe to embrace a Roman soldier?"

"Not in public—but here, it's okay. What is all the secrecy about?"

"Please come inside." Paul sat on his mattress and Quintus in a chair. "My Master has told me to pass through Rome and head out west for Spain. I can only stay a few days."

Quintus stood up. "You have done wisely to come in secrecy. There is turmoil brewing between the senate and the emperor."

"Is that something new?"

"Ha! You're right. I'm glad I'm in charge of slaves and criminals—like you!"

Paul returned the smile. "A slave of my Christ . . . that I am. I have peace in sharing tonight, but Luke and I will most likely leave tomorrow."

"Then I will see that several men escort you out of the city and bid you farewell."

"One more thing: have you heard from Peter or his son-in-law, John Mark?"

"They passed through several days ago, headed south. I was unable to see them but for an hour before I had to go transport some slaves."

"Do they know you have a place of meeting here?"

"Yes, and I invited Master Peter to stop here anytime for a place to sleep and to speak."

"Then will you have him send word back to Antioch of Syria as to the work of ministry he is accomplishing? There are many Christians who are anxious to hear from him."

"I will do my best . . . say, I want to show you something in the reading room." He stood up and motioned for Paul to join him. They walked down a breezeway and stopped at another door that opened inside the main house. Inside the large room was a smaller room with books, papyri, and parchments. Paul stopped at the first pile of parchments and began thumbing through them.

"I see you have some of the writings of Plato and Socrates."

"Yes. I even have a few by some fellow named Moses." He smiled. "Don't suppose you know of him do you?

"Oh, a little."

Quintus brought over a large canvas of rolls of papyri. "Now this here is my most popular group of writings." Quintus pulled out a large roll and began opening it.

Paul looked at the title: "To the Romans." He looked at the pages and then he looked at Quintus. "This is the letter that the Lord instructed me to write."

"Yes; and look at this." He pulled out another. "Here's the one you wrote to the Galatians; and this one is to the Corinthians; plus I have a copy of all the others you've produced."

Paul was astounded. "Oh my."

"Paul, these are the most requested letters of all the writings I have. Six scribes work on copying these letters every week—one scribe a day, six days a week."

Paul flipped through several pages of the Romans papyri. "How careful are they being copied?"

Quintus smiled. "I knew you would ask that. The six scribes proof each other's copy. Then they follow their copy while someone reads the original aloud."

Paul looked toward the heavens. "My Lord, I pray Your hands, Your eyes, and Your mind be upon those who make copies of Your words."

"Amen," Quintus said.

"How many copies have been made?"

Quintus scratched his head. "I think about two dozen? Maybe more . . . I'll have to ask Carolina; she keeps the books on this project. Everyone wants to read about the things of Jesus; but . . ."

"But what?"

"Well, we're lacking on some of the instructions about leaders for the fellowships . . . and we're having a hard time distinguishing some of our Christian foundations from the Jewish religion."

"Oh . . . well, I wasn't writing on those issues. I thought they were simply letters from my heart to the fellowships to which I was writing." Paul continued to look over the pages of his letters. *Perhaps I should write more . . .*

Carolina entered the room. "The evening meal is prepared."

"Please," Quintus said. "Come now and let's be refreshed."

Luke looked around the room. "I see no familiar faces . . . except Quintus, of course."

"Of course," Paul said. "Yet, they still act as one body—Romans, Gentiles, and Jews—one body in Christ."

Quintus walked up to them with someone else. "Men, this is Jonas, a former priest who now acts as our elder of the fellowship."

"Grace and peace to you," Paul said as he embraced Jonas.

"And our Lord's grace and peace be upon you as well, Paul."

"And this is Luke, my companion and personal physician."

"A pleasure to meet you both. Paul, everyone will expect words from you tonight. How shall I prepare our fellowship?"

"Oh, let's begin with singing a few psalms, shall we? And then let's pray for one another as needs are shared. Then I'll preach."

Paul preached for several hours and closed his message with a request: "I need all of you to support our efforts to plant new fellowships in Spain. Our Lord has commanded me to go farther west until I reach the end of the earth. But I cannot go alone. Luke, my physician, is going, but we need a group of men to go with us—men who may know some of the dialects spoken, and men who aren't afraid to travel back and forth, alone, for supplies.

"If you feel our Lord speaking to your heart about this ministry, please come to me after we dismiss." Paul then closed in prayer.

After he prayed, the people began leaving. Two men came forward. "I believe I am one who needs to go with you. I am Obadiah; I am a scribe for the tax office. I know many of the dialects spoken in Spain, for that is where my parents migrated from when I was just a boy."

The next man spoke. "And I am Sophocles. I was born in Rome and have run the western routes as a courier for many of the officers of the imperial army. I know the way of the sea."

"Then the two of you will report to me in the morning," Paul said. "Doctor Luke will inspect you both to ensure you're ready for the trip."

Paul prayed most of the night. Something was amiss. The next morning, he spoke with Luke. "Luke, I struggled in prayer last night. I keep getting this feeling I am overlooking an important item for our journey."

"I struggled also. Finally, the Lord reminded me that I must complete the writings of His life and ministry." He put his arm on Paul's shoulder and smiled. "And a journal of our travels."

"That's what I'm missing—a scribe! The writings must continue."

"I am that someone," Luke said. "I only need to find the time to do so."

"Time . . . that precious commodity that seems to elude us all. And yet, our Lord never moved or spoke except that which His Father told Him to do." Paul turned to Luke and looked him straight into his eyes. "If Jesus took time to pray and find the Father's will, then you and I must double our prayer efforts to fulfill all things He has commanded."

Luke nodded in agreement.

✝✝✝

Poppaea looked at the head carefully, while Nero turned his aside. "I tell you," he said, "it *is* her." Satisfied also, Poppaea ordered the head of Octavia taken away to be incinerated, apart from the rest of her body which was in exile in Campania.

She walked over to her new husband and moved his hands across her face and arms. "This skin is deserving of only the greatest man in the empire." Nero dropped his face upon her bosom while she ran her fingers through his curly hair.

He lifted his head and smiled. "With Octavia, Plautus, and Sulla out of the picture, the empire is mine to build! We will celebrate!"

"Yes!" she said. "What Rome needs is a party!"

"And I know just what we need: an exhibition match in the arena!" But she frowned. "What?" he asked.

She walked over to the window, ran her fingers down its sill, and rubbed them together. "That place is so dirty; the dust chaffs my skin." She turned to him and nestled up close to him again. "Can't we find another place?"

"Where, my love? You name the place and I will build it for you!"

She walked over to the doors that looked over the lake built in honor of Marcus Agrippa. "There, my emperor!"

Nero walked over to her side, looking out over the lake area. "In the lake?"

"Drain it! Pack it with sand and mortar. And let the emperor lay in his bed, if he wishes, and watch the battles!"

He laughed. Then he looked out over the lake. "By the gods, I think you have a fantastic idea!"

Within days, Nero ordered the lake drained. A few months later, construction began on a new arena for gladiator battles. He also constructed it to where it could be refilled with water, using it to reenact sea battles.

However, with Poppaea's lavish lifestyle and no one managing Nero's uncontrollable spending, the empire's budget shortfalls began weakening his reign and his popularity.

†††

Elijah cried out in the middle of the night. Mary quickly nestled him to her side and began nursing him. She smiled as she stroked his fine black hair. *My Lord, You have given me someone new to love. I would have never known such love if I had not seen You.*

"Mary, My child?"

Mary was quiet; she thought she was hearing her Lord in a dream.

"Mary?"

She looked at Elijah nursing. Then she realized she was not dreaming. "Yes, my Lord? Are You speaking to me?"

"Yes, My child, I am speaking to you. Your husband is going to hear from me to go to Capernaum and proclaim My salvation. You must be brave and support him by cleaning fish and rearing up young Elijah. Some will accept the message of salvation, but many more will reject it and rebel against you and your family. Do not be discouraged, but be prepared to move farther north to Caesarea-Philippi. There are many people there and in Dan that need to hear the message. You will stay there and build a fellowship of believers."

"My Lord, what will become of Elijah?"

"I will call him into My ministry. That is why you must continuously teach and train him in My words and in My ways. The day will come when you must release him into My calling."

Tears streamed down her cheeks, some of which dropped onto the face of Elijah. He jerked a little, but continued nursing. "Thank you, my Lord, for speaking to me. I—we—are yours . . . and Elijah will grow up to know You. Eliezer and I will train him to listen for Your voice."

"My voice is in My words. Listen to them as I instruct My followers to write them." The voice of Jesus began to fade out. "Listen to My words and obey them . . ."

The morning crow of a rooster finally awakened Mary. Elijah continued to sleep as she arose from her bed and walked outside to fetch a bowl of water. Eliezer was up and feeding the chickens a little grain. She stopped and smiled at him.

"What?"

"Oh, nothing."

"I've seen that look before and it's not a 'nothing' look." He walked over and kissed her. "But whatever it is that you want, I'll do my utmost to get it." He kissed her again.

"It's nothing I want—it's something I heard."

His eyebrows raised up a half-inch. "Gossip? Now you know how some people talk."

She grabbed his hand. "Have you heard from the Lord?"

He looked into her eyes, momentarily, and smiled. "Apparently the Lord doesn't keep secrets."

"And? . . ."

"If I am to proclaim more and clean fish less, then you are going to have to grow that little man up as quickly as possible."

She smiled and embraced him from his backside. "I think Elijah and I can hold our own. As long as we are obeying our Master, He will meet the needs of His children."

Nine months later

It had been ten months since the birth of Elijah. Eliezer increased his time proclaiming the way of salvation through Jesus, while his wife and Mary, the mother of Jesus, cared for Elijah and the fishing business. Jude continued his trips from Galilee to Samaria and Judea, proclaiming the way of salvation and checking on the existing fellowships.

Jude was in Jerusalem and stopped at the villa of Joseph of Arimathea. He did the customary knock at the front gate. When he knocked, the gate slowly opened by itself. As he walked through the empty courtyard, he remembered the years when there was much activity going on and the Holy Spirit was very active among the followers. Now it was desolate. He looked through several rooms—empty. Then he walked to the stables in back, where he saw Joseph.

"Joseph?"

Joseph stopped shoeing a horse and put the horse's hoof down. He wiped the sweat off his brow and then wiped his hands.

"Jude!" He walked over to him. "I'd embrace you but you caught me at a very dirty chore."

"Quite alright; it's a pleasure seeing you again."

"And look at you! You've grown some since your last visit."

"Older and wiser, I pray." Jude looked around. "Anyone else staying with you now?"

"Oh, just Hamath. The others come and go but rarely stay—except Matthew. He spent a number of months here working on his story about Jesus. It's a bit quieter these days inside the villa . . . I wish I could say that for the fellowships in the area."

"How's that?"

Joseph picked up a brush and began untangling the horse's mane. "The high priest has infiltrated our fellowships with so-called Christian priests. They were first welcomed into the fellowships but then they began refuting many of our practices and beliefs.

There's also a lot of deception going on. As so-called priests, they demanded funds from the fellowships, saying it was their right to be supported by us. But later, we discovered that they spent our support on strong drink and women of ill repute."

Jude stared at Joseph as though he'd seen a ghost. "I can't believe what I'm hearing. How can the followers of our Lord allow such deception?"

Joseph stopped brushing for a moment and looked away. "One notable difference: our elders do not spend adequate time before the Lord in prayer and in His words as you and the apostles did. Pride has crept in; they rely on their abilities to recite our old covenantal laws and even sing many psalms . . ." Joseph turned back to face Jude. His eyes were moist as he continued speaking in a broken voice. "But they do not speak with a passion . . . they do not have the burden and brokenness of the years past. The glow of our Lord's presence has diminished . . . the fire of the Holy Spirit has gone out."

Jude looked to the ground and shook his head. "The prophet Agabus was right; the Spirit has left this city."

Joseph nodded his head. "And our land. I did not believe it at first, but now I agree with you. That's why I'm moving my stock and relocating to Antioch."

"Relocating? Really?"

"Yes, I no longer associate with the Sanhedrin council. I'm selling or leasing out my properties locally. With our Lord's favor, I will sell enough to enlarge my stables in Antioch and then set up additional stables toward Rome."

"And what of Nicodemus?"

"He has retired from the council, but has too much family in the area to move with me. He has children in Bethany, Bethlehem, and Hebron, so I expect he will stay nearby."

"And Hamath?"

"Hamath? Oh he's pretty stubborn—says he can't move; but I think I've made him a deal on stable management that he can't refuse. He's building me a large cart that will support him and much of my stable gear." Joseph smiled. "He'll go with me."

Jude returned the smile. "And how are John Mark's parents?"

"They're managing their fellowship well. They are our largest group in Jerusalem now. Jacob reads the writings of our brothers well enough to refute the babblers that come in the fellowship. He shows them the door." He laughed. "Several priests came in with two temple guards and were going to take over when Hamath came up to them and tried to smile . . . that was the last we saw of them."

"Jacob will miss the big fellow when he leaves."

"The priests won't know that." They both laughed. "Will you stay with us tonight?"

Jude shrugged his shoulders. "Is it safe?"

"Yes, quite safe. Hamath will be back from the errands he's running for me and will be in the room next to yours."

"Okay; and perhaps later we can get together and pray for our city."

"You go get cleaned up and I'll prepare an extra plate—oh, and don't forget that we have a meeting to go to tonight over at Jacob's house."

"A meeting . . . tonight? I didn't think you were having a meeting tonight."

"We weren't—until you showed up. The followers will want to hear a report from you and the wellbeing of your mother. Now you can't disappoint them, can you?"

Jude smiled. "You are right as usual, Joseph. I'll go clean up."

The meeting went well. Jude shared how the work was developing throughout the region. He also gave an update on his mother and Mary of Magdala. Now the three men were walking back to Joseph's place for a time of prayer. They had to walk slowly, for Hamath now walked with a limp.

"That wound still bothering you, Hamath?" Jude asked.

He grunted.

"He's fine in the stables," Joseph said, "but walking gets to him."

Jude smiled. "I don't like to walk either, so I ride your donkeys as much as possible."

"They're my most reliable animals for this terrain . . . but I'll take a good horse any day."

When they settled down at the villa, Jude and Joseph got on their knees to pray. Hamath remained standing and eventually left.

Jude stopped praying when he heard him leave. "Is that normal?"

"Oh yeah; he says he prays a lot by himself, but is uncomfortable trying to pray with a group. For one thing, he can't get up and down easily . . . he doesn't like attention."

The men continued praying for about two hours before going to bed. Jude made himself comfortable in his bed and closed his eyes. But before he fell asleep, the Lord spoke to him.

"Jude, my child."

"Yes, my Lord?"

"The false brethren are trying to corrupt My children. You must write a letter to warn the brethren of the false teachers. Do so before you leave!"

"But, Lord, who will I get to help me?"

"Ask and you shall receive the necessary items for writing. Stay with Joseph until you're finished. My children will suffer many tribulations soon. They will need a fresh word from Me."

Jude fell on his face again in prayer. "Yes, my Lord; I will start tomorrow."

†††

"It's all rubbish, I tell you—rubbish!" Nero looked out his window. "This palace is a mockery to the empire!—to my divinity!"

"But you have all the available space around this facility," the senator said. "We can't go house to house and order Romans to surrender their homes."

Nero turned to him. "Has Caesar lost his honor before men? Must I remind them that I watch over their property?"

The senator looked into his eyes. It was always a risk to challenge Nero. "Perhaps Caesar should be grateful for the largest palace ever built for an emperor?"

Nero turned away. *I need more leverage with this imbecile.* "You may leave for now." The senator bowed and exited.

Tigellinus, co-commander of the Praetorian Guard, walked in. "So, did you get some land?"

Nero growled like a wild beast. "I must find something in which to charge this senate. I've got to get the upper hand on this sparring match. Think with me; what have they done recently?"

Tigellinus looked at the floor as he scratched his head. "Don't they keep records of charges and hearings? Perhaps we can dig up a discrepancy or two?"

Nero smiled and put his arm around Tigellinus's shoulder. "You see, my friend, there is some genius in that thick skull of yours. Tonight we go to the senate archives for a little reading."

AD 63-64

*P*aul stood at the bow of the ship as it neared the eastern coastland of Hispania. Three weeks of sailing port-to-port finally produced the land of the empire's western border. Although the Celtic and Iberian cultures were dominant, the area had become more and more Romanized. No matter; Paul was anxious to get on land and start his mission work.

Luke walked up. "It's so peaceful from the sea."

Paul ignored Luke's small talk. "The Lord told me that this was a pagan land with the need for His salvation."

Luke gently turned Paul's head and stared into his eyes. "It will be more difficult for you to introduce Jesus to the world's population if you cannot see." Paul relaxed a little, as Luke did his usual eye examination. "I will make a new batch of salve for your eyes."

Paul smiled. "Are you as careful with your writings as you are with my eyes?"

"Strange you should mention that. I have reached a place in the writings that completes the physical life of our Lord."

"Did that long night with Peter help you?"

"Not really . . . well, some; but the Spirit gave me much of the details so that I could connect all the pieces."

"That is what I like to hear. The blessed Spirit is preparing His word. Let's have a look at it when we settle in for the night."

Nimes was a busy port city. The empire worked feverishly to make it look and feel like Rome itself. Paul, Luke, Eubius, Prudens, and a few others walked slowly through the main part of the city. Paul stopped abruptly. "There," he said as he pointed to a makeshift villa. "Surely there are some rooms for us to rent for the week."

Luke looked at the shabby mud-caked walls. "You are a man of great faith. Let's hope they recognize Roman coins."

Later that afternoon, Paul sat with Luke as they read over the story of Jesus. Tears filled Paul's eyes as he read. He lifted up a sheet of the papyri: "Blessed be Your holy name, my Lord Jesus. You are providing Your words for all ages—for all nations."

"Amen," Luke responded, as Paul continued praying.

"O Lord, the Almighty God. Keep my physical eyes dim, as You wish; but I beg of You to sharpen my spiritual eyes for Your glory and for Your kingdom to be established in this land. In Jesus' precious and anointed name I pray, amen."

Luke looked at Paul and then back at the sheets of papyri. "This is His story," he said quietly.

"Yes it is. And we must protect it and have copies made as soon as possible. Tomorrow we must find a local scribe who can copy this while we journey west to the sea."

The morning sun awakened Paul's entourage. As each began cleaning their faces, Luke noticed Paul had already left the room.

As soon as he could, Luke went searching for him. Paul was seated under a small tree near the villa entrance.

"Did you sleep?" he asked Paul.

"Enough. The Lord awakened me early. We discussed the agenda." Paul looked at Luke. "Luke, we must travel in haste for there are some who are tracking me down."

"Huh? Why? Why would anyone track you down way out here?"

"It is the Lord's directive. I do not question my Master—I only obey Him."

"As you wish."

"As soon as everyone is refreshed, we must meet for our duties."

After few pieces of fruit and juice, Paul called everyone's attention. "Men, we will divide into three groups and travel to the western shore, stopping in any town that gives us Godspeed. The Lord has promised that He will go before each group to prepare the way. Cresens and Eubius, would you be team leaders?" They nodded approval. Great; now I want Luke and Linus to stay with me. Who will volunteer to stay here in Nimes to oversee the copying of Luke's letters?" Claudia raised his hand. "Okay then, the rest will divide up between the other two teams."

Cresens chose Obadiah and Sophocles. Eubius chose Aristocles and Nikaristos. Paul looked at each group assembled. "Men, we do not know what lies ahead, but our Lord is with us. Let us retreat into a time of prayer, seeking His directions."

†††

For several weeks, Nero and Tigellinus secretly brought the ledgers of the archives to Nero's reading room. Page after page was read, but they could not find a flaw or weakness in the senate's deliberations.

"I'm tired of reading," Tigellinus said. "Can we do something else by which we get the senate in hot water?"

Nero didn't speak. He was reading over a hearing about ten months ago.

"Have you found something?"

Nero put his finger to his lips. "Shhh," he said. "Who is Paul of Tarsus?"

"I don't know; why?"

"It says here that he was a Jewish criminal—yet a Roman citizen—who had appealed his verdict to me . . . Did I ever hear this Jew from Tarsus?"

"I don't suppose you did, Divine One."

"That means the senate broke this man's legal right to a trial by hearing; and it also means that they bypassed me in their verdict and dismissal of this man."

"That's terrible! Hey, weren't the Jews a part of the prophecy of Tiberius? Did he not say our gods are to 'straighten them out'?"

Nero smiled. "The senate has voted against our gods? Where is justice when you need it?"

"Someone needs to pay for this atrocity!"

Nero stood up as he ripped the page out of the archives' binding. "I want this Paul of Tarsus returned to me as quickly as possible. I will use him as my leverage for more land acquisition."

"How do we find him?"

"He's a Jew, isn't he? I'll call my generals in tomorrow and will put a bounty on his head—a bounty big enough that all in the empire will be looking for this criminal."

†††

Looking west from Nimes, a mountain range jutted in the distance. Paul, Luke, and Linus had obtained a map of the trade routes to the west, along with three donkeys, and enough supplies to get them down the trail for a few months. Although the native tongue was foreign, the empire had been in the region long enough for Latin's language of commerce. This was good for Paul and Luke.

Each community through which they traveled welcomed strangers from the east, as people were always curious about news from afar. Paul wasted no time in proclaiming the good news of salvation in Jesus, the Lord confirming the message with signs and healings. In town after town, new fellowships were formed as they headed west into Hispania.

For months, the gospel spread to the west. Then one day it happened. Paul halted his donkey. The others stopped as well. "What is it?" Linus asked.

"Shhh," Paul responded. They listened. "Did you hear that?"

Luke listened more intently. "Breakers?" he asked.

Paul smiled. "You have good ears Doctor Luke. Let's go!" Paul kicked the sides of his donkey to get the animal trotting. The others followed suit.

Within the hour, the three were at a precipice, gazing across a mass of water with waves breaking far below them. The wind rising upward from the cliffs caused an array of sounds.

"The call of the Great Sea," Linus said.

Paul took in a deep breath of sea breeze. "So this is the western edge of the empire."

"Don't forget the warnings about the call of the sea," Luke said.

Paul glanced at Luke. "I think the call of our God can snuff this strange noise out. Let's travel south and see where the locals gather."

It wasn't long until they saw smoke on the horizon. The smoke eventually revealed a small community along a crevice that allowed for a road to the seashore. Dozens of boats were sprawled along the shoreline. People were busy bringing in a catch of fish or working on some other craft related to the sea.

The three walked their animals down the main road as they peered into everyone's shop. Finally, they reached the shoreline. After tying the donkeys to a post, all three walked into the water. Although salty, the cool sea water was a welcome relief from the many months of traveling. For a time, the three just relaxed in the water, acting like children who had found a new place to explore.

Finally Paul had enough. He headed back to his donkey and rested on the ground, watching Luke and Linus splashing water everywhere.

Luke was next to retreat back to the animals. He fell to the ground beside Paul. "What a delight!"

"Yes . . . such refreshment in God's great ocean. But . . ."

"But what?"

"My eyes, Luke; they're burning again."

"Oh . . . I had forgotten those precious eyes of yours. Let me wash them with clean water and put more salve in them."

Paul looked down to the ground and closed his eyes. "I can still see this majestic place of beauty—even with my eyes closed. Thank You, Lord, for eyes with memory."

Several hours had passed; now the three men were back in the town area seated with some of the local people. The locals were curious about the man with eye patches who was creating a tremendous picture, with his hands, of the handiwork of God's creation. Soon his message turned to the One who brought deliverance to all people.

"Each of you," Paul said, "has knowledge of a need for peace on your insides. We have all sinned against the Creator God and we deserve the penalty of our sins. But God, through His mercy and grace, has given His only, uniquely born Son as a sacrifice for all sin for all time. It is in the name of His Son, Jesus, that you can find forgiveness and fulfillment in your life."

After several hours of proclamation, Paul called on his listeners to bow down with their heads to the ground and ask for forgiveness and ask to receive the Christ. Many did; some, however, mocked his testimony.

"He speaks of God's power to save," a man said, "yet he is blind himself."

"These patches are to heal my physical eyes; but the healing God offers, is for your blind souls. This flesh is temporary, but your soul lives eternally . . . Luke, tell of the difference in physical and spiritual sight."

While Luke began speaking, another man stood up and walked away. Luke continued giving his testimony of how he saw the miracles of God and how he became a follower of Jesus Christ.

About that time, the man who had walked away was guiding another man toward Paul. "Here, man of God!" he said. "This man fell upon some rocks and lost his hearing and his sight. He has a wife and five children who need him to see again. You heal this man and we will all follow this Savior of yours." Some of the other men spoke in agreement.

Paul stood up and motioned Luke to his side. They walked over to the man. Luke gently touched the man's eyelids and slowly raised them up. The man jerked a little but cooperated.

"I see some separation in the eyes. The trauma must have severed his main optic nerve."

"And his ears?" Paul asked.

Luke motioned for a torch. "Hold this, Paul, and let me look down into them." He studied the each ear for a moment. "Hmmm."

"I've heard that sound before," Paul said.

"What does this sound mean?" asked the man standing with them.

Paul couldn't help but smile. "Nothing at all."

Luke smiled back at him. "It's hard to tell; there is some scar tissue inside his ear."

"Linus, come join us," Paul said. "Luke, do you have any oil or salve on you?"

Luke pulled out a small flask. "Since being around you, I always carry a little oil and salve."

"Give it to me." Paul then instructed Linus and Luke to put oil on their fingers and anoint the eyes and ears of the man. Paul then joined them by placing his oily hands on the man's forehead. "Our Lord Jesus, we know not how this man feels about You because he can neither see nor hear. But that the others may see, hear, and believe, we ask You to heal this man right now, that Your glory may fill this town."

As the three of them held on to this man, he began to jerk and let out a yelp, as if he had been speared. He fell to the ground on his knees, causing all of them to fall; yet, they maintained a hold on him. Again, the man yelled out loud: "Help! Help!"

The other man was about to jerk Paul, Luke, and Linus off his friend, when suddenly he heard a familiar voice:

"Ghandlan, stop!" He did. "I . . . I see you! Ghandlan, I see you!"

"Antonio? Antonio, can you hear me?" Silence invaded the scene momentarily.

"Yes . . . YES!" he said. "I can see and hear again!" Ghandlan looked at Paul and his companions. Then he fell to the ground before them. "You are gods! You are gods!" When he said that, all the others in the gathering fell to their knees and bowed to the three strangers who had come into their community that day.

Paul stood up, while wiping his oily hands. "We are not gods. We are simply the representatives of the one true God who has given us this sign to confirm our message of salvation. There is salvation in no other god, but through the true God's Son, Jesus Christ. If you will confess with your mouths, Jesus as your Savior and Master, you also may become His representatives—His adopted children!"

Within the hour of the healing, every man and his family were confessing Jesus as Lord and were bringing their local idols to a large fire for burning. After the precious metals were shaped into small pieces, they gave them to Paul as an offering of thanksgiving.

For three days, Paul remained with the townspeople and taught them the ways of salvation. Luke helped a local man copy down a small portion of the story of salvation in Jesus Christ.

Paul was anxious to move on. "We must continue traveling north along the coastland until we meet up with the others," Paul said.

"How are we going to shake this scribe off our trail?" Luke asked, as he pointed to the fourth person.

Paul lifted his hand toward the man. "Stop!"

"But sir," the man said, "we must have as many words as possible about our Deliverer."

"Look at me; I will have copies of some of His writings sent to your community. I can't just spit out words while I am maneuvering my donkey down a trail. That's not how it works." The man looked dismayed. "Get alone and spend time in prayer. The words of the Christ will come to you by His Holy Spirit. The writings will come your way in due time."

"Yes, Master Paul."

"My friend, Jesus is your Master—mine too! We must all go to Him daily for instructions in righteousness and ministry." Paul smiled at him. "Live by faith and not by sight; trust Him for words to say when needed." With those words spoken, Paul pulled on his reins and turned his donkey northward. Luke and Linus waved at the man and then fell in behind Paul.

The new follower of Jesus watched as the three men disappeared from the horizon. "Live by faith," he whispered. "Live by faith—not by sight."

†††

The guard on duty knocked on the door facer. "Enter," the general said.

"Sir, the soldier you requested is here."

"Send him in."

The soldier walked in, military style, and stood at attention.

The general stood up. "At ease, soldier. State your name.

"Quintus, sir; eleven years as a soldier."

"Then you must know that this conversation must be kept among us soldiers."

"Yes sir."

"You were assigned guard duty to a Jewish prisoner for two years, is that correct?"

"Yes sir."

The general walked over to a pile of papers. He looked at one in particular. "A 'Paul of Tarsus' was his name."

"Yes sir, and a fine prisoner he was, sir."

"I'm not interrogating you on his character. I want to know what became of him."

"He had a day set to meet with the senate council and he was released."

"Soldier, I'm asking you again: What became of him?"

"Sir, he received his certificate of passage back to his homeland."

The general changed the conversation. "Are you rich, soldier?"

Quintus hesitated. "Sir, I am paid well for my assignments and have no complaints."

"Then you'll not complain with your new assignment. I am placing you in charge of twelve soldiers to hunt this Paul of Tarsus down, arrest him, and bring him back to Rome."

"Sir?"

"You heard me. You and your men will leave as soon as possible and head for Tarsus. You will be paid double while on this assignment, and will be hailed as a hero for bringing in a man sought after by Emperor Nero himself. There's a bounty of a year's wage and property on the Baiae for the capture of this man."

"But sir, what if I can't find him?"

"You will find him or you will be banished from Rome—you and your men. Now take this order to the commander of the barracks and select your soldiers. Tomorrow morning, assemble here with your men for further instructions. You were with him for two years . . . surely you picked up on his habits."

Quintus snapped back to attention. "Sir, are we finished?"

"Yes, go your way. I want you and your men here by the third hour of the day tomorrow."

Quintus dismissed himself from the general's office. *Paul must be alerted!*

† † †

For four months, Paul and the others went from town to town and village to village, explaining Jesus as the Deliverer of sins and as the Christ. Many signs confirmed their testimonies and proclamations. Finally, they all regrouped at Nimes.

"Men," Paul said, "tonight, we must gather for prayer and worship. Then we must decide how to best circulate the Sacred Writings our Lord has given us. But for now, go out into the market and refresh yourselves in the beauty of God's handiwork."

As the men disbursed, Luke remained with Paul. "Let's have a look at those eyes."

Paul smiled. "Luke, must you remind me?"

Luke said nothing as he spread both eyelids open, looking into one eye. "Hmm." Paul said nothing. He looked into the other eye for about a minute. He stepped back and looked at Paul. "Your eyes are getting worse."

"I know . . . Is there anything we can do?"

"I can strengthen the salve, but you will have to wear the patches longer . . . that's all I can offer you. Your eyes have taken a terrible beating and I am amazed that you can see at all."

Paul closed his eyes and turned his head as if he were experimenting on an idea. Then he opened his eyes and stared at his hands. "Luke, you must become my eyes. Wherever I go, I will need you to read to me from God's words."

"I would be honored to do all that and much more."

"One more thing: as much as is possible, tell no one about my blindness. I do not want to be a distraction from the proclamation of the gospel."

✝✝✝

"No sir, I have not seen or heard from my brother."

"If you do, you must warn him of a huge bounty that has been placed on him for his arrest and return to Rome."

"I will . . . and thank you, sir, for your kind warning. And may I say who has given me this warning?"

"Just tell him a soldier who was chained to him—one whose heart became unchained." Quintus turned from Paul's mother's house and returned to his men. "He's not here."

"Where do we go next?" one of the soldiers asked.

"Antioch, Syria—and from there, Jerusalem."

"But the centurion and his men told us last night to stay clear of Judea. They are poised to invade that city."

"Then we must arrive before the generals cut the city off. The emperor wants this Paul alive."

One of the soldiers complained. "This is not what we were told to do!"

Quintus mounted his horse and faced his men. "Listen to me—all of you! We have been given orders by the emperor himself to track down and capture this man. I have been placed in charge of this assignment. If any of you wish to disobey my orders and return to Rome, then do so at your own peril. You will be treated as a traitor and severely punished by the emperor. If you wish to rebel under my command, then do so right now! Otherwise, you will stop any objections to my orders. Is that understood?"

The men looked at each other, but remained in their ranks.

"I would much rather be in Rome with my family," Quintus continued. "And someday I will—but not until we reach the far ends of our empire. Now get on your horse and follow me."

Paul's sister went to her mother's bed. "They're gone now, Mother." She gently wiped her mother's forehead with a damp cloth.

"Oh my dear, I pray they do not find our dear Saul."

"The Lord knows where he is and that is all we need to know. In fact, this answers your prayer Mother."

"Oh? It does?"

"Yes; we now know that he is alive and that all of the Roman Empire is searching for him."

Her mother closed her eyes. "You're right . . . You're right, he is still alive."

"Now you just relax and keep those eyes shut. You need to rest." Esther slowly left the room. *My Lord,* she prayed, *please tell Paul that his mother will soon pass on to be with You.*

† † †

"I tire of waiting—where is that man?!" Nero was furious.

The general was fearful, but dared not show it. "I have a dozen of our finest soldiers tracking him, Divine One, and notices have been delivered to the far reaches of the empire. He will be found!

Nero turned to the general. "Double the reward and the land holdings! Send couriers out again and, this time, have them notify all neighboring empires that twenty thousand Roman gold coins will be the reward for any man of any country who turns this man over to our authorities."

"Yes, Divine One; I will expedite the orders!"

† † †

"Today?" Peter asked. "Are you certain of this?"

Julius, a servant of Nero's household, nodded his head. "The order was clear—the reward for Paul has doubled and couriers have even been sent into the farthest points of the empire and foreign countries."

Peter looked at Perpetua. "Then we must meet for prayer tonight—at Quintus's villa. Julius, be secretive about it, but let the others know of tonight's meeting."

"Yes, Master Peter, I will."

"This doesn't sound good," Perpetua said.

"No, but our best offense is to cover Paul in prayer. The report we get is that he and his group are converting many of the Gentiles. His work must continue unabated."

"Speaking of which, when will we catch up with John Mark and Pet?"

"Soon, Perpie . . . soon. Perhaps we should leave tomorrow and go farther north."

"That sounds great!" She stood up and embraced him. "I did say I wanted to come to this city; but, my dear, I long to see the country again. I miss the smell of the fish of Galilee."

"That's our Lord's decision; we must wait upon Him, my love."

The villa was fuller than usual. Carolina busied herself by offering anyone a drink. Peter came up to her. "Dear Carolina, have you any word from your husband?"

She shook her head. "The last report given to me was that he had left Tarsus and was traveling farther east."

"Good; he continues to draw attention away from Paul's location."

"I'm afraid the news worsens," she responded.

"How so?"

"The reward is so great that many centurions have mobilized their men to search every city and seaport."

Peter patted her shoulder. "Our Lord is aware of this . . . we must place it in His hands." He then turned to the others. "Everyone." The place quieted down. "This is a most important meeting tonight. Our brother Paul is in danger of being arrested and returned to the emperor. I want us to dispense with the traditional songs and readings. Let us gather in small groups and pray for Paul and his group tonight. Then later on, if it is appropriate, we will sing and read together."

People began gravitating into smaller groups and some began praying immediately. Peter looked around for a moment. *My, what a group. I hardly know these people. Lord, You have blessed the church in Rome.* He then bent his knees and fell on his face praying.

For several hours, prayers were lifted up from the villa of Quintus. The more they prayed, the louder they became. It was so loud that no one heard the arrival of soldiers surrounding the villa. A centurion entered the courtyard and broke down the front door. Screams erupted from the crowd of believers as they stood and ran out of the room.

"There is no escape!" the centurion said. "Stop! All of you! I have over twenty men surrounding this house!"

Peter stood up. "You do not need the women and the children, sir. Please allow them to leave."

The centurion walked up to Peter and slapped him. "Did I ask for your opinion?" Peter said nothing more. The centurion turned to the women. "Which one of you is the wife of Quintus?"

Carolina stepped forward. "This is my home and these are my invited guests. Why have you disrupted our gathering?"

The centurion reared back and slapped her face, harder than he slapped Peter. "Your husband and you are harboring those who refuse to worship our gods and the Divine One. He will not be pleased when he gets my report." He turned to the rest. "I am looking for Paul of Tarsus." He looked at Peter. "Are you him?"

Peter hesitated a moment . . . "Yes, I am Paul of Tarsus. Now let the others go!"

The centurion smiled. "Let them go? I will let them go . . . to the prison! Guards! Take them all to the prison." He stepped up into Peter's face as two soldiers held Peter's arms. "And we will interrogate everyone here until I am satisfied that you are indeed the criminal the emperor seeks. And you had better not be lying to me."

†††

"So this is the amphitheater of the three Gauls."

Paul turned to Luke. "Please, describe it to me."

Luke looked around. "Oh, I'd say its layout is similar to the one in Rome . . . except it is not dug down into the ground and it's smaller and it's not as tall—but wider."

Paul kept his patches on. "Oh well; perhaps I'll see it another day. We must look for a synagogue.

"In Lyon?" Crescens asked. "Surely not."

"Let the locals judge on this matter," Paul said.

"It's getting cold," Eubius said. "How much farther north do we travel Paul?"

"Until we will find the islands of which our Lord has directed us."

"The islands of the Britons?" Luke asked.

"Yes; we must tell them of a Deliverer—and they'll be happy to hear that it's not the Roman Empire."

One month later

"Where are we?" Linus looked at what appeared to be a tent city.

"The Saxon Shore," Paul said.

"I have heard of this place," Luke said. "A shoreline of Roman forts and ports." The others just looked on.

"And the seaport to the islands of the Britons," Paul said.

"Do we go farther?" Cresens asked.

Paul thought for a moment. "Only Luke, Linus, and I will cross over the channel. I want the rest of you to minister to the Romans and the locals here. Travel up and down the shoreline for several months and then return to this port. Perhaps we will have finished our work on the islands."

A week later, Paul and his group arrived at the docks of Londinium on the Thames River. The city was dirty and you could hear Roman soldiers cracking whips as they led horses and servants through the streets. Occasionally, a centurion would stop

Paul and ask who they were and what was their reason for being there.

"We are ambassadors from another country," Paul said.

"Which country?" he asked.

"Paradise."

For several weeks, Paul and company tried to venture out into the countryside to share the gospel of Jesus to the locals. However, due to the recent battles with Queen Boudica, the outskirts of the rebuilding area of Londinium were heavily guarded by Roman soldiers.

Linus looked at the other two. "You think, perhaps, this is a sign that we should turn back and join the others across the water?"

Luke looked at Paul. "We can probably offer medical assistance to the Roman officers."

"Yes, perhaps we can negotiate."

"Take your patches off." Luke went and spoke to a centurion.

Soon he returned to Paul with the centurion. "I am Dokeomis; your doctor says you can offer assistance in return for protection?"

"Doctor Lucius is well known for his healing powers."

"Very well; we suffered many casualties farther north at Camulodunum. General Paulinus is camped there and report has it that he has malaria."

"That is my specialty," Luke said.

Dokeomis turned and called several men over to him. "See that these three men go with our next ship to Camulodunum. Make sure they are delivered to the general."

Camulodunum had been the capital city of the locals for many years. It was a cleaner city than Londinium and many of the locals were now being used to rebuild the city. Paul and company arrived about a week later and were sent to the general's quarters.

Gaius Suetonius Paulinus was lying down when they entered the tent. After a brief interrogation and search, the three were allowed inside his sitting room, adjoining his bedroom.

Luke motioned to Paul and Linus. "Linus, you wait here. Paul, I'm going to need you inside." Luke and Paul were shown in to see the general.

Paulinus was breathing heavily and was covered in blankets. Paul addressed him. "General, I am Paul of Tarsus and this is Doctor Lucius of Cilicia." He opened his eyes, but did not respond. "My doctor healed me of your same dreaded disease, but you must do as he says."

Luke motioned to a servant. "Bring me fresh water, some cloths, and two small cups." Soon Luke was mixing up a liquid from the herbs and spices he kept in his bag in case Paul had a relapse. Luke dipped a small cloth into the mixture. "Sir, suck this gel out of the cloth; let it remain in your mouth until it breaks down into a liquid and then swallow it."

The servant took the cloth and smelled it. Then he handed it back to Luke. "You first," he said.

Luke took the cloth and handed it to Paul. "You may need this more than I."

Paul took the cloth and lifted it up in the air. "Lord Jesus, use this salve to heal the general of his malaria." He then began sucking on the cloth.

While Paul sucked on his cloth, Luke dipped another into the mixture and gave it to the servant. "Give this to the general if he wishes to get well." This time the general moved his hands toward the servant and took the cloth. Together, they managed to get enough of the cloth into the general's mouth for him to suck the gel. This procedure went on for about thirty minutes. Luke continued wiping the general's face with fresh water. He turned to the servant. "Continue to give him this gel through the night. See that he allows it to turn to liquid in his mouth and then he must swallow it." Luke stood up, motioned to Paul, and, together, they joined Linus in the sitting room.

"I believe he will survive," Paul said.

Luke shook his head in question. "This is as worse a case I've ever seen, Paul. We must wash ourselves thoroughly and continue in prayer. If he shows signs of improvement tomorrow, he should recover."

The three were given a place to rest for the night near the general's tent. After a meal, they began worshipping and praying.

Early the next morning the three were awakened by several soldiers. "You are commanded to go to the general's quarters immediately!" The soldiers escorted them over to the tent and into the sitting room. "Sit down."

Paul looked at Luke and Linus. "This may be our longest day yet."

"Or our shortest," Luke said.

Two guards opened the door to the bedroom while two servants assisted the general slowly into the room and seated him. He managed a slight smile. "That medicine tastes poorly," he said. "Do you mind if I chase it down with strong drink?" He continued to smile.

"Only a sip or two of fresh wine—mildly fermented," Luke replied. "You mustn't dilute the mixture too quickly."

"Thank you for coming," he said. "I am Gaius Suetonius Paulinus. What needs do you men have while on this island?"

Paul stood up. "Sir, I am Paul of Tarsus, and this is Linus and the doctor is Lucius of Cilicia. We have come to speak to the locals about a spiritual matter concerning the salvation of their souls."

The general stopped smiling. "You came from Asia and risked your lives just to tell these barbarians about a salvation of their souls?"

"These barbarians, as you call them, are humans for whom the Son of God died."

"Which god?"

From that question, Paul spoke of Jesus, the Son of God and Savior for all men.

"I can only permit you safety as long as you remain inside our barriers. I will allow you to assemble the servants, after the final meal, and then you may speak to them."

"I understand," Paul said.

"Remember," Paulinus said, "only four or five evenings, for we are subject to rebellions at any given time." Then he turned to Luke. "Do I need more of your medicine?"

"Yes, you do; I will instruct your servants in gathering some local herbs to mix with green pond water."

The general looked sternly at Luke. "You had me sucking on green pond water?"

"The green alga has medicine in it; as long as it is filtered and cooked slowly in some bee's honey until it forms into a gel, it will do its trick."

The general wanted to say more, but showed signs of weakness.

"Get him back to his bed," Luke ordered. Several servants helped the general to his bed as Luke followed them. "I'll show you how to mix this formula," he said to a servant.

Paul looked at Linus. "Let's go and discuss a suitable meeting area for our messages."

AD 64-65

While Paul and company were on the islands of the Britons, Crescens, Eubius, and their team members returned to the seaport where they had separated from Paul and his team. While waiting for Paul's team, they shared the gospel with as many of the soldiers and servants as were allowed. The Holy Spirit gave them utterance so that the message was clear to those who had ears to hear.

For three months, the teams on the mainland continued witnessing to the locals. Finally the day came when Paul, Luke, and Linus joined them again. This time their gathering was different. Soldiers marched the three back to their comrades. Dokeomis was among the soldiers. "This is where we leave you," he said to Paul. He pulled out a pouch of coins. "Oh, the general ordered me to give you this." He tossed a bag of coins to Linus. "These may buy you passageway back to your homeland. And stop by the livery stable in our camp; we could use some good donkeys for carrying loads. We'll trade you some horses for them." He motioned to a couple soldiers to lead the way to the stables. "See that these men get horses and supplies for their pack animals."

"Thank you, sir," Paul said. "You have been most kind to us. And thank the general again, if you should have the opportunity."

Dokeomis smiled. "No; he and others need to thank you for the good news of the gospel. I pray it brings civility to the Britons and lasting peace to our empire." He turned around and headed back to his vessel.

"What was that all about?" Eubius asked.

Luke smiled. "Malaria."

Paul looked at the others. "So tell me, was your visit at the Saxon Shore profitable?"

"Was it ever!" Eubius said. "Many responded to the gospel message."

"And blessed be our Lord," Cresens said. "We found several fellowships of believers amongst the locals."

"Christians?" Paul could hardly believe what he heard.

"Yes!" Aristocles said.

"How can this be?" Luke asked.

"Ever heard of the Apostle Andrew of Bethsaida?" Cresens asked.

Paul rehearsed the name: "Andrew; Andrew . . . Yes! That's Peter's brother!

"Well he and a Simon the Zealot have been in the area southeast of here, sharing the gospel of Jesus," Aristocles said.

Luke smiled. "I suppose this means we don't have to stop in every town and stay a month?"

"You're right, Luke," Paul said. "But we will stop along the way and discover what our Lord is doing as we return to the south."

"South!" Eubius said. "I love that word. There my feet shall thaw out!"

Linus took the reins of Paul's horse as they began the Roman road south through the Gauls. The majestic mountains appeared as a wall in front of their every day. After several weeks, they arrived at Augustodunum of Lugdunensis.

"I remember this place," Paul said.

"We didn't pass this way before, Paul," Luke said. "Let me check you for fever."

"No, I didn't mean it that way. I've heard the name of this place before." Paul rehearsed the name through his mind for a few minutes. "Augustodunum . . . Augustodunum." Then he smiled. "Now I remember: the man and his son in Ephesus—the son had a demon that the widow lady exorcized. They live near this town in Germania."

Luke looked at Linus. "He has a good memory."

"Yes he does," Linus said.

"I must enquire about him." Paul visited several shops before someone knew the answer. "Yes," a shop owner said, "I know Junius and Antony very well. They come into town one evening a week to help the poor and to tell us of God and His Son, Jesus."

"Do you remember which night they come?" Paul asked.

The man thought for a moment. "Yes, I believe this is the night for them to come."

"Excellent!" Paul looked at the others. "Men, we lodge here tonight!"

"I'll see if I can find lodging," Linus said.

"They meet at the stable," the shop owner said. "And I'll help you find that lodging."

Paul acknowledged with his head. "And will we see you at the meeting?"

"Yes; my family and I have become followers of God and Jesus."

After the evening meal, Paul and company walked to the stable. There were about a dozen men standing around, along with the women and children. Although the dialect was foreign, Paul knew enough to greet others. He also remembered that Junius and his son knew Aramaic, so Paul began to speak to several other men in Aramaic.

One of the men turned toward Paul. "I recognize that voice," he said.

Paul came toward him with a smile on his face. "Junius?"

Junius looked at him. "Rabbi Paul?"

"Yes! It is I!" Paul reached out to embrace him, but Junius quickly bowed down before Paul.

"Oh, Rabbi Paul! How much I have prayed for this day to occur!"

Paul bent down in front of him. "Junius, you don't kneel to me; get up and let me greet you!" Paul grasped him, lifted Junius up, and embraced him for a few moments.

"Oh, Rabbi Paul, I nearly forgot—" He turned his head toward a group of men near the stable. "Antony? Antony? Where are you son?"

A handsome young man came out of the stable area. "Here I am, Father."

"Antony, it's Rabbi Paul from Ephesus; remember him?"

Antony walked up to them. "Remember? How could I ever forget the experience of receiving Jesus and getting my life back?" Antony bowed down before Paul.

Paul grabbed him and embraced him. "What a joy it is seeing you both! I thank our God for allowing this meeting to occur."

For the rest of the evening, Paul, Junius, and Antony gave testimony to the saving grace and power of God to the others. Some of the men had already become followers of Jesus; but that evening, five more men asked to receive Christ as their Lord and Savior.

"We must leave now, Paul," Junius said. We have another town to travel to tomorrow."

"Two fellowships?"

"Actually there's six or seven."

"How did all this come to be?"

"Many people in many towns knew the story of my son's condition. When we returned, our Lord burdened us to go to each town and testify how Antony was delivered. When they saw him and heard the testimony of the power of Jesus' name, many called upon Him for deliverance. Paul, we saw many people delivered from demonic oppression. Antony knew exactly how to deal with them."

"He's a miracle son."

"Yes, indeed."

"Someday, you and Antony will need to return to Ephesus and visit the widow lady."

"Perhaps we will." Junius embraced Paul and got on his horse. "Antony? Son, we must go now."

Antony left the group he was talking to, came over to Paul, and embraced him. "I am so happy to have seen you again. I will pray for your safe journey back to your homeland."

"Bless you, my son," Paul said. "And may your testimony continue changing many lives." Then Paul watched them as their horses trotted them away.

Luke wandered over to Paul's side. "Sorry I missed that episode in Ephesus."

Paul continued to gaze down the street. "I nearly missed it myself. I saw a simple widow lady, looking for a miracle. But God saw a willing vessel—an open vessel—for Him to fill."

Towns like Lugdunum, Vienna, and Arelate became resting points for Paul and company. They had been away from Rome for nearly two years now and were anxious to see familiar territory again.

At Nimes, they found Claudia and a fellowship of believers that had formed since their departure. Soon after the welcoming embraces, Luke led Paul into a room where he redressed Paul's eyes. How is your vision now?"

"I see men as trees."

"That's good. Let's keep the patches off for the evening fellowship time and see how they feel." Paul did not object. "Paul?"

"Yes?"

"Why can we heal others and yet not ourselves?"

Paul thought for a moment. "That's a good question . . . I've asked the Lord to remove this malady from me—just like I did for the malaria—but He has told me that He is stronger when I am weaker. I believe the miracles we have seen at certain times were to affirm His power to deliver people from their sins. Miracles seem to awaken people who are entrenched in deep paganism and are under the sway of the wicked one.

"If you remember, our Lord told me that I would have sufferings in my ministry to others. This sickness of mine drives me to a total dependence on Him for my strength."

"It just seems that we could be more effective if signs and miracles were in all our meetings."

"If that were to happen, I'm afraid people would follow us just to see physical healings of all sorts; they would not come to Jesus just for Him alone. This flesh of ours is tainted with the sin nature. God does not intend to restore this corrupted flesh; He has far greater plans in immortality. And Luke, remember, we have something far greater than healing."

"Really? What's that?"

"We have the Healer living inside us."

Luke smiled. "I think the Lord chose you because you have a way with words . . . Thanks for the lesson."

After supper had ended, Paul met with Claudia and discussed the spreading of the gospel copies throughout the region. "This book needs to find its way into Germania and the Britons."

"But they do not understand the Greek language," Claudia responded.

Paul rubbed his beard. "Then we must pray for future translators so that all peoples may read and understand the words of our Lord."

Everyone made their way to the fellowship to worship the Lord. As soon as they were recognized, several of the men pulled Paul and Luke aside.

"Master Paul!" one of the men said. "You mustn't walk about in public! Don't you know you have a new bounty on your head?"

Luke spoke first. "What do you mean?"

"We took supplies into the Roman camp where we heard several soldiers talking about how they hope to be the ones to capture Paul of Tarsus because of the huge reward and recognition from the emperor himself."

Paul was unmoved. "I think I've been hunted most of my Christian life. Why should I worry now?"

"Master Paul, the emperor has offered two-years of wages and a large parcel of land on the Baiae. It is the largest reward ever offered for one person."

Luke looked concerned. "Paul, perhaps you should go back to your room?"

"No! I am not afraid of the emperor. My Lord is much greater than he; and, besides, He may still allow me to give a testimony before him."

"Still, I will have these men form a group to scout the area to see if there are any strangers among us who may look like soldiers in disguise."

Paul faced Luke. "Whatever it takes to satisfy you is fine with me. Just remember, I am crucified already in Christ our Lord; it is no longer I who lives, but He lives in me. And the life I now live is a life of faith in Him who loves me and has given Himself in my behalf."

The service went on without any disruptions. Prayer lasted for several hours for Paul's safe journey back to Asia. After everyone went to sleep, Paul stepped outside, under the stars, for some privacy. He looked into the sky, but could only see little fuzzy balls of light. *My Lord, I love the beauty of the stars. I remember, as a child, forming the stars into groups: some into angels and some into demons who would battle the good angels. Of course, Your angels always won the battles.*

"My Master, I am Yours to do with as You please. Let me be faithful to You to the finish line of my life. Let me be a part of Your harvest for the souls of people until my last breath. Be my strength, O Lord, I pray! Guard my tongue, guide my steps, give me wisdom . . . and go before me in power!" Paul knelt down and wept.

"Paul? . . . Paul?"

"Yes, my Lord?"

"Your days are numbered; you will not survive your next capture. However, I will use your dying to overwhelm the emperor's power—both you and Peter."

"Can the emperor be converted?"

"He has much blood on his hands and will not turn to Me. His selfishness has consumed his heart; his evil deeds will be counted against him in the day of judgment."

"Then I am ready to go to him."

"Not yet, Paul. I want you to write a few more letters and help compile a treatise to My people. Don't rush your encounter with the emperor; he will find you at the right time and place. Go about your travels and listen to My Spirit; I will be your traveling guide. And rejoice in Me always—again, I say, rejoice!"

Paul smiled. "I remember those words. Thank You, Lord, for Your abiding presence." Paul stood back up and looked into the heavens. For a few minutes he could see the stars again clearly. He looked back down. *Just as I remember them, Lord . . . just as I remember them.*

A barking dog awakened Luke. He rose up and looked around. Everyone was still asleep—except Paul's bed was empty. *Does he ever sleep?* Luke got up to go find Paul. He was outside, sitting against a tree, snoring. *Now that's what I was hoping to see.*

Luke walked over to Paul. "Paul? Paul?" He touched Paul's shoulder.

"Huh? What?" Paul felt Luke's hand. "Oh, it's you, my son. I guess I fell asleep outside."

"Yes, I suppose you did. Let's go inside and let me clean your eyes."

Paul blinked a couple of times and tried to focus on the tree next door. "Still fuzzy trees."

"Yes, but it is a tree you're looking at this time." Luke helped him to stand. "Come on, let's go inside."

Luke helped Paul stand. "We must return to Rome," Paul said. "The fellowships there need to circulate our reports."

† † †

The slums of Rome appeared more dismal than before. The group had dismounted their horses and left them at a local stable. As they neared Quintus's villa, Linus motioned for the others to stop. He walked a little farther to the corner of a house to peer down a side street. Then he returned to the others. "There are several soldiers down beside the side entrance. Wait here until I get inside and find out what is happening." Paul was in the middle of the group with his face partially hidden by his headdress.

Luke nodded to Linus. "We will backtrack to the next side street and wait for you in the back."

Minutes later, Linus returned. "We cannot enter the villa of Quintus. One of his servants gave me instructions on another place for us to go. Follow me."

The group walked back several streets and turned down a small alley beside a market place. Hidden from the main street was another villa, surrounded by a five-foot high stone wall. The wall contained jagged spear-tipped sticks at its top.

Linus knocked on the wooden gate.

Through a small opening came a voice from inside. "Yes?" Linus spoke softly to the voice and the gate was opened. The group was shown to a large room. "Stay until I announce your arrival," the servant said.

Paul looked around until he saw what he was searching for: a bench. He walked over to the side of the room and sat down. Luke followed him. "Paul—"

"I know," he interrupted Luke. He smiled as he raised his head a bit and closed his eyes.

"I need to take care of my patient." He peeled Paul's eyelids back, one at a time. "Hmm."

"There goes that dreaded sound again."

Luke continued examining Paul's eyes. "Actually, it's a good response. Your eyes appear a bit clearer."

"Good! Now I can get rid of these patches."

"Not so fast; I want you to wear them at night."

"After the meetings."

"Of course; but after the evening fellowship, I want them on while you sleep. Then tomorrow I will make a new assessment."

"Yes, Doctor Luke. Now where is Linus? I want to know what is going on with Quintus."

Soon Linus appeared with the villa's owner. "Paul, this is Zinkros."

Paul stood up. "Grace and peace to you." They embraced.

"And greetings to you. Please, sit back down and rest yourself."

Paul and Luke both sat down. "This is Luke, my personal doctor," Paul said, motioning toward Luke.

"Greetings, Doctor Luke." Zinkros smiled and acknowledged Luke's presence. Then he turned back to Paul. "Sir, you are a wanted man. Your description has been posted in the market places throughout the empire. Quintus is my brother-in-law and has been sent to the east to search for you."

Paul stroked his beard. "I see."

"The reports I get say that many bounty hunters are searching for you in many cities—even into neighboring countries. Nero has promised twenty thousand gold coins for your capture in any country—but he wants you alive."

"Why is the emperor seeking him out so seriously?" Luke asked.

"He wants to show how incompetent the senate has become and how strong he is in conquering the enemies of the empire. He found out that Paul was released before he had a chance to judge his case. He is using Paul to gain an advantage."

Paul leaned back against the wall. "Well, here I am . . . and right under the emperor's nose."

Zinkros studied Paul for a moment. "Quintus described you well, so you had better stay put inside the villa." He pointed to a door. "This entry has several rooms—one of which contains a door under the floor rug; it leads to an underground lodging area. This will be your quarters while you're in Rome." He turned toward it. "Come, follow me."

Paul, Luke, and the others followed Zinkros and his servants to the entryway of their new quarters. The entry opened into a large room. There was a large table in the middle—large enough to seat over a dozen people. Around the room were sitting areas, several doors, and a large open fireplace. In front of the fireplace was a small table with a large rug underneath it.

Zinkros pointed toward the doors. "Your party can lodge in those rooms over there; Paul, you and your doctor will lodge here." He moved the small table and rolled the rug back, revealing a door in the floor. His servant lifted the door up. There was a small stairway with a handrail on one side. Several torches were hanging on the wall. A servant stepped down a few rungs, grabbed a torch, and held it up for another servant to light.

"Before going down," Zinkros said, "I want to speak to you all." Everyone stopped talking and listened. "The cost of housing a fugitive is death. Me, my family, and my servants are putting our lives on the line for this accommodation. You must not draw attention to yourselves and you must be careful what you say on the streets. There is a back way from the villa that you must use. As soon as is possible, some of you will find other Christians with whom you must lodge. The bounty hunters and the soldiers are assuming Paul is traveling with a minimum of six people, so keep your group to a maximum of four while outside on the streets."

"Uh, sir?" Paul asked. "Are you a Christian?"

"Yes I am."

"And where do the Christians meet for worship and training?"

Zinkros looked around him. "Do you know all these people in your group?"

Paul joined his gaze around the room. "Luke, be my eyes for me, please?"

Luke looked around the room. "Yes, these are the ones who went with us to Spain—except your two servants there—and you, of course."

"We meet in the catacombs outside the city on the east side. There are also some catacombs on the south side of the city where other fellowships meet."

"Are Christians banned from public gatherings?" Paul asked.

"Not yet; but if we meet publicly, we get interrupted by men looking for you."

Paul lowered his head. "Oh dear."

Luke diverted the attention. "Let's have a look downstairs. I think we need to rest for a while.

"One other thing," Zinkros said. "Your apostle friend, Peter, was captured. He claimed he was Paul. After further flogging and interrogation, they realized he was not you. Last I heard, he and his wife remain imprisoned."

Paul continued to look at the floor. Luke spoke up: "Do you know the whereabouts of his daughter and husband?"

"Somewhere north of Rome is all I know."

Outside of Rome, in the area called the catacombs, there were caves large enough for the Christians to meet in worship. While Paul enjoyed worshipping with fellow believers, his heart ached for sharing the gospel. After several meetings in secret, he decided he'd had enough.

"I'm leaving Rome," Paul announced to Luke.

"Leaving? Paul, we just arrived and you are carefully hidden here. You can't just go out on the streets again."

"The Lord has called me to be a witness and to share the good news of salvation. My calling is out there—in the public arena."

"But what about the reward for your capture? Everyone is looking for you!"

"Then the Lord will blind their eyes. I can't stay here and be hidden. The Lord has told me that I would be captured and would give my testimony to the magistrates."

"I think that has already occurred once . . . don't you remember?"

Paul smiled, as he looked at Luke. "You can stay, if you wish, but I must go."

Luke studied the face of his dear friend. "You still need your doctor . . . when do we leave?"

"Tomorrow."

"Where are we going?"

"We're sailing to Crete. They say Titus is there and I long to see him."

"And what of Peter?"

"The less he knows, the safer he will be. We must instruct the others not to tell him of our whereabouts. In fact, no one else must know where we are going."

† † †

The worship service was one of the finest Paul had seen and experienced. The Sacred Writings were read with brokenness and the people sang the psalms with fervent hearts and voices. Hardly a dry eye remained by the time Titus stood to speak.

"The Lord be praised for His indescribable presence here tonight. Listen while I read to you some of Paul's instructions to our Corinthian brothers and sisters." He then read from one of Paul's letters to the Corinthians. After reading a few verses, Titus explained the setting and the application the verses brought for the fellowship in Crete. For about an hour, he exhorted the people from God's word.

Slowly, the fellowship dispersed, everyone leaving except a middle-aged man with an elderly person, wrapped in an outer garment. Titus approached them. "Grace and peace to you; I don't think we've met. My name is Titus."

"Titus."

Titus looked more intently. "Luke? Is that really you?"

Luke put his finger across his lips. "Shhh."

Next, the elderly man spoke quietly: "If you don't recognize him, I know you won't recognize me." He pulled his headdress up and smiled.

"Paul! Oh blessed be our Lord Jesus! Paul!" Titus embraced them both as he began to weep.

"My son," Paul said. "You must control yourself; my name mustn't be spoken in public."

Titus began to wipe his face. "Yes; yes, I've heard you have a large price on your head."

"I came to see you and see how the ministry was growing here in Crete."

"Oh Paul, our Lord is building a fine group of Christians here. Many are coming to Jesus for deliverance. There are at least a dozen assemblies here on the island and many more needed."

"And who is helping you?"

"Philip and Nathanael—the apostles—came through and helped me for about six months. Then they headed for the mainland of Phrygia."

"That is good."

"But we could sure use a message or two from you."

"From what I heard tonight, you're doing a fine job."

"The Lord is gracious to use me." That being said, the three walked over to the house next door, where Titus was living with some believers. Paul and Luke spent the rest of the evening with him, speaking of all the travels to the west of Rome.

Paul arose early and went outside to listen to the sea waves breaking against the rocks. This atmosphere was such a comfort for him. He loved the sea and was always amazed at its size. "My Lord," he prayed, "You have such a bigger plan for the world than I can see. Please help me see Your plan for the remainder of my days."

The Lord answered him: "Paul, help Titus and Timothy by writing down My instructions for the leaders of the local fellowships. There will be times of discouragement and opposition after your departure. Give them personal encouragement as well."

"Yes, Lord, I will do so."

"There you are!" Titus said. He walked up to Paul and looked out over the rocks along the coastline. "I love to come here as well; it's so soothing."

"Yes it is . . . Titus, while I'm here, I'd like to meet with the men that you sense can be trained to become elders for each fellowship."

His eyes lit up. "That would be great! I have been asking our Lord for wisdom in leading each group."

"We must learn that we cannot do everything to keep each fellowship active. We must set aside abled men who sense a call from the Lord to be elders and deacons. Both are vital for each fellowship to grow strong within."

Titus embraced Paul. "That's just what I needed to hear. What a blessing to have you here."

"And what about me?" Luke asked, as he came up from behind the two.

Titus reached out and embraced both men. "You also, Luke; you also."

✝✝✝

Peter stretched out on the stone bench in his cell. He recalled one of the early psalms John designed for the followers to sing. He hummed a few lines and then began singing aloud. This was his daily routine. Once he got it started, his wife, Perpetua (a few cell doors down), joined in the singing.

At first, many of the prisoners would shout out complaints and insults. But after a few months, Peter and Perpetua began hearing other voices join them in the praise songs. It was now the delight of the prison as it encouraged those who seemed to have no hope left in their lives. Today, however, would be different.

Two guards walked down the corridor with the prison official in charge. One each of the guards stopped at Peter and Perpetua's cell door. They began unlocking them as the singing stopped.

"We're moving you two," the official said.

"Where?" Peter asked.

"You are being assigned to a house, by order of the general."

Peter stepped out of his cell, looked toward his left, and saw his wife step out as well. They both exchanged a cautious smile as they were led to the front of the prison.

The official wrote a few words on some papyrus, stamped it, and sealed it. He handed it to one of the guards. "See that Arston gets this when you arrive."

The guard took the papyrus and lifted up a chain with two shackles attached. "You two raise a hand and attach this to each other.

"Gladly," Peter said.

Just outside the prison wall sat several small houses with barred windows and doors. The guard stopped at the second one and unlocked the front gate. He opened it and walked them to the front entrance. "Your hands," he said. They both extended their arms and he unshackled them, but left their leg shackles intact.

Peter lifted up one of his legs. The guard smiled. "That stays on." Another official walked out of the house. The guard held out the papyrus. "I believe you are expecting these prisoners?" Arston grabbed it and walked to the gate. The guard looked at the two prisoners and smiled. "Hope you can convert ol' grumpy with your singing."

Arston walked past Peter and Perpetua without saying a word. He stopped in the doorway and looked back at them. "If you expect me to show you the place, you'd better keep up." He then walked on into the front room.

"After you, Perpie."

She smiled. "You're so polite."

He whispered: "Just staying as far away as I can from him."

Arston showed them each room and gave them instructions on when they could draw water for cleaning clothes and personal baths. He finally returned to the front door. "A guard will be posted outside your gate. This front door will remain unlocked until darkness. You will have one month to pay for the use of this house."

"What?!" Peter said. "Pay?"

"You don't think you will have this luxury for free, do you? Tomorrow, your guard will lead you to your former lodging where you can get word to your friends to come up with the money: four silver coins or two gold ones each month."

"We didn't ask for this!"

"Peter, hush!"

Arston smiled. "You better listen to the lady or you'll be back in the cell block . . . and maybe this time I'll put you farther back where it's nice and damp." He turned around and walked out the gate.

Peter stared at the gate as the guard locked it. Perpetua came to his side. "Why are they being so nice?" she asked.

"They want to know who our friends are so they can find Paul."

"Oh . . ."

"There's always a price for Roman 'luxury'."

✝✝✝

Thirty miles from Rome sat Nero and Tigellinus. They had just finished a night of gambling in the confines of a luxurious spa. Several merchant marines allowed a prosperous night for Nero, as many allowed him to win just to stay on his good side. Tigellinus didn't care what he won because he always managed to help Nero spend his winnings.

"It's still hot!" Tigellinus complained. "Come on, Nero, let's go for a swim."

Nero shrugged his shoulders. "I'm too tired and intoxicated to do anything else tonight."

Tigellinus laughed. "Did I hear you correctly?"

Nero smiled as he threw a wine cup at his companion. "You'd better thank the gods that I'm not sober or I would have you cut open." They both laughed as they fell onto their beds. Several male servants came over to undress them. By the time they were undressed, both of them were asleep.

"Divine One, wake up! Wake up!" A servant was beside Nero's bed. "Divine One, you must wake up!"

Nero groaned. "Huh? . . . What is the meaning of this? You better have a good reason for awakening me before dawn." Nero rubbed his eyes. Tigellinus was awakened also.

The servant pointed out the window toward Rome. "We've received word that there is a large fire spreading throughout the city! Look! Look!"

"What?!" Nero stood up and walked over to the window. Toward Rome, there was an orange-red glow over a large portion of the city. "By the gods! Quick, make my carriage ready! I must return to the palace!"

In a matter of minutes, both Nero and Tigellinus were racing down the road toward Rome. As they neared the city, the fire was all around them. Nero's carriage was halted by a roadblock the soldiers had formed.

"Make way for the emperor," cried one of Nero's guards.

"No, Divine One," a soldier said. "Fire is crossing the road and it's too hot for the animals. You will be suffocated by the smoke."

Nero stood on top his carriage. He could see the flames lapping over the housetops. Even worse, he could hear the screams of people as the fire showed no mercy on those who were caught in its pathway.

✝✝✝

"Guards! Unlock this gate!" Peter rattled the front gate. The fire was approaching the prison area, but the guards had left their posts to go home to save their families.

"Peter!" Perpetua shouted from the broken-down front door.

"Woman, go back and get a sack of food and water—I'll get a blanket!"

Soon, both were back at the locked gate. Peter threw the blanket over the barbed top of the gate's fixture and tugged on it. It became stuck in the barbs. "Quickly," he said. "Climb over and I will throw you the sacks!" He helped her climb over the gate. Next, he hoisted himself over with both sacks wrapped around his shoulders. He managed to retrieve a torn portion of the blanket.

"Run for the prison! There's a dungeon beneath the ground!" They both ran to the prison gate. It was locked and the guards were gone! The gate and walls were twice as high as the gate they had just scaled.

"Look for some rocks, Perpie! We need to get higher!" They both began kicking among the weeds as sparks began falling all around them. Small fires were lighting up nearby.

Then she saw it. "Peter!" She ran out into the street and picked up a ring of keys.

"Bring them quickly, my dear!" Peter began trying each key until he found the right one. The gate unlocked and they ran toward the prison. As they entered, they heard prisoners crying out for help. Peter and Perpetua ran to each cell door and unlocked each one. "To the dungeon!" Peter shouted.

"No!" cried out some of the prisoners. "I have family nearby—I must try to save them!"

Most of the prisoners ran down into the dungeon, carrying water buckets and other supplies. Nearly one hundred prisoners made their way down deep into the ground, hearing less and less of the ground-level screams.

Peter sat next to Perpetua on a bench. "I pray those prisoners were able to save their families," he said. She took the keys from Peter and kneeled down. Soon she found the right one and unlocked both their ankle shackles. He smiled at her and lifted his shackles. "No wonder I was having difficulty climbing over that gate."

"I think perhaps now would be a good time to invite these men to pray with us?" she asked her husband.

"I think you're right . . . I think you're right."

†††

In Antium, Nero watched the fire continue engulfing his city. Tigellinus had fallen across his bed, asleep from exhaustion. He pulled out his lyre and strummed a melody as the orange-red glow slowly changed to a shadowy grey against the morning sun. His glazed look suddenly turned to anger. *Where are our gods!*

The following day, Nero slowly made his way through the charred remains of the area next to the palace. His horse snorted occasionally, clearing the soot from his nose. Tigellinus stood behind Nero in a chariot. "What a mess!" He jumped off the chariot, creating a cloud of soot as his sandals disappeared underneath the grey ash. "By the gods, they must hate us!"

Nero remained stoic. "Who hates us?"

"The gods; they let this fire ruin a third of our city."

Nero slowly eyed the area, studying the terrain. "The gods? I am the voice of Apollo. All other gods are subject to me. They tell me that this fire has created an opportunity."

"You risk receiving the blame for this 'act of the gods'. . . Opportunity?"

"Opportunity, my friend . . . I seek a Christian rebel, so the Christians retaliate by creating a diversion—a fiery diversion."

Tigellinus wiped the ash off his hands and onto his outer garment. "I don't understand; how do we get to that rebel through such a mess as this?"

"We'll keep interrogating them until one snaps. In the meantime, I will rebuild from this golden opportunity. I will erect a palace—a temple!—like no other Caesar!" Nero stepped down into the ash, grasping a handful, allowing it to trickle from his forming fist. "Gold from ashes!"

† † †

"Corinth?" Luke asked.

"Yes," Paul answered. "We can blend in with the crowds; plus, I want to check on the fellowship there . . . and then perhaps to Ephesus."

"Ephesus?" Luke ran his hand through his short-but-curly brown hair. "These are places the bounty hunters and soldiers will expect you to visit."

Paul smiled at Luke and put his arm on his shoulder. "My dear doctor, the Great Physician bids me to keep an appointment with Him."

Luke looked into Paul's eyes—this time not for medicinal purposes. He saw the peace of God in a willing servant. "Then let us go together to meet Him."

"Not too fast!" Paul's smile turned into a stern look. "My son, when we arrive in Corinth, I want you to find someone—Artemas or Tychicus, perhaps—to deliver the letter I have written to Titus. I promised him that I would get it back to him in Crete as soon as possible."

Paul put his hand in Luke's curly hair and rubbed it briskly. "In Corinth, you will keep a distance from me in the public arena. Our Lord has other plans for you than a capture. You must remain available to finish the writings He has appointed us to write."

† † †

Capernaum seemed more restless than the years ago when John last visited. Roman soldiers appeared in groups of a dozen or more, walking as if they were expecting an ambush. John stopped his donkey and walked down a side street. Soon he arrived at the house of Jacob and Elizabeth, Perpetua's parents.

"Greetings!" John spoke up as he opened the front door. "Is anyone here?" When no one answered, he walked out back to a bench under a tree and fell asleep.

"John? John?" She shook him again. "John?"

John opened his eyes and focused on the woman in front of him. "Mary?" She smiled. "Mary! Blessings be mine, I've found you at last!"

"And where have you been looking for me?"

"Oh, nowhere until now; but I didn't expect it to be this easy."

Mary helped him to his feet and they embraced. "I have been waiting for your arrival."

John rubbed his eyes. "You have?"

"Yes, my child; our Lord told me you were coming." She then looked around as if she were being spied upon. "And not a minute too soon, I might add."

"Yes, I felt a bit of edginess on the streets. What's happening?"

Mary looked south. "Our kindred are rebelling against the emperor in Judea. There are reports that Jerusalem has shut its gates and all Romans have been ousted."

"A rebellion? The city gates shut?"

"Yes, and the leaders of the rebellion are here trying to recruit Jewish fighters."

"Oh my."

"That's why we must leave as soon as you are refreshed. Our Lord has spoken to me about traveling with you to Ephesus."

"We'll need to go to the market and restock my donkey for the journey."

"I have already collected supplies for our trip." Mary pointed at a couple of donkeys tied to a tree nearby. "One is for me and the other to carry our supplies."

John smiled. "He's in touch with you."

"On a regular basis, my son."

"And what about Peter's family?"

Mary smiled. "Let's go inside and prepare an evening meal. I'll let Elizabeth and Jacob fill you in on their plans . . . then tomorrow we leave."

John embraced her again. "You are much more than a mother to me. I am so happy and honored that our Lord chose me to bring you under my care."

John prayed as he brushed and fed his donkey. "My Lord, thank You for this place and Your people who have watched over our mother until I returned. I ask for Your guidance as we travel to Ephesus."

The Spirit interrupted John's prayer: "Go to Antioch and report to them all that you know of My work in Rome. Warn them of the pending conflict in Jerusalem."

"Yes, my Lord." John turned and headed for the house.

While eating, John asked a few questions. "Where is Mary of Magdala and her family? Are they well?"

"Yes, they are well," Jacob responded. "They moved to Bethsaida a year ago. I saw Eliezer about a month ago; he was here buying some knives. He said they were moving farther north to Dan."

"Oh . . . a fishing business in Dan?"

"I asked that very question, John. He said that the mountains supply the Jordan with plenty of fresh water and that there was a sizeable lake there. But his main job would be his proclamation of the gospel." Jacob leaned over to John as if he was going to tell a secret. "Plus, a lot less Roman soldiers there too."

"I see. Perhaps you and Elizabeth will join them someday?"

"The invitation has been given. We'll have to wait and see what happens around here."

Elizabeth stopped talking to Mary and looked at John. "Surely everything in Jerusalem will be settled soon, don't you think?"

"No!" John and Mary said together.

"Pardon me," Mary said. "I didn't mean to sound harsh."

John smiled. "You weren't harsh, Mother; I think it was our combined voices." He then turned to Elizabeth. "Our Lord has told me—us—that there is a coming conflict in Jerusalem. That's why we must move on tomorrow to Antioch."

Jacob looked at his wife. "Then perhaps we should prepare for a trip to Dan ourselves."

"But what if Perpetua and Peter return, looking for us?" Elizabeth asked.

"I spoke with your children in Rome," John said. "They intend to stay in Italy for some time. And I doubt they will return this way when the conflict begins."

"Oh dear." She grasped Jacob's hand. "Maybe we could travel west to be closer to them?"

"Ha! I think John here can tell them of our whereabouts . . . John?"

"All the missionaries report to Antioch because of the financial support the fellowships there give to them."

Jacob looked at his wife. "See? If we move anywhere, I say we should go to Antioch."

"But they're mostly Gentiles," Elizabeth said.

"Well, don't Gentiles eat fish?"

"Yes they do," John said. "Plus a whole lot more."

Elizabeth frowned. "Perhaps Dan would be better."

Mary put her arm around Elizabeth. "Just ask our Lord where you should go. He will tell you where and when."

John grabbed another piece of bread. "You can always join us at Ephesus." He smiled at them both, but they gave him no response.

†††

Corinth was as busy as ever. The docks were full of ships, loading and unloading cargo for the across-the-isthmus route tugging. Although he wanted to stop and share the gospel to many onlookers, Paul lowered his headdress, allowing much of it to cover his face.

At first, Luke lingered behind Paul about a dozen steps; but Paul kept stopping to look at the people, causing Luke to catch up. "This isn't working, Paul."

"What?"

"You're not walking fast enough."

"Look at the people, Luke . . . so many do not know about deliverance in Christ. It burdens me so!"

"You're a wanted man, Paul. You must ignore the people and walk to Junius's house where the fellowship meets."

Paul wiped tears from his eyes. "You're right. Perhaps you should lead the way and I will follow you."

Luke obliged. "This way."

The villa of Junius had a few additional rooms than before. Luke stopped at the tree next to the synagogue. Paul stared at the synagogue. "No, Paul; don't even think about it."

He smiled. "If I keep my face covered, they won't know it's me."

"Trust me; they will know it's you as soon as you open your mouth. Now let's see who is at the villa." Luke grabbed Paul's arm and helped him walk through the front gate. They knocked on the door. Soon, the wife of Junius opened the door.

"Yes, may I help you?" she asked.

Paul stretched forward as if he were telling a secret. "Does the grace and peace of the Deliverer abide here?"

She smiled. "Yes they do, as well as the Deliverer Himself."

"May we come in?" Luke asked.

She backed up while opening the door. "Please come in."

"Thank you, dear woman," Paul said. "Is Junius nearby?"

"Please come in and recline. I will serve you a drink and then find him."

"You are most kind," Paul said.

She brought them some water and placed some fruit and bread before them. "Please refresh yourselves while I find my husband. He should be nearby."

"Thank you," Paul said.

She stopped and looked at Paul. "I do not recognize you, but your voice is very familiar. Who may I tell is visiting us?"

Luke smiled at Paul. "See, Paul, I told you your voice would give you away."

She took a second look at him. "Are you Paul, our apostle?"

Paul smiled at her, but spoke to Luke. "You gave her my name."

Luke smiled. "Oh, excuse me."

Paul slowly removed his headdress. "My dear, it is very important that you do not tell anyone other than Junius that I am here."

"He has a price on his head," Luke explained.

"Everyone knows that. Dozens of people and many soldiers have sought for you."

Paul's smile left his face. "Recently?"

"Maybe two or three weeks ago was the last time our gathering was interrupted by several men with swords. They looked at every man and had every man walk a distance to see if they matched your description. Fortunately, our men are tall—you have been described as short."

Paul did not respond, but Luke continued. "Anything else we should know?"

"The soldiers have offered a huge reward for information that leads to your capture. They have described you as a Jew, short in statue, receding hairline, and that you walk with a limp."

Paul remained silent. "Thank you; now if you don't mind, we'd like to speak privately with your husband." When she exited, Luke patted Paul's shoulder. "Don't despair, Paul. Our Lord knows where we are."

Paul's eyes were moist. "I do not fear being captured—nor do I fear the emperor. But I did not think of how others might be affected by my presence. Luke, I cannot bear thinking that others may be harmed because of me."

Luke looked at him. "I think it's too late for that, Paul." He sipped some water from his cup. "Every person you have brought to face their sins and then led them to Jesus have come in harm's way. Didn't you once say that we must all enter the kingdom of our Lord through many tribulations? I would not have been stoned in Philippi had I not known the Jesus you led me to."

Paul wiped his tears. "You're right . . . you're right. I mustn't forget the way of our Master."

"Good. Now take some bread and eat—and drink some water."

"Paul!" Junius embraced him. "I can't believe you're here. I thought surely you would have been captured by now."

Paul managed a slight smile. "You remember Doctor Luke?"

I don't think we've met, but I've heard a lot about you."

"Quite alright," Luke said. "I like being unknown."

"You won't be unknown for long hanging around this guy. The whole empire is dreaming of catching him—the reward, you know?"

"The reward—of course!" Paul said.

"Do you know it is the largest reward ever offered for a single man?"

"We've heard that," Luke said. "Is it safe for us to be here?"

"Ha! The last bounty hunters that came here were witnessed to by so many that they literally ran down the street to get away from us. You're safe for now. But watch out for the soldiers. They're the ones I would fear."

Paul looked at them both. "Is it possible for me to speak to the fellowship?"

Junius came over to Paul and put his arm on Paul's shoulder. "I believe most of our people would never sell you out for any amount of gold . . . but, you know how greed can grip a man's heart. The soldiers have offered five thousand gold coins for your capture."

"Five thousand?" Paul repeated.

Junius nodded his head. "So, you are at risk wherever you go and you increase the risk every time you speak in public."

Paul walked over to a window. He stared at the movement of people, listening to the noise of life. Then he turned to the others. "God has called me to proclaim His words—not to hide for fear of physical harm. I wish to speak at the next meeting of your fellowship."

There was silence. Luke then stood up. "Let's not advertise it, but speak at the end of the service."

"That's a good idea," Junius said. "Let the people participate in the service as usual, then I will recognize you as a guest prophet."

Paul decided to come into the fellowship by himself as the service began. He sat in the back and uncovered his head. Several men looked at him and smiled, but did not seem to notice him as Paul. *Lord, be my protection and my guide.*

The service began with a reading from the prophet Isaiah by an elder. After that, several people prayed randomly. Junius then led the fellowship in the singing of several songs from the psalms. After that, he spoke before the usual time of offering support for the fellowship. "Today, we will hear from a prophet who travels throughout the empire, sharing the gospel of Jesus, our Deliverer. I want you to pray for him and for his ministry. Also, I want us to give an offering to his work after he has shared his message to us today. So give as the Lord burdens your heart."

Next, Junius led the fellowship in another reading from Paul's letter to the churches in Galatia. Then there was a time for much prayer. Many prayed aloud; others whispered their prayers, agreeing with what was spoken aloud.

Paul noticed that there were several languages being used in the prayer time. Occasionally, someone would interpret a prayer from one language to another. All praying was edifying to the whole fellowship—no confusion or misunderstanding of what was being said. *Lord, I thank You that Your words to this fellowship were heeded and beneficial. Now be in control of the words I speak to this Your fellowship. In Your precious name I pray, amen.*

After a season of prayer, Junius stood before the fellowship. "My brothers and sisters, I usually take a portion of the Sacred Writings and proclaim or teach the meanings behind them. But I yield my time to a guest prophet. But before he comes, I want you to know that he speaks at great peril to his own life. Therefore I beg of you to keep his name a secret in the public arena." He then motioned for Paul. "Paul?"

As Paul made his way to the front, gasps and whisperings were heard throughout the room. Paul turned around to face the fellowship. He placed his finger over his lips. "Shhh," he said quietly. "My beloved family, of whom I have prayed for daily for many years. Allow me to speak softly this evening." The whispering stopped. "Most of you know that I am being sought after by the emperor and that there is a large sum of money to be gained by the one who turns me in. Any of you would become wealthy by doing so. But I want you to know that I do not count my life or my belongings as any good thing when I consider what my Lord Jesus has done for me and has given me. I look at me in a mirror and see nothing worthwhile. When I reflect on what I have done to some Christians in my past, I see myself as the chief of all sinners.

"The words we heard earlier from the prophet Isaiah are very helpful to me. Here was a giant of a prophet of God; yet when he saw the glorious presence of Him, he prostrated himself before God as a dead man—a man with unclean lips, condemned! I feel that way when I consider myself. But I do not look back—I do not live today based on who I was yesterday. Every new day given me is a new day for me to press forward with the gospel message—the great news!—that Jesus has given me a new life. I am dead to myself, but alive in Christ Jesus, who is the Lord of my new life. My old life has passed away; behold, all things are new today!"

Paul continued to share his heart and his journey, using the readings from both Isaiah and Galatians. After about an hour, he began to close the message. "Now today, you have a choice. You can reject this message and leave here unchanged. Any one of you could go to the docks or to the city magistrate and turn me in and receive this world's riches. Or you can allow this message to edify your very spirit and nature and be changed forever. You can keep my whereabouts a secret, thus allowing me to speak to others who may benefit from my proclamations. And finally, some of you may not have experienced the deliverance from your sins that Jesus offers. If you wish to be saved today, please come to me or Junius after the final song and we will be honored to help you through the process of being born again . . . Junius?"

Paul stepped to the front row of benches, knelt down, and began praying.

Junius stepped to the front and faced the people. "Let's pray now for our brother and do not forget to support his ministry with an offering."

As Paul continued praying, he felt many hands placed on him and coins placed beside him. When the room became quiet, Paul stood up. Only Luke remained, sitting near the back. Paul motioned for him. "Come here, my son."

Luke slowly made his way forward. "Just you and me."

"And the Master. Would you pick up these coins and put them in our pouch?"

"Yes, Paul . . . Junius left."

"I suppose he had some business to tend to with the others—or perhaps someone needed to come to Christ for salvation."

Luke looked to the rear again. "I pray everything is okay. It doesn't feel safe anymore."

Paul grabbed his shoulder. "It is not for us to worry about safety. We do what we can for our Lord and if He permits calamity then it will benefit the Kingdom's work somewhere down the road of life."

"So where to next?" Luke asked as they neared the doorway.

Paul thought for a moment. "I would love to visit Ephesus one more time. Perhaps Timothy is there—and the widow lady; she would love to hear of the work in Germania."

"Taking a ship to Ephesus might not be wise. Too long in one place . . . people have time to study others and may realize who you are. We should travel by land."

"Athens, Philippi, and Troas?"

Luke managed a smile. "And all points in between."

As they stepped outside, Junius was walking toward them. Paul was about to call out to him, but Junius put his finger to his lips. "Follow me," he said quietly. The three walked to the back-side of the villa.

"Is something wrong?" Luke asked.

"Several of our men noticed two or three new faces in tonight's meeting. They left shortly after Paul began to speak. I have set up some spies of my own to see if they can find out who they were."

"We should leave tonight," Luke said.

"No," Junius said. "Let's wait and see what we discover. It could be nothing. Come, let's go inside for some refreshment be-fore—"

Suddenly a scream shrieked from within the house. "Marsella!" Junius cried out. He ran toward the back door.

Luke looked at Paul. "Go!" Luke pushed Paul toward the side of the villa as he ran toward the back door as well.

Paul made quick steps to the corner of the house, hearing more commotion inside. It sounded like soldiers. Alongside the house was a large tree—the same tree where the Corinthian fellowship began. He moved to the backside of it and stopped. For a few minutes he heard the clanging of swords against armor with an occasional shout from several men.

Then it became quiet. Paul looked up the tree. *No, can't climb there.* Next, he looked toward the front and over toward the synagogue. He started toward the synagogue, walking behind several bushes. He checked the door—locked! Near the back wall was a window. He quickly made his way to the rear, found a rock, and placed it under the window to help him get inside.

Once inside, Paul noticed a candle still lit. He took it and made his way to a small room on the side. There, he sat down to collect his thoughts. "My Lord, is this how I'm to act? Must I run from my enemies? And must my friends suffer because of me? What shall I do?" Paul continued praying as he listened to the commotion outside.

Then the Spirit spoke to Paul. "Paul! Do not fear man, for I am with you always. Walk to the front of the house and get the soldiers' attention. They will release your friends in order to capture you. As for you, it is time for you to go before the emperor."

Paul remained quiet for a moment. "Yes, my Lord. I will do as you say."

"Bring them to me," the lead soldier ordered. One by one, Luke, Junius, and his family were escorted to the front gate by several soldiers. The lead soldier eyed Junius and Luke. "Are there any other men?"

"No," a soldier replied. "Just these two."

The lead soldier took out a sheet of papyrus and held a torch near it for light. "Neither of you are short nor Jewish. Walk about in a circle." He studied them as a soldier made them walk. "No limp."

"Maybe our source was wrong in sighting this criminal."

"Maybe." The lead soldier put his papyrus back into his pocket. He then pointed to Junius's wife. "Bring her to me."

"No!" Junius said.

"Oh?" the lead soldier said. He pulled out a small dagger. "Perhaps this Paul will magically appear if I start carving my name across her pretty face." He pulled her closer to him.

A voice yelled out from the street. "Let her go!"

The lead soldier pushed her away and looked into the darkness. "And who is ordering me to stop?"

"I am Paul of Tarsus and I will surrender to you as long as you release these people. Otherwise, I will run off into the dark and you and your comrades will be known as the soldiers who let the emperor's criminal get away."

"We have horses."

"But I know places between these houses that your horses cannot pass. Good luck finding me!" Paul turned to disappear into the dark.

"Wait!" The lead soldier released his grip from Marsella. "We don't want these people. You walk over to the horses and I will let each one go, one-by-one, until my soldiers have you."

"Run, Paul!" Luke shouted. "We'll manage!"

"I wouldn't do that," the lead soldier said. "I can still work out information from these three if you run."

"Luke," Paul said, "the Lord told me to do this. It's in His hands now. You must trust Him." Paul began walking toward the horses. The lead soldier motioned to his men. They released Junius and Luke and walked toward the horses in the street. When he was comfortable, the lead soldier walked out into the street with his men and approached Paul. He raised his hand back to slap Paul.

"I am a Roman citizen," Paul said.

The lead soldier lowered his arm, pulled out his papyrus, and read it again. Then he raised his arm and slapped Paul. "Doesn't say you're a citizen in my report, so I'm covered." He laughed as Paul wiped the blood from his mouth. "Tie him up men. This catch is going to make us rich."

✝✝✝

For miles, a haze surrounded every road out of Rome. The fire had been out for days, but the smoldering embers and the clean-up detail kept the air filled with ash. Peter turned and looked at Perpetua behind him. He smiled.

"What?"

"Oh nothing."

"Come now; tell me what's funny."

"You look like a street beggar, with all that ash covering you."

She started brushing off her outer garment, creating a small ash cloud. "Oh, you would laugh. I pray we can get a bath soon. I'm so dirty."

"Perhaps in the next town we will find some Christians to help us."

"And perhaps they will know something about our children."

"It's getting dark." Perpetua was tired and concerned that they may not find a safe place for sleeping.

"The ash cloud makes it appear later than it is." Peter squinted his eyes, trying to make out the road ahead. "I believe Monterosi should be in our sights soon." About that time, a man appeared ahead of Peter, walking toward them. "Pardon me sir? Monterosi?"

The man smiled and pointed his finger behind him, to the north. "You are very close; not too far." He then continued walking south.

"You see," Peter said. "I knew we were close."

Soon, they were walking through the main street of Monterosi. Peter turned in circles as he walked along the road. "I should recognize something or someone soon . . . THERE!" He pointed. "That's the shop where I led a man and his wife to Jesus. Come quickly, Perpie!"

Perpetua was too tired from walking all day to be excited about anything. *My Lord, please make this a place where we can stay and refresh ourselves.* By the time she made it to the shop entrance, Peter was already in a full conversation with a man.

"Perpie, you remember Antwan, don't you?" She managed a polite smile.

"You look awful," Antwan said. "And Rome is a mess! I am happy to see you got out safely."

"Antwan, Perpie and I need to get cleaned up, eat, and rest for the night. Can you help us?"

"Oh, pardon me for not seeing the obvious. Yes, yes; my family and I will take good care of you. Please give me a minute to close my shop and I will take you home with me. My wife will be happy to see you again . . . and your daughter?"

"We are looking for her and her husband, John Mark. Have you seen them?"

Antwan was about to speak when Perpetua fainted from sheer exhaustion. "Oh my!" Peter said, while catching her fall.

"Here," Antwan said, as he handed Peter a cup of water and a small cloth. "Give her a drink and moisten her head while I close up."

When Perpetua came to, she was lying on a mat in Antwan's living room. A young girl was wiping her head with a damp cloth. Perpetua managed a smile. "Mother, she's awake!" The little girl smiled back at Perpetua.

"Where am I?"

"I am Catalina," the mother said. "And your helper is Angelina."

"Father and Master Peter brought you from the shop," Angelina said with a smile. "And I helped." When she said that, she started rubbing Perpetua's head with the damp cloth.

Perpetua reached up and stroked Angelina's hair. "Yes you have. I have a daughter too."

Angelina's eyes lit up. "You do! Is she coming to see you? Can she play with me?"

"My dear, she is not with me and she is married."

Angelina's face showed disappointment. "Oh."

"Let her rest," Catalina said, as she returned to the room. She knelt down and gave a small cup to Perpetua. "Here is a warm cup of tea."

"Thank you."

"The men went back to the shop to fetch some blankets and pillows. Your husband removed your clothing and I am soaking them in the back."

Perpetua felt underneath the blanket that covered her. "Oh . . . he did."

"They should return soon and then I'll have some food for us to eat."

"Thank you. You can't imagine how grateful we are for your kindness."

"Peter spoke to us several years ago, in our shop, about the eternal deliverance of our sins through Jesus the Messiah. We became followers of Jesus."

"Was I with him?"

Catalina thought for a moment. "I believe he said you were with your daughter and her fiancé at another shop looking for wedding materials. He left later to find you; but I don't think you came in."

Perpetua managed to sit up and prop herself against a chair. She sipped some more tea. "Mmm, this tea is so refreshing. We haven't eaten all day."

"Peter said the two of you had been walking from Rome. Is it as bad as it looks from here?"

"Very, very bad. Many people suffered and died in the flames."

"Oh my!" Catalina looked at Angelina who had already moved over to some of her dolls, wiping their heads with a damp cloth. "That is so sad."

"Many homes were destroyed."

"Yes, we have seen many travelers come from Rome the last two days. I suppose they will either stay locally or return to Rome when the ash is removed."

At that time, the men returned, carrying pillows and blankets. "Perpie!" Peter said. He dropped his armload and knelt beside her. "How are you?" He began stroking her hair.

"Much better now, thanks to these wonderful people."

"Jesus is good to us," Peter responded. "These folks are believers and have invited us to stay with them until we decide where to go next."

Antwan walked over to them. "You are welcome to stay here as long as you have the need. There is a small room in the back where we'll make a bed for you, and there is water for bathing out back."

"And the meal is ready when you are," Catalina announced.

"I'm ready!" Angelina said, while dropping her doll and the cloth on the floor."

Perpetua smiled at her. "So am I, Angelina."

†††

"Will you turn your life over to Him for deliverance—for eternal salvation?"

"No . . . I'm not ready to take such a blind leap of faith, as you call it."

"Jesus says He is the only way to have your sins removed. Without Him, you will die in your sins and be eternally condemned to a place of judgment."

"Ha! That is what you say. I've not heard of anyone else in Terni who has forsaken their gods to follow this Man whom you say rose from the dead."

John Mark saw that he was getting nowhere with this local city magistrate. He stood up and looked at the officer. "It is getting late and I must return to my home. May I pray for you?"

"Yes, of course; pray to your God for me. Be sure and tell Him that He must reveal Himself to me with more than a crazy man's words in order for me to be converted."

John Mark quietly opened the door to his two-room cottage. "Oh, there you are," Petronilla said. "I was wondering if I would have to send out some soldiers to hunt you down." When she saw his face, she dropped her stirring spoon, wiped her hands, and came to him. She embraced him tenderly. "Another day of rejections?"

Tears formed in his eyes. "I can't seem to get the message across to this man. He won't listen to my words."

She held him at arm's length. "Listen, my father was rejected many times in Judea and Galilee. Not everyone will be willing to let go of what they have in their hands for that which their hands cannot hold."

John Mark pulled away from her and sat down. "Today he called me a crazy man—the man for whom I write now thinks I'm crazy. How long before he fires me!"

Petronilla sat down beside him. "And when he does, we will move on to another village. Jesus did not tell us how many we would bring to Him; He told us to be faithful and proclaim the good news of salvation. We must be faithful wherever He leads us.

"Listen, perhaps you're trying too hard to make it easy for him to receive Jesus."

John Mark looked at her. "What? What do you mean?"

"I listened to Father numerous times in Jerusalem. He stood before our Jewish leaders and said they crucified their Messiah—they were guilty of murder! I was so afraid they would stone him . . . and some rejected him, but others received his message. And to them who received his words, they became followers of Jesus and were baptized."

"I wish I had your father's boldness. Peter was fearless."

She put her arm around John Mark and rested her head on his shoulder. "You don't need to copy Father's traits; you just need to let Jesus use you and your gifts for ministry. You have traits that my father does not have."

"Such as . . .?"

"Patience . . . and pity. He would not have given your magistrate another opportunity to hear the gospel; but you continue returning to this man and you continue sharing your testimony and the gospel. In time, I think your boss will believe."

John Mark reached and grabbed her hand. When she raised her head from his shoulder, he kissed her. He pulled her over onto his lap and kissed her again. "How blessed I am to have such an encouraging wife."

She smiled. "And I love you just the way you are."

"You do?" She nodded her head. "Am I a good husband?"

"The best husband for me. Your patience and your persistency are qualities that I admire. You are a great husband . . . and you will make a great father as well." She took his hand and pressed it against her abdomen.

He smiled as he carefully felt her abdomen. "How blessed we are to be given a new life share with our parents and with the Lord."

"Yes . . . which reminds me: When are we going to get word to our parents about the baby?"

"If I'm fired, it may be soon, my love."

"Then I'm praying you get fired immediately!"

"Don't say that! I love copying the magistrate's orders into Greek and Latin."

She laughed. "We'll see; we'll see."

John Mark hurried into Dachmon's room. "You wish to speak to me?"

"Yes; I need for you to deliver an important document to the governor's home in Monterosi. He'll need to read it and write out a response. Stay with him until he completes it. Make extra copies of it; He should keep a copy and I want two copies: one for me and one for the family for whom it is written."

"Yes, your Honor . . . Sir?"

"What is it?"

"I have no animal on which to travel."

"Oh; okay, I will arrange for you a chariot and horse . . . And take your wife with you, if you wish. There is a beautiful lake there and the governor's guest housing is very accommodating. I will send word with you of your good work here."

"Thank you, sir!"

He smiled. "And keep praying to your God for me."

"Yes sir!" John Mark took the pouch from Dachmon's hands and left his office. *Thank you, Lord, for answering my prayers . . . and thank you for Pet!*

† † †

Peter rowed the small fishing boat to another cove. *Okay Lake Monterosi, it's time you gave me some fish for tonight's supper.* He cast his small net into the water. After a few minutes he reeled it in—one small fish! "Ugh! At this rate I'll never catch enough for supper." He looked around to make sure no one was on shore, close enough to hear him talking to himself.

Peter was about to give up, when he recalled a similar event he experienced with some of the disciples and Jesus. "Cast the net on the other side of the boat," Jesus said. He remembered how dumb he thought Jesus was for making such a suggestion. *Jesus, a carpenter, was telling professional fishermen how to fish? Oh, but how wrong I was! I now thank You, Jesus, for being my wisdom and for making a believer out of me.*

Peter smiled as he gathered the net in his hands. He looked at the other side of the boat. *Okay; why not?* He cast his net to the other side of the boat. In a few minutes, he reeled it back in. This time, the net had at least ten nice-sized fish. He put them in the boat and laughed. *Lord, are You trying to teach me something again?*

"Perpie! Perpie!" Peter ran into Antwan's house. "Look what I caught today! Twelve fish!"

Perpetua stood in front of their room's door, smiling. "That's a wonderful catch, Peter."

Peter looked at her. "Wonderful? There's no greater catch today! We are going to eat fresh fish tonight. I can't think of anything greater; can you?"

"I don't know; I wouldn't count all your fish before they are roasted."

"What does that mean?"

Perpetua stuck her hand into their bedroom. "I'm thinking I may have a better catch than you."

A puzzled look spread across his face. "Perpie, you're speaking to me in riddles."

"Take a look at this catch!" She pulled Petronilla out of their room.

"Pet? Oh, blessed be my soul!" Peter dropped his fish onto the floor as he ran to embrace his daughter.

"Father!" she screamed, as she ran to meet him. John Mark stepped out of the room and smiled as he watched the two spinning around in the room.

"Whoa!" Peter said, as he slowed down. "I'm getting too old for this!"

"Really? I bet you danced more than this when you caught that string of fish."

Peter laughed. "You know I did, but I was in a boat—and not spinning!" Everyone laughed, as Peter saw John Mark. "My son!" Peter walked over to him and embraced him. "How I thank our Lord for your love and care for my daughter."

"The pleasure is all mine, Father."

Peter backed away and retrieved his fish. "Now I understand why the Lord gave me such a large catch. We have two extra mouths to feed."

Petronilla walked over to her mother and grabbed her hand. Then she led them over to her father and grabbed his hand. "Two extra mouths to feed?" she asked as she placed both of their hands on her abdomen.

Peter was puzzled. "What? What is the meaning of this?"

Perpetua put her spare hand to her mouth. "Oh!" she exclaimed. "You're . . . you're with child! Oh Peter! Our baby is having a baby!"

Peter's puzzled look was replaced with a widening smiled. "A child? We're having a baby?"

Petronilla pointed to John Mark. "Actually, John Mark had a part in this as well."

Peter began dancing with Petronilla and Perpetua, and then moved over far enough to grab John Mark. "Let's dance the night away!" Peter said. For a few minutes the four danced in a circle. Then Peter stopped. "Oh my, what are we doing?"

"What?" Perpetua asked.

"Pet needs to sit down . . . rest. We don't want to harm the child."

"What?!" Petronilla said.

John Mark laughed. "Father, I have tried that already. Trust me, it won't work."

"This baby isn't slowing me down one bit," Petronilla remarked. "So don't you be telling me to sit down." She smiled as she hugged her father and then her mother. "I am so thankful we found you here. John Mark and I have been praying for weeks about how to get this news to you and his parents. And now look at us here, living less than a half-day's journey from each other."

Perpetua spoke up. "Well, let's start preparing this meal and we'll get caught up on all the family news while eating."

About that time, Antwan entered through the back door where the women were preparing the meal. "I must speak to you all."

Perpetua saw the seriousness of his face. "Peter! John Mark! Come in here please."

Peter rushed in first. "What is it? Is Pet okay?"

"Antwan has a message for us."

Antwan trembled as he spoke. "I just received word that we Christians have been blamed for starting the fire that burned Rome."

"What?! Peter exclaimed. "How can that be?"

"My friend simply said that the emperor has blamed us and plans to bring in every Christian for interrogation."

†††

The sea breeze was irritating Paul's eyes again. He looked at his chains and wondered if the soldier assigned to him would loosen them enough for him to rub his eyes with a cloth. *Maybe if I bent over far enough, I could touch my eye . . .* As he bent over, the chain tightened around his neck, stopping him short of the connection between eye and hand.

The soldier pushed Paul's head back up. "Sit up!"

"Sir, I have an eye infection that needs attention. I need a small piece of cloth and some clean water."

The soldier looked at Paul and then laughed. "Ha, ha, ha! I was warned about your requests. Word has it that you can slip through the links of a chain . . . but not on my watch! Now sit back before I tighten these chains further."

Paul closed his eyes, drawing his mind away from the burning pain. *My Master and Lord, give me a mind and a heart that is drawn closer to You than ever before.* Then he thought about Luke. *Lord, please bring Luke to me safely. Spare his life, I beg of You.* Paul prayed often as the days passed on while sailing between Macedonia and Italy.

"You will stay imprisoned here in Three Taverns until Rome is cleaned up and the emperor is ready to judge you." The soldier slammed the cell door, locked it and walked away.

Paul looked around. There was one torch outside his cell and a stone bench inside his cell with a pile of straw and one blanket. A few distant groans informed him that he was not alone. He sat down for a few minutes, thinking through the events that led him to this prison cell.

"My Lord, You saw this before I was ever born. Let me see this from Your perspective. Remind me of my duties while I am in man's prison. Let me share the freedom I have on the inside."

"Paul?"

"Yes, my Lord?"

"Write a letter to Timothy. He needs words of encouragement on how to teach others the true words of the faith. Speak words from your heart; challenge him to be faithful to speak My words of truth.

"There is coming a day when many will soften My message in order to live comfortably. Remind Timothy of Jannes and Jambres who tried to battle against the teachings of Moses. Those who wish to live a holy life must obey My words. And they will be persecuted—persecuted by My enemies and confused by deceitful imposters within the fellowships.

"Paul, tell Timothy to use the words of our Father as his foundation for holy living. Teach them to others! Remind him of your own persecutions for living righteous before me. Warn him of Demas who wants recognition as My messenger. He has usurped My authority and he wants a holy life without sacrifice. Also, remind Timothy of the trouble you had with Alexander the coppersmith in Troas. He is an imposter—an enemy of My cross!"

Paul laid flat on his face as the Lord spoke to him. "Yes, my Lord; I will speak from my heart to my son, Timothy. Guide my every thought, O Lord. Breathe the breath of life in Your words. And Lord, please protect him from the imposters."

"Protection is in My words. My words are truth. Tell him to proclaim My words and to always be ready to defend them from the imposters.

He will be victorious if he studies my words and waits for My Spirit to rightly interpret them to him."

After praying for several more hours, Paul fell asleep from exhaustion.

"Well, well, look who's back in prison."

Paul did not move from his straw bedding. He wanted to keep his irritated eyes closed. Then he heard his cell door unlock. It sounded as if several people entered his cell. He sat up, but kept his eyes closed. "Please pardon me if I don't open my eyes. They're infected."

One of his visitors called out: "Guard! Bring this man a pail of water and some clean cloths."

Paul thought he recognized the voice. "Quintus? Is that you?"

Quintus put his finger to Paul's lips and whispered to him: "We must remain strangers."

The guard returned with the materials and gave them to Paul. "Our orders are to keep this one on a short chain. The emperor is paying big money to see him."

"I know the order," Quintus replied. "I also know that the emperor would like to see this man's eyes opened. This man usually travels with a doctor as his companion. Where is he?"

"He was given to us alone. No one came with him."

Quintus stood up and faced Paul. "Your personal doctor . . . what is his name?"

"Luke; Luke of Cilicia, sir."

"I'll have the authorities look for him. In the meantime, I'll have one of the local doctors tend to your eyes." Quintus turned and walked out while the guard shut and locked the door behind him.

I guess I should have asked for some food.

Several hours later, the guard brought Paul some food. Then, after eating, a local doctor came by to inspect Paul's eyes. He tried to open one eye, but it was matted shut. "Hmm."

"I've heard that noise before," Paul said. "What is it this time?"

"How long have you had this illness?"

"Off and on for over twenty years, but the sea mist irritates them tremendously and the damp prison cells keep them matted."

"I see."

Paul smiled. "Well, I'm glad one of us can."

"Pardon?"

"'See' . . . I'm glad one of us can see."

The doctor wasn't warming up to Paul. "I must go to my home and mix you up a small batch of salve. When you receive it, use a piece of clean cloth to coat both eyes. Cover them with cloth and tie them so that they stay on your eyes. I'll be back in a day or so to check on you."

"Thank you doctor; do you have a name?"

"'Doctor' will be enough for now."

"Doctor, when you return, please bring me a papyrus roll and quills that I may prepare my words for the emperor and my friends."

The doctor stared at Paul for a moment. "I'll look into it." With those words, he turned and walked away.

Paul found his way back to his straw and blanket and laid down, covering his head to help keep the prison dampness from his face. Once again, he prayed for several hours before falling asleep.

A week passed. Paul's new doctor saw him twice. The salve solution was softening the matted area of his eyes, but he had yet to open them. He thought he could possibly force them open, but was afraid of damage. He didn't want that to happen without

Luke nearby. *My Master, please send Luke to me. And, if possible, I would like to hear Your Sacred Writings read to me. How I hunger for the hearing of Your words!* Paul held back his tears for fear of causing further delays of opening his eyes. He covered his head again in his blanket.

The following day began with a familiar voice: Quintus. "Guard, open this cell." The door was opened and Quintus came in. He handed the guard Paul's pail and yesterday's food can. "Go freshen his water . . . and get him something to eat!"

Paul smiled. "Thank you, officer."

Quintus knelt down in front of Paul so that he could speak softly. "How are you holding up?"

"Well, I suppose. Any word about Luke?"

"I think he traveled to Rome, but when he saw the devastation, he continued north, hoping to find Peter."

"Oh."

"The word is out that you are here now, so you can expect some visitors soon."

"Will they be allowed to visit me?"

"Not in this horrid place. Trust me, Paul, be thankful that you cannot see, or it would probably turn your stomach. Listen, I'm trying to work on a deal that will put you in a house like before in Rome. I've got to negotiate a deal with the local magistrate. You may have to translate some Greek to Latin or vice versa. The fire destroyed many policy manuals and records that the authorities are trying to rewrite. They could use a good translator such as you, but there is a holy fear that you may escape. There is a death penalty for those in charge of you, should you escape."

"Are you in charge of me?"

"Not technically. My team of soldiers was the one who caught you in Corinth."

Paul's left eyebrow rose. "You had me arrested?"

"Not personally. I had my men spread thin through the Isthmus of Corinth. There was a spy among the Corinthian fellowship. He heard you speak and left early to find several of my men. These soldiers became greedy and took it upon themselves to turn you in without my approval."

"Oh; I understand."

"I'm glad you do. The soldiers in Rome had my wife arrested for harboring some Christians; but when they heard that my men had captured you, they released her."

"The spy at Corinth . . . do you know his name?"

"I think they called him Demas."

† † †

"My fellow-captive in the ministry." These words of Paul were embedded in the mind of Demas. Try as he may, he could not eradicate them. To the west, Mount Olympus jutted high above the other mountains. Demas tried to avoid looking at it as he continued his journey north to Thessalonica. But even Mount Olympus seemed to condemn him for becoming a traitor to Paul.

The two large sacks of gold coins were now a heavier burden on his heart than on his donkey. He turned around to see if anyone was following him. He studied the faces of everyone on the road that passed him, headed in the opposite direction. *I'm a traitor! No! Stop saying that! I will use the money to help others after I have acquired a suitable place to live.*

Demas thought he might settle in Berea, but then remembered how Paul had boasted in the Berean's love for the truth of God's words. So Thessalonica was his destination now . . . or would it be as bad as Berea? He continued thinking. *I must continue my travels to a place where Paul is not known . . . Byzantium! Yes, I will go there and blend in with the locals—a place where Paul is not known.*

†††

The night air breeze made for a comfortable place to sleep. Peter rolled over next to Perpetua. "Are you awake, Perpie?"

She turned to face him. "I am now."

"Sorry; I was wondering what we will name the baby?"

"Depends."

"On what?"

Perpetua closed her eyes. "Depends on whether it's a girl or a boy. Now let's get some sleep.

Peter rolled back over on his side. "That wasn't funny."

Antwan and his wife prepared an early breakfast for everyone. They had some meats at their shop to trim before the morning customers arrived, so they left before the others were awake. Perpetua and Petronilla were the first to get up. They met together to pray and to discuss preparations for the coming baby. Peter and John Mark remained in the bedroom to pray as well. Afterwards they discussed the events surrounding the fire of Rome.

"I've never seen such poorly built houses as those in Rome," Peter said. "No wonder the fire destroyed them all."

"I wonder where it started?" John Mark asked.

"Who knows; we were under house arrest by the prison . . . in chains!"

"I'm grateful the Lord spared you."

Peter felt his ankles. The scabs and scars remained where the chain and ankle bracelets rubbed against his flesh. "Yes, our Lord spared us. There must be something else to do while we await His return."

Petronilla came into the room. "We have breakfast on the table; please come and join us."

After breakfast, Peter and John Mark stepped outside to look at the horse and chariot.

"Your magistrate let you travel in this?"

John Mark patted the horse. "Yes . . . Pet and I took turns with the reins . . . a great way to travel."

"And when do you return?"

He thought a moment. "After the records are signed by the governor, copies must be made. Then I return them to my boss. It could be several weeks or a month."

Peter looked at John Mark. "Is your magistrate a Christian yet?"

"Not yet. I have shared the gospel with him, but he hasn't come around to believing. He says he needs more than words from me."

"This means he knows you are a Christian."

"Yes; I'm not sure what to do, now that we may be hunted down."

"He needs to become a Christian right away."

"Just before leaving, he told me to keep praying for him. That's the first time he's ever spoken favorably about my witnessing and praying."

"You never know, John Mark, what it will take to turn someone's heart toward Jesus and the gospel. Keep praying, my son."

Antwan came into the yard with a man. "Peter!"

The morning sun made it difficult for Peter to identify the man with Antwan. "Yes, my brother?"

Antwan stopped. "Peter, this man says he knows you."

The bearded man came in closer for Peter to see. "Have we met before?"

"Yes, Master Peter; I am Apollos of Alexandria."

"Apollos? My dear brother!" Peter embraced him. "What brings you to Monterosi?"

John Mark approached them. "Apollos, I am John Mark. I met you once when I was traveling with Paul."

"Yes, I remember you—Paul was always telling you to 'write this down.'" They all laughed.

"That was me."

"Not only was he writing," Peter said, "but somehow he found time to win the affection of my daughter and marry her!"

Apollos smiled. "Sounds like you have been a busy man."

"Has he ever!" Peter said. "They just announced to me yesterday that I'm going to be a grandfather . . . Hallelujah!"

Apollos embraced John Mark. "Praise be to our Lord Jesus for new life."

Peter motioned for them all to recline under a nearby tree. "Tell us now, why have you come? And how did you find us?"

"My apologies in that I bring a disturbing report. I felt the Holy Spirit leading me to Rome. As I approached the city, I received numerous reports of the great fire. I decided to walk around the city and head north. A few miles south of here, I ran into a small group of Christians. I shared my burden about coming to Rome.

"They invited me to stay with them and pray, asking our Lord what to do. For two days, we prayed. Suddenly, a man stood up and prophesied, saying that I must find Peter and John Mark in Monterosi, get them, and return to Three Taverns where we'll find Paul in prison. And that is why I've come here."

Peter was silent momentarily. He stood up and walked over to the front gate. Apollos and John Mark joined him. "Three Taverns . . . that's south of Rome."

"Yes," Apollos replied.

"Several days ago," Peter said, "while I was praying, I felt a burden to go to that town. But I was so exhausted from traveling that I dismissed the thought. I wanted to get far away from Rome." Then Peter began to weep. "Did I miss hearing from My Lord?" He raised his hands to the sky. "My Lord, have I been too preoccupied with saving myself that I missed Your call?"

John Mark put his hand on Peter's shoulder and comforted him. "Father, if you hadn't been here, I would not be with you now. And Apollos did say the Spirit wanted us both to go with him."

Peter wiped his eyes and looked at his son-in-law. "You're right, John Mark. The Spirit knew we would be here and Apollos found us."

Apollos stood up. "God's timing is always best."

"But what about the women?" Peter asked. "Pet can't go there with child."

John Mark thought for a moment. "I know what to do. Mother and Pet can remain here until my records are completed and then return them to Turni. The magistrate knows Pet and I'm sure he'll understand my delay in returning."

"Is it safe for them to see him?"

John Mark thought about it for a moment. "Pet knows his wife. I'm sure she can communicate with her as to their safety . . . he asked me to report to a friend of his in the senate to get an update of the affairs for our region. I still can do that and Pet can convey that message."

"How will you do that?"

"The senator doesn't know I'm a Christian."

✝✝✝

Gaius Calpurnius Piso pounded the wooden podium. "He's mad, I say!"

The chief senator waved his hand toward Piso, the speaking senator. "Lower your voice or we may be in danger of our own lives. I agree, but is there enough of us who are willing to act upon it?" He looked around the room at the three dozen senators, most of whom made no motion nor did they speak.

Piso stood up. "If we do not act, who or what will he marry next? How many more cities will he burn to obtain the gold necessary to finish his palace? How many more necks will he crush under his feet?"

"Is it really that bad?" another senator asked.

Piso pointed to another senator. "I will let our treasurer answer that . . . Orbus?

Orbus Egenus stood up. "My fellow senators, as you know, we are fighting wars on several pioneer fronts. We have promised many financial benefits to our soldiers for their longevity in service. As it stands today, we are four months in arrears in securing our military promises."

"Thank you, Orbus," Piso said, as Orbus sat down. "Nero has ruined our city's wealth. With no money to pay our soldiers, it's only a matter of months until we lose all our empire's protection . . . yes, it's really that bad, my friends."

"Then who will plan and lead the assassination?"

Piso remained silent as he looked at his fellow senators. No one stood up . . . "Then I will," he said. "But no one must tell anyone about this plan. Will you stand in allegiance to silence?" Everyone stood up. "Good; I will hire a group of freedmen to help me."

✝✝✝

Paul shivered under his blanket. *The prison cell must be under ground level. It's cold, day and night!* Paul remained wrapped up in his blanket, on his straw. The eye salve allowed his matted eyes to open, but his vision remained blurred. In the dim light of the cell, he could only recognize moving, blurry images.

The prisoners remained relatively quiet, except for an occasional groan. Paul wanted to sing and perhaps cheer the others up, but his cold, shivering body made it impossible to speak intelligently. *My Lord, I am Yours. Please come and take me away. I have no use for the kingdom in this place.*

A clanging of soldiers' gear interrupted his brief prayer. Paul's cell door was opened. "Well, look who remains in prison." Paul recognized Quintus's voice and knew he had to act cold toward him. Quintus turned to the guard. "Has the doctor checked on this prisoner's eyes lately?"

"Sir," the guard replied, "he was here several days ago and said there was nothing else he could do."

Paul remained covered in his blanket. Quintus took his sword and pulled the blanket off Paul's head. He knelt down and turned Paul's head to inspect his face. "By the gods!" Quintus cried. "This man's face is rotting!" He stood up. "Find this prisoner some quarters above ground."

"But sir, we been ordered to—"

Quintus turned his sword toward the guard and brought its tip to the guard's throat. "I am under the orders of the emperor himself to bring this man to trial—get him above ground now!"

The guard backed out of the cell. "Yes sir! Right away!"

When the soldier disappeared, Quintus knelt beside Paul. He grabbed the pail of water, rinsed out a cloth, and wiped Paul's face. "Paul, please forgive me; I have been on several assignments for the emperor, trying to accumulate your records. The fire has made havoc of the archives."

"No need to apologize, dear Quintus. I know you're trying your best to help me. And our Lord has comforted me through all this."

"I will find another doctor to see to your illnesses as soon as possible."

"Please, Quintus, find me Doctor Luke. I need him badly."

"I will, Paul; I will send couriers into Macedonia to see if he is with the fellowships there. Just don't give up hope. Rome is still in a mess and it may take months to get you before Nero."

"Nero? Does he still insist on seeing me?"

"He plans to use you as an example of the incompetence of the senate. So don't give up. You may be Rome's last hope for a new emperor."

"Yes; our Lord may use this flesh once more to accomplish His will." Paul turned his head away from Quintus and closed his eyes. Quintus pulled the blanket up to cover Paul's head. "Quintus, find me Luke."

††††

Apollos rode his donkey as a man on a mission. He wanted to go straight through Rome, regardless of the danger. Peter and John Mark, however, convinced him to go around the city and stop at several areas where fellowships once met.

Apollos stopped and turned his donkey around to face his two companions. "I am simply trying to find Paul as soon as possible. The Spirit tells me that he needs help."

"And help him we shall. But if he is able to speak, he will ask about our brothers and sisters in the devastated areas of Rome. We must get an update on our way to see him."

Apollos moved his donkey to the side. "Then lead us on this search and I will follow."

Peter smiled. "Thank you; let's ask the Spirit to guide us."

††††

"Towel, please?" A servant helped Paul out of a public bath-house outside the prison.

One of the two soldiers assigned to him growled to the other. "This prisoner is getting better service than me! I'd like to slit his throat and be done with him."

"We have orders from two centurions and a vice-general to protect this man. He now has a doctor visit him every day. You touch him and we'll both suffer the consequences."

The servant helped Paul dry off and put on some fresh clothing. "Thank you, young man. Could you bring me my medicine and cloth?" The servant walked carefully over to the soldiers. One of the soldiers growled as he handed the medicine over.

"Hurry up over there, slave! It's time to eat."

Paul looked in their direction. "Just one moment please." The warm bath gave Paul better eyesight, but he knew the salve would blur things up again. He applied the medicine and then raised his hands toward the guards. "I'm ready. Could you please help me walk? I cannot see very well."

"Can't we just push him back into the water and sit on him?"

The other guard looked at his comrade. "Don't even think it."

Once back into his house, Paul was chained to a fresh guard. He then sat down and ate some stew and bread. While eating, he heard several voices approaching. Soon the front door opened. It was Quintus.

"Guard, release yourself from this prisoner until we are finished in here." The guard removed his chain, dropped it on the floor, and walked out past a group of men.

"Paul, I have some guests who have come to see you."

Paul tried to make out who was entering the house, but could not do so. "My apologies, dear ones, but my eye medicine only seems to blur my eyesight further."

"Paul, this is Peter speaking to you."

"Peter?"

"Yes."

"And I'm John Mark."

"And I am Apollos. Greetings my brother."

For a moment, Paul was speechless. "Oh, dear brothers, come to me. Let me feel your embrace."

One by one, each man embraced Paul as he wept.

Quintus turned around. "I'll be outside while you men visit."

Paul used his medicine cloth to dry his tears. "How did you find me?"

Apollos motioned for Peter to speak. "It's a long story, but the short version is that the Holy Spirit sent Apollos from Macedonia to Rome to find us and you."

"Oh that blessed Spirit of Christ—always watching over us!"

"Yes."

"But why? Why have you come?"

Peter yielded to Apollos this time. "Paul, as I was praying, the Holy Spirit told me to find you and to help you put together a treatise to our Hebrew kindred. Our Lord wants to put together an important letter to help our people understand the new priesthood of Christ."

"Plus a whole lot more," Peter added.

"This has been a burden of mine for many years now," Paul said. "I just couldn't figure out how I could do it while on the run as a fugitive."

"Well here we are," John Mark said. "You speak and I'll write."

Paul turned back toward his table and felt for his glass of juice. He managed a couple of swallows before speaking again. "I . . . I'm not sure I have any words from the Lord by which to speak. I am so weak these days."

Someone new walked into the house. "Perhaps I can help."

Paul recognized the voice. "Luke!" He stood up, waiting for an embrace from his missing companion.

Luke walked over to Paul and embraced him. For a minute or two, both of them clung to each other. Finally, Luke pulled away from Paul. "Let me have a look at those eyes."

Paul laughed. "Same old Doctor Luke."

Luke placed his fingers around Paul's eye to lift up his eyelid. "Hmm." Paul smiled, but didn't say anything. He was thankful to the Lord for hearing that familiar sound from his doctor. "What is this solution that you've been putting on your eyes?" Luke smelled it. "Yuck! It stinks!"

"That's what I've been trying to tell these doctors around here."

"I need to find a stagnant pond—one with plenty of frogs."

Peter spoke again. "Uh, yes, a stagnant pond. We'll get to that as soon as we finish our gathering here."

"Yes," Luke said. "Our gathering . . . I was sent here by our Lord—with the help of Quintus's soldiers. We collided near the Puteoli Harbor."

"Apollos says we are to compile a letter to our Hebrew brethren," Paul said. "But I'm afraid I haven't any words to say."

"Oh, I think you do," Luke said. "In fact, I have your old canvas satchels full of your words—notes that you put together many a night when we were traveling."

"You found those notes?"

"When we were separated at Corinth, I traveled to Philippi to my uncle's villa—the place I left them years ago. I always knew we would need them some day."

John Mark spoke up. "I also have numerous notes from Barnabas that the Lord gave him. They also speak to our people."

"It sounds like a plan is coming together," Apollos said.

"Where are my scribes, Phygelus and Hermogenes?" Paul asked. "They helped me copy previous letters."

"We do not know," Peter responded. "Since the fire, many have fled the city . . . Some even died in the flames."

"Oh," Paul said.

"Time is short; we must start this project." Peter looked out the front window. "Now if we can just get the soldiers to cooperate."

"I can take care of that." Paul stood up. "Walk me to the front door." Luke and John Mark helped Paul to the door. "Quintus? Quintus, sir, I need you."

Three months later

"**G**et this area wiped down!" Nero cried out. "I want our deities centered on Apollo." Several artisans cleaned the floor and positioned the busts of the Roman deities. They moved Apollo, god of *Sol*, to the center.

"Stop!" Nero cried. "Who is that?"

"Apollo, Divine One," the head artisan said. "You said to put the god of *Sol* in the center."

Nero approached the head artisan and slowly placed his hand on the artisan's neck. "I am the god of *Sol*. I am Apollo. You will put my statue in the middle. Is that understood?"

"Yes, Divine One; as you wish." Nero released his grip and let him hurry off to another room.

"Anicetus, where are my gold crafters?"

"Divine One, they await more gold—we have no more gold."

"We've run out of gold?"

"Yes, several days ago."

Nero walked over to a window. "Where is the gold I need to finish this palace?"

Anicetus joined him by the window. "There is one place spoken of by many travelers that has an abundance of gold."

"And where might that be?"

"In the treasuries of the Jerusalem temple."

Nero faced Anicetus. "And why do I wait for it? I want it now!"

"There is much resistance to our presence there. The report says that we—the non-Jews—are not allowed inside the temple lest we defile their holy place."

Nero's face turned red as he became angry. "Shall I, the god of *Sol*—the god of all light!—shall I be deprived of that which I have created? Without *Sol*, there would be no brightness for gold's beauty. All gold is mine!"

"But Divine One, we need strength in numbers to take the gold of Jerusalem."

"Who's in charge in Judea?"

"I think it's—"

"Don't say it! Send Vespasian and his sons to Jerusalem. Tell him his emperor needs the gold to finish the repairs of Rome. Tell him to beat the rebellion down." Nero looked toward the east. "There can be only one golden house for god—only one golden palace." Then he remembered an old Roman prophecy. He clinched his fist and raised it toward the east. "'Straighten them out'! 'Straighten them out'!"

"Must you come in so late?" Poppaea was perturbed at Nero for his long nights at the races.

Nero had been drinking. "Does not the emperor have freedom in the pleasures of his empire?"

"It is I who is great with your child. Shouldn't you want to spend some time with me in preparation of the birth?"

"I did, during our first child, and she died as a baby. My staying away may allow this one to survive infancy."

"That was the fate of the gods. It was not to be that she lived. But I am alone day and night. Our baby needs your affection . . . I need your affection."

Nero turned away from her and walked to a nearby window. "I did not marry you to show affection. I married you to produce an heir for the empire." He then walked over to her and, with his hand around her neck, he pushed her against the wall. "And if I wanted someone around to nag me all the time, I would not have killed my mother!"

Poppaea gasped. She remained silent for a moment. "You said she had an accident."

Nero knew he had said something that could cost him the empire, if it got back to certain members of the senate. "Why do you make me say things that should remain hidden?" He squeezed her neck. She could hardly breathe. "Why can't you be happy being the emperor's wife?!"

He threw her down beside her bed, as she gasped for breath. The jolt of the fall created a deep throbbing pain in her abdomen. Fluids, mixed with blood, began flowing from her uterus as her pain became sharper.

Poppaea grasped her abdomen. "My baby! My baby!" She looked up at Nero. "Please, Divine One, help me!"

"You need help?" He stepped back and saw the pool of bloody fluid. "Here, let me help you." He bent forward as if he were going to lift her onto the bed. Instead, he reared his leg backwards and aimed a deliberate kick into her abdomen.

"Aughh! No!" Her voice weakened as she tried to shield his attack. "Our baby . . ."

He kicked her again . . . and again. The blood flow increased, soaking the tapestry beside her bed. In his drunken rage, Nero did not stop kicking her until her body lay lifeless on the floor. Panting for breath and sweating profusely, He looked down at her. "There's the help you need, you ungrateful woman . . . Servants!"

†††

Lying on his bed, Paul could hear the chatter of the group in the front room as they continued compiling the important letter to his kindred. He hid his head under his blanket to reduce the noise. *My Lord, I praise You for using me in my last days to assist in this final letter. I pray this message will illuminate the minds of Your chosen ones and lead them to the truth. Your word is the truth.*

"Paul?"

"Yes, my Lord?"

"You must write to Timothy again. He needs to be reminded to endure the hardships of the ministry and to keep himself pure. Imposters will come, like Demas, who will try to teach false doctrine. As suffering and persecution increases, many will want their ears tickled with soft words from my proclaimers. They will act like righteous proclaimers, but will lack power from My Spirit or My words to genuinely convert the lost and dying."

"Yes my Master." Paul remained quiet before the Lord for a while, renewing his strength. Then he lifted himself from off the floor and slowly made his way into the other room where everyone was working. "My brothers, how are you with the letter?"

Luke was the nearest to him. "We have compiled most of the major thoughts you gave us, but it still needs more input. John Mark and I have integrated the thoughts of Apollos, Barnabas, and Peter. But it needs your input to make all the pieces flow as one."

"Then you will read it to me later today."

Peter approached Paul. "We should finish soon. John Mark and I need to journey north."

"Bring the finished pages to me. Luke and I will go to the back room and inspect them."

Paul made his way to his sleeping area. Luke followed him with the beginning pages of the letter to the Hebrews. He added some oil to the lantern and began reading to Paul.

Paul listened intently as Luke read throughout the morning and into the afternoon. Occasionally, he stopped Luke, allowing the Lord to lead them in making a few clarifications. By evening, Paul and Luke had completed the letter the Lord had given them all.

"Finished," Luke said, as he tidied up all the loose sheets of papyri.

"Not quite, my son. I have one more short letter that I need you to write for me. It's to Timothy."

By evening time, Paul and Luke returned to the front room. "Finished?" Peter asked.

"Yes, I think so. The Lord gave us a few more words, but this should be all."

"Then John Mark and I will depart as soon as we have a copy."

Paul embraced Peter. "My brother, how I praise our Lord for this time together. May what is written bring all our fellowships together as one."

"They will," Peter said, "if they will but allow the Holy Spirit to speak to them through His words and maintain its sound teachings." Peter patted Paul's shoulder and joined the others in reading the finished copy and making preparations to start the copying.

Luke joined Paul as he reclined at a table. "So what's next?"

Paul patted his eyes with a damp cloth. "I must go before Nero . . . I will not survive this encounter with him, but it is the Lord's will that I testify before the emperor and the senate."

"Then I will go with you and testify in your behalf."

"No!" Paul turned and faced Luke. "You must stay away from this hearing. No one is safe around Nero. I want you to be in charge of copying all the letters and distributing them throughout the empire." Paul grabbed Luke's arm. "Luke, promise me that you will do as I have requested."

Tears welled up in Luke's eyes. "Now you're hurting *my* eyes." He wiped his tears. "I promise."

Paul reached over and embraced him. "You have made my fellowship with pain more tolerable. I praise our Lord for your faithful companionship. Always remember, I will see you again in our Lord's glory."

Paul stood and got the attention of the others. "When you are finished reading, Luke will be in charge of making copies and distributing them."

The next morning was spent in prayer and the copying of the letter to the Hebrews. At lunchtime, the change of the guards also brought a change in the fellowship around Paul. A new centurion entered the house. "Which of you is Paul?"

"I am."

"I am Randolphius, friend of Quintus. He says it is time for you to travel to Rome. We will leave at sunrise tomorrow. The rest of you will depart before the sun sets today. That is all for now." Randolphius left the house to speak to the soldiers in the front yard.

Peter looked at Paul. "The Lord's timing."

"Yes; He has done well."

Peter embraced him. "I will do my part in spreading the word. And I will keep an ear out for your hearing."

"Peter, stay away from Nero. The Lord said he would not listen to the words of my defense. He has chosen to rebel against our God."

"Don't let me be your concern. You remain focused on your testimony before that anti-Christ."

Paul turned to them all. "Let us depart in prayer. Keep your hearts turned toward our Lord. Finish the race He has set before you. Run to win! Sow the seeds! Be faithful to the end . . . remember my chains . . . as well as the chains of other believers who will follow in His steps. The grace and peace of our Lord be with you all. Amen."

"Amen," the others replied in unison. Then they prayed.

The wooden wheels on the cart allowed every bump to res-onate through the body of each prisoner. Stuffed into the cart like sheaves in a bundle, each prisoner had ample reason to growl and complain every mile from Three Taverns to the heart of Rome. Yet Paul said not a word. He managed to get Luke's eye salve on his eyes one last time before they were separated.

The painful trip finally reached the central prison of Rome. Paul slid his patches up above his eyes to see the old place where he lived for several years. Although blurry, he noticed the houses were gone—burned to the ground! As he looked around, he saw many charred metal bars mended together by newer metal wire with stone bases—a temporary fix for the prison's perimeter walls.

A soldier came and unlocked the cart's rear ramp. "Get out you scum! We haven't all day!" Each prisoner was chained to one another, meaning everyone had to work together to get down the ramp without falling. Paul, however, could not see very well and stumbled down the ramp.

A soldier cracked a whip across his back. "Watch your step, old man!"

Paul managed to get up quickly and get in step with the others as they walked toward the prison door. "State your name!" a sol-dier commanded, as they entered through the door. Each, who could understand the language, gave a name. Those who did not understand were given a number by the guard.

Now it was Paul's turn: "Paul of Tarsus."

The soldier looked up at Paul. He smiled. "So you're the fa-mous prisoner, the one who has made several of my friends wealthy." He stood up and unchained him. "Stand over here until I'm finished."

Paul moved over to the side. "I do not wish preferential treat-ment. Put me in the cells with the others."

The soldier turned to Paul and spit in his face. "There's your preferential treatment! Ha! I'm putting you in a place where I can keep a close watch over you." He motioned to several guards. "Give this prisoner his preferential chains and lock him to the wall by the entrance." Both Paul's wrists and ankles were secured in iron sleeves with large chains run through each and then bolted into the side of the entryway chamber. There was no bench, so Paul sat on the ground in the hot sun.

For several hours Paul sat there with his eye patches over his eyes. He prayed for a while and he dozed off for a while. The attending guard finally completed the check-in of the prisoners. Several cart loads of prisoners were brought into the prison that day. Many more were led in by foot. Paul could perceive that the guards were tired of dealing with prisoners and ready to change shifts. He remained as quiet as possible.

The guard put away his records into a canvas bag and then walked over to Paul. "You will stay out here tonight. Here's a blanket; the guards will bring you some water and a cup of food." He looked toward the prison door. "Trust me, after all those prisoners were pushed into those cells in there, you got the best place of all."

"Thank you, sir."

The morning sun arose from the backside of the prison. Between the soldiers' laughing and cursing, and occasional screams from the prison cells, there was hardly an hour of quiet throughout the night. But Paul had managed a few hours of sleep. He looked at his empty food cup. Ants had managed to claim anything that was left inside it. He then picked up his water cup for a last swallow he had saved. But, alas! It was full of bugs that were attracted to the torch by the prison entryway. He managed a small sip into his mouth, but spit it out.

"Water, please?" he asked a nearby guard. The guard came over and grabbed his cup. When he saw the bugs in it, he turned it upside down and knocked the bugs out; then he poured some more water in it and handed it to Paul. "Thank you."

A chariot pulled up to the prison gate. Several soldiers got off the chariot and proceeded to walk toward the entryway. They stopped in front of Paul.

One of them stooped down to inspect the prisoner chained to the entryway. "You're just the one I'm looking for." Paul recognized Quintus's voice but did not reply. "Soldier, lock this prisoner to the inside of our chariot. I'll get his release papers."

The soldier dragged Paul over to the chariot and secured his chain to the outside. "Sit on the ground here until we leave."

Quintus soon returned to the chariot. "Put the prisoner inside the chariot."

The soldier looked puzzled at Quintus. "Sir, there's hardly room for two and he smells."

"Then you may walk alongside the chariot. I want this prisoner inside the chariot. He may be interviewed by the emperor today."

After a few minutes of travel, the chariot stopped in front of Quintus's villa. "Take him inside to my servants," Quintus commanded the soldier. "I want him cleaned and fed before we enter the senate chambers."

Paul remained quiet around the soldier, but he thoroughly enjoyed the bath and fresh garments given him to wear. Next, he was led to a table where fresh vegetables and fruit lay. Then Quintus showed up. "Take your leave of us," he told the soldier. "There's food for you in the main dining area."

After the soldier left the room, Quintus sat beside Paul. "My brother Paul, you are expected before the senate at midday. I will try to help you through this process, but my general will be there and the full senate. We are expecting the emperor to arrive thereafter."

Paul looked at Quintus. "You have done more than a prisoner could ask. I am grateful to you and your service to me."

He looked away from Paul. "If I let you escape, I and my family will be killed."

Paul grabbed his arm. "Quintus, look at me." He turned once again and saw the peace of God in the face of Paul. "No heroics, my brother. Our Lord has told me that I would not survive this meeting; but He told me to give my testimony before the emperor. I must pass on into the presence of our Lord, but His words will remain. There are many who are charged with distributing the words of our Lord. Do your best to assist in this distribution."

Tears filled the eyes of Quintus. "I will, Paul, I will."

"Remember, these words are from our Lord and our God. They must be carefully copied and rechecked to assure their correctness. His words, empowered by His Spirit, are the hope for your children and for the salvation of Rome."

"I will guard the words of our Lord with my life."

"Now release your emotional ties with me. Treat me as a prisoner so that I may get my hearing before the emperor. Put your trust and guidance on Jesus. Protect our fellow Christians here as much as you possibly can."

Quintus wiped his tears and stood up. "We must go. Let us walk out the back to the rear gate. From there we will walk down the road to the front where the chariot awaits us."

Paul thought it a little strange to go in that direction; nevertheless, he followed Quintus out the back door. When Paul stepped out into the back yard, there were several lines of believers formed to create a path to the gate. As he walked passed them, not a word was spoken—only touches from those who could reach out to him.

It was the same outside the rear gate. Many believers were standing along the roadway to bid a silent farewell to Paul. He looked at Quintus. "Tell them later to stay the course and finish the race. And tell them I shall see them again on the other side."

†††

Nero enjoyed the tasty treats spread out before him. He especially liked the fresh wine and drank it profusely. Then he stood up and threw his cup onto the floor. "Servants!" Several ran up to his side. "Prepare me for the council." Immediately, they began fitting him with the golden breastplate and arm and shin shields. Next, several rings were placed on his fingers. Then he was given the scepter of the Caesars.

Nero stood before the polished glass to observe his stature. He smiled. "Let us go and break the senate's back." Anicetus and Tigellius smiled as they fell in behind the emperor and his servants.

Mixed with his power was Nero's love for the theatrics. Horns blew while dancers performed in front of his appearance in the chamber. The senators were seated in a semi-circle formation, with many rows. They stood as Nero entered the main arena and walked to his seat near the podium.

Paul was seated behind a curtain for the moment. His eye patches were now a thing of the past. Iron sleeves remained on his wrists and ankles, but the chains had been removed. While the introductions of the chamber continued, Paul heard yet another voice.

"Paul? Be courageous before the emperor. You will be given a chance to say a few words. Let Me be your voice—your words."

"My Master, will he listen to You?"

"No, he will not; but there are some in the chamber who need to hear Me. Some of them will listen and eventually their children's children will allow this empire to fall."

Paul closed his eyes. "Thank you, Lord, for Your grace, Your mercy, and Your calling in my life. You are faithful and You are righteous."

The guard punched Paul's side. "Stand up . . . When you are positioned before the emperor, you will bow before him. And don't try anything stupid or you may not see anything else outside this chamber." The guard raised his sword and pointed it toward Paul's neck. "Do I make myself clear?"

Paul smiled at the guard. "I only request that you listen carefully to my words today; then judge for yourself who is the one who offers hope for this nation."

"Present the accused," the call came from the chief senator. Two guards took their swords and marched Paul out into the chamber's walkway. Slowly they walked to the center, in front of the podium. Paul faced the chief senator and bowed; then he turned to Nero and bowed more fully.

"Be seated," the senator said. "This is Paul of Tarsus, charged with inciting a rebellion against our most noble government by speaking such accusations against our gods that would cause instability and civil unrest to the outer reaches of our borders. He is also a member of a sect of the Jews who are called, Christians. They were recently accused of starting the great fire of our beloved city." The senator then turned to Paul. "Do you have a representative to speak in your behalf?"

"Most Honorable Senator, I wish to speak in my own behalf."

"So noted. You may be given a limited time to speak now." The senator sat down as Paul walked closer to the senators. Nero sat opposite of the senators.

"My honored representatives of our esteemed and blessed state, I, as a Roman citizen, have been accused by a written record originated in the mind of a writer who does not exist. Today, you will not find any man seated in this chamber who has any evidence of these accusations written of me."

"Stop!" Nero stood up as Paul faced him. Once again Paul bowed. Nero stepped down and walked over to Paul. "Look at me."

Paul straightened himself up and looked at Nero. For a moment there was silence in the chamber as Nero looked into the eyes of a holy man—eyes unlike any he had ever seen. He quickly turned his head and stepped away.

"Is Zeus one of your gods?"

"No, he is not, most Honored One."

Nero, now at a distance, spun around. "How about Hermes? Is Hermes your god?"

"No, he is not."

"What about Apollo?"

Again, Paul responded negatively.

Nero approached Paul, but maintained a distance from him. "What about your emperor? Am I a divine one, selected by the gods?"

Paul bowed once again as he spoke. "Most Honored One, I hold you in high regards as the leader of our people."

"Answer me! Am I divine?"

"Only in the eyes of men have you been called divine."

"What does that mean? Answer me clearly!"

Paul stood straight again and faced Nero. "Most Honored One, there is only one true Divine One. He is the God of creation. It is He who made all things since the beginning of time. For centuries He presented Himself through a people whose charge was to show all nations His power and His holiness. This God sent His only begotten Son—born of a virgin—to redeem mankind from their sinful state of being."

"Born of a virgin?" Nero smiled. "How can this be?"

"The Spirit of the Creator God overshadowed her and she conceived. This child became a man and lived among us in the regions of the east. He proclaimed peace with God and told men to turn away from their evil deeds and turn to God, His Father, for the forgiveness of sins."

"And does this Son of your Creator God have a name?"

"Jesus, most Honored One; His name is Jesus."

Nero walked back to his chair and sat down. "This Jesus . . . wasn't He crucified for crimes against your people?"

"Yes, most Honored One. False charges—like those against me. However, three days later, He rose up from His death chamber—alive."

Numerous senators began murmuring to each other. "Silence!" Nero ordered. He returned to Paul. "And you say there is a dead man walking among us today . . . alive?"

Paul knew where Nero was going with his line of questioning. "Yes, but not physically walking around."

"A ghost then, perhaps?"

"A living Spirit; Jesus is among us today as the Spirit of the Creator God. His Spirit resides inside every man and woman who has repented and called upon Him for deliverance from their sins."

Nero took a small cloth and held it close to a torch. As the cloth began smoldering, he blew on it to create a swirl of smoke. "Is He like smoke, here one moment and gone the next?"

"No, most Honored One, He is not smoke."

Nero dropped the smoldering cloth and stomped on it. "THEN WHERE IS HE?!"

"In the life of all who come to Him in simple faith."

Nero paced the floor in front of Paul. "You say this Son of God lives inside you?"

"Yes."

"Is He all-powerful?"

"Yes."

Nero turned to the guards. "Remove this deranged prisoner from the center court." Paul was quickly moved back to his previous seat.

The chief senator stood to speak, but Nero stopped him. "I'm not finished." Nero walked out into the center court. "Several years ago, this senate released this deranged man, allowing him to go into the four corners of our empire, proclaiming a Deliverer from our sins. He was accused of blasphemy by his own people, the Jews . . . blasphemy against this man's own God—this 'Creator God' as he calls Him. He, as a Roman citizen, appealed his case to Caesar—to me. Yet, I never heard his case until now."

Nero looked at the senators closely. "You released one who has tried to usurp the gods of our empire—the gods of our stability! And why didn't you interrogate him? Why is it that only now do we hear of his rebellion? We could have averted this destructive fire, had you done your duty.

"Maybe you are afraid of this man and the Christians. Are you afraid of his God?" He turned to the chief senator. "Archilus, are you a Christian?"

"By the gods, no!"

Nero walked back and forth before the senators. "Are there any Christian senators among us?" No one responded. Nero walked back to his seat. "Bring the prisoner before me."

Paul felt the tip of a sword push into his side. Without a word, with a soldier on each side, he stood and slowly walked toward the emperor. He was led to the front of Nero where he stopped.

"There's not enough room for two gods to lead the empire. Either your God shall take over now by saving you—since He's all powerful—or I shall continue to rule as the face and presence of Apollo." Nero leaned forward toward Paul. "If your God is God, then I should expect Him to save you from dying."

Paul raised his head to look at the emperor. His eyes pierced into Nero's darkness. "He already has. I am crucified with my Master, and yet I live by His presence living in me."

Nero felt the burn of holiness from Paul's eyes and quickly turned his head. "Stop speaking to me in riddles!" He sat there momentarily, nervously tapping his fingers on the chair's arm. "You say you are already crucified with this Jesus and yet you're standing before me alive. So, crucifixion is the way to live as a Christian?" Paul did not speak. "Then I shall order all Christians to be prepared for their new life by crucifixion."

Archilus stood up. "Divine One, now you speak in a riddle. Whatever are you—"

"Silence in the chamber!" Nero cried out. "Scribe, record this edict: The main highway into Rome will be lit by the bodies of Christians as they are crucified on crosses."

"And what is their crime?" Archilus asked.

"I blame them for the instability of our empire. These crazed Jews—and now many Gentiles!—create disturbances wherever they go. They burn animal sacrifices—these burnings which started the fire that nearly consumed our great city." Several gasps were heard as the murmurings increased.

"You would crucify innocent citizens just to light a path?" Archilus asked.

Nero faced him. "They're not innocent!" Then he faced the chamber. "Have you not heard anything in this chamber? These Christians are telling us in order to live we must die! In order to be forgiven by their God, we must sacrifice ourselves—you heard the man: BE CRUCIFIED!"

Nero turned to the soldiers. "Take him outside to the punishment foyer. Make his head ready for removal. Let's see if his all-powerful God shows up to rescue one of His 'crucified' servants."

The murmurings increased as the soldiers led Paul out a side door. Nero pointed to the open viewing section. "Anyone want to join me to see whose god is going to reign today?" He let out a shrilling laugh as he grabbed his lyre and took a front seat by the window. Archilus and a few other senators assembled around him to watch.

Paul's face was pushed down onto a large wooden block. His arms were bent backwards and tied together; then they were tied to his feet. Ropes were then tied around him and the block. Through all this, he said not a word.

Nero strummed his lyre as he watched. When the soldiers were ready, he stopped strumming and looked heavenward. The room became quiet. "I hear no rumbling of a rescue," he said. "Maybe your God is asleep? Where is His power?"

Paul quietly replied, "Maranatha . . . maranatha." Then he closed his eyes.

After a brief moment of silence, Nero motioned to the executioner, who raised his axe and, with one powerful swing, severed the head of the apostle. There was silence.

Nero stared at the lifeless body. He smiled. "That's what I figured. Bring the head to me." The head of Paul was presented to Nero. He raised it high. "This is the payment for rebellion! This is the sacrifice I require for my forgiveness! My temple shall be built with the gold of this phony God. His temple in Jerusalem is mine! Soon Rome will sparkle with the beauty she deserves. I shall raise her up out of this ash heap. Rome will be glorious again!"

Nero turned to Archilus. "Prepare my *toga picta* for the *triumphator*. Make ready the procession as we celebrate the defeat of the God of the Jews and Christians. Let us send a clear message throughout the empire that Apollo, god of *Sol*, has triumphed over his enemies. Let us feast and play games for a whole week!"

Quintus looked on, beside the general. "May I gather this body and return it to his family?"

The general nodded his head, approving the request. "Perhaps something humane can come out of this monstrous fiasco," the general said.

✝✝✝

"Paul has been beheaded!" A servant of Quintus ran down to the villa where Peter and John Mark remained.

Peter stood up. "Are you certain?"

"Yes! My Lord instructed me to spread the word. My Lord intends to bring his body back here soon! I must run and tell some of the Christians to beware of capture. Nero wants to crucify the Christians!" Then he disappeared through the back gate.

"Father," John Mark said, "what are we to do?"

"Wait for Quintus; perhaps he has an idea what to do with the body."

Quintus walked alongside the ox-driven cart that carried the body of Paul. At the back gate of his villa stood Peter and John Mark. Quintus was visibly shaken. "I wanted to intervene, but . . . but he told me that our Lord was aware of his termination. He told me not to protect or defend him."

Peter thought of Jesus' prediction of his final days. "The Lord works through our tribulations. I'm sure He told Paul what to expect."

"He was certainly bold in telling the emperor and senate about salvation through Jesus," Quintus remarked. "I only wish they had listened."

"The words of our Lord will touch some hearts," John Mark said. "It may take some time, but it will happen."

"What are we to do with his body?" Peter asked.

"I thought that over while walking here. There are some catacombs south of the city where Christians meet secretly. I think that would be a fitting place to lay his body."

"Yes, I agree," Peter said. "Shall I get some men together to help?"

Quintus shook his head. "No; I think it best we keep his burial place a secret. Nero remains unpredictable. Which reminds me: he intends to arrest Christians everywhere and crucify them along the city's main roads. He plans to light our main street with the burning bodies of believers. The man is wicked and sick in his head."

Peter looked at John Mark. "We should plan on leaving late this evening. This news needs to travel fast—faster than the soldiers and couriers. Perpie and Pet remain vulnerable with your magistrate's knowledge of your Christian faith."

"Then let's hurry and make ourselves ready for the journey. I have my records from the magistrate's senator. He should be pleased with my work."

"Is there a bounty on Christians?" Peter asked Quintus.

"I did not hear of one, but I left my general there for further meetings. If so, I will send word to you."

"And what will you do, my brother?"

Quintus looked toward his house. "We will go underground with our Christian meetings—perhaps the catacombs. Pray for us; I do not know how this decree will affect my servants or comrades who know of my Christian faith and the faith of my family."

"We will pray . . . and we will pray for Nero's plans to be shipwrecked."

† † †

"Any news?" John held Mary's hand as the man from Caesarea caught his breath.

"Nothing about Jude; but the Romans have closed all gates into the city. With the massive buildup of soldiers, it's just a matter of time before Jerusalem will be under siege. Many Romans have been killed and some of the priests—the Pharisees—are allowing the Zealots and Sicarii safe haven in the temple area. Many refugees from Galilee are trying to enter the city as well."

"Have the Christians left the city?" John asked.

"Yes; most have fled toward Damascus and here."

John looked at Mary. "Antioch is no longer safe for us. We must travel to the west—to Ephesus."

"Oh, my son, I am getting old; I will only slow you down. Perhaps you can let me stay here with some friends."

"No, Mother. I promised Jesus I would take care of you. He told me to take you to Ephesus."

Mary began weeping. "But what about Jude? I just can't leave him out there by himself."

"Jesus will be with him. He will tell Jude where we are located."

At that moment a loud rumbling sound increased by way of the sea. "More soldiers have arrived at the docks and are marching in this direction," the man said. "You must leave quickly. The mother of our Lord must not be captured!"

John grabbed her arm. "Come quickly, Mother. We must remain out of sight." He looked at the man. "Tell the others that we are leaving for Ephesus. If you see Jude, tell him where we are going." John embraced the man as he covered his face and left the house. Then he looked at Mary. "Come; we must pack our donkeys and leave."

The gateway through the mountains of Cilicia to Cappadocia was as brutal as ever for travelers. But, for a Jew, the culture could be more difficult than the travel itself. Entering Cappadocia meant entering a primarily Greek culture, filled with foods and idols from which a Jew was forbidden to touch or even look upon.

In Cappadocia, John, Mary, and a few additional Christians continued their westward journey toward Ephesus. In Derbe and Iconium, they heard of the wonderful acts of the Spirit through the ministries of Paul, Timothy, and others.

Mary looked at John, as they settled down to a Gentile meal at the home of Timothy's relatives. "I know these foods are now acceptable, but can you tell me what is more acceptable to my tastes?"

John smiled. "I don't see anything your taste buds will reject. But eat small portions for your stomach's sake."

"I don't think that will be a problem."

Antioch, Pisidia was the next city for John, Mary, and company. From there, they passed through Philadelphia and finally arrived in Ephesus.

"This is Ephesus," John said. "A place where God is doing an amazing work."

Mary smiled as she looked around. "I am amazed at how salvation has spread throughout the Gentile nations. Our Lord is truly gracious, showing mercy to all mankind."

"And those who are Christians show His love as only He can give. And I especially love the people of Ephesus."

John, Mary, and company were directed to the house of Simon, the former Jewish priest who was now the elder of the Christian fellowship. John helped Mary off her donkey and they walked up to the door of Simon's house. When he knocked on the door, a woman opened it.

"Grace and peace to this house," John said.

She smiled. "And grace and peace to you . . . John, isn't it?"

"You know me?"

"Yes; we met briefly when the Apostle Paul last visited. He introduced you to our fellowship."

"Yes, that was the last time I was here. But I thought Simon was not married. Are you his sister?"

She laughed. "Only in the sight of our Master, Jesus." She opened the door. Please come in and allow me to refresh you and your company while I explain the rest of our story."

John motioned for everyone to follow him inside. "Dear woman, this is—"

She interrupted John. "Forgive me, my name is Sarah." She bowed her head.

"Okay," John said. "Sarah, this is Mary of Nazareth." Mary smiled. "And these are fellow believers from Antioch, Syria."

"Mary," Sarah asked, "Are you John's mother?"

"How did you know?"

"The way he treated you when you first came in."

Mary wrapped her arm around John's arm and leaned her head against it. "He hasn't always been my son, but took the place of one of my sons when He died."

"Oh; I didn't mean to bring sad memories to your heart. Please forgive me."

"No, you haven't brought sadness, but joy to my heart."

Sarah's curled up eyebrows revealed her puzzled mind. John jumped into the conversation. "Her Son was Jesus of Nazareth."

"Jesus of Nazareth," Sarah repeated. "Jesus of . . ." She stopped. Then she fell to her knees. "Oh my! You're talking about my Jesus? You're the mother of my Lord?!" Sarah bowed her head.

Mary lifted her up. "My dear Sarah, you don't bow to me . . . we only bow to our Lord and Savior Jesus. He was the one who died for my sins and yours. He alone is worthy of our praise, adoration, and worship. *I* bow to Him."

"It took me some time to get used to her as equal to me," John said. "But she's right. We bow to Jesus as our King—our Lord."

Sarah kissed Mary's hand. "How blessed you are to have seen our Lord grow up to become our Deliverer."

"Yes, I am blessed. But He said one thing that took me some time to understand. He said, 'How blessed are those who will not see Me in the flesh and, yet, will believe in Me as their Savior.' His teachings on seeing Him as Savior by faith instead of by sight required His sacrifice in order for me to really receive Him as my Lord and Savior."

Sarah hugged her. "Oh my dear Mary. To see Him suffer for our sins . . ." She began to weep. "I can't imagine me having to see one of my boys go through that."

John changed the subject. "You have boys?"

"Yes—three of them. Fine boys they are." Sarah motioned for everyone to sit on benches and chairs around a central table. "Please, allow me to refresh you as I finish explaining who I am."

As the group reclined, several servants quickly removed everyone's sandals and began wiping their feet. "My name was Felicianna. I was married to a boat builder. We had three sons—sons who he trained in the boat business as well. He died in a boating accident."

"Oh my," Mary said. "How tragic."

Sarah nodded. "Yes, it was devastating to me and my boys. Fortunately, the boys were young men and continued our family business. However, my grief led me to run from my home and onto the streets. I lived on the streets among the beggars and the lame for years."

Sarah sat in front of Mary while the servants placed drinks before everyone. "Then came a man into our town who spoke of a Deliverer that could save us from our wrecked and idolatrous lives. His name was Paul." The group smiled. "I didn't believe it at first, but suddenly his presence began healing people who were lame. Some said it was his smell—others said it was his sweat! I didn't care which it was, but was determined to help my lame street friends. So I asked Paul to wipe his sweat on some cloths I had obtained."

"The widow lady!" John shouted. She smiled. "Paul spoke of you often; that's how I remember you."

"Yes, he called me that. He not only healed my friends of their lameness, but he healed us of our spiritual deadness." She looked up to the ceiling in reflection. "Oh what a day it was when we burned all those things related to our idolatry."

"But you're married now," Mary said.

"Yes; once I got delivered from my sins, I began serving our Lord through our street people. My boys were saved as well so we had no shortage of resources to help our Christian fellowship grow. Simon, our priest-turned-elder, and I kept getting into each other's way so much that he finally said, 'Look, if we got married, we could sure save a lot of time walking between two houses.' I had moved back into my house by then. I saw the sparkle in his eye and knew this had the approval of our Lord. So we got married and I changed my name to Sarah."

"What a wonderful story," Mary said.

Sarah looked at both Mary and John. "So what's your story? What brings you to Ephesus?"

"The Lord told us to come here," John said. "Our people, the Jews, are rebelling against the empire, causing a war to break out in Judea and Galilee. Since, as they say, we all look the same, we had to spread out to avoid being arrested or killed. Even now we must dress like the locals wherever we go to avoid being stopped."

"Well, I have bad news for you. The Roman soldiers are gathering Christians and hauling them off to Rome. Nero says we are to blame for that huge fire that took place there about six months ago. Ever since he beheaded Paul, he's been hunting us down."

"Beheaded?" John asked. "Paul, beheaded?"

Sarah looked surprised. "You haven't heard?"

John looked at Mary and the others. "No, we've been traveling for some time."

Sarah stood up and walked over to a shelf. She picked up a few pieces of melted silver, remembering the day Paul had told her to use the melted silver and gold to help the poor. "Yes, he's with your Son now, Mary."

Mary held John's hand as they and the others ingested the news of Paul's death. "Were any others killed?" Mary asked.

"Not from this message. The courier also told us that the emperor had put out an edict to arrest any Christians they could find and to bring them to Rome to be burned on crosses. He said they would make good street lamps for the main highways into the city."

John patted Mary's hand. "I pray Peter, John Mark, and the others are safe."

† † †

"Are you sure? John Mark asked.

"Yes!" Petronilla shouted. "The baby is coming!"

John Mark jumped up. "But it hasn't been nine months—barely eight!"

"Babies don't count days! Quick, awaken Mother and Father!"

John Mark ran out of the former back door, down a short corridor, to a small bedroom. "Mother! Father! Wake up! The baby is here!"

Perpetua jumped up. "What! The baby is here?!"

Peter rose up straight in his bed. "It's here? Why didn't you tell us?!"

"I did—I am! Pet just woke me up and said the baby is coming—now!"

"You men get out of my way!" Perpetua ran out of the bedroom, shouting, "Fetch me a pail of water and some clean linens and cloths!"

Three hours later, as the sun broke over the eastern range, the shrill of several women were heard as a baby made its first cry.

"You hear that?" John Mark asked Peter. "It's crying!"

"Yes, they do that you know," Peter said. "Now get in there and find out if it's a girl or a boy."

John Mark stood up and walked over to the adjoining door. The women were still shrilling out of jubilation. (Several neighbors had come over to help.) "Hello?" John Mark asked.

Peter walked over toward John Mark. "Move aside, son." He opened the door. "Hey! We want to see that baby out here!"

Perpetua was holding the tightly-wrapped newborn. She turned, walked past Peter, and handed the child to John Mark. "Here's your new son." She placed him in John Mark's arms.

"A son?" John Mark was smiling as tears welled up in his eyes. "A son! I have a son!"

"Let me hold him," Peter said. John Mark carefully handed the baby to Peter. "Oh what a beauty! What a beauty!" Peter began crying as well.

John Mark took the baby away from Peter as soon as Peter would allow it. He brought his boy close to his face and smelled him. "Brand new."

Peter laughed. "That's the way they come—brand new."

The baby made a couple attempts to cry out. John Mark looked puzzled. "Did I do something wrong?"

Perpetua came to get the baby. "I think he needs to meet his mother's food source."

"Oh." John Mark quickly handed him over to her.

"In the meantime, Father," Perpetua said, "you must come up with a name for your boy."

Petronilla smiled as the baby was brought to her. "John Mark and I have discussed a name for him . . . tell them, dear."

"John Peter; we will call him John Peter."

Peter looked at John Mark. "A fine name indeed. I like that name!" He embraced John Mark. "Praise be to our God for a new son!"

"Grandson," Perpetua said.

"Grandson, son—what difference does it make? He's ours! He's our new boy!"

Perpetua could sense Peter's next stage of excitement. "Why don't you men go outside and celebrate while your new boy gets nursed."

Peter clasped John Mark's hand and, together, they headed for the front door to make some noise.

† † †

Apollos listened to the waves crashing against the rocks as he looked out across the Great Sea. When he was troubled or trying to make up his mind, he would always head to the seashore at Alexandria.

Now he was in Cenchrea, listening to the waters of the same sea. "My Master," he prayed, "what am I to do with this threat of arrest from Nero? He killed Paul; does this mean You allow Your servants to be captured and tortured?"

"Apollos, read My words from Paul and the others. What do they say?"

Apollos thought for a moment. "That You will always be with me . . . That You see all things and nothing happens without Your knowledge . . ."

"My love and My presence is sufficient for your every moment. Walk in My presence, My child; do not fear any man or any circumstance that man may put you in, for I am there beside you at all times."

Apollos was now flat on his face as he spoke to his Lord. "My Lord, where do I go now?"

"Return to Corinth; they need a firm, stable voice. Pour your life into the people. Train those who are willing to become disciples of My cross. Corinth is a gateway to many nations. Use it to spread My word and My salvation. Read and explain My words. Let My Spirit transform the fellowship."

Apollos stood up and looked at a few ships as they prepared themselves to enter the Corinthian isthmus. "Yes, my Lord, I see my mission now. Thank You for Your guidance and Your patience with me." He then turned and walked back to the road that enters Corinth.

†††

Luke's uncle knocked on the door. "Please come in," Luke said.

"Luke, you've been reading and copying for several hours. You should go outside and rest your eyes and mind for a while."

He looked up from the papyri and smiled at his uncle. "Johannes, you should have been a doctor."

Johannes smiled. "One doctor in the family is enough. I just want the doctor to care for his own body."

Luke stood up and stretched. "You're right; I need to get outside and take in some fresh air." He took a couple swallows of water and stepped outside his uncle's villa in Philippi. He leaned against the iron rod fence and watched the people walk past for a while. *If only Paul were here . . . he would be out there speaking with those people and sharing the gospel.*

Luke bowed his head, as he thought about Paul . . . something he did frequently. "My Lord, I am spreading Your words, as You instructed; but I miss being out among the people with Paul. Oh I miss him so."

The Lord spoke to Luke in his heart. "Luke, my dearly loved one, be faithful in distributing My words. See that they remain accurate so that the many fellowships may know how to combat those who deviate from the truth."

"How shall I do that?"

"Evangelize by using My words. Visit the fellowships around you. Listen as you hear My words proclaimed as I wrote them to my selected ones. See that they maintain sound doctrine. Warn them of the false prophets who want to be heard and who are satisfied that they have a name among the fellowships.

"My words are truth. I will bring conviction through the explanation of My words. My Spirit will breathe life through the reading and preaching of them. The gospel is found in the explanation of My words. Keep proclaiming and copying them."

Luke wiped the tears from his eyes. He was humbled that the Lord would give him the direction and encouragement he needed to continue copying the new covenant of truth. He turned away from the street and headed back to the house.

Johannes was sitting at the table when Luke returned. "Luke, sit with me for a while . . . please?"

Luke smiled. "It's always a pleasure to sit with you. What's on your mind?"

"Well, I've been thinking about you and your ministry. Luke, yours is as important as anyone's in getting out the message of salvation through Jesus."

"And . . ."

"And . . . I have another villa in Boeothia, near Tipha, overlooking the Gulf of Corinth. It's a quiet place—a great place for writing and relaxing. I think it would be ideal for you and would give you more room with fewer distractions. I have several servants there who will see to your basic needs."

Luke thought for a moment. "Sounds like a great opportunity and a great place for me to continue my main work."

"Great! I will write you a letter of passage so that you may use all my resources for your work. I will also inform my couriers of your need to travel and to distribute your letters. They're some of the finest."

Luke stood and embraced his uncle. "Johannes, thank you for your kindness and support. You are such a blessing to me."

"I should thank you for searching me out and introducing me to my Lord and Savior. I can only offer you a temporary place; you, however, offered me an entrance into an eternal place—a place where I now commune with my God. You have given me the greater gift."

AD 67

"Kill the women and children as well?"

Vespasian looked at the centurion. "Kill anyone who tries to breach our access into this disgusting city." The centurion snapped to attention, turned around, and left the tent. Vespasian sipped some wine and immediately spit it out. "Would someone please find me some Roman wine and remove this local stuff from my tent!" A servant grabbed his bottle and ran out the tent. *Jews . . . they can't even make strong wine.*

Titus entered the tent. "Father, does it go well with you today?"

"Don't even ask! These barbaric, religious-crazed people are running toward our lines, shouting out something about defiling their temple."

"Oh, that place!"

"Yes; that place where Nero thinks there is gold. My spy tells me that the priests have long pilfered the gold and have lied to their own people."

"Maybe we have a second opinion on that place."

Vespasian turned to his son, a top general of the Praetorian Guard. "What do you mean?"

He smiled. "I captured one of their leaders in Galilee . . . a Joseph ben Matityahu."

"And what does he know?"

"He's been trained in some of the finest schools of our empire. A smart fellow he is. And I bet he knows what is going on behind those temple doors."

"Then bring him to me and let's see what will loosen his mouth."

Titus snapped to attention and left his father's tent."

Perhaps he'll talk . . . at least we have eliminated another rebel leader. Vespasian grabbed his empty cup to sip his drink . . . "Where's that useless servant of mine!"

† † †

"Stop!" Titus ordered. He looked at his prisoner, Joseph, and then at the soldiers. "Let's take our 'captain' through the base camp before we report back to my father." The group turned about forty-five degrees to the west and proceeded to a ridge. When they arrived, they stopped to view the valley below them.

Joseph could not believe his eyes. Tens of thousands of small tents were all in neatly kept rows, as far as the eye could see. He knew then the futility of the Jewish rebellion.

"Seen enough?" Titus asked him. Joseph didn't speak. "Then perhaps my father will get you to open up . . . Guards!" They turned Joseph's horse around and led him back to the main camp on the southwest side of Jerusalem.

Joseph was led into the reception tent and chained to a stone bench. Soon Vespasian entered the tent. He walked up to Joseph. For a moment they both looked at each other. "Unchain the captain." Titus looked on as Joseph was released from his chains. "Bring us something to drink—Roman wine this time!" Vespasian smiled. "No offense, I hope."

"None taken," Joseph replied.

As soon as the wine was poured, Vespasian raised his cup. "To peace in Judea."

Joseph slowly raised his cup. He had not eaten or drunken all day, so he gulped it all, nearly choking on it.

Vespasian laughed. "Slowly, captain; this isn't your local stuff." Vespasian finished his as well. "I have a proposal for you, Captain . . . what's your name?"

"Joseph."

"Captain Joseph; yes, I have a proposal for you. Your armies are currently outnumbered about ten-to-one. I could call on the emperor to send more troops, but I'd like to think that some of your leaders are men of good intelligence . . . men like yourself.

"Now, Emperor Nero thinks there's enough gold in your temple to pave a road with it from here to Rome." Titus and several centurions laughed. Vespasian smiled, as well as Joseph. "Yes, I agree that *is* a lot of gold. But, nevertheless, we're going to go in there and see for ourselves. The problem is that your priests have allowed your rebel forces to lock themselves inside the temple and adjoining buildings. Now I'm thinking perhaps someone like you might be able to talk some sense into their heads. You see, some of your extremists have put on women's garments so they could get close to my men in order to slit their guts open. This has so angered my men that they want to kill all your women and children as well." Vespasian leaned over closer to Joseph. "Wouldn't you hate to see all your people slaughtered over a stockpile of gold?" Vespasian stopped to let that thought sink in. "We need more wine over here." The servants came and filled both cups.

Joseph took a sip and swirled the juice in his cup. "What do you wish me to do?"

Vespasian took a large gulp of wine. "Lead a delegation of my men to speak to your leaders in the temple. Negotiate terms of surrender."

This time Joseph laughed. He looked at Vespasian. "You apparently don't know the resilience of the Jews."

Vespasian showed anger. "You mean stubbornness."

"Call it what you may; but I doubt they will listen to me."

Vespasian stood. "They will listen to you or they will die."

Joseph stood as well to face Vespasian. Several soldiers pointed their spears toward him. Vespasian motioned them to put their spears down.

"I will do as you say," Joseph said, "but I know my leaders will never surrender. They believe God is going to protect them."

"Which god?"

"The one true God—the Creator God."

"We'll see." Vespasian motioned to Titus. "My son will fill you in with the details."

† † †

"A blee, blee, blee, blee," Peter said. "A blee, blee, blee, blee." This time his wiry beard tickled little John Peter's face. The baby smiled. Peter held his little grandson in his lap while bouncing his knee. "We're riding on the camel," he kept repeating.

"Father, you're going to make him spit up his lunch." Petronilla came and sat beside him.

He handed John Peter over to her. "He's such a handsome child."

"'Handsome'? Father, he's not even six months old. Don't you think it's a bit early to say he's handsome?"

Peter rubbed his grandson's hair. "Well I think he's handsome. We don't like 'cute' and 'beautiful,' do we son."

Petronilla leaned on her father. "I just pray he grows old enough to be a handsome man for God's woman in his life."

"Whoa there, my Pet. Let's get him old enough to talk and fish before we get him betrothed."

John Mark walked into the yard. He smiled as he kissed Pet and grabbed John Peter. "How's my son today?"

"Fine," Petronilla said. "Waiting for his father to come home."

"Well, I'm home . . . in one piece, for now."

Peter noticed a bit of concern in John Mark's statement. "Yes, and what's pulling on you?"

John Mark glanced at him. "We need to talk . . . Pet?"

She took John Peter from him. "I'll leave you two alone . . . for a while."

They watched as she went inside the house. "Tell me more," Peter said.

"The magistrate knows my family is Christian and he has kept us safe thus far; but there is an uprising of Jews throughout the empire. The rebel leaders are calling for Jewish men to fight the Romans in Judea."

"I've known that for about a year now."

"Yes, but the hatred expressed to my magistrate for Jews is weakening his ability to keep us safe. Father, today he told me that he cannot promise I will be safe this close to Rome anymore."

Peter rubbed his beard as he looked to the east. "So what are your plans?"

"He has offered to write papers that will allow me to go to another area, as long as it is not close to Judea."

"Oh . . . Any place popped up in your mind?"

"Cyprus; they know me and they have seen the power of our Lord work among them."

Peter thought for a moment. "Or perhaps Crete? I think Barnabas is in Crete."

"Perhaps—even Malta has seen God's delivering power. I believe these islands have a more Christian influence with less conflict than other places along the Roman highway to the east."

Peter smiled. "I think I'll let you convince the women while I go down to my fishing hole and pray a while."

John Mark smiled. "I will—you go."

Peter walked down the street to the path that led to the local river. From there, he walked along the riverbank, northeast for about a mile. He stopped and looked at the rock ledge that jutted over the river, making a good place to sit and fish.

Behind the rock ledge was a place where he had placed some straw for times of prayer and relaxation. This time, instead of climbing up on the ledge to fish, he headed straight for the straw where he immediately began praying.

"My Master and Savior, I bring to you the predicament of our family and our future ministry. How shall I instruct John Mark and the others? And what of the fellowships in this area and in Rome?" Peter continued to pray, worshipping God, face down. After about an hour, the Lord spoke to him.

"Peter?"

"Yes, my Lord?"

"My beloved child, you and your beloved wife will leave with John Mark and Petronilla . . . but you must stay in Rome to write a final letter and to encourage the fellowships there."

"Write? Lord, You know I'm not much of a writer."

"I have someone there who will put your words—My words—on papyrus for you. When you settle in to write, I must speak some strong words, warning our fellowships about future imposters who will try to sway them away from Me. These imposters refuse to allow My words to speak in their behalf. They think their thoughts are more acceptable than mine. Peter, allow Me to write through you to save My children from these imposters."

"Yes, my Lord. I will go there and I will write in Your behalf."

"Peter, if I tell you that there is a cost for this privilege of writing for me, will you still do it?"

"Yes, Lord, you know that I will do it!"

"Peter, what if I told you it would cost you the life of John Peter. Will you still write for me?"

Peter rose up from his face upon the ground and sat on his knees. He trembled at the thought his Lord just presented him. *Lord, my grandson? Writing a letter would require my grandson?*

Peter continued to tremble as he lowered his head once again . . . he began to weep. "My Master, I love you; but you know my heart. I love this little boy you've given us. I cannot easily give him back to You. I hardly know him!" Peter tried to dry his tears on his sleeve. "Yet, I know You give us no bad thing or situation that You don't use it for Your glory and honor. If my writing and the life of young John Peter brings You glory, then so let it be done. I am Yours first and foremost. And You are first in my life." Once again, Peter burst into tears.

"Peter! I see and hear your heart. Your pain and your offering of sacrifice are received. Your grandson will live a long, fruitful life."

Peter raised his head and lifted his hands high into the air. "Thank you, my Lord! Praise be to Your name!"

"There is more, My child. Although your grandson shall live, you will sacrifice your life for the benefit of all who will receive your letter." Peter lowered his hands and head. "My beloved child, you will be tortured by those who attempt to find your letter. Be strong and courageous and you will follow My example."

"Lord, how will this happen?" Peter expected the conversation to continue, but there was no further response from the Lord. He remained silent for a moment. "Let your will be done."

"We must separate," Peter said to John Mark and Petronilla.

"Father, why?" Petronilla asked.

"It is too risky." Peter looked at his daughter, John Mark, and little John Peter. He trembled as he continued to speak. "Our Lord has different plans for your mother and me." John Peter crawled over to his grandfather; Peter picked him up and hugged him. Petronilla came over and hugged her father as well.

"No Father; John Mark and I can offer you safety with the magistrate's papers."

John Mark handed Petronilla a sheet of papyrus. She handed it to her father and knelt down. As he looked at the letter, she placed her head onto his lap. "Abba, Father, let us stay together."

Peter wept. "My child—John Mark!—listen to me. Our Lord has told me to stop in Rome and write a letter. Our safety is greater when we obey His commands. You must go on without us. Trust in the Lord and not in conventional wisdom. Put your faith in Him."

For a few minutes, all four adults wept as John Peter continued crawling in and around them.

Perpetua had the donkey loaded down and was waiting for Peter. He finally let go of John Peter, mounted his donkey, and began the trek toward Rome. "Remember," Peter said, "wait one or two days. We will be on the west or south side, depending on where the followers are gathered."

John Mark put his arm around Petronilla while she held their child. Her tears were the only words she could express at the moment. "We will lift you both up to our Lord daily," John Mark said. "May His grace and peace follow your every step."

Perpetua looked at Peter, as her daughter's family disappeared from their sight. "Are you sure this—"

"Yes," He interrupted her, "I'm sure. I have wrestled with our Lord about this in prayer. He is sending us to Rome."

She turned her head toward the front of her donkey. "Then His will be done."

† † †

"It's Joseph ben Matityahu, most Excellent One."

Theophilus, the high priest, turned to face Phannias, the chief priest. "Joseph, the Galilean?"

"Yes; captured by the Romans several weeks ago. He wishes to speak terms of peace in behalf of Vespasian."

"Peace?!" The high priest turned toward the wall. *Grandfather, speak to me!* (But Annas had died many years ago.) "Keep them in the Court of the Gentiles. Tell his delegation that I must consult with the others." Phannias left the room. "Guards!" Several guards appeared. "Find me any council members in the temple and bring them to me immediately."

Theophilus looked at the fifteen priests who had assembled. He saw fear in their eyes. "Come now and be you like men of courage. Stop this appearance of doom and gloom." No response was given. "Very well; follow me to the outer court where a delegation awaits us."

As they walked toward the porches, Phannias spoke to Theophilus. "What are you going to do?"

"I will listen to their terms for peace—their terms for leaving Jerusalem."

"I don't think that's what they will offer."

Theophilus turned to look at Phannias. "Then this will be a short visit."

Joseph stood beside Titus as the high priest and his council arrived. Joseph bowed. "Hail to the leader of our people!"

Theophilus stepped to the front of Joseph and extended his hand. Joseph kissed it. "Please rise and state the reason for your stand before me."

Joseph motioned toward Titus. "This is General Titus, son of Vespasian, ruler of the armies of Rome." Theophilus nodded his head in acknowledgement. "He brings you terms for a peaceful resolve between our people and his."

Joseph stepped back as Titus and two soldiers stepped forward. "My father wishes to spare your people the total destruction of your temple and city. If you will surrender all the treasures of this place and have your men lay down their weapons, we will spare you of future battles."

Theophilus laughed. "And that is your terms for peace? Make us your slaves? Rape our temple of her treasures reserved for our God?"

Phannias interrupted: "What if we offered you a payment of, say, ten thousand pieces of gold and silver?"

"Silence!" Theophilus cried. "I am the one who speaks for our God and our people."

Titus smiled. "I did not come to negotiate a deal; I come to offer you life or death."

Joseph stepped forward. "Listen to the general, most Excellent One. There are hundreds of thousands of soldiers at his disposal."

"Yes," Titus replied, "listen to your captain. Let him tell you how we captured your forces in Galilee."

"No, you listen to me, General. This is not Galilee! This is the temple of the Most High God and He will fight our battle for us! It is you who will beg our God for mercy as He slaughters your armies."

Titus's face turned red hot. He turned to Joseph. "We're finished here; get us out of this place!"

Joseph nodded toward the high priest. "As you wish." Then he turned with his delegation and left the temple area.

The priests watched as the Roman delegation left the area. "This is suicide!" Phannias said to Theophilus.

"Suicide? Come now, Phannias; they will return to negotiate."

Phannias grabbed the arm of the high priest. "They will return to burn this temple and city to the ground!"

"Let go of me!"

"Maybe we should listen to Phannias and Joseph," another priest said.

"What! And bow to these Gentile dogs?!"

Theophilus rushed on ahead, leaving Phannias and the rest of the council. Phannias watched as he disappeared into the temple corridors. Then he looked at the others. "Do any of you wish to die for the temple treasures?"

"What choice do we have?" another priest asked.

"Go before the people and relieve the high priest of his duties. Get another high priest who will negotiate with the Romans."

†††

Peter knew of several locations on the west side of Rome where some Christians used to reside. The area on the west had less fire damage—one reason that Nero had accused the Christians (although there were more Jews living on the west side than Christians). It was a dusty day with sand blowing through the streets. Most people who braved the outdoors were wrapped with several layers of cloth over their faces. This made it near impossible to distinguish one person from another.

In front of a house Peter recognized, he spoke to a man by the gate. "Sir!" he shouted over the wind. "Is this house one who seeks a Deliverer for the Jews?" The man nodded an affirmative and motioned for Peter and Perpetua to tie their donkeys and enter the house. Once inside, they began to unwrap themselves from the layers of cloth and sand.

"Whew!" Peter said. "What a blustery day." He bowed his head briefly. "I am Peter and this is my wife, Perpetua."

The man smiled. "And I am Daniel, son of Joshua of Samaria. He pointed to the woman who was helping Perpetua remove her outer garments. "And this is my wife, Ruth." She acknowledged Peter with a smile. "Welcome to our humble abode."

"Grace and peace to you. Thank you for allowing us to enter."

"It is our privilege to assist a fellow Jew. But I must warn you to keep your head covered while visiting Rome. The emperor is hunting us down like wild beasts."

"Then you and your family are followers of Jesus, the Deliverer?"

"Yes! Hunted followers at present!"

"That we are."

"Please, recline with me." He turned to Ruth. "My dear, find something to drink for our guests." Ruth left the room and Perpetua followed her. "Now tell me, what brings you to Rome?"

"Our Lord has instructed me to write a letter to our fellowships . . . He told me to return to this city."

Daniel studied Peter more closely. "And you say your name is Peter?"

"Yes, Peter of Bethsaida, apostle of Jesus the Deliverer."

Daniel dropped his head to his knees. "Oh, blessed one, I did not realize it was you!"

Peter lifted Daniel's head. "Daniel, I am a man such as you. Do not bow to worship me."

"But I do praise our Lord for you. Your letter and the others' letters have been essential to our fellowships' understanding of how to live for Jesus."

"Praise our Lord, for He has blessed us with His words." Peter looked more intently at Daniel. "My brother, I need a scribe to assist me with this writing duty. Do you know of anyone?"

"There were several in times past, but I have not seen nor heard of them since the recent diaspora."

Peter nodded his head. "I understand. How about you?"

Daniel shook his head. "No, my Lord, I cannot write well . . . but my wife teaches our two children in the Greek language. Both she and my eldest son are quite proficient in reading and writing."

"Then, my brother, you are an answer to my prayers."

"Only one problem . . . we have no writing utensils or papyri."

Peter smiled. "My son-in-law has provided me with a pouch full of those things."

Daniel smiled. "Then the three of you may use the dining table as soon as you're ready."

Inside the house, Rome appeared like every other city. Occasionally, Peter would stretch himself by walking out behind Daniel's house. For the most part, however, he, Ruth, and Joshua (Daniel's eldest son) remained indoors listening to and copying Peter's words from the Lord. They prayed often, seeking God's wisdom and illumination.

Perpetua shielded her face and would go walking to the local market. Sometimes she stopped at Daniel's small jewelry shop and helped him clean some of his displays. One day was particularly warm, so she removed her facial covering while cleaning a display stand. She was so involved in her cleaning that neither she nor Daniel recognized a group of Roman soldiers a few shops from them, staring at Perpetua.

Two of the soldiers split up while one soldier walked up to her. "Hey, you!" His abrupt voice startled Perpetua. She stood straight up and became motionless. He moved about in front of her, studying her face. "You're new here."

By now Daniel had walked to her side. "She's a visiting friend of mine. As you can see, she has revealed the beauty of my fine jewelry—here, take a look at this piece." Daniel tried to remove the soldier's attention away from Perpetua.

The soldier looked at Daniel and then pushed him backwards. "I wasn't talking to you!" He then grabbed Perpetua's arm. "You look like a fine specimen of these foreigners." He pulled her closer to him.

Perpetua knew the soldier had a lot of armor on, but he was not shielded in the knee area. She immediately swung her foot around, kicking the back of his knee. "Aughhhh!" he cried out as he lost grip of her. She ran down the street toward the house. "STOP!"

Perpetua turned and looked back. The soldier was no match for her speed—but alas!—she ran straight into the arms of one of the other soldiers. He grabbed her and knocked her down to the ground. With one large foot on her abdomen, he held her until the other two soldiers arrived. He laughed as the other soldier limped up to them. "She packs a mean kick there, doesn't she?"

The limping soldier did not laugh. He reared his powerful leg back and kicked her in her knee. She screamed in agony as the pain shot up and down her leg and abdomen. "Now taste your own medicine, you foreign harlot!" He looked at the other two soldiers. "Take her to my barracks. The emperor is not getting this one until I'm finished with her."

† † †

Peter smiled as he inspected the final page of his letter. He looked at Ruth and Joshua. "Finally! The letter is complete." They both smiled. "Tonight we celebrate."

"I'll prepare a special meal for us," Ruth said. "Joshua, why don't you run and help your father and Perpetua close the shop. Tell them to come home now, but don't say why."

Joshua bolted for the front door, but before he could get to it, the door opened slowly. Daniel stumbled in, dirt all over his clothes, and signs of anguish on his face. "Father!" Joshua cried. "What has happened?"

Peter and Ruth entered the front room. "Daniel?" Peter asked. "What happened to you?"

He continued weeping uncontrollably. "Oh, it happened so fast! I couldn't stop them!"

"Stop who?" Peter asked. Then it hit him. "Where's Perpie? Daniel, where's my wife?"

"They took her, Peter. I tried to divert their attention and she managed to escape one of them, but there were too many!"

Peter ran over to Daniel. "Who took her?! Daniel, WHO TOOK HER?!"

"Roman soldiers. She kicked the chief one and knocked him down to the ground. But the others caught her. Then the one she hurt came up to her and kicked her and ordered the others to take her to his barracks."

Peter stood up and looked at Ruth. "Whatever happens, guard that letter!" Then he bolted out the door. By the time Daniel could get up and look out the door, Peter had disappeared down the street.

The Roman soldiers were assigned in small squadrons throughout the city. Still, there were at least twenty-five assigned to every set of barracks. Peter had been in the city enough to know where many of the barracks were located. However, the fire had destroyed some causing the others to overflow with soldiers.

Outside one set, he listened carefully, hoping to hear something that would alert him to Perpetua's whereabouts. Several soldiers were talking at the gate, but no other noises were out of the ordinary.

Peter ran down the street to another set of Roman barracks. This time, a dozen or so soldiers were out by the gate. "It's not fair," one of the soldiers said to another. "I was enjoying a good rest—then he kicks us out."

"Just wait until you're the commanding officer; then you'll be whistling your own tune." The others laughed. At that time, a woman's scream was heard. Peter recognized it. The scream came from the rear side of the complex. He walked briskly to the corner and then ran down the side fence. As he neared the corner of the barracks, he saw Perpetua strapped to a post. The commander pulled back his whip and laid its tips across her barren back. She screamed again.

Peter leaped over the fire-charred fence and with all the speed he could muster ran past two watching soldiers and knocked the commander off his feet. He kicked the commander several times in the face before he grabbed the whip and cracked it at the others. He backed up to Perpetua as he cracked the whip.

"GUARDS!" the commander cried. "GUARDS!" Suddenly there were about a dozen soldiers surrounding the two. The commander's eyes were swollen from Peter's attack. "Somebody help me up!" Several soldiers helped him up while the others closed the circle around Peter and Perpetua.

The spears and swords were no match for Peter and the whip. He dropped it and turned to Perpetua. As he pulled her clothing up onto her shoulders, he spoke to her in their native Galilean dialect: "I love you, my dear Perpie. Our work is complete now; soon, we'll be together on the other side."

"Yes, my brave husband. We'll soon be with our Lord. Then our love will be complete."

A soldier knocked Peter down to the ground. "Shut your mouth you disgusting swine!"

"Tie him up!" the commander ordered. Peter and Perpetua were tied together, back-to-back with the post between them. He still could not see due to Peter's damage to his eyes. "Bring me to his front." The assisting soldiers obliged. "Give me the whip and heat me up the irons."

The commander took the whip and stepped back a couple of steps. "Release me." When the soldiers released him, he immediately cracked the whip across Peter's chest. Then he did it again . . . and again . . . and again!

Peter groaned each time the whip cut through the hairs on his chest and ripped holes in his flesh.

"I may not have the satisfaction of seeing this," the commander said, "but I will have satisfaction in knowing that my face will be the last one you'll ever see." He turned his head. "Bring me the irons!" Two soldiers came over, each one carrying a red-hot iron poker. "Help me guide my arm." He looked toward Peter. "An eye for an eye!" he cried as the soldiers helped him burn out Peter's eyes."

"AUGHHH!" Peter screamed.

"NO!" Perpetua screamed with him as she felt the jerking of his body against hers.

"Be strong, my Perpie," Peter said to her again in their native dialect. "The Lord is with us!"

"Take them away," the commander ordered. "Prepare them for the lighting of the highway as our emperor has ordered."

When their ropes were loosened, Perpetua immediately turned and helped guide her husband away from the whipping post. A soldier came over and wrapped some of her clothing around her eyes. "Ha! Look! The blind leading the blind." He then pushed Perpetua into Peter, causing them both to stumble.

Next, their hands were tied and ropes were tied around their waists. Peter had lost so much blood that he could hardly stand on his own two feet. Perpetua continued to assist him. "Lean on me, my love. I will guide you to our crosses."

Peter finally spoke. "Just as our Savior said would happen to me. Oh, Perpie, Jesus is with us—He knew this would happen!"

"Yes, my dear Peter. And He will see us through this."

"Oh, praise be to His name! He *is* on the other side! The soldier was wrong . . . I see another face! His face! Soon, my love, we will be with Him in Paradise. Soon, real life begins!"

"Say no more, Peter. Save your strength for the walk to the cross."

"Yes, dear Perpie, and the fellowship of suffering will soon be complete."

†††

Petronilla smiled as she watched John Peter pull on the reins of their donkey. The donkey continued to stop each time the reins were pulled.

"Keep this pace up," John Mark said, "and we'll arrive at Puteoli in time to celebrate his Bar Mitzvah." He turned his donkey around and was soon at their side. "Hand me the reins." Petronilla pulled the reins out of their son's clutches and handed them over to John Mark. John Peter began crying.

"See what you've done," Petronilla said with a playful pout-looking face. She found a cloth camel figurine and gave it to the tearful lad riding with her. Once again John Mark took the lead down the Roman road to the coastline, looking forward to as much distance from a turbulent Rome as possible.

Petronilla looked back in the direction of Rome. Although it was out of sight, she couldn't help but wonder about her mother and father. "When did Father say they would leave Rome?"

"He didn't say," John Mark said.

"Why couldn't they come with us?"

"Your father simply said that the Lord told him to go to Rome and write a letter."

Petronilla watched John Peter playing. "Father hates to write . . . he doesn't have the patience to write."

"I'm sure our Lord had His reasons for selecting your father."

"I hope Mother reads it carefully before they send it out."

Petronilla kept much of her face hidden as she held on to John Peter while they walked to their ship's boarding area. Roman soldiers monitored the docks, ever watching the business transactions. With the help of his magistrate's letter, John Mark received exceptional treatment on their journey to Crete.

On board, the three found the meager accommodations as a welcomed respite for their journey. John Peter was asleep, so Petronilla lay down beside him. "I'm going out to watch the shoreline," John Mark whispered. She nodded her head and closed her eyes.

Several hours later, John Peter was seeking more bread and nourishment. The ship would make a stop on the island of Malta before voyaging east to Crete. John Mark helped Petronilla by taking his son up on deck to see the water. At other times, he read from the life of Jesus he had written and from Peter's first letter. Then he would pray. One day while praying, he heard from the Lord.

"John Mark?"

"Yes, my Lord?"

"Seek out Barnabas on Crete, for he has words by which to direct your future ministry."

"My Lord, can You not speak directly to me?"

"It is not good for my children to rely on direct revelation from Me. My Spirit will use My words to reveal your directions. In time, My words will be compiled to reveal my New Covenant for My chosen ones. Use My words to reveal My will for the people."

"Yes Lord, I will seek Barnabas when we arrive."

John Mark shared his prayer conversation with Petronilla. She was interested, but she also had another question. "Did the Lord speak of my parents?"

"No He did not. I regret that I did not think to ask Him."

She lowered her head. "That's okay. I just have this gnawing feeling in my heart that they're in trouble."

† † †

Although in a separate cell, full of women, Perpetua could hear the groans of her husband as his eyes remained untreated after they were gouged. She wept and she prayed. *Please, my Lord, ease the pain of our beloved Peter.*

"Perpetua?"

She looked up and around, but saw no one speaking to her. Then she remembered Peter's many conversations about how the Lord spoke to his mind—his heart. She fell to her knees and bowed her head to the floor. "Speak, my Lord, for I hear you."

"Peter's groans are more for you than the pain of his eyes. He prays for you constantly. Let him know you're okay by singing some of the psalms he and John put together years ago. Your songs, bathed in My words will not only comfort you both, but will also be a testament of My presence with you now. Do not be afraid of tomorrow; rejoice in this day I have given you as a testament of My salvation."

"Yes, my Lord. I will sing unto You with all my heart and voice."

Peter groaned yet once more. "My Lord, where's my Perpie? I miss her so."

Someone slapped him. "There's no 'Perpie' in here, so shut up!"

Suddenly, a hush fell among the cells as a lone voice was heard up the corridor. Someone was singing! "It's an angel!" one of Peter's cellmates cried. "I hear an angel!" Several men fell to their knees in fear.

Peter stood up. "Yes, it is an angel . . . PERPIE!" he shouted. She continued to sing. He felt his way to the front of his cell, listening to her sweet voice. Soon he recognized the song and began singing it with her, quietly at first, but increasing his volume as others listened.

After a few repetitions, some of the prisoners began singing with them. The singing continued for about thirty minutes, until a guard came down the corridor raking his sword against the cell bars. "Silence in here!" the soldier cried out.

"Or what?" Peter asked. "You're going to pluck my eyes out?" He smiled at the guard while pushing his face against the bars. His face was so repugnant that the guard turned and walked away without another word.

Peter turned and walked to the backside of the cell. Someone grabbed his arm. "Sir," a prisoner said, "allow me to help you." He was escorted to a bench. "I apologize for slapping you earlier. I just couldn't imagine anything good coming out of this place."

"There is one who is good—His name is Jesus. And He can be with you anytime, anywhere."

"I have heard of this name before—in the streets of Rome. His followers are called Christians. Are you a Christian?"

When Peter heard that, he remembered how his Lord had told him that there was a reason for his coming to Rome and for being caught. *My Master, thank You for reminding me that there is a bigger picture going on before me. Forgive me for not sharing Your message of hope sooner.* Peter then began sharing the gospel to many of the prisoners—the same gospel being heard up the corridor in the women's cell. And that night dozens of prisoners were set free in Christ.

The prisoners knew it was morning based on the food that was brought to them. Since all the cells were beneath the ground, daylight was not an option. But this morning was different—quieter. Many prisoners had confessed Jesus as their Lord and it was showing in their attitudes.

Another set of soldiers walked down the corridor. "Peter of Bethsaida, step to the door." Several men helped him to the front. "The rest of you step away from the door." As they did, the soldiers unlocked the cell door and pulled Peter out into the corridor. "Come with us."

As they led Peter up the corridor, he heard another cell door open and close. "Perpie?"

"Yes, I'm here beside you."

"How sweet," a soldier said, as he pushed them forward.

"Let me guide you," Perpie said as she grabbed his hand.

A soldier was about to separate them when another stopped him. "Let her help him. This will make it even harder for them later."

Outside, Peter groaned as the sunlight heated up his eye sockets. "Where are we going?"

"The commander wishes to see you again—what's left of his eyesight." They continued walking toward the backside of the prison, where they were once again tied together to a post. Peter could feel and hear the tearing of their clothing. Soon they felt the stinging of the whips against their bodies. According to their turn, each let out a yelp when struck.

The commander stood and was assisted to the whipping posts. "You thought I was finished with you two last night?" He walked over to the front of Peter and spit in his face. "You may have ruined my eyes, you foreign scum, but I will have the last laugh."

Peter heard him step around to Perpetua's side of the post. "Sir?" Peter said, "I have some information that may help your vision."

The commander removed his hands from Perpetua and was assisted back to Peter's side. "What can prison scum offer me to restore my sight?"

Peter then began explaining the gospel of Christ and how it could give him a new vision for life. "With Christ in your life, you will see life with spiritual eyes and see the Creator God through His Son, Jesus."

"Guard!" the commander shouted. "Tie a cloth in their mouths. I don't need a prisoner's God." The guards did as commanded. Perpetua's hands were able to touch Peter's arms, so she kept them there as much as possible.

"Take and prepare them for crosses. The emperor has requested some light for tonight's party. And see if you can find at least four more Christians to join these two. Make sure they bleed out and are soaked for the lighting."

The soldiers separated the two and led them both to crosses. "So this is the way to your leader's kingdom," a soldier said to Peter. "Crucified, just like Him!"

"Soldier?" Peter asked through his cloth. The soldier pulled the cloth down. "Sir, I don't deserve to be crucified like Him . . . perhaps you could hang me upside down?"

The soldier stared at Peter in disbelief. "I . . . I've never heard of such a request." He pulled the cloth back over Peter's mouth.

Once again, Perpetua began humming psalms to her husband. Peter heard her and joined in the humming as they were tied and nailed to crosses. With cloths stuffed in their mouths, they hummed psalms to each other as their blood was slowly let out. Then, within the hour, they were in the presence of Jesus . . .

"To be absent from the body [is] to be present with the Lord."
2 Corinthians 5:8

† † †

"It's beautiful!"

"It's an island," John Mark replied.

Petronilla continued gazing at the mountains that dropped right into the sea. "Well I love it!" She lifted John Peter up to view the coastline. "See the cliffs?"

Phoenix was the first town on the island of Crete that John Mark and family would search for Barnabas. They visited several fellowships, but found no Barnabas in the area. "He was here about six months ago," one elder said.

Next stop: Fair Havens. Once again, John Mark led them to a known house of Christians. A man was grooming a horse outside his door. "Pardon me, sir, would you know if Elder Barnabas is in town?"

The man put his brush down. He motioned for John Mark to come nearer. John Mark handed the baby to Petronilla and stepped up to the man. "Now who did you say you were?"

"John Mark, cousin of Barnabas. And this is my family: Petronilla, my wife, and John Peter."

"My name is Samuel, elder of the fellowship. This is Barnabas's horse. He went for a walk, but should be back soon."

John Mark turned and smiled at his wife. "May we wait here?"

"Not only wait, you may stay here as long as you wish." He embraced John Mark. "We are your family in Christ. Please, let's go inside and allow me to introduce my family to you."

"Samuel, my brother," Barnabas said as he open the front door. "I've brought a couple new friends with me; may they dine with us?" A man and woman stepped inside the house with Barnabas. Samuel walked in from the back room and embraced him. "This is Jonathan and Mariah, new believers in Jesus."

"What a blessing and honor to meet new members of the family." Samuel acknowledged Mariah and then embraced Jonathan. "Welcome to my home."

"I told them of your fellowship and how important it was for them to connect to the other believers here."

"That is wonderful! And Barnabas, I have a couple new friends of mine to introduce to you." Samuel stepped back to the doorway and motioned for his friends.

"Barnabas!"

"John Mark?"

John Mark ran and embraced his cousin. "Barnabas, I've missed you so!" They held each other for a few minutes.

"I'm speechless."

"Now that's a rarity," Samuel said, smiling.

Petronilla brought in John Peter. "Who is this?" Barnabas asked as he released John Mark and grabbed John Peter.

"This is John Peter," John Mark said.

Barnabas raised him high above his head; John Peter began to cry. "Oh my; did I hurt you little fellow?" He lowered him down and handed him to Petronilla. "Maybe a little too much excitement?"

"He's not used to these surroundings," Petronilla replied.

"He'll be fine," John Mark said. "Just give him a few minutes to get used to that ugly face of yours." Everyone laughed—everyone except little John Peter. He continued clinging tightly to his mother.

Barnabas looked at John Mark. "I can't believe we're together again—oh! I nearly forgot. This is Jonathan, of Crete, and his wife, Mariah."

Petronilla walked over to Mariah and embraced her. "A blessing to meet you." She bowed her head and smiled.

"They just now became followers of Jesus," Barnabas said.

"Well they are welcome here as family," Samuel responded. "Let me find the wife and tell her."

Petronilla stopped Samuel. "Don't bother, I'll take her back to the cooking area and we ladies will take care of the introductions."

Samuel smiled. "Now that's what I call sweet fellowship." The men laughed as they headed outdoors.

While Samuel talked with Jonathan, John Mark and Barnabas walked along the docks, sharing their ministry stories.

"And your Roman boss never received Jesus?" Barnabas asked.

"Not to my knowledge. But he did help us leave Italy, writing papers for our free transportation to here."

"That's encouraging."

"Yes."

"And you say Peter and his wife remained in Rome?"

John Mark looked to the ground. "Yes; he said our Lord told him to go there and write a letter."

"You don't seem happy about that."

"Barnabas, Nero is hunting down Christians and hanging them on crosses along the main roads to use as torches to light the streets. I am concerned about Peter and his boldness."

Barnabas looked down as well. "I see what you mean . . . do you expect to hear from him soon?"

"I don't know."

"Well, if the Lord told him to go there, then we must trust the Lord's guidance."

"Yes, God's will is best. But Pet really misses them—and so do I."

Barnabas put his arm on John Mark's shoulder. "Let's talk about your ministry . . . where are you headed?"

"I'm not sure just yet. I thought maybe we could hang out with you."

"Is that what the Lord told you?"

"He hasn't said. He only said for us to come find you."

"I'm flattered, but I have no word from Him either." Barnabas looked at his cousin. "But it's no time like the present to start praying for His revelation concerning you."

John Mark looked at his cousin and smiled. "You are such an encourager."

† † †

"Where is my gold?!" Nero turned to Anicetus. "Where is it?"

"The Jews are stubborn. Vespasian has the city of Jerusalem under siege, but there is a rebellion going on inside the city itself."

"And what concern does that have to me?"

"Wait, Divine One, and the blame for their destruction will be on their shoulders and not yours."

"Wait . . . I detest that word!" Nero was about to continue his ranting when he saw several young freedmen walking past his gaze. "Wait . . . Anicetus, did you see that man?"

"Which one, Divine One?"

He pointed: "There, that one! Look at him. Doesn't he remind you of someone?"

"I'm not sure—"

"Guards!" Several guards appeared. "Stop those men there and bring them to me."

Within minutes, the guards brought in four men. All four bent their knees and bowed before the emperor. "Stand up," Nero said, "all of you." As they stood, Nero continued to look at each one. He pointed at three of them. "You three turn around and step away." As they did, Nero continued to circle one of the men. "Anicetus, do you see her?"

Anicetus walked in a little closer. "See who?"

Nero reached out and touched the face of the freedman. "Sabina . . . Sabina, you have returned."

Anicetus stepped back and looked at the young man and then at Nero. "Sabina?"

"Sporus, Divine One; my name is Sporus."

"Silence!" Nero responded. "Show me your arms." Nero began caressing the young man's arm. "Sabina, you have returned to me." Sporus tried to lower his head, but Nero grabbed his chin and lifted it up. "When I speak to you, you will not lower your head unless I command it. You are now Sabina." Nero turned to Anicetus. "What does my Sabina need to make her more beautiful?"

"A bath, perhaps? And a shave?"

Nero was not amused and shot a glaring glance at Anicetus. "Guards, take Sabina to my chambers and prepare her for my visit. Find out where she has been."

"And what of his comrades, Divine One?" a guard asked.

"You mean, *her* comrades? Interrogate them and report back to me." Nero smiled at Sporus/Sabina as the four were removed from his presence.

Anicetus stepped over to Nero's side. "Are you sure about this, Divine One?"

"What do you mean?"

"Well, this Sabina is different from the first one. Don't you have concern as to what others will think or say?"

Nero growled at Anicetus. "I am the Divine One. Gods may choose whomsoever to be their partner. Go now and have her fixed so that she may be made as beautiful as before."

Anicetus backed away from Nero and quietly left the room. *The senators are correct. This emperor has lost his mind.*

† † †

John remained secluded in his room, praying and seeking answers from his beloved Lord. "My Lord," he whispered. "Peter and Paul have joined you now. How do I comfort your people with this news? How do I calm their fears?"

Jesus spoke to John. "By My words, My beloved one. My Spirit will use My words and bring hope to all who believe in Me. John, you must maintain your focus on Me. I will give direction to you and My fellowships by My words. The Spirit will direct you and others compiling My writings and spreading them throughout the world. Do not fear man, who can only destroy your body; rather, fear Me by allowing My words to rule inside you."

"Lord, what about the others? Where are the other apostles? Do we need to come together again? And what of Jerusalem?"

"You follow Me; I will guide all My followers to places where they will give testimony of Me and My plans. Do not let their whereabouts concern you."

"And Jerusalem?"

"Stay away from there. The leaders continue diverting My chosen ones from Me. I will allow the Romans to destroy it."

John remained quiet for a while. In his mind and heart, he began to rehearse the words of his Lord. He thought of some words of the prophets that spoke of the Son of God. Immediately he saw the correlation of these words to the life and ministry of his Lord.

"Write, My beloved child; write the things that I bring to your remembrance."

"Yes, my Master . . . I will write."

John stood up and straightened up his garments. He made his way to the dining room of the house that he and Mary now occupied by the gracious gift of Sarah's family. A note from Mary was propped up beside a bowl of fruit. She had left to go with Sarah to minister to the poor and lame people of Ephesus. "My son," her note continued, "here is some fruit and there is bread in the basket. I will return before dark." John smiled as he thought of Mary. *She never tires of serving our Lord.*

A knock on the door interrupted John's thoughts. He opened it partially. "Yes?"

"Is this the house of my Lord's mother?"

"Yes, and you are?"

"Apollos, a proclaimer of the way of deliverance from our sins and the corruption of this world."

"Apollos! Yes, my brother, please come in." John opened the door fully, allowing Apollos to enter. "Please forgive my reluctance; the Romans are using anyone and everyone to entrap us and carry us away to Rome."

Apollos received John's embrace. "Yes, I am aware of this plot to destroy us."

"But of course. By the way, I'm John."

"John, the beloved apostle?" Apollos bowed. "It is always an honor to meet those of you who knew our Lord so well."

"And it is always my joy to meet those who did not see Him and yet believe as strongly as I."

"I did meet him once, near the Jordan, when I was but a lad."

"Oh really? The days of John the Baptizer?"

"Yes; my parents and I listened to John on several occasions. One day Jesus came by us and spoke to me. That was the day that changed the lives of my family and me."

John smiled. "Yes, He has a way of doing that."

Apollos changed his smile to a serious face. "John, I come with a troubled heart."

"Come, sit down and tell me what is on your heart." John handed him a piece of fruit and retrieved some flat bread for their consumption.

"This edict from Nero . . . it has gripped the churches of Macedonia with fear. No one will go out with me to share the gospel anymore." Apollos pulled a cloth out from under his outer garment to wipe his nose and eyes. "The people want me to share the words from our Lord but they have no intent to go out and proclaim what they have heard. It's breaking my heart and it's causing a lot of bickering in the fellowship." Apollos wiped his eyes again.

"Oh . . . I understand. I also see this happening in our Asian fellowships. Fear has indeed gripped our people, thus keeping many from sharing their testimony."

"I told the fellowship at Corinth that I would go away for some time alone until I get a word from our Lord about this fear. As I was praying, the Lord told me to come find His mother in Ephesus and wait here until I get a new word from Him.

John stood up and raised his hands toward heaven. "This is why You told me to write, my Lord! I praise You and bless You for Your everlasting peace and grace. Your love for your children is never ending!"

Apollos joined John in standing and began weeping. "Yes, Jesus, You are the all-knowing One—the One who is all-powerful and everywhere!" Together, they praised and worshiped the Lord for about an hour.

"Well this is a lovely sight to see," Mary said as she entered the house with Sarah. John and Apollos were now on their bellies, face down.

"Looks like Jesus has been visiting here," Sarah commented as she helped Mary bring in some food.

John and Apollos sat up and smiled. "Mother," John said, "this is Apollos."

Apollos stood up as Mary approached him. "Oh, my dear son," she said as she embraced him. "I've heard so much about your boldness to proclaim our Lord to others."

"You have?" he asked.

"Yes! I have. Our Lord has spoken to me about you on several occasions."

"He has?" Apollos was at a loss of words.

"Yes, and He told me that none of us should be worried about the fear of some, but to continue proclaiming His faithfulness and gospel to the people."

Apollos raised his hands to heaven and began praising the Lord once again.

"Here we go again," Sarah said with a smile.

"I'll take him to my bedroom while you ladies start the supper meal."

"Sounds great," Mary said. "Sarah, you go get your husband and come back for a night of fellowship."

† † †

*L*uke looked back at his donkey in tow. The animal was weighed down with a canvas full of papyri and parchments. After a week of traveling, he was anxious to get to Philippi. *I pray Johannes is home.*

Several hours later found Luke in front of his uncle's villa. He dismounted from his donkey and found his way up to the front door and knocked. The door opened just enough for someone inside to look outside. "Luke?" The door then swung wide open. It was Johannes. "Luke! What a surprise!" They embraced in the doorway momentarily. "Come in, come in."

Luke stepped inside the door. "So good to see you are home. I was afraid you might be off on a business journey."

Johannes laughed. "That sounds like me. But I have slowed down a bit, with all the Roman turbulence and all. Enough about me; tell me how are things in Boeothia? Are my people serving you well?"

"Everything is great—they're spoiling me!"

Johannes laughed. "That's what I wanted to hear. Now tell me what brings you back to Philippi?"

Luke pointed toward the door. "My writings; the donkey has quite a load."

"You stay put and I'll have someone fetch them." Johannes walked away and disappeared momentarily. Soon, he and a servant were bringing in the canvas bags. "Whoa! You weren't joking when you said you had a load."

Luke smiled. "No interruptions allow for a lot of writing."

"That indeed." They placed the bags next to a table. "Tell me, what have you written this time?"

Luke pulled out some papyri. "I have completed the story of how the gospel spread from Judea to Rome."

Johannes inspected a few pages and read a few lines. "This is good, Luke—no, this is excellent!" He continued reading.

"I have many pages. The Lord allowed it to flow through me. Then one day, it stopped."

"Stopped?"

"Yes; just as I was about to go into detail about Paul's prison time in Rome, the Lord said, 'No.'"

Johannes looked up from the pages. "Do you think He will say 'continue' later on?"

"I don't think so. I waited for days in prayer, but nothing has come from Him."

"Then it must be complete." He laid the pages down. "What now?"

Luke rubbed his eyes. "I need some copyists. Can you help me find some?"

"I will get the word out. In the meantime, you must rest your eyes."

For once, Luke did not object. He knew he had strained his eyes from much writing.

Several weeks later

Luke inspected each page from the three copyists. He read them aloud, making a few corrections on the copies that were different from the original.

Johannes came in from outside. "How's the work coming along?"

"Fine," Luke said. "Only a few minor corrections. These men are great!"

"Philippi's finest." He smiled. "Now what are your plans for the three copies?"

"I want one to stay with you, one to go to Ephesus, and the final one either to Antioch, Syria, or Alexandria."

"Antioch is too close to Judea—there's a war going on over there. Alexandria, on the other hand, sounds better. There's a lot of Jews there that need to hear of the gospel spreading into the non-Jewish world."

Luke looked closely at his uncle. "Now when did you start taking an interest in the Jews?"

"When I began following my Jewish Savior, of course. Luke, I've been listening to the local priests reading from their Sacred Writings. Those parts that I understand keep pointing me to Jesus. It's like history being revealed to me."

"Really?"

"Yes, really. I listen quietly and when he asks for questions I raise my hand and ask questions . . . it's that simple."

"Uncle Johannes, you simply amaze me sometimes. Perhaps our Lord is leading you to proclaim His word?"

Johannes looked down at the canvas bags. "Perhaps." Then he looked seriously into Luke's eyes. "The only problem I see is that those of you who have been called of our Lord to proclaim His word are either mocked, beaten, or die a cruel death—maybe all three! . . . I think I will be a little more discreet in sharing His word."

Luke thought of Peter and Paul for a moment. Then he rubbed his legs where he was injured from his previous encounter with the angry Jews in this very town. "Perhaps you're right . . . just follow His lead and He will guide you."

"Yes, my nephew, by all means, follow His lead. Now tell me, how do you plan to get these books to the proper fellowships?"

"Let's pray about it and see what He has to say."

† † †

"NOOOOOO! It isn't true! It can't be true!"

John Mark tried to pull Petronilla closer to him, but she broke from his hold and turned away from him. "My dear Pet, Barnabas received the news from some of his workers who just returned from Rome."

She fell to the floor and leaned her head against the wall, sobbing. "Noooo, noooo, noooo! They can't be dead—not now!"

John Mark knelt on the floor beside her. He was sobbing as well. This time she turned to him and embraced him, weeping uncontrollably. "Why, My Lord, why?" John Mark didn't speak, allowing her to mourn the loss of her mother and father, Perpetua and Peter.

Barnabas sat in the opposite corner of the room, keeping young John Peter occupied while his parents grieved over this tragic loss. Petronilla looked over at him. "Are you sure?" Barnabas nodded his head. "Then we must go and bury them—a place where it's safe."

"Quintus, the Roman guard, sent word that he would place the bodies near Paul's. That's the safest place right now." Barnabas did not mention that the bodies had been set ablaze on crosses.

John Peter ran over to join his parents on the floor. They opened their embrace to allow him to join them. His giggles and baby talk brought smiles through the tears of mourning. "We can go back, can't we?" she asked her husband.

"Not at this time, Pet; it is not safe."

"But can't we do something?"

John Mark remained silent, but Barnabas spoke up. "We can have a memorial service here among the believers. I'll see if we can erect some memory stones nearby—a place to go and sit and pray."

Petronilla lowered her head on John Mark's shoulder. "My Lord," she prayed, "please put a stop to this emperor's madness."

† † †

"The gods will bring you great fortune," Nero said to Milichus.

"And to you, Divine One, for you have elevated my fellow freedmen in the affairs of Rome."

Nero turned and stared into the faces of Piso and Seneca, who were chained against the prison dungeon wall. He slowly stepped up into Piso's face. "You thought you could remove me with your cries for justice?" Nero then whispered into Piso's ear. "The emperor must understand the methods of the dark world in order to rule his servants."

Next, Nero turned to Seneca. "And you, my old confidant; are you a part of this assassination attempt?"

"No, Divine One! I did not know of the final outcome of this dishevel."

"But you never warned me. You knew something was going on, but you remained silent. You are no friend if you know the truth but do not speak out." Nero motioned to a guard. "Gather a few guards and let this one go to his villa and let his blood flow before his family."

As Seneca was carried away, Nero turned back to Piso. "As for you, you and your comrades will be executed before the senate as a testimony of the outcome of treason."

Nero turned and exited the cell, but before he left earshot he heard Piso shout out, "There are too many of us! You will not survive this so-called cleansing of your enemies!"

"What is your report?" a Praetorian general asked Nero as he returned from the prison area.

Nero looked glaringly at the general. "You report to me!" He stepped up closer to the general. "I am a god; I report to no mere mortal."

The general returned an equal glare but said nothing. Nero then turned away and headed toward his palace. "Where's Sabina and Pythagorus?"

The general looked at several guards. "Set up a meeting with the other commanders immediately." Then he turned toward the emperor's palace. *You will not be a god much longer.*

† † †

One month later

Vespasian studied the unsealed letter from Rome. "Guards! Bring me Titus! *So Nero will be replaced soon? . . . By whom?*

Titus walked into the tent of his father, Vespasian. "Yes, Father? You requested me."

"Read this." He tossed the letter to him.

Titus sat down and began reading. "Nero replaced? By the gods! Who will replace him?"

"My question also. There is no one in Caesar's lineage; it must be a general."

"Galba? Otho?"

"Perhaps; this is from Galba's secretary. But just in case, bring your legion in and let's surround this city until it is subdued." Titus stood up and started to walk out. "Oh, and send Joseph over to see me."

"Yes, my Father."

"You wish to see me?"

"Yes," Vespasian said. "Sit with me." Joseph sat down across the table from the general. "I have called for King Agrippa to come in for a visit. You two have some things in common: you want your people to live and you want this temple of yours to survive my attack. Perhaps, between the two of you, we can come to a resolution."

Joseph stared momentarily at the general. "I do not think my and the king's views are the same."

"How so?"

"The Zealots and the Sacarii are at each other's throat for control over the city. They hate each other and are continuously fighting for control of the temple."

"And which of the two is the strongest?"

Joseph stood up and walked over to an opening facing Jerusalem. "The one who controls the temple."

At that moment, Agrippa entered the tent. "General, you wish to speak to me?" He then looked over and saw Joseph. "Is this not the captured leader of the Galileans?"

"Sit please," Vespasian gestured to the king. "And please pardon the place; I haven't the luxury of time and servants to find a more suitable place for a visit."

Agrippa took a seat and motioned toward Joseph. "And why is he here?"

"I sent for him. I am announcing my plans to the both of you and wish to hear of your views . . . Joseph, join us." Joseph walked back to the table and sat with the two leaders.

Vespasian looked at the two men. "I am ordering my men to tear down the walls of Jerusalem and we will march to the gates of the temple. If the temple is not surrendered to me, it too shall be razed to the ground."

Agrippa stood up. "The temple? Surely you won't destroy our temple!"

"I won't; but your people will by not surrendering."

"Then I will speak to them . . . right away!"

Vespasian turned to Joseph. "Your two mites' worth?"

Joseph looked first at Vespasian and then addressed the king. "Most Noble Agrippa, I know you mean well in your efforts, but Jerusalem is fighting from within. If the commander waits another year, Jerusalem will drop in his hands like an over-ripened fig."

"That may appear so to you, but I believe they will listen to their king." Agrippa turned to the commander. "Give me until tomorrow. I will appeal to the people to listen to me."

"My son should be here in five days with additional troops. You have until then to convince your priests to hand over the temple."

Agrippa nodded and left the room. Vespasian motioned to a servant. "Bring us a drink."

Vespasian and Joseph sat down once again. Both took turns sipping the Roman wine. "Ahh, didn't I tell you our wine was much better than the local stuff?"

"Certainly stronger."

Vespasian laughed. "I like you; you would make a good Roman." He gulped down his drink. "But you have to learn how to drink Roman wine."

Joseph smiled as he took another sip. "Perhaps, in time, sir."

"So, do you think the king has a chance?"

"No, sir. I know my people better than he does. They will die first."

"People of conviction."

Joseph did not agree. "People who are blind to the truth."

"Truth?"

"Sir, when Titus returns, you will have, what, 80,000 foot soldiers?"

"Somewhat."

"That's 80,000 against 20,000—that's 20,000 *only* if they will stop fighting each other long enough to join together."

Vespasian smiled. "I like your summation. You're right."

"The king's motive is to somehow save face long enough with the priests to get some of the temple treasures for himself. He is not interested in saving our people."

"Joseph, you have perception like a commander." Vespasian became silent for a moment. "I want to make you an offer: After this siege is over, return with me to Rome as one of my advisors. I will make you a citizen and pay you well."

Joseph stood up and bowed to him. "Commander, you would do that to me?"

"Yes; killing you would be such a waste of good talent. You see the bigger picture and I think you see the future of your people."

"But I am still a Jew. Doesn't the emperor dislike Jews?"

"The emperor? Oh, Nero? Pay no mind to him. His reign should end before we arrive."

Joseph looked at Vespasian. "Then I will accept your offer."

"Great!" Vespasian reached out and grasped his arm. "Then it is agreed. From henceforth, I shall call you Josephus."

✝✝✝

"Jesus is that Deliverer—not from your physical oppressors, but from that which enslaves you far greater: your spiritual oppressors and your sins. Turn yourselves over to Him and He will set you free. Jesus said He was the way to salvation—He is the truth! If any of you have not turned your life over to Jesus, then see me or any of the local elders. We will assist you with His understanding. Amen."

Luke then walked over to the front bench and knelt to pray. He did this after every message that he preached. Johannes began singing a psalm. Soon, many joined in the singing while a few others came to the elders who were standing next to Johannes.

After about ten minutes Luke stood up to face the front. Johannes spoke to the elders and then quieted the fellowship. "My fellow believers, we have twelve men and women who wish to announce their followship of Jesus. Tomorrow morning, we will gather just southeast of the city and baptize these in the name of the Father, the Son, and the Holy Spirit. Please, if possible, meet us there for this joyous occasion."

Numerous "amens" were heard as the fellowship broke up for dismissal. As the crowd thinned, someone grabbed Luke's shoulder. He turned around. "Timothy? Timothy!"

Timothy smiled. "I got word in Troas that you were in Philippi, so I had to come see you."

"What a blessing! I was just praying for a way to get a large book to Ephesus and Antioch."

"You've written more?"

"Yes; when I arrived in Tipha, I met the governor of Boeothia and he listened very intently to my presentation of the gospel. Soon he became a follower of Jesus and asked what he could do to help spread the words of Christ. I gave him a copy of my version of the life of Jesus. Then the Lord told me to finish the story of the spread of the gospel throughout the Roman Empire and give the governor a copy of it as well."

"Luke, can you trust him?"

"What do you mean?"

"Aren't we Christians still hunted down by Nero? Governors still get rewarded for capturing enemies of the empire."

Luke smiled. "I wouldn't worry. He is so excited about becoming a Christian that he changed his Roman name, Antony, to a Christian name, Theophilus. He even allowed me to address my books to him for better security across the regional borders."

Timothy's eyes lit up. "Awesome!"

"'Awesome'? Oh yes, I heard Paul mention that word before. Anyhow, you need not worry about Theophilus. But I need you to transport this second book to Ephesus. From there, I pray they will copy it and distribute it."

"Consider it done, my brother . . . And did you know that the apostle John and Jesus' mother, Mary, are dwelling in Ephesus?"

"No, I did not know. Are they well?"

"John is fine; Mary is getting up in age and doesn't get out as much as she used to when she was in Jerusalem. But she has plenty of stories to tell and the children love to hear her tell the stories about Jesus when He was a boy."

Luke stopped to ponder that thought. "You know, it's hard to imagine Jesus was a boy like us."

"Well He was a boy . . . but I doubt He was like us—or like me!" Timothy laughed.

"Are you saying that you were a bad boy?"

"I wasn't all bad—I was crippled, you know; but I was no saint either."

"Say, I don't mean to change the subject, but would you give your testimony in our next service? I'm sure there are some members who need to hear of your disability and how Jesus gave you victory over that obstacle."

"Sure, I'd love to!"

"Great! Let's go find my uncle and we'll tell him."

† † †

"Has the Lord spoken to you yet?"

John Mark reached over and rubbed Petronilla's hair. "Not yet, but let's keep asking."

She smiled as she kissed his neck. "He's spoken to me."

John Mark sat up in their bed. "He's told you where we're going but hasn't told me?"

"Must be something wrong with your praying. You and that cousin of yours haven't gotten into any trouble lately, have you?" She laughed quietly as she turned away from him.

"Where'd He say we were going?"

"I'm not telling you; you have to find out for yourself."

John Mark got up from the bed. "Well I'm going to the other room and pray until I hear from Him."

She pulled a blanket onto her shoulders. "Don't wake up John Peter when you return."

John Mark settled down near the fire and lay on his belly. "My Lord? I ask once again, where do You want my family and me to go to represent You?" He thought about his question and then prayed again. "My Master, I apologize for being so abrupt. I want to spend time just to worship You. You don't need to answer me for I do not deserve hearing one syllable from You. Please forgive me for being so selfish. You are God and there is no other."

John Mark spent several hours praying and singing a few psalms he learned from the fellowship in Jerusalem. Then he fell asleep on the floor by the fire.

In a dream, he saw him and his family proclaiming the gospel to people in a foreign land. He also worked as a translator for the local officials, translating Roman documents in Hebrew and Arabic. One day, Petronilla took their son and daughter on a long trip. Soon, they saw the Great Pyramid. "Look, Mother," John Peter said. "There's a pointed hat on that hill."

John Mark woke up—it was a dream! *Pyramid? A long distance? . . . Alexandria!* He got up and ran to the bedroom. "Pet! Pet! Wake up!"

"Ummm, wake me up tomorrow."

He looked around. "I think it is tomorrow . . . Pet, wake up! I know where we're going!" John Peter began stirring in his little bed beside theirs. "Pet!" He shook her again.

This time she sat up. "Shhhh, he's stirring."

"I don't care; listen, the Lord showed me in a dream that we're going to Alexandria."

"That's nice; I already knew that. Now let's go back to bed." She laid her head back down.

John Mark lay beside her. He was smiling as he thought about how the Lord had spoken to him in a dream. *Alexandria . . . Alexandria . . . Thank you, Lord, for Your revealing power.* He then turned over and whispered something in her ear. "The Lord showed me something else about our future family."

Petronilla opened wide her eyes. "What? What did He say?

John Mark yawned. "Umm, something about children."

"More children? Did He say we were having more children?"

He turned away from her. "I'm not telling; you'll just have to ask Him yourself."

Soon, she could hear John Mark snoring as she lay wide awake, asking the Lord what He revealed to her husband.

†††

"You wish to speak to me, my Father?"

Vespasian motioned for Titus to sit down. "Yes." He grabbed another cup and handed it to his son. "There's word from Rome that Nero has traveled to Greece with his clowns."

"You mean his circus?"

Vespasian laughed. "Call it what you wish; he's gone and Rome is conspiring to kill him."

"Again? I thought the incident with Piso was enough to quell any future conspiracies."

"Rome is broke. Our men are not getting their promised wages while Nero seeks everyone else's gold. He is no leader who thinks first of his own welfare." He looked straight into his son's eyes. "Titus, we must garner the strength of the military if we are going to survive the next few years."

Titus looked perplexed. "Isn't this thinking first of our own welfare?"

"No, my son. It is for the stability of the empire. The barbarians that surround us will slaughter our people if they see us as weak. We must fortify our ranks to maintain the laws of our land."

"What is your proposal?"

"Nero has given me orders to secure the rebellion of the Judeans. No one will question my travels through the region to check on our legions. I will obtain the trust of the vice-commanders and centurions so that when the civil war begins we will have a sizeable trust in our leadership."

Titus took another sip of wine. "Then you should go to Egypt first."

"Egypt? Isn't your brother Domitian stationed there?"

"Yes. And a large fleet of ships is stationed there as well."

Vespasian thought for a moment. "We will go together."

"Together? But what about Jerusalem?"

"Josephus is right: there's so much in-fighting there that they'll not miss us for another six months. By then, we and your brother shall be back. Have our soldiers back away from the city gates enough to let them think they have won this battle. We'll take enough soldiers and gold with us to make an impression on the Egyptian leaders and our centurions."

"Father, do you want to be the emperor?"

Vespasian stood up and turned toward an opening where he could see outside. "First, let's allow Galba and Otho to fight it out—and maybe Vitellius will want a piece of the action. Let's see how they plan to handle the situation."

Three days later

"I must speak with Commander Vespasian," Agrippa demanded.

"He's gone," a guard said.

"Gone? That's all?" The guard did not move or speak. "Where is he?"

"He left strict orders to say no more."

Agrippa was angry. *I am the king of Judea and this commoner won't speak to me?* "Where is his counsellor?"

The guard pointed to another tent nearby. As Agrippa made his way to the nearby tent, he began thinking of the things to say to this counsellor to show his displeasure in the arrangements.

When he arrived, there was another guard at the entranceway. "I am King Agrippa II; I must speak to the commander's counsellor immediately."

The guard turned to go into the tent. "One moment." He disappeared behind the canvas doorway, but soon returned. "You may enter."

The counsellor was seated at a table, writing on a stack of papyrus. Before he could stand, Agrippa began speaking: "Sir, I demand to know where the commander is right now!"

Josephus stood up and bowed. "My king."

"Wha…What! You? The commander's counsellor?"

"Yes, Your Majesty. I am Josephus, high servant and counsellor of Commander Vespasian."

"I cannot believe this! I am speaking to a traitor of our people!"

"Traitor? I was captured by the Romans. My punishment is to be his servant and to be relocated to Rome."

Agrippa shook his head. "Where is the commander now?"

"I cannot say; he did not tell me. He only said that he would be back soon and for me to be his mediator between the Romans and the Jews."

Agrippa smiled. "He's afraid, isn't he?"

"I don't think so, Your Majesty."

"I think he is."

Josephus walked to the backside of his tent and pulled open the back flap. "There are about 60,000 soldiers in the valley below us. The commander took 20,000 with him. Those in the valley below us have pledged to keep Judea under control until he returns. My advice to you is to try and negotiate terms of surrender before he annihilates our people and our temple."

"Are you trying to advise me?" Agrippa walked toward Josephus, but before he could reach him, two guards intercepted his move. Agrippa stopped.

"As I said, I am appointed by the commander to speak in his behalf. If you want to help our people, you will go back to the temple and start the negotiations."

"So, I see. Very well then; please let the commander know that I paid him a visit."

✝✝✝

"Where's John?"

Elder Simon studied Timothy's face. He appeared anxious. "Our last report said that he and Mary were in Laodicea . . . Timothy, is everything okay?"

"Yes, my brother, I want to show him a new letter from Luke."

"The Apostle Philip is among us now. Would you like for one of our young men to find him?"

"Philip? Are there any other apostles with him?"

"No, but he's awaiting John's return to give an update of the apostles."

"Then yes, I'd like to visit with him."

"I'll have one of our young men bring him to the guest quarters."

Timothy patted him on the shoulder. "Thank you, Simon." Timothy walked his donkey toward the guest quarters. When he saw them he could almost envision Paul sitting on the tree stump under the tree. *My Lord Jesus, I miss Paul so much. I beg of you to give me strength to proclaim Your gospel as did Paul.*

As Timothy made his way around to the back side of the quarters, he saw a familiar face. "Priscilla!" He dropped the reins and ran to embrace her.

"My dear Timothy, look at you!" She held him back at arms' length. "You look so, so—"

"So much wiser?" He smiled.

She laughed. "You took the words right out of my mouth."

"Where's Aquila?"

"Oh, out drumming up business as usual. You know him; he doesn't like for me to be idle." This time they both laughed. "Well now, I suppose I should prepare another seat at the dinner table."

"Yes, and I'm starving for some of your great cooking."

"I'll get right on it."

"Say, have you seen Philip?"

"The apostle? Yes; he's in the marketplace, sharing the good news."

Timothy hesitated. "Oh . . . well that's good."

Priscilla walked back over to Timothy. "My son, do not be afraid; he's gentle and has the love of our Lord written all over him—just like Paul." Timothy's smile returned. "Now go get yourself cleaned up and rest awhile. I'll send someone to your room when dinner's ready."

"Which room?"

"Oh, just find one that looks empty and claim it as yours."

"Timothy." Philip reached out and embraced Timothy as he walked in. "I've heard so much about the witness you have been for many years."

Timothy was taken aback momentarily. "Philip, it is you I should be speaking of in praise."

"No, my brother, we're all equal in God's kingdom. Jesus chose us commoners to introduce salvation to all nations."

"Okay, okay," Aquila said. "Let's break up the embraces and get down to the serious stuff—food!"

Timothy laughed. "I couldn't have said it better myself."

After blessing the meal, everyone began eating. "This is delicious!" Timothy said.

"Yes," Philip agreed.

Priscilla smiled. "Thank you."

"Philip, what brings you to Ephesus?" Timothy asked.

"The civil unrest continues to grow out of Judea. My kinsmen are at war with the Romans there, so it became necessary for us believers to separate ourselves from the beliefs and practices of our forefathers."

"I see," Timothy said.

"Jesus taught us to live peaceably within our government, as much as is possible."

"Even when our government is seeking us out to make us human torches in Rome?" Aquila asked.

Philip took a large gulp of goat's milk. "That's a good question—one that needs to be addressed in this meeting."

"Meeting?" Timothy asked.

"Yes; I've sent word out to several posts, asking our fellowships to find the apostles and bring them in for counsel on the Lord's directives."

One week later

Priscilla, Aquila, and Mary made the meeting area as comfortable as possible, bringing in bread, fruits, vegetables, and drink for the fellowship of saints. Others in and around Ephesus were praying for the apostles and elders during this meeting.

John looked over the group. In attendance were Philip, Simon the Zealot, Matthew, and Andrew. Also attending were Timothy, Luke, Junius, Titus, and Barnabas. And there were numerous elders from the local fellowships of Asia, Syria, and Macedonia. Finally, there were Phoebe, Lydia, Mary (the mother of Jesus), and Priscilla.

Philip stood up and raised his hand. "My brothers and sisters, thank you for responding to my call for this meeting. Before we open up for discussion, let us spend some time in prayer for the families of Peter and Paul and for the many around us who are sacrificing much in order to spread the gospel of deliverance."

For about an hour, prayers were offered to the Lord for wisdom and guidance, as well as for those who were suffering.

Finally, as the prayers were subsiding, Philip stood up again. "The Lord impressed on my heart to call us together for an outreach report and for our future ministry. First, let us hear from Matthew."

Matthew stood up. "The ministry to our kinsmen in Judea is virtually outside of Judea now. I remain transient as the Romans seek to gather us all in as prisoners of the empire. The leaders of our forefathers have renounced us as fellow members of our Judean beliefs. I believe our Lord's predicted judgment of our land has come to fruition."

"Any word from Eliezer and Mary?" Mary asked.

"Last I heard, they are in Dan and have started a new fellowship," Matthew responded.

"Any news from the east?" Philip asked.

"Thomas, Judas (the Less), and Nathaniel remain in Mesopotamia and continue to work toward the Far East. They reported six months ago that the Lord was confirming their work with signs and miracles. They continue translating His words in several far eastern languages. That's all I know."

"Thank you, Matthew. Simon or Andrew?"

They both stood up. "Brethren," Simon said. "The Gauls up north are a tough breed, but we have seen some openings to the gospel. They are still fighting with the empire in certain extreme areas and look upon us with some suspicion. But the Spirit is alive there and we have seen many fellowships begin.

Our greatest need, like the others, is the translation of our Lord's words into the local dialects. We find that His words continue to have convicting power for salvation. His blessed Spirit has done amazing things for us. The biggest concern I have is that most of the men and women cannot read or write in their native tongue." Simon began showing some emotions. "How will they read God's words?" Simon sat down.

Andrew continued the report. "I have managed to enter the Isles of the Britons. Paul and his group have also made an inroad to the locals and the Roman camps there. It's been truly amazing to see the openness of the gospel, but, as Simon said, there is still some fighting going on against the empire."

"Thank you, brothers, for your report," Philip said. "John?"

John stood up. "My dearly loved brothers and sisters, these reports further confirm our Lord's involvement in the spreading of the gospel. Even among much suffering, His word still brings conviction and comfort to the masses.

"Mary and I continue visiting and encouraging the churches in this area. Paul, Barnabas, Timothy, and others have done an amazing ministry here."

Philip turned to Mary. "Do you wish to add to John's report?"

Although a bit feeble, Mary managed to stand on her own. She wiped her tear-filled eyes. "My children, I pray daily for you all. I am so blessed to hear of our Lord's work throughout the lands . . . When He speaks to me, He reminds me not to forget the poor, the prisoners, the widows, and the orphans. John and I see this need increasing as the war against our Savior increases. Let us never forget His love and His heart for the defenseless among us."

As Mary sat down, Philip stood once more. "Brothers and sisters, Timothy and Luke have an update as well."

They both stood up. As Timothy spoke, Luke passed around several large books of papyri. "Thank you all for allowing us to be a part of this. Luke was led to a secluded region in order to compile the journeys of the acts of the Spirit-filled. I wish there were enough copies to give you each a personal one, but time just didn't permit the detailed copying needed to keep them true to the original. In time, we hope to have more copies made so that every region may have one as a resource by which we may share. So, for now, one can be shared among the three main regions. We'll continue to copy some for this area."

"Luke?" Philip asked. "Do you wish to add to this report?"

"I want to say how grateful I am to be a part of this group. For Jesus to allow the gospel to spread throughout all regions is just a sampling of how gracious and merciful He is and has been to all people groups. His love and salvation continue to bridge ethnic groups; we are truly one people in Christ."

Philip stood up again. "Now, is there anyone else who wishes to speak?"

Barnabas gave a brief report of the ministry on the islands in the Great Sea and told of John Mark's journey to Egypt.

Next, Lydia stood up. "My brothers and sisters in Jesus, as I travel throughout the region, I see great prejudices toward the followers of Jesus. I have tried to remind people that we're all humans of great value to the one God, but prejudice runs deep in our cultures. This is something I wanted to share with you.

"I also wish to say that because of my business, I have been blessed to provide nearly one-half of my profits to our Lord's work—primarily to pay our scribes for their hard work copying these letters. The Word of God is very active and powerful when it is heard and understood. If any of you need financial assistance in getting copies made, please let John know and I will do what I can to assist you."

"Thank you, Lydia," Philip said. "And thank you all for gathering and for the wonderful words of encouragement. I know this may possibly be our last gathering as a group like this, but do know that John plans to keep Ephesus as the main connection point of us all. If possible, send a report this way every year and we will continue praying for one another and assist as much as our Lord allows.

"Our emperor continues to promote abominable acts that are contrary to our Lord's instructions. The empire appears to be weakening from within. The senators are divided, but all want the removal of Nero. However, they continue hunting us down and enslaving many believers in Rome. So be diligent and discreet in the sharing of the gospel.

"If there are no further reports, then after our evening meal, let us worship together. Timothy, would you exhort us in our Lord's words during the worship time?"

"Me? Uh, sure; if that's okay with everyone else."

✝✝✝

"The soldiers in our northern borders are leaving their posts."
Nero looked at Sabina, his eunuch "spouse."
"Why? What is happening to our leadership?"

"Word has it that their families have not been paid for many months now."

Nero picked up his lyre. "Don't they understand that the gods do not pay mortals, but the mortals must pay the gods?"

Sabina rubbed the curls that hung from Nero's head. "My love, do not let the mortals disturb you. They will come to their senses or they will receive the fate of your wrath."

At that moment, two guards approached them. "Divine One?" one of the guards asked.

"Why do you trouble me at this time?"

"There is a rebellion among the soldiers."

"I know this; I have heard of the rebellion in the land of the Gauls."

"No, Divine One; this comes from Spain. General Galba has been announced as the new emperor in your place."

"What!" Nero stood up and began beating his head against a post. "What madness has befallen our people!"

"What shall we do?" Sabina asked.

Nero looked at the guards. "Save me from this dreadful state!"

"You must leave Greece and return to Rome for your own protection."

Nero was now pounding his head with his fist as he walked in circles. "What do you think, dear Sabina?"

"I do not know. Their suggestion sounds right though."

Nero looked at the guards. "Prepare my entourage for the return trip to Rome. We must leave right away. And make sure my instruments and props come with us."

"Word has it that Nero is returning," a senator said to the chief senator.

"Good! He should be back in time for his own dethroning."

"And will Galba take the throne?"

The chief senator looked at the near-empty senatorial chamber. "Not without a fight. I will propose that Vitellius ascend in Nero's stead."

"Why Vitellius?

"He was the first to come to his senses and allow his soldiers to leave the land of the Gauls." He turned to the senator. "It is time to see who, among our generals, is the rightful and noble leader of the empire."

†††

Titus approached his father. "Father?"

"Yes, my son?"

"The report is true: Galba and Otho are fighting in the west and Vitellius is heading south to Rome."

Vespasian stood up. "Then I will send our fleet from Egypt to control the seaports. Put on board as many of the foot soldiers as possible. Have the remainder travel around the sea until they arrive in Nicopolis. I will send the ships to them to board. Have them arrive at Puteoli as soon as possible."

†††

Several months later

"We summoned you four times," the chief senator said, "but you ignored our edicts."

Nero faced the Senate. "I will renounce my sins to the people."

"You have depleted the state's funds."

"I will stop the add-ons of the Golden House."

The chief senator stood up. "Guards, remove the emperor and put him under house arrest."

"No! You cannot do this to me. I am your emperor!"

"The senate has voted Vitellius as our emperor. He will determine your fate when he arrives."

The commander of the Praetorian Guard watched as Nero was removed from the senate chambers. He whispered to his assistant: "General, who is winning the battle in Spain?"

"We think Galba has the upper hand."

"Have the all the vice-commanders and centurions meet me in an hour at my quarters."

"They can't do this to me!" Nero shouted. He turned to Sabina. "I will poison them all."

"Careful, my love; the walls have ears."

There was a knock at the door. Sabina opened it. "What are *you* doing here?"

"I am Acte; I need to speak with Lucius."

"You may not!"

"Stop!" Nero stood up and walked quickly to the door. "Let her in."

"Do not trust her!"

Nero studied the face of his former mistress. "Why have you come?"

A tear revealed her heart. "I love you; I've come to ask you to resign your position—to stop fighting your removal."

Nero rubbed her hair. "My dear Acte . . . I know of no emperor that has resigned. It is unthinkable."

"But they will banish you!"

Nero hung his head on her bosom. "You must go now. Let your emperor decide his fate."

"No! Please do not order me away!"

He looked over to his body guard who gently, but firmly, pulled her away from Nero and walked her out of the room. The sobs from her voice grew dim with each second.

"Sabina, perhaps the Egyptians will receive me—or the Parthians! Yes, they owe me favors!"

Sabina sat Nero down on a couch. "Why do you run away? Is it a bad thing to die nobly?"

Nero began sobbing. "The death of such artistry! Should the world be deprived of such greatness?" He stood up and walked to his balcony. He then stepped onto the railing, three stories above the lower marble foyer. "Help me, Sabina! Help me finish the task!"

Sabina stood at a distance. "No! I cannot bear to watch such a performance."

A freedman servant, Phaon, was nearby. "Divine One, let's rush to my cottage! There, you may find time and rest your thoughts."

Nero crawled down from the railing. "My loyal Phaon, how can I get there?"

"I have servants clothing—I can dress you as my comrade."

Nero embraced him. "May my fellow gods, show us favor as we travel."

One hour later, Nero, Sabina, Phaon, and several additional servants arrived near Phaon's villa. Phaon stopped the group. "They may be checking for you; follow this path to my servants' quarters and remain there until I send for you."

Nero looked down the dark and thorny path. "I don't think I can get through these thorns!"

"Shhh," Phaon said. "This is your only hope. Now go!"

A servant went first, then Sabina, and finally Nero. The thorns were snagging each one's clothing. "Ouch!" Nero cried in a muffled voice. "These thorns are stabbing my toes."

Sabina removed his outer garments. "Use these to cover your steps."

Several minutes later, a small house appeared. "There," the lead servant whispered. "We're almost there." Nero entered the house and went into the bedroom where he fell onto the bed and covered his head with the covers.

Sabina came into the room. "My love, here is some bread and water; please refresh yourself."

"No! No bread—just water."

Another servant entered the room. "Divine One, my Lord Phaon said that the guards are searching for you. He wants you to travel south to the gravel mines and hide yourself." He handed a note to Sabina, who read through it quickly.

"What does it say?" Nero asked.

Sabina hung his head down. "The senate has declared you a public enemy and that you shall be punished by the way of the ancients."

Nero tore the letter from Sabina's hand. "Me, their god?! Publicly stripped and flogged to death?!" He crumbled the letter and threw it to the floor. "Servant of Phaon, have your people dig my grave immediately!"

"No!" Sabina said.

"I will not be humiliated before my enemies. Servant, obey your emperor!" The servant bowed and left the room. Sabina remained on the couch while Nero crawled into a corner of the room, muttering to himself. "My life is vain . . . I am despised by all! . . . Is this the reward for being the greatest Caesar? . . . Oh death, come quickly!"

Within the hour, several servants, Phaon, and a scribe came into the bedroom. "Divine One," Phaon said. "The guards have entered my compound. They are searching for you."

Nero pulled out two daggers, positioned them against his throat, and spoke to himself: "Nero, be a man and thrust them in!" But he could not do it. "Sabina, help me!" Sabina ran out the room. "Phaon, please help me."

"I cannot do so!"

Nero looked at each servant—none offered to help.

"I will help you," the scribe said.

"Oh, the gods be favorable upon you!" He walked over to Nero and clasped his hand around Nero's.

"Put your other hand on mine," the scribe said, "and slowly fall backwards."

"Please don't allow them to sever my head! Please!" Trembling, Nero slowly gripped the scribe's hand. "I hear the approaching hooves of the horsemen!" Then he fell backwards, allowing both daggers to plunge into his throat.

The scribe backed away from the bleeding body, ensuring that Nero's hands remained on the daggers. "Tell no one," he said to Phaon.

About that time, an officer walked into the room. "Too late," Nero whispered. "Too late."

The officer walked over to inspect the wound. He stood there until Nero took his last breath.

After a brief moment of silence, Phaon stepped over beside the officer. "He was an emperor; let him be recognized and buried as such."

"There is no money for such recognition and fanfare."

Phaon nodded his head. Then he remembered Acte's offer. "I will collect the necessary funds for the event."

The officer turned to walk out. "I will inform the Senate."

✝✝✝

Barnabas had his entourage ready to leave Ephesus. His plans were to travel to Cyprus by way of Antioch, Syria. John and Philip stood by the group as they mounted their horses with the donkeys in tow.

"Why Antioch?" John asked.

"Joseph of Arimathea has joined my stock of animals with his there. I want to make sure everything is well with him."

"Farewell then, my brother. Please give the fellowships our love and blessings. And please, send us a report each year."

"I will, my friend, I will."

John and Philip watched as the group slowly vanished into the eastern horizon. "I get the feeling we will never see him again," Philip said.

John did not act surprised. "The Lord's will be done."

Three months later

As Barnabas neared the southern route into Antioch, a large mass of travelers was headed north. He finally had his group stop and dismount. "Say there, sir?" he asked a man. "Why so many leaving Antioch?"

"The rebellion has reached the city," the man replied. "Many soldiers are ransacking the whole city, looking for anything to help them survive."

"Why so many soldiers?"

"Word is that Nero is dead and there is unrest in Rome. Several generals are fighting for the emperor's position."

Barnabas thanked the man and then turned to his group. "Men, if we are to survive this trip, we must get off the main highway and enter Antioch in the cloak of darkness. I know of a route east of the city where there is a small stable. We will keep our animals hidden there.

After securing the animals, Barnabas and his men found their way into Antioch. He wanted first of all to visit the assembly buildings of the fellowship to see if it was still intact. Then he wanted to visit the stables. It was late, but the fires of many burning houses kept the city adequately lit—too lit for Barnabas! He motioned for two of his men to move over one street while four others remained with him. As they neared the assembly area, Barnabas saw the buildings smoldering from a previous fire. Oc-

casionally a robed figure would run past the area—someone trying not to be identified.

For a moment, the seven men stood there, observing the remains of the once flourishing center of Christ's followers. "Let's
walk over to the guest housing," Barnabas said. The group
walked a couple of blocks southwest where once again there remained only gutted, smoldering frames of houses.

"This is not good," one of his men said to him.

Barnabas stood there and stared at the buildings. Finally, he
turned to the others. "We must go to the stables. A couple of you
go first; then two more will be about a block away. Then I and
the rest will follow you. Try not to get any attention drawn toward
you. Stop and hide if you encounter any soldiers."

Luckily, it appeared that the soldiers were finished with the
ransacking. As Barnabas neared the stables, he was amazed that
they were still standing. *What could this mean?* As the group entered the first stables, he could smell the scent of animals. "They
must have just left," Barnabas said.

The group continued walking through the first set of stables.
As they neared the next set, they heard a donkey starting to bray,
but it was immediately muffled. Barnabas held up his hand;
everyone stopped. He motioned for two men to slowly enter the
stall area. Suddenly a large man appeared with a threshing rod!

"Stop!" Barnabas said. "We mean you no harm!"

The man said nothing . . . but then he grunted as he pointed
the rod toward the men.

"Hamath? Hamath, is that you?"

He grunted again. "Who's asking?"

"It's Barnabas, Hamath!"

Hamath lowered his rod. "It's our last animal—noisy one at
that."

Barnabas passed the men up front and approached Hamath.
"Where's Joseph?"

He grunted again. "Took many of our horses to the docks and put them on a boat. Out in the sea somewhere. Soldiers took all our donkeys and camels . . . Too many men for me to fight, so I remained in this stall with this small donkey. They did not want to fight for this small one."

Barnabas smiled. "I'm relieved to see you again, Hamath. But what of the Christian fellowship?"

Hamath propped on the side of the stall. "Some have fled for the mountains while others remain in villages nearby. They're caught between the soldiers and the Jews. Many remain hidden in caves."

Barnabas looked around. "May we rest here for the night?"

Hamath grunted. "There's straw and a little grain for animals the stalls—nothing for you to eat though. Soldiers took most of the supplies."

"That's okay; we have food. Tomorrow, we will go to Seleucia and find Joseph."

The short trip to Seleucia was a sad one, as Barnabas recalled the once beautiful seaport. Now it had the markings of a ruined city with the smell of dead animals and people in the air. The soldiers had moved on to the north. However, Barnabas remained on alert as they neared the docks. He inquired as to which ship was leased to carry a large stock of animals. After receiving a few names, he proceeded in the direction given.

At one such dock, Barnabas watched as some workers helped maneuver a ship into position for tie-down. After it was secured, the crew members disembarked and walked past Barnabas and his men. Near the end of the crew, the captain set foot on the dock.

"Captain?" Barnabas asked.

"Listen," the captain said, "if you need this ship, you'll have to wait a week until me and my men check on our families."

"I was wondering if you had transported a large number of animals?"

"Yes; to Cyprus—away from the soldiers."

"That's good. I am joint-owner of the animals and I was wondering if you know where my partner might be?"

The captain rubbed his beard. "What is your name?"

"Barnabas."

"Yes, he did mention your name. He's in Salamis, looking to put the animals with the rest of your stock."

Barnabas looked relieved. "All is well."

"I wouldn't act so relieved. It's only a matter of time before the Romans search out the islands to supply their war machinery. There's a civil war going on, you know."

"Everywhere, my friend, everywhere."

"I've instructed my men that they better stay close by in case I have to get back out on the water for protection."

"Is there really protection out there?"

The captain smiled. "Their vessels may be larger, but I can maneuver this baby through some of the rocky passageways near Cyprus; it's our only place of refuge."

Barnabas pulled out his pouch of coins. "I want to go to Cyprus as quickly as you and your men will allow it. I have a few horses and donkeys east of Antioch that I want to bring with us."

The captain studied Barnabas and his pouch momentarily. "Give me three evenings. During the fifth watch of the third evening, bring your men and animals here and we will set sail before the sun rises."

Three days later

Getting the horses and donkeys to the dock was relatively easy compared to getting Hamath to go with them. When he saw the docks and the moon glistening across the sea, Hamath stopped and grunted.

"Come, Hamath," Barnabas said. "I need you on Cyprus."

"I can't swim."

"None of us can swim to the island. Remember, all the other stock made it there and so can you."

Hamath stared out over the moonlit horizon. "What if we miss the island?"

Barnabas withheld his laugh. "The captain has equipment that steers him in the right direction. You know, after a donkey has traveled a certain way for months, he begins to know instinctively where to go. The same is with the captain of the ship. Trust me and him on this, my friend."

"What if I'm too heavy?"

"Just remind yourself of the many horses that have been boarded onto the ship. So far, none of them have capsized a boat."

Hamath let out a long grunt and looked at Barnabas. "I will trust in my Jesus to get me across this water, just as the story of His walk across the Sea of Galilee." Then he looked sternly at the smiling Barnabas. "But after this is over, you'd better not mention this to anyone."

"The lips of my men and me are sealed," Barnabas said.

† † †

AD 69

"Say, 'Father.'"

"Fadder."

Petronilla smiled. "That's good, John Peter! Father." She waited. "Father."

"Fadder." He smiled and ran over to the door.

"Soon . . . Father will be home soon." She stood up and went into the area where she prepared food. The two-room house was small, but she was grateful for the Christians who gave it to them.

John Mark slowly opened the front door. He saw John Peter seated on the floor, playing with a cloth camel and horse. He got on his knees and began to make camel noises. John Peter stopped playing, turned toward his father and cried out, "Fadder, Fadder!"

John Mark reached out as his son lunged into his arms. "My son!" John Mark then wrestled his son to the floor and buried his head into his son's tummy."

John Peter let out a squeal of delight as his father tickled him. Petronilla smiled as she watched her two men play on the floor. Her only regret was that her father and mother would not see their grandchildren grow up. She gently felt her tummy, anticipating another new arrival in several months.

John Mark finally got off the floor long enough to kiss his wife. "How has Egypt's most beautiful mother felt today?"

She embraced him. "Better, now that you're home . . . And how has your day been?"

"Interesting."

"Oh? Just 'interesting'?"

"Well, it's hard to tell if my job of translating Arabic to Greek to Latin is all that beneficial sometimes."

"What? Some secret letter or code?"

"I wish; no, this was an order to arrest all Jews who meet on the Sabbath."

"What?!"

"Yes; it seems that the Jews in Judea think they have pushed Jerusalem out of the Romans' reach. You see, Vespasian withdrew his troops about a year ago when the generals were fighting for Nero's position. Now that Vespasian is the emperor, he has sent his son back to Judea to conquer the grand old city."

Petronilla looked away. "War; why can't our cultures coexist?"

"Because most of the cultures' gods do not promote peace. Only Jesus said He represented ultimate peace. Real peace comes from within a person."

"Yet so many reject our message . . . why?"

"It's a struggle within a person—two natures that war against each other. Remember Esau and Jacob?"

Petronilla returned to her dinner preparations. "So does this new order mean we are in danger now?" She turned and faced her husband. "Can John Peter and I go outside to visit the market?" She started to cry.

John Mark stepped over to her and embraced her again. "Pet, my love, nothing has changed yet. The papers have not been distributed and I do not think they will mistake us as Sabbath-worshipping Jews." He rubbed her hair and felt her tummy. "Besides, our Lord has given us another child with whom to share the gospel." John Mark kissed her again. "Remember, your father said that Jesus suffered, leaving us an example to follow in His steps."

After the dinner meal, several Egyptian couples came to John Mark and Petronilla's house for a study of the Sacred Writings.

John Mark had made some advances among the servants of the governor. Some had made decisions to follow Christ. These two couples, however, were still seeking for answers.

"Tell me again," one of the men said, "how do Christians differ from the Jews?"

John Mark explained the old covenants of the Jews and how Jesus fulfilled them with His permanent sacrifice, thus allowing eternal peace with the one true Creator God.

"How does this deliverance differ from the sacrifices we make to our Egyptian gods?"

"The Egyptian gods require numerous sacrifices every year—just as the Jews," John Mark said. "But Jesus' sacrifice was for all wrongs for all time. His bodily sacrifice as the only begotten Son of God satisfied God's wrath upon all wrongs for all time."

"But will I not continue to do wrongs?" one of the men asked.

"Yes; that is why the Spirit of Jesus remains in the life of a follower. When a true follower commits a wrong, the Spirit convicts the follower of the wrong, which leads him to confess it before Jesus through His Spirit. If a follower confesses that wrong, our Savior promises to forgive us of the wrong and clean our guilty hearts and minds of all unrighteous deeds.

"Jesus once told my father-in-law that a man may take a bath and be entirely clean. When that man walks to a neighbor's house for a fellowship meal, only his feet are wiped clean at the entrance—not his entire body. So it is when you come to Jesus for eternal washing. You are clean within; you may get dirt on your feet as you walk, but only that dirt needs daily cleaning when you come into His presence for fellowship."

The man looked at his friend and then back at John Mark. We and our wives want this eternal cleansing of our wrongs before the Creator God, We want to turn from our gods and turn to the Son of God—your Jesus—for eternal life."

The wives carefully laid their sleeping children's heads from off their laps and scooted up next to their husbands. John Mark explained that each person must make this decision from their own inner selves and that they should be baptized later, showing that they had made this commitment. The four adults agreed and accepted Jesus as their Lord and Savior.

After the others had left, Petronilla came and embraced her husband. "This is worth all the dangers and sufferings we may encounter for being Christians."

"Yes, Pet, it is. Just seeing the change of their facial expressions is worth the many times of explaining it to them."

"And the wives want to learn so much as to what pleases Jesus. I told them to come over during the day and I will teach them things from the apostles' writings."

"That will be wonderful . . . Now I must get some rest. I have some final documents to translate tomorrow. And you need your rest for Sarah's health."

Petronilla smiled. "My love, I have been thinking; perhaps we should give Sarah an Egyptian name as a secondary name."

John Mark turned toward her in the bed. "What? Why do you think that?"

"I think it may help us fit in with the locals better and allow them to see our love for our surroundings."

"I'll have to think on that . . . You mean something like Sheba or Cleopatra?"

"Yes, something like that."

"Let's pray about it some before we make a decision."

"In the morning?"

"Yes, right after our readings in the Writings, we will pray."

Petronilla smiled as she snuggled beside her husband. *Sarah, you will have a kind and compassionate father waiting for you when you are born.* Then she closed her eyes and fell asleep.

† † †

AD 70

*G*eneral Titus looked around the table. "Give me an update."

"The gates are under our control now," a centurion said, "And the walls have our soldiers guarding them."

"Then what is the problem?"

"Sir," another centurion said, "their shrine to their God is filled with fighting men. They believe they are protected inside that 'temple' of theirs."

Another centurion spoke. "They say their God will slaughter any who try to defile that place."

Titus slammed his fist onto the table and stood up. "And you believe in their superstition?!" No one responded. "I can't believe you think their one unseen God is mightier than all our gods combined!" He began walking around the table, looking into the eyes of all his leaders. "Your silence at this table can be heard across the valley and into their temple. But I am going to deafen their ears with the destruction of their famed city. Tomorrow, I want every wall—every stone!—to be crushed into powder. I want this city to be only a memory in their crazed minds. The blood of every male, female, and child will fill the streets." Titus pulled out his sword and struck it into the table. DO I MAKE MYSELF CLEAR?!"

"Yes sir!" the centurions said as they stood to their feet.

Some more leaders stood up. "Yes sir!"

Now everyone in the room was standing. "YES SIR!"

The high priest managed to squeeze past the zealots who had taken custody over the temple. Most of the council had fled the city weeks ago. Now he was left obeying the commands of the smelly defilers. *Their smell is a stench in God's nostrils!*

"Hey Rabbi," one of the zealot leaders called out. "Me and my men need more water and more meat."

The high priest would tell them to get their own supplies, but he wanted to keep these occupants out of the storage cellars, the place where the temple treasures remained secured. "I will send some priests to get more." He motioned for the priests to go downstairs. The few temple guards remaining followed them to keep the visitors out.

"Jonathan! Jonathan!" The shouts came from a watchman atop a temple steeple.

"Yes! What do you want?" The commander of the zealots turned from his study of the temple maps.

"The eastern city walls are being battered by the Romans!"

Jonathan stood up. "Signal the outer spies to give us a head count of the soldiers." He turned to several others. "Go and alert our men to focus everyone toward the eastern walls. Shower them with arrows and stones."

Two hours later, a report came to Jonathan: "Commander, our spies signal that there are four legions of Roman soldiers on the southern and eastern side of the city."

"What about the other two sides?"

"As many as before."

Jonathan looked at the maps again. "How are the men in battle?"

"Famished, sir; they haven't had but one meal in two days and barely enough water to drink."

"Why? Where are our supplies?!"

The high priest walked over to the table. "I warned you not to hold up inside the temple. Our tunnels were only intended for traffic in one direction. Your men have trampled upon each other trying to go both ways. We've spent hours pulling out the dead bodies."

Jonathan had fire in his eyes as he looked at the priest. "You want to see more dead bodies in here?" The priest shook his head slightly. "Then you'd better find us more food and water—now!"

The priest slowly turned and walked away.

A knock was heard on the temple doors. A guard looked outside and came running to the commander and whispered in his ear.

Jonathan walked over to the doors with the guard. "Open the doors."

As the doors slowly creaked open, a plume of dust was whisked inside. Jonathan walked through the doors and onto the porch. From the Court of the Gentiles, walked King Agrippa, Josephus, a dozen of the king's servants, and six Roman soldiers—all unarmed.

"We come to offer terms of surrender," Josephus said from a distance.

"STOP!" Jonathan cried. The king's entourage obeyed, as they were encircled by dozens of Jonathan's soldiers.

Agrippa stepped forward with Josephus by his side. "My fellow kinsman, I beg of you, for the love of this sacred place, tell your men to lay down their arms. If they do so, General Titus has promised to leave our temple in one piece and to spare your lives and the lives of your families."

Jonathan scraped the ground with his sandal. Then he looked up at Agrippa. "Your Majesty, I thought you were coming to announce the terms of the Romans' departure from Judea. You are supposedly *our* king, are you not?"

Agrippa looked in astonishment. "You don't understand; they have over 80,000 soldiers surrounding our city. You cannot possibly win this confrontation. Think about your family!"

"Family? The Roman soldiers killed my family several years ago when we had no more money for their emperor's building plans." He glanced at the Roman soldiers. "I think about my family every day."

Jonathan turned toward Josephus. "And you, Joseph, commander of the Galilean army; do you think of your family?"

"Every day."

"And now you side with the murderers of them?"

"Only to save what is left of our kinsmen. Jonathan, this is our only hope."

"Ha! I know how murderers treat their captives. I place no hope in their terms of surrender and you are a fool if you do." Jonathan took his foot and drew a line in the dust. "You tell your general that whoever crosses this line with their weapons drawn will feel the wrath and fury of those who battle for a cause—for the fate of our people, our land, and our God." He then turned around and walked back into the temple.

Agrippa and his entourage turned around and walked back out into the street.

One month later

General Titus stood where the western wall of Jerusalem used to stand. The city had been systematically razed to the ground, street-by-street, until now, only the temple remained standing. He turned to his centurions. "Go in and kill the remaining rebels and their priests—leave no one alive! Then check every room. Make sure all gold, silver, precious stones, or any artifacts have been removed. After that, burn it to the ground. Destroy it like the rest of this pitiful city." He mounted his horse, slowly turned around, and headed back to his headquarters.

At the evening meal, Titus and his leaders celebrated the final days of the siege of Jerusalem. There was much merriment occurring, with the exception of one lone figure. Josephus sat in a corner, writing out the story of the fall of Jerusalem.

Titus made a surprise approach to Josephus's table. "You should celebrate with us."

"They were my people."

"And I saved your life! And I offered them salvation as well, but only you and your king were smart enough to come to terms with reality."

"They believed our God would save them . . . but He didn't."

"A year ago, they were killing each other. On whose side was your God then? My father was right: give them a year and they will kill themselves. I just helped end the conflict a little earlier.

"Josephus, my father and I see value in your wisdom. You will travel back to Rome with me and there you will publish your historical works and become famous among all peoples—including your own someday." Titus lifted him up out of his chair. "But right now, you will join me in the celebration."

† † †

"Aughhhh!" Petronilla cried out.

John Mark put a cloth in her mouth, "Shhh, my love. We must be quiet."

The contraction eased momentarily. "John Mark, I can't do this on my own; I need your help."

"Okay." John Mark positioned himself. "I am ready, but keep the cloth in your mouth. There may be soldiers in the area."

Beads of sweat formed across her brow as the next contraction began. "Aughhhh," muffled through the cloth as she clamped it between her teeth. "Aughhhh!"

Soon, the cry of a baby rang out into the small room. John Mark began wiping little Sarah off and severing the cord from her mother. Petronilla lay on the bed of straw, panting for breath.

"Take her, my Pet, while I clean you up." He slowly wrapped her in cloths and handed her to her mother.

Petronilla smiled as she looked into the face of her newborn. "She's beautiful, oh so beautiful."

John Mark continued the cleaning process. "God makes no ugly babies in this family." He looked up at her and smiled.

Petronilla felt another contraction. "Aughhhh."

"What is it!? Another baby?

"No; the contractions may continue for a little while." She groaned again.

"You're still bleeding. Stay put; I need to get more cloths." John Mark stood up and went into the cooking area. He found one large cloth and brought it back. He replaced the others and put them in a pail of water to rinse. "I need some fresh water, my Pet. I must go to the well down the street. You'll be okay until I get back?"

"Yes, but hurry."

He knelt down and kissed little Sarah; then his wife. When he stood up, he looked in the corner at John Peter and smiled. "And he slept through it all. That's my boy." Then he turned and left the room.

The community well was about three houses down the narrow street. John Mark was used to people coming and going to the well. However, since the latest edict was out against the Jews, he tried to keep himself from strangers whenever possible. Tonight, however, he was not thinking of anyone who might be out. Several women were gathering water, so he patiently waited his turn. Because of his hurry, he had not put on his Egyptian outer cloak. While he waited, three soldiers walked up from behind him.

"Who are you?" a soldier asked.

"Listen, my wife isn't well and I must get some water for her."

Another soldier pulled out a small sword. "You're not going anywhere until you tell us who you are."

Before he could make another move, John Mark was surrounded by the three soldiers. "I work for Governor Narkiksias; now please let me go!"

Two of the soldiers grabbed John Mark's arms and legs. The other one raised his garment. "A Jew!"

"No! I am a Christian! Now please, I must get back to my ill wife!"

"A Jewish rebel! We've got orders from the general to bring you in, dead or alive." The soldier's sword was now pressed against John Mark's throat. "Which shall it be for you?" John Mark stopped struggling and dropped his bucket. "That's what I thought. Now tell me, Christian Jew, which house is yours? We'd like to meet your wife."

One of the other soldiers laughed. "Yeah, we want to introduce ourselves to her."

John Mark remained silent and made sure his glances did not reveal his street. "Tie his feet and arms," the lead soldier said. "Perhaps he will speak after we drag him around the area for a while."

The soldiers removed his sandals, tied his feet together, and then tied his wrists together above his head. Next they took a rope and tied it to the rope around his wrists. For an hour, the soldiers dragged John Mark through the streets, hoping he would reveal his house . . . but he didn't.

"It's getting late," the lead soldier said. "Let's walk him back to the jail. Go get our horses."

When the horses arrived, one of the soldiers tried to stand John Mark up. "Uh boss, we got a problem."

"Which is . . .?"

"The skin around his ankles and heels is gone—just blood and bones. He can't walk."

"Then put him on your horse and carry him."

"I ain't putting that mess on my horse!"

The lead soldier got on his horse. "Then drag him to the jail. I don't care how you get him there, just get him there!"

Petronilla continued to bleed. She had managed to nurse Sarah a little, but knew that something must have happened to her husband. She slowly placed Sarah next to John Peter in his straw bed. Now she limped over to the front door and looked out. It was dark. John Mark had taken the outside torch and there was only one table lamp lit inside. She looked at the lamp, but did not think she could hold it and walk. She looked outside again.

"My Lord," she prayed. "I need Your help." Although she and John Mark had been good witnesses before their neighbors, none of them had become Christians. "Lord, please send me someone."

A knock came upon her door. She slowly limped to the door. "Who is it?"

"It's Cleonna, your neighbor. I thought I heard a baby cry. Are you okay?"

Petronilla opened the door. Cleonna was holding a pail and a bundle of cloths. She smiled. When Petronilla saw her smile, she slumped to the floor and fainted.

Petronilla awoke in a dark room, alone. Her head ached and she felt weak. At first she wasn't sure if she was dreaming or if her surroundings were real. She felt her abdomen. *My baby!* "Help!" Her mouth was too dry to squeak out more than a faint whisper. She cleared her throat and tried again. "Help!" She slowly moved off the bedding and raised herself on her knees. Next, she raised a leg up to get one foot on the floor. Leaning against the wall, she managed to stand up. She felt her body to make sure of her clothing.

Petronilla slowly made her way to the door, but before she could open it, someone opened it for her. "Oh! Petronilla! You startled me!"

She recognized the voice. "Hannah?"

"Yes; please, let me help you." Hannah, a member of their local fellowship, put Petronilla's arm over her shoulder and helped her to the main room.

There she saw John Peter playing with Hannah's young son. Then she saw the little bundle. "Sarah!"

"Sit first," Hannah said. "I'll bring her to you."

Once Hannah had her seated, she hurried over to pick up Sarah and bring her to her mother.

Petronilla smiled as she gazed upon her beautiful newborn. Suddenly she remembered. "John Mark! Where is my husband?"

"Ezekiel has gone to enquire at the governor's palace. Don't be concerned; he will find your husband."

Petronilla looked toward the closed window. "It is daylight; how long have I been sleeping?"

Hannah looked over her shoulder at Sarah and smiled. "Your neighbor came to get us before daybreak. She said she was afraid to move you from your house, so Ezekiel fetched Samuel and brought you over on a gurney. I went as well to get the children and brought them over. It's about noon now."

"Noon? Oh my; Sarah must surely be hungry!"

"No need to bother; I nursed her."

"*You* nursed her?"

Hannah smiled as she held up a skin. "With goat's milk. And did she like it!"

Petronilla smiled. "I suppose she did; she received plenty of it from me for nine months." They both laughed as little Sarah moved her lips in a sucking mode. "No goat's milk this time, little princess."

†††

Ezekiel made his way through the jail cells, looking at each man. He stopped the guard. "That's him! Please open the door."

The guard looked at Ezekiel as if he wasn't going to open it. "By order of the governor himself, open the door."

"He's a Jew. We have permission to hunt down Jews."

"He's also the governor's chief translator and interpreter . . . he's not going to be happy if this man is damaged."

The guard slowly unlocked the cell door and opened it enough to allow Ezekiel in. Ezekiel quickly walked over to John Mark's still body. He first saw John Mark's raw and bleeding ankles and heels. He grabbed a handful of straw and carefully tried removing some of the soil from John Mark's ankles. When he tried, John Mark groaned and moved his legs.

"Don't move, my friend," Ezekiel whispered. He turned to the guard. "Untie his ankles and hands." The guard did not move. "Untie him now or I shall report you to the governor myself!" The guard stepped into the cell and pulled out a long, curved dagger and quickly cut the ropes. "Get me some fresh water, a cup, and some cloths."

The guard left as Ezekiel continued surveying John Mark's body. *My Lord Jesus, Your servant, John Mark, is hurt badly and has lost a lot of blood. He needs Your healing hand.*

✝✝✝

"Who cleaned me?"

Hannah smiled. "Your neighbor found her way over here and helped me remove your baby waste."

Petronilla smiled. "Thank you; and I will thank her later."

"You were very weak, but we managed to get some fluids in you—camel's broth."

"My neighbor is not a Christian."

"She told me that; but, after what the soldiers did to your husband last night, she said she and her husband want to have a faith in God as you two have."

"John Mark? She saw John Mark? Tell me, is he okay?"

"Ezekiel is checking on him now. I'm sure he'll find him and get back to us soon."

"Please tell me, what did she see happen?"

Hannah looked away. "We mustn't talk anymore now; you must rest so that Sarah will have plenty of her mother's milk."

Petronilla wanted to press Hannah for more information, but it was all she could do to keep nursing Sarah. Soon she had fallen asleep, while Sarah continued nursing.

✝✝✝

Ezekiel managed to trickle some water into John Mark's mouth. John Mark swallowed occasionally, but choked on the wet fluid more often than not. Apparently he had passed out while being dragged through the streets, because both his shoulders were rubbed raw to his collar bone. His hands were also bleeding and numerous fingers were either broken or out of joint. *This is inhumane!*

Several guards and soldiers came to the cell. "Remove this man!"

Ezekiel ignored the command. "I am here with the governor's consent."

A soldier walked into the cell, grabbed Ezekiel's arm, and raised him up and away from John Mark's body. "I don't answer to your governor, so stand back."

The guard smiled as he watched the other soldier push Ezekiel to the opposite cell wall. "Are you also a Jew? You don't look like a Jew."

"I am an Egyptian—a counselor of the governor. And be assured he will hear of your inhumane treatment of this prisoner."

The first soldier took his foot and rolled John Mark over on his back. John Mark's face was caked in mud and debris, with dried blood from every facial opening. "Inhumane? This is no human—it's a dog!" He turned to the guards. "Get this animal out of my jail and take him to the dunghill."

Ezekiel objected. "No! You can't do this. The governor needs him; STOP!"

Both soldiers pinned Ezekiel to the wall as the guards dragged John Mark out of the cell. "Tell your governor that the emperor's orders precede his. And if he wishes another dog, go fetch him a nice Egyptian one." The soldiers laughed as they threw Ezekiel to the floor and locked him in the cell.

He stood up. "Let me out!" I am not a prisoner! Let me out now!"

"We'll send the guards back once they have disposed of the animal." They laughed as they walked out of the cell area. Outside, they stopped beside the guards who were wrapping some dirty rags around John Mark's body. "Set him afire when you dispose of him. We don't need to have this one return from the dead."

† † †

When she awakened, Petronilla noticed that Sarah was once again lying on a bed of straw beside the other preschoolers. The sun was near dusk and she was propped beside a wall, still weak from having lost a lot of blood. She heard some talk outside the house, in the back yard. One voice sounded like a man's. *It's Ezekiel; perhaps he has found John Mark.*

Slowly, she raised herself up and onto her feet. Her steps were shortened as she limped toward the back door. When she stepped out, she saw Ezekiel, Hannah, Samuel, and his wife, Rachel. When they saw Petronilla, they stopped talking. Hannah and Rachel walked over to her.

"Oh, my child," Hannah said. "You should be resting! What are you doing out here?" Hannah tried to turn her around. "Come, sit with us while Rachel and I prepare the evening meal."

Petronilla would not budge. "I want to know if Ezekiel found my husband." Ezekiel looked in her direction, but said nothing. "Ezekiel, please tell me if you found John Mark."

The women released their grasp from her as Ezekiel and Samuel walked over. "My dear woman, I found John Mark in the Roman jail."

"Good; tomorrow, I wish to see him."

"Oh no, you can't; he was beaten badly. I was able to treat him for a time, but then the soldiers came and removed us."

Petronilla was upset, but she thought she misunderstood his words. "'Us'? What do you mean, Ezekiel? Did they take John Mark to another prison?"

This time Ezekiel was equally upset. "Oh, dear Petronilla, they locked me up in his stead and told the guards to dispose of his body. I was told he was taken to the dunghill and burned."

Petronilla's knees became weak and she stumbled to the ground. "No, Ezekiel!" She began sobbing. "Surely not! Ezekiel, we must find him!"

He looked at her. "They kept me locked up for three hours. I do not know where he was taken." By now, all of them were on the ground, surrounding Petronilla and weeping out loud.

Petronilla's consciousness left her again.

† † †

Barnabas and his men unloaded the horses and donkeys from the ship and proceeded to his stable near the docks in Salamis. It had always been a profitable venue for him on the island because of the many tourists who came there. However, today the streets did not seem as cheerful as before the war with the Jews. Many

Jews escaped Judea and surrounding states and came to Salamis. Groups of Roman soldiers were scattered along the thoroughfare from the docks.

Barnabas looked at his men. "Be on your best behavior men. The soldiers are looking for a reason to fight."

Hamath motioned for Barnabas to come near to him. "What if someone recognizes me? Remember, I fought off a few soldiers on the mainland just a few days ago."

Barnabas looked Hamath over. "Well, you're too big to hide." He thought for a moment. "How about you walking between two horses? We'll lead them down to the stables two-by-two and you stay by their heads."

Barnabas grabbed the reins of two horses and brought them side-by-side. "Now you hold the reins tight, in the middle, and walk them down the street . . . Follow me." Hamath did as told and began following Barnabas while the others fell in behind Hamath's two horses.

As they neared the stables, Barnabas recognized several of the keepers. "Peace to you Olegaisius and Nathan!" The men recognized his voice and returned the greeting. "How goes the business?"

"A bit cautious these past few weeks," Nathan said.

"What troubles have your concern?"

Olegaisius motioned with his eyes down the street. "Soldiers' post down by the trees. They have harassed us several times this week, saying that soon these animals will belong to them."

"Has Joseph registered a complaint?"

"Yes, he has. A few days ago, he went to the centurion and complained about the harassment."

Barnabas looked toward the trees. "And where is Joseph today?"

"He went to the governor's palace, seeking papers to protect us from the Romans."

Barnabas looked up the hillside at the governor's palace. He remembered going there many years ago and sharing the gospel with the governor. He turned to the others. "Hamath, you and the rest stay here. I'm going to find Joseph."

Barnabas registered at the gates of the governor's palace. "Have you been here before?" a guard asked.

"Yes, over a decade ago. I brought the good news of Jesus Christ to the governor back then. I was a welcomed guest and he told me I could drop in to visit him any time I was in the area."

"Remain here." The guard walked away and spoke to several more guards. One of the guards left the others and walked toward the palace. The first guard returned. "We will announce your arrival. Wait over there." The guard motioned Barnabas toward a bench under a tree by the road's edge, overlooking the city.

Barnabas stood there, looking over Salamis and the docks. He could see the stables and the grove of trees where dozens of military tents were set up. He prayed silently: *My Lord, how long will the Romans continue to scour our lands and our properties? How long will they resist Your message of deliverance and eternal salvation?* His prayer was quickly interrupted.

"Barnabas! Barnabas!"

He turned around. "Joseph!" Barnabas began walking back to the gate. The guards opened the gates and the men embraced. "Joseph, my heart rejoices to see you again."

"And so does mine, my brother." Joseph held him at arm's length. "How long has it been?"

"Too long!"

"And how did you manage to find me?"

"Oh the big fellow at the stables in Antioch."

"Hamath! Oh, the Lord bless him. Is he well? You know I tried to get him on the ship with the stock, but he would not . . . I was afraid he might be slain in the raids."

Barnabas pointed toward the city. "He's at the stables right now."

Joseph smiled. "Well praise be to our Lord! Miracles still happen."

"Joseph, the men say they are being harassed by the soldiers?"

Joseph stopped smiling. "Yes, and that is why I'm here today—trying to buy some time and, hopefully, some leverage."

"Perhaps I can help. I visited the governor over a decade ago and he was very kind to me."

"Oh, I'm afraid he was ousted about four years ago. A dispute with Nero's taxing process."

"Then how did it go with you?"

"He wants two of our finest horses and two donkeys for a paper that says we are his property."

"What! He wants our finest *and* he also wants to own us?"

Joseph looked to the ground. "I'm afraid the disease of greed is spreading throughout the empire. He said we may continue leasing the animals and pay him half of the profits, after the up-keep expenses."

Barnabas felt a surge of heat rise from his neck upwards. "Come walk with me." The two men walked away from the palace gates over to the tree. "Joseph, we cannot afford the men and ourselves with only half of the profits."

Joseph sat on the bench and faced Barnabas. "I know."

"What can we do? We lost many animals in Antioch. There aren't enough animals."

Joseph glanced over at the gate. "He doesn't know how many animals we have. I suggest we move some of the stock to another place after dark."

Barnabas lowered his voice. "This is outrageous! Must we steal our own animals?"

"It's our only hope of survival. We either do our trading in secret or become servants to the Roman governor."

"Have you agreed to do this?"

"I was negotiating with him when word of your arrival came to his ears. He gave me permission to come out here to discuss it with you."

For a few minutes, the only noise heard was from a flock of seagulls passing nearby. Barnabas looked out over the city. "Let's move half of the stock tonight. I have a small parcel of land toward the mountains. There is no stable, but there are several caves among the rock formations to shelter the animals."

"And what about the men?"

"I will explain to them the situation and see if they wish to participate."

Joseph stood up. "Then I will return inside and agree to his terms. As soon as you get there, go ahead and divide the stock in half in case they send a guard down with me. Get our half out of the stables."

Barnabas and Joseph pulled two horses and two donkeys from the stock. "These should make the governor happy," Barnabas said.

"They're our finest," Joseph remarked. "Hamath, are you and the men ready?"

Hamath looked into the moonlit sky. "Too much moon. The horses are not used to this terrain. Very risky."

"Sorry, my friend," Joseph said. "The governor did not allow for us to pick our night. Spread the animals out until you get past the Roman camp."

"Olegaisius and Nathan know where the caves are located," Barnabas said. "Allow them to lead the stock."

"Weapons?" Hamath asked.

Joseph pulled out a large canvas and unraveled it. Six long swords and a dozen daggers glistened in the moonlight. "It's all I have."

Barnabas looked at the weapons and then looked at the men. "This will not protect you from the Roman soldiers. If you are stopped by them and wish to live, you must drop your weapons. Run if you can—leave the animals." The men looked at each other. No one picked up a weapon. "Then let's gather for prayer."

The torches in front of their camp provided the soldiers with plenty of protective light. Slowly, the men walked the animals through a gulley on the opposite side of the wide road in front of the soldiers' camp. One dozen men and sixty animals walked through the gulley, using small torches covered in part by clay jars.

From the rear, Hamath herded the animals. The group was about two-thirds past the camp entrance when a snake slithered between two donkeys. Suddenly the donkeys began braying and kicking. This caused several horses to snort and whinny. Several of the men looked back at Hamath. "Go!" he said. The command was relayed to the front as all the animals picked up the pace.

Hamath looked at the camp and saw six soldiers running in their direction.

"STOP!" a soldier shouted.

Hamath took his staff and beat the rear of donkeys to keep them moving. As the soldiers neared his location, he stopped and faced them. The soldiers stopped when they saw him. Some of them drew their swords and others drew their spears. Hamath stood there and managed to show his unusual smile while pounding his staff into his palm.

"Drop your weapon," a soldier said. "Now!"

Hamath could hear the herd getting farther away.

The soldiers lined up, three in a row. They moved in closer to him. "Hey, didn't we meet in Antioch a few months ago?"

Hamath said nothing—only smiled.

"Yeah," another soldier said. "This is the man that broke the arms and legs of several of our men." Two of the soldiers came in closer. "You won't get away this time." They lunged at him with their swords and shields. Hamath easily knocked both of their swords away from his body. Then he pushed his staff into their shields and caused them both to fall onto the ground.

Two of the other four rushed in with spears, but once again Hamath was able to swing his staff and break their spears in half. But while he did that, the other two soldiers threw their spears at Hamath. One spear caught Hamath in his shoulder and the other in his thigh. He looked at the spears that had pierced him. Blood was trickling out at both wounds. He managed to grab each spear and slowly pulled them out, tearing the flesh around the entry area.

One of the first soldiers managed to retain his sword and now swung it toward Hamath. It lodged in the calf of his injured leg. Hamath maintained his stance and once again swung his staff knocking two soldiers down. He reached down and pulled the sword out of his leg. He was about to swing the sword back toward the soldier when he felt several stings in his chest. On the road stood three soldiers with bows, reloading them with more arrows.

Hamath looked at the arrows that had entered his body. This time he dropped his staff, as he reached for the arrows. But before he could grasp them, three more arrows struck him—two in his abdomen and one in his neck. He slowly fell to his knees as the soldiers surrounded him.

But when he looked up, he saw, on the road beyond the soldiers, a man in white apparel. The man smiled and lifted out His hands toward him. When Hamath saw the wounds in His hands, he smiled . . . and grunted.

†††

Joseph and Barnabas stood together in a receiving room near the governor's judgment hall. Two soldiers came to the door. "Follow us," one of the soldiers said. The four of them walked out into an open area where there was a table with a canvas covering a large item—an animal or something.

Next, the governor walked out from another entrance. He walked up on the other side of the table. "Remove the canvas," he ordered. When the soldiers pulled the canvas back, there laid the mangled remains of Hamath. Joseph and Barnabas were shocked at the sight of the body. The governor looked across the table at them. "He was a friend of yours, helping to move a large herd of horses and donkeys."

At first, neither of them spoke. "If you wish to be spared of this man's fate, you had better start answering my questions." The governor moved even closer to their faces. "Where are those animals?"

Barnabas pointed to Joseph. "This man had no involvement in the movement of my stock last night."

"Barnabas!" Joseph said.

"It's me that did this."

"And why did you?" the governor asked.

"Because they are my animals and you have no right to them. I delivered four of my finest to you."

"And how would I know you gave me the best if I cannot compare them to the rest?" He walked to the front of Joseph. "I gave you an offer that would have given you a good job and an enjoyable life on my island. And this is what I get for my offer?"

Joseph fixed his gaze upon the governor. "Your Honor, we serve another king in another empire. We dare not—we will not!—bow to your orders."

The governor backed up. "Another empire? Are you spies?"

"No," Barnabas said. "We are ambassadors of a heavenly kingdom and our king is Jesus Christ."

"And where is this 'heavenly kingdom'?"

"Within us," Barnabas continued. "And within everyone who repents of this earthly kingdom and turns to Jesus for deliverance."

The governor turned and walked back to the other side of the table. He looked down at Hamath's body. "Is this man alive now in your heavenly kingdom?"

"Yes," Joseph said. "Alive and fully clothed in a new body."

"Then, when you see him, tell him that my soldiers had the best night ever last night when they shredded his body to pieces. And let him know that I have several dozens of them searching now for the stock that you tried to hide from me." Then he motioned for the guards. "After I leave, see that these two 'ambassadors' join their friend in their kingdom." As the soldiers grabbed Barnabas and Joseph, the governor looked at them both. "And tell your King Jesus I would love to meet Him someday."

"You will," Joseph said. "Someday, you will."

"Better to meet him now in repentance and faith," Barnabas said, as the governor walked away. "Governor, it's not too late to make Jesus your king!"

The governor spoke no more and soon disappeared behind the doors he had previously entered. The soldiers removed Hamath's body from the table and tied both Joseph and Barnabas to it. Soon, two large men appeared with hatchets. When the order was given, the heads of Joseph and Barnabas were severed from their bodies. Now, they joined Hamath in the presence of their Lord.

†††

"**Y**ou wish to see me, my Lord?"

Vespasian motioned for Josephus to enter. "Yes, Josephus. Come, sit with me." He walked into the emperor's sitting room. Vespasian motioned to a servant. "Drink some good Roman wine with me."

The servant poured Josephus a cup of wine and handed it to him. "Thank you my Lord." He sipped it.

"Have you had enough provisions for your writings?"

"Yes, I have; and I have written many hours of all that has transpired throughout the empire."

Vespasian swished the wine around in his cup. "War—it's a terrible way to maintain peace." He looked at Josephus. "I hope you understand why I had to subdue your people. I'd hate for them to read from your works that I mistreated them. It might incite a future rebellion."

Josephus lowered his head. "I would not intentionally write to cause future harm, my Lord. But I trust you will allow me to write the truth."

"Truth? Isn't truth a relative term?" Josephus did not respond. "I go to war for truth and my enemy forms a battle line against me for truth—his truth versus mine! Tell me, how can one know who is fighting for truth except he who studies the foundation of the conflict? And how can my enemies know my foundation except someone tells him or he reads from the archives?"

"My Lord, I will speak from your foundation—I will tell your truth."

Vespasian stood and motioned to another servant. "That you will. And to help you, I will assign you a team of scribes who will read every line you have written and report back to me if there is any questionable 'truth'." Josephus stared at the floor. "My servant will introduce you to my scribes."

Josephus stood up. "As you wish, my Lord." He then walked out of the room with the servant.

Vespasian watched him leave. "Guards!" Quickly, two guards appeared at the door. "Bring Titus to me."

Titus had returned to Rome to parade the spoils of Judea with his father. He walked into his father's sitting room. "Yes, my Father?"

"Please sit with me for a few minutes—bring us some wine," he ordered a servant.

"Tell me, my son, how did we fare with the spoils of Judea?"

Titus smiled. "Enough to rebuild all of Rome!"

"Good. I want to first reward our soldiers who have fought for our empire. Then I want to build an arena of such might and beauty that no one would dare challenge us again. A place for all civilization to gather for games of strength."

"And we'll always be indebted to the Judeans' gold for such an arena."

"No!" Vespasian threw his cup down on the table. "They cost me years of my life in a tent. I want you to return to Judea and hunt down every Jew until there are none in Judea and surrounding areas. Bring some of them back to serve in rebuilding our city."

†††

*M*e, *using a cane?* Luke smiled. *If Paul were here, he'd
laugh.* He slowly managed his eighty-four year old
body outside to view the bay. Boeotia was as beautiful as ever.
His uncle, long since passed away, had bequeathed the properties
to Luke. But what was Luke going to do with the place? He had
no wife or children.

"Paulus?"

A servant came to Luke's side. "Yes, Master Luke?"

"Paulus, please fetch a scribe from the town. Tell him I need
a legal document drafted."

After several hours, the servant returned. Luke had fallen
asleep in his chair outside. "Master Luke, please wake up. I have
brought you a scribe from the governor's palace."

"Oh? Yes, yes. That is fine. Please bring us something to
drink."

"Master Luke?" the scribe asked. "What is it that you wish
for me to write?"

"Bonarius, is that you?"

"Yes. Do you have a new book from your God for me to
write?"

Luke smiled. "No, Bonarius, He has not given me any additional books to write. But I do thank you for the many copies you
have provided these past years.

"Today, I wish to pass my land holdings on to others."

Bonarius pulled out his quill and papyrus and laid them on
the nearby table. "If I remember correctly, you have this 200-acre
villa and a 150-acre villa near the town. Is this correct?"

Luke thought for a moment. "Yes, I believe that is correct.
Paulus, is that correct?"

Paulus stepped outside on the porch from the adjacent room. "Yes, Master Luke, that is correct."

Bonarius began writing on the papyrus. After a few minutes, he stopped. "Sir, what do you wish for this 200-acre villa?"

"I want it sold and the proceeds delivered to the Christian fellowship my uncle started in Philippi."

Bonarius continued writing. "And who will oversee this transaction?"

"Well, I do expect you to be paid your customary fees for all the transfers necessary. And, Paulus, will you deliver the proceeds to the fellowship? I'll cover your expenses."

"Yes, Master Luke, as you wish."

"Good," Bonarius said. "Now who gets the smaller villa near town?"

"Paulus."

"Yes, Master Luke?"

"No, I'm not calling you. I'm bequeathing my second villa to you."

For a moment, Paulus could not speak. "No, Master Luke, you can't mean that!"

"I do mean it. Don't you have a large family still?"

"Yes, but I—"

"And didn't they all respond to the gospel of our Lord?"

"Yes, but I—"

"Then it's settled. Bonarius, see to it that Paulus becomes the legal owner of that villa."

"Yes, Master Luke, I will draw up the documents and make copies for each recipient." Bonarius stood up, bowed, and walked away.

"Paulus, come sit with me." Paulus came over to Luke's side, but was afraid to sit down. "Come now, my friend, and please sit. I have much to say to you."

"Master Luke, I . . . I don't know what to say."

"Say nothing—just listen. These properties were gifts to me from my uncle. I did not deserve them, but they became mine nonetheless. To this day, I have used them to do our Lord's will. And what a blessing this place has been.

"For many years, my uncle and I have paid you a servant's salary. When he passed away, your salary was mainly what you and I could cultivate from the land. And yet your family continued to grow. Your family pitched in and maintained both properties in exchange for areas to grow crops and raise farm animals.

"Now it is time for you to receive the fruit of your labor."

"Oh, Master Luke, how can I thank you?"

"You already have, Paulus. My last request is for you to remain with me until I pass on to my forefathers. When this property is sold, I want you to return my body to the fellowship at Philippi. Keep enough to cover you and your family's expenses for the Philippian delivery. Do you have any questions?"

"No questions, Master Luke. Only deep gratitude to our Lord for His abounding grace."

"Yes, His grace is bountiful. Let's spend some time in prayer. And after that, would you read to me from the writings to the Hebrews? It blesses me so."

AD 82

"Who are they?" Polycarp asked Timothy.

Timothy watched from a distance. "They are Christians from another town, herded like animals into the slavery of Rome."

"What can we do?"

Timothy thought for a moment. He looked down at his once renewed legs and remembered how bold he became with his renewed strength. Now he was dependent on a cane. He looked again as the six men in chains were walking toward them. "Offer the soldiers a cup of fresh water. Perhaps they will allow us to comfort their captives."

Polycarp and several elders ran to get a bucket of water. They stood by the roadside, each with several dippers in hand and held out the water.

A soldier halted the group and grabbed the dipper, drinking the water as half of it ran off his chin. "More," he commanded. A second dip into the bucket brought forth the results Timothy had prayed for.

Several more soldiers came and grabbed the other dippers, drinking profusely from the bucket. Timothy approached the soldiers with Polycarp carrying a large basin and several cloths. "Please," the aged Timothy asked, "may we remove your sandals and refresh your feet?"

The soldier in charge looked around and then up and down the street of Ephesus. "Don't try anything stupid or I'll put you at the end of these chains and drag you to the docks."

Timothy and Polycarp smiled as they removed each soldier's combat sandals and began washing their feet. Meanwhile, a group of elders passed the dippers among the captives and wiped the blood stains from the abrasive cuts of the chains on their wrists and ankles.

The chief soldier studied the faces of Timothy and Polycarp. "Why are you doing this?"

"It pleases our God," Timothy replied.

"Which god?"

Timothy looked at the soldier. "The Creator God—the One who made heaven and earth and all living things—including you and your captives."

"More water please," the soldier said. He drank another dipper full. "Does your God fight?"

"Once, He did."

"Yes, and lost or else you wouldn't be serving me . . . lace up my sandals. Men, time to get going." He stood up as Timothy, Polycarp, and some of the elders assisted the soldiers with their sandals. "Does your God have a name?"

"He sent His Son—Jesus is His name—to die for the sins of man in order to offer peace to all those who seek Him as their Deliverer." By now everyone was standing.

"I've heard of this Jesus. Many speak of Him as a weak man, always teaching His followers to turn the other cheek when someone hits them. Is that what you teach?"

"What I and my friends have done for you now—does that make us weak? Or does it bring peace to your heart?"

"I'm not allowed to have feelings for others. We fight to maintain peace."

"The peace for which you fight brings calm throughout an empire. The peace I speak of brings calm in your heart—a calm that can last for all eternity. Jesus offers eternal peace."

The soldiers were back in place and about to leave. "I envy you," he said to Timothy and Polycarp. "I wish I had that kind of peace. But, as you can see, I have a duty to the empire. I don't have time to appease your God with good deeds."

"Our Deliverer can meet you anywhere, any time. His salvation is not based on your good deeds, but upon your willingness to turn to him in repentance and faith. Call upon Jesus for your eternal salvation."

The soldier smiled. "I'll give it some thought. And tell your Jesus that your deeds did indeed bring peace inside me. You are not weak. Now we must be gone." He motioned to the other soldiers and they left.

Polycarp smiled back as the group began walking down the street. "They're from Antioch—the captives."

"Oh?" Timothy replied.

"Yes, one of the men said they were chosen among the fellowship to surrender to the soldiers in order to go to Rome to become witnesses for Jesus."

Timothy watched the captives pass by, each one's face glowing with the love of Christ on it. "We must tell John."

John's back was now bent over. He couldn't move as fast as before, but he always managed a smile when fellow believers approached him. "Timothy! And my dear Polycarp! How blessed I am to see you. Come and sit with me and we can enjoy some refreshing water and fellowship."

"My Master," Polycarp said. "We just ministered to some fellow Christians as they were being marched to the docks."

"More captives," John said. "May our Lord give them all a peace that surpasses all understanding."

Timothy smiled. "And they had it on their faces, John—the peace of God."

"Yes? Our Lord has a way of doing that."

"They said they were chosen to be captured so that they could go to Rome as witnesses," Polycarp said.

"Oh," John said, while looking to the ground. "They're giving their physical lives in order to save men for all eternity."

"In prison?" Polycarp asked. "Why not remain free and spread the gospel throughout the land?"

"Most will," Timothy said. "But those in captivity need to be set free in their hearts."

"Yes," John said. "Listen to the wisdom of Timothy." John sat down again and drank some water. "My beloved Polycarp, you must return to Smyrna and have the fellowship pray for the captives. Timothy and I will do the same here with our Ephesian brethren."

John and Timothy walked a short distance with Polycarp and some of his elders, as they began their journey back to Smyrna. At an intersection, the group stopped, embraced each other and separated.

John watched Polycarp and his men walk away. "Our Lord continues maturing a people for His work," he said to Timothy.

"Yes, John, He does." He looked at John. "And it looks like He's done so at the right time. You and I are about run out of energy—and usefulness!"

"Ha!" John laughed. "Speak for yourself, old man!"

Timothy and John walked back a few streets. "John, here's your street. I think I'll walk over to the main thoroughfare and look at the vegetables and spices."

"Okay; peace to you my friend."

Timothy loved to walk through the market area and smell all the fruits, vegetables, and spices. As he approached the main street, there was a great commotion going on—a parade of some sorts.

"Great is Diana!" he heard the shouts. "Great is our fertility goddess!"

Timothy could not believe how people of supposed intelligence could excuse their immorality through a lifeless idol. He watched as about two dozen men marched down the street past him.

"Great is Diana! Great is our goddess of love!"

Timothy could restrain himself no more. "Great is your immorality! Great is your idolatry!"

The marching men stopped. "Who said that! Who dares blaspheme our goddess?"

"You blaspheme the Creator God with your immoral practices and idol worship."

Four of the men ran over to Timothy. "You will ask Diana for forgiveness or you will suffer the consequences."

"I have found forgiveness in my Lord Jesus Christ. And He will forgive you of this idolatry if you will repent and turn from your wicked ways."

"You call our worship wicked!?" One of the men slapped Timothy, knocking him down.

"Listen to me," Timothy said. "Jesus can release you from your inner sinful drives. You don't have to keep chanting to Diana and purchasing her harlots."

Two of the men lifted Timothy to his feet. "I think this old man needs to go with us and observe the pleasures of Diana and her servants."

"Yeah," the other one responded. "Let's give him an eye full!"

"No!" Timothy shouted. "I'll never go into that evil shrine."

As he resisted, several of the men managed to tie his hands together. Timothy, however, still had a lot of strength in his legs. He jerked back, causing two of the men to fall backwards. "Aughhh!" one them responded.

Timothy turned to run away, but the rope tied to his hands somehow got tangled up between his feet causing him to stumble and fall.

By then, four other men had grabbed the rope and dragged Timothy into the street. "Let's help him to the temple," one of them said as the others laughed. They tied him to an ox and proceeded down the street, dragging him up the hill to the temple.

When they arrived at the main entrance, the temple guards would not open the gates. "Let us in!" someone cried. "We have a sacrifice for Diana."

A guard looked at the ox and Timothy, who was still lying on the ground. "The ox can come in, but not the old man. He's too dirty and bloody—he'll defile our hallways."

The men looked at each other. "Then what can we do to give him to Diana?"

The guards turned away. "Take him to the side over there," one of them said. "Tie him to the side wall and there you may sacrifice him to her."

The men looked at each other. "Let's get this over with." So they took him to the side of the temple and began tying him up. However, his feet were raw from the dragging so that he could not stand."

"Tie ropes under his arms and lift him up onto the wall," one of them said.

Timothy was dazed from the painful trip up the hill. "My Master," he prayed. "Do not let this sin prevent them from finding You as their Savior from this cruel idolatry."

"Shut up, old man. We gave you an opportunity to walk with us. This is your own fault."

"Listen to me! Jesus has brought us together so that you may hear of His love that satisfies your every longing—more so than these harlots!" The men said nothing as they finished strapping him to the wall. "I beg of you, please turn from your wickedness and come to Jesus. He died to cleanse you of your sins and to make you complete again."

No, you listen to me," one of them said. "You will die so that we can be clean enough to go inside the temple."

"This act will only make you feel worse inside—listen to your hearts!"

The men backed away from Timothy and collected some rocks from a ditch nearby. "Great is Diana," they shouted, as they began stoning him. "Great is Diana!" Soon the rocks had done their damage and Timothy breathed his last.

John looked on as several men cut Timothy's body from the wall. He turned and walked back to the small cart that he had ridden to the site. "Take me to the proconsul's office."

The cart driver looked at John. "Master John, perhaps you should wait until we finish with Timothy's burial?"

"No! Put his body next to mine and take me over there now."

About thirty minutes later, the cart stopped in front of the city's governing offices. Several men helped John off the cart. Then they assisted him as he walked to the front gate. "I wish to speak to the proconsul."

A guard looked John over. "He's busy. Come back next week."

"Tell him the Apostle John wishes to speak to him now. He will see me."

Once again, the guard studied the face of John and then turned around. "Wait here."

A few minutes later, the gate opened and John and his helpers walked in. "Follow me," the guard said.

Flaggelan, the proconsul, sat in his judgment seat, awaiting the apostle. John was assisted into a small chair by his attendants. "You are the Apostle John?"

"Yes, your Honor."

"And what is so important that you demand to see me without due process of an appointment?"

John stood up. "Your Honor, I just watched my attendants cut down the body of my friend from the outer wall of the temple of Diana. He was stoned to death by a group of men."

Flaggelan motioned to a guard. They spoke in private. "We have no report of such an event."

"It just occurred today, your Honor."

Flaggelan stood up. "Until it is registered with the court, I cannot act upon an event based on your words. Make a formal complaint and we will look into it."

Flaggelan stepped down from his chair and was about to leave the room when John shouted: "YOU WILL STAND IN JUDGMENT IF YOU IGNORE THIS TRAGEDY!"

He stopped and turned toward John. "Listen, I don't care if you're somebody's apostle or Zeus himself. I do not judge based on hearsay. Now be gone or I'll have you locked away."

"The governor will hear from me if you ignore this!"

Flaggelan motioned for two guards to join him in front of John. They pulled their swords as they approached John. "Are you a Roman citizen?" John did not respond. Flaggelan studied him a little. "Aren't you a Judean?" Again, no response. "Listen to me, I have orders from the emperor himself to arrest and banish any and all Jews who cause trouble in my district. I think you just qualified for an arrest." He turned away from John. "Take him to a holding cell while I think about his punishment."

"Your Honor," one of John's attendants said. "He's an old man. He can be of no service to the emperor. Please, allow us to return him to his quarters."

John wanted to object but the proconsul cut him off. "I said *I* would decide. Now unless you men wish to join him and his fate, I suggest you leave immediately."

John raised his hand toward his attendants. "Go, my little children, and see to Timothy's trip to his burial grounds. I will see you again."

During the night, John was awakened by the guards and taken outside. There, a cart awaited him.

"Where are we going?"

"You are taking a little trip," a Roman soldier said. "Now get in the cart or I'll make you walk to the docks."

"The docks? You can't just move me in the night without my friends knowing it!"

The soldier smiled. "The proconsul can deal with dogs anyway he pleases—especially old ones!" The other soldiers laughed as John was pushed into the cart.

Within minutes, the cart arrived at the docks. "Get out, old man." A guard grabbed John's wrist and pulled him out of the cart.

John stood beside another man in chains. "Where are we going?" John asked the prisoner.

"Patmos," the prisoner said.

Patmos was a small mining island, used primarily to retrieve large cut stones for building projects. Many Roman slaves lived and died there. John looked at his new home from the ship. It was beautiful—too beautiful for mass banishment.

The soldiers turned John over to the local centurion. He glanced at John and back at the soldiers. "He's too old. Take him back!"

"Orders from Flaggelan—keep him here."

"I can't use a worthless old man in the mines."

"I can carry a bucket of water," John said. "And a dipper."

The centurion looked at John and then at a soldier. "Fill me a bucket with water and bring it here."

Soon John was toting a bucket of water around the centurion's office, offering everyone being processed—including the soldiers!—water to drink.

Near sundown, the centurion closed the offices and walked over to John. "I guess you think you have won special treatment today?"

"I ask for no special treatment; I'm here to serve."

"And serve you will." He motioned for a guard. "Show this man a place to sleep in the closest cave out there." Then he turned back to John. "In the morning, you will help in the kitchen. Then report back to my office for further instructions."

† † †

"There is only one master and god in this empire—me!" Domitian stood before the senate. "You will consult me before making any changes of rule for the empire."

The senate remained quiet until he left the chambers. "Tyrant," someone said. The whispers became louder within seconds.

The chief senator stood. "Men of the senate, it is of no value to the empire to dispute titles. Nothing has been said that changes our method of rule, so let us continue our duties of the state."

"And they call this Jesus their Master and God?" Domitian asked.

"Yes, *Dominus et Deus* (Lord and God)," Nerva, his advisor, said. "To them, He remains alive as a Spirit."

Domitian became angry. "And where does His Spirit reside? Surely not in Jerusalem!"

"No, *Dominus et Deus*. The Spirit of Jesus dwells in their hearts—a place, they say, where no man can remove Him."

"We shall see about that! Write a decree calling for the arrest and enslavement of all Christians. Place a day's wage as bounty for every Christian caught and turned over to a Roman camp—dead or alive!"

† † †

AD 85

*T*hough old, John managed to walk through the Roman camps and mining areas, offering water from mid-morning to late afternoon. And on the first day of each week, he held a pre-dawn worship service for any who wished to know more about Jesus. Many men came to know and confess Jesus as their Lord and Savior. John was so respected among the soldiers that he was allowed visitors from the mainland—especially from his fellowship in Ephesus.

One morning, after a pre-dawn worship service, John slipped and fell, twisting his ankle. He was taken to a camp clinic where his ankle was bandaged. "Stay off this ankle for two days," the doctor said.

"But I must do my chores each day."

"I will go to the centurion and explain your case. You stay off your feet for two days . . . Guards, see this elderly man to his quarters."

John was returned to his part of the cave where he slept at night. Only a fire in the middle and several wall torches lit the dark area. *Well, I guess I should consider this as good fortune, for it gives me an extended time for worship and prayer.* And so John began praying and singing the psalms he had memorized over the many years.

After several hours of communing with his Lord, suddenly a loud noise interrupted the quietness of the cave and the light in the room increased sevenfold! A voice thundered: "I AM! The Alpha and the Omega—the Beginning and the End! What you see, write in a book and roll it up to send to the seven churches of Asia!"

John turned around to see what was happening. He shielded his eyes against the bright light. *My Master, what is this? Brilliant, golden lampstands with candles!* John could not gaze at the brilliance of the Son of Man, so he fell on his belly as a dead man.

But then the figure touched him. "John, don't be afraid. I am the First and the Last, the Eternal-Living One—He who died and now lives forevermore. Behold! I possess the keys to death and the grave. I have come to speak to you—to unveil to you things that are and things that are yet to come. I want you to write down everything I reveal to you. Then I want you to give this revelation to the messengers of the fellowships at Ephesus, Smyrna, Pergamum, Thyatira, Sardis, Philadelphia, and Laodicea."

John rose up and looked around. There by the campfire was a stack of papyri and writing utensils. He limped over to the stack and then bowed before the figure. "Yes, my Lord. Speak and I will write all that I see and hear." For the next eight hours, John remained uninterrupted as he was carried about in the Spirit and wrote. For him, time stood still.

When it was over, the light of life glowed over John's body. Then the figure reappeared. "Just as suddenly as I appeared to you this day, so will be My return. And I will reward everyone according to their service. Behold! I am He who died and now lives forevermore. I am the Alpha and Omega—the beginning and the end. How blessed those will be who obey My commands! And cursed is anyone who tampers with the words of this prophecy. Spread this prophecy to all fellowships. And the Spirit and My fellowships—My Bride!—say 'Come!' And they who hear and thirst for the water of life, I say 'Come!' Come of your own volition—take eternal life freely!"

As the figure left the cave, John continued worshipping the Lord. A slave walked in and saw John's body glowing. He immediately ran out of the cave and found a soldier. "Help the old man! His body is on fire!"

When the soldier ran into the cave, he abruptly stopped. Then he fell on his knees. "He is not on fire, but has the glow of the gods upon his body!" The soldier backed out on his knees and then ran to get the centurion. "Sir! You must come with me to see the old man!"

When the centurion arrived, John's glow was fading. But it was enough for the centurion to see the glow of God on his body. He bowed his head and knelt. "What has happened to you, John?"

John smiled. "My Lord has come to me and has given me a book to distribute to my Christian fellowships on the mainland."

The centurion looked on the floor and saw the many pages of papyrus. "Where did you get these pages?"

"My Lord has provided all things for me."

The centurion bowed his head again. "Forgive me, John, for mistreating you. Please don't command your Lord to harm me!"

"Sir, neither my Lord nor I shall harm a single hair on your head while the day of salvation remains. I am here to proclaim His salvation and freedom from all oppressors. My Lord Jesus offers you peace from this sin-oppressed world."

"Then you must come and stay at my house! You must tell my family about Jesus!"

John looked at his foot. "I'm afraid my ankle remains sprained. Please allow me to rest one more day and then I will speak to you, your family, and all those who are in the camp."

The centurion turned to the soldier. "Run! Get a gurney and enough men to carry him to my house."

†††

Years later

"The emperor is dead!" a courier shouted as he galloped on his horse through Ephesus. "The emperor is dead and now Nerva is emperor!"

A young man ran into the house. "Master John, Domitian is dead and Nerva has taken his place!"

John raised himself from his small cot. "My child, why all the excitement?"

"Master John, you don't have to worry about the emperor anymore. Domitian's bounty for Christians is dropped!"

John thought for a moment. "Perhaps; but the evil one will never stop trying to destroy our testimony. He will either attack us from the outside or from within. We must never let our guard down."

"Yes, Master John."

"My child, could you find an elder and tell him I wish to speak to our fellowship soon?"

"Yes, Master John, I will go now and search for one." Before John could say another word, the lad ran out of the house.

John smiled as he watched the lad run. He remembered those times when he would challenge Peter to a foot race in Jerusalem. *My Lord, soon I will join Peter and the others around the throne to worship You in Your presence and in Your glory again. I am ready, My Lord.*

The fellowships in Ephesus were now six in number. When the word spread that John wished to speak, all six fellowships gathered in a field next to where John stayed. He was brought out in a gurney and placed in a large chair, under a tree.

An elder stood and read from the gospel that John had written. After that, several prayers were offered. Then there were several psalms sung, one of which John had put to music in Jerusalem. Next, all became quiet, waiting on John to speak.

"My dearly loved children, the day is soon approaching when I shall join our brothers and sisters in the throne room of our Lord and God. So I say to you, love one another as Jesus loves you. Hate no one, for God is love. Keep His commands ever before you—every day! Live in the true light of His words.

"Remember that your sins are forgiven because He died for you. When you sin, confess it right away, for the Just One will faithfully forgive you right away and purge you of all unrighteousness by His mercy.

"Do not be deceived by the charms of this world. The great deceiver of our Lord will try to turn you away from Christ through this world's charms. Use your anointing from Him to expose all forms of darkness. Let His truth keep you holy and separated from the world. If you abide in Him, His word will abide in you.

"If you maintain His abiding presence, the world will always hate you because His presence in you will expose the dark deeds of the world—even among your fellowships! Listen to me and discern the spirits to see if they are from our Lord. In the last hour, many deceivers will prowl throughout the world and will try to overtake your fellowships. But you!—be overcomers! For He who resides in you is greater than all the deceivers put together—far greater than the Evil One himself!

"Proclaim Jesus Christ as the Son of God. That message will reveal to you if Christ abides in a person. And the message of Christ dying on a cross will purify the love of God in your fellowships. This message will reveal the true followers of Jesus, the God and Savior who gives eternal life."

John pulled himself up out of his chair. Tears were trickling across his cheeks. "My little children, I must leave you soon. Be faithful to the end. Take His words and let the Holy Spirit reveal His truth through His words. Be careful to copy His words and spread it through all lands. Create and support fellowships wherever you go and proclaim His words. And let His love dwell in your hearts always. Amen."

John sat down. An elder came to him and gave him a clean cloth to wipe his tears. Then he embraced John. Soon, a long line of people stood before John, each person wanting to embrace him.

After about an hour, John asked to be taken back to his small cot in the front room of the house. Once inside, he refreshed himself with some juice and bread. Then he lay down to sleep, for his message had worn him out.

During the night, John was awakened by a voice. He thought he was dreaming, but when he opened his eyes he saw Jesus standing, in all His glory. John closed his eyes. "My Master, forgive me, for I am too weak to bow before you!

Jesus spoke to him: "My dearly loved one, you have walked with Me for a long time on this earth and I have so enjoyed our time together here. But it's time for you to come and enjoy My presence like never before."

And John fell asleep and did not awaken in his flesh anymore, for Jesus took him home.

Bibliography

The Scriptures used in this series are paraphrased by the author. Any similarity with any copyrighted editions of Scriptures is purely accidental. The author has consulted the following works:

Baker, Simon. *Ancient Rome – The Rise and Fall of an Empire* (Croydon: BBC Books, an imprint of Ebury Publishing, 2006)

Blond, Anthony. *A Brief History of The Private Lives of The Roman Emperors* (London: Constable & Robinson Ltd. 1994)

Complete Word Study New Testament with Parallel Greek, by Spiros Zodhiates, ed. (Chattanooga: AMG Publishers, 1992)

Chronological Bible, Edward Reese, ed. (Nashville: Regal Publishers, 1977)

Gibbon, Edward. *The History of the Decline and Fall of the Roman Empire: Abridged Edition* (London: Penguin Books, 2000)

Green, Bernard. *Christianity in Ancient Rome: The First Three Centuries* (New York: T & T Clark International, 2010)

Interlinear Bible, Greek / English, Volume IV, New Testament, Jay P. Green, Sr., ed. (Hendrickson Publishers, 1985)

Jones, Timothy Paul. *Bible Time Line: Genesis to Revelation – 2200 BC-AD 100* (Torrance, CA: Rose Publishing, Inc. 2001)

Kerrigan, Michael. *Dark History of the Roman Empire – From Julius Caesar to the Fall of Rome* (London: Amber Books Ltd., 2008)

Liberty Annotated Study Bible, King James Version, Jerry Falwell, ed. (Lynchburg: Liberty University, 1988)

New King James Version (Nashville: Thomas Nelson, Inc., 1982)

Novak, Ralph Martin, Jr. *Christianity and the Roman Empire: Background Texts* (Harrisburg, PA: Trinity Press International, 2001)

Sterling, John. *An Atlas Illustrating the Acts of the Apostles and the Epistles* (London: George Philip & Son Ltd., 1954)

White, L. Michael. *From Jesus to Christianity – How Four Generations of Visionaries & Storytellers Created the New Testament and Christian Faith* (San Francisco: Harper Collins Publishers, 2004)

Ziffer, Walter. *The Birth of Christianity from the Matrix of Judaism* (Bloomington, IN: Author House Publishers, 2006)

Internet sites consulted:
en.wikipedia.org/wiki/List_of_High_Priests_of_Israel;
freebeginning.com/new_testament_dates/index.html;
generationword.com/bible_school_notes/Timeline;
and *bible.ca/maps/*

About the Author

Johnnie R. Jones was saved in Hawaii in 1971. He was licensed to preach in 1974 and ordained in 1976. He has pastored churches in Virginia, Alaska, and Texas. He is a graduate of Tunstall High School, Dry Fork, Virginia; Dallas Baptist University, Dallas, Texas; and Southwestern Baptist Theological Seminary, Fort Worth, Texas. After high school, Johnnie served four years in the U.S. Air Force.

Johnnie has written articles for several magazines and daily newspapers. He is chief editor and publicist for SYD Publications, McKinney, Texas. He has authored eleven books and booklets.

Johnnie is currently founder and revivalist of His Abounding Grace Ministries, Inc., McKinney, Texas. This is volume three of a series of novels based on the first century A.D.

Contact Information

His Abounding Grace Ministries, Inc. (501c3 nonprofit)

Website: www.HisAboundingGrace.org
Email: jj@HisAboundingGrace.org

About the Acts Novel Series

There is no literary work greater than the Holy Bible. Whether you read in the Hebrew Bible (called the Old Testament by Christians) or the New Testament, you will find a God who consistently works among people to bring holy living, justice, and peace. Specifically, in the New Testament you will find the Creator God presenting a solution to mankind's fundamental need of deliverance from its sin nature—that part of mankind that is egotistically self-serving.

In *Acts of the Spirit-Filled*, you will experience the passion, drama, and results of first-century people who choose between good and evil. You will discover how God provided them with a solution to their basic need of deliverance. The timing and scenes of *Acts of the Spirit-Filled* are from the Book of Acts of the New Testament. If you have read this particular book in your Bible, you know there are many gaps surrounding many of the events that occur. For the most part, we have to use our imaginations as to what led to certain events, trips, and crises of the early followers.

Acts of the Spirit-Filled fills in many of the gaps in the Book of Acts with fictional dialog, narration, and historical events that allow the reader to experience the emotions and drama of the New Testament characters who participated in the birth of the church.

The *Acts of the Spirit-Filled* series is comprised of three volumes. Volume One covers the events of Acts, Chapters 1-12; Volume Two covers Acts, Chapters 12-24; and Volume Three covers Acts, Chapters 25-28, plus historical events that lead up to the end of the first century.

Other books by this Author

Acts of the Spirit-Filled: Volume 1

Martyrdom. Fraud.
Stoning. Beheading.
Miracles. The early church
experienced it all!

© 2013; 322 pages

In his dramatic novel, *Acts of the Spirit-Filled*, Johnnie R. Jones helps the reader envision how common, oppressed people became empowered by God's Spirit and turned their world upside down with a powerful Gospel. Interweaving fictional dialogue, narration, and historic events, Jones paints a graphic picture of the struggles, trials, and passions that propelled Christianity forward during a dark and dangerous time.

This theatrical account of the early church is the first volume in Jones' Acts series and is based on events described in Chapters 1-12 of the New Testament Book of Acts.

The *Acts of the Spirit-Filled* series is available in paperback and eBook editions at **www.HisAboundingGrace.org** and **www.crosshousebooks.com**.

Acts of the Spirit-Filled: Volume 2

© 2013; 397 pages

In the days of the early Christian church, new believers faced opposition from both the religious pluralism of the Roman Empire and the traditional monotheistic religion of the Jews. This resulted in a violent intolerance toward the budding Christian faith.

In this second volume of the Acts of the Spirit-Filled novel series, Johnnie R. Jones brings to life a sometimes-incredible story of spiritual fire through prisons, demons, and bloodthirsty oppositions from religious and city leaders—all based on real events documented in the Bible's Book of Acts.

This theatrical account of the early church is the second volume in Jones' Acts series and is based on events described in Chapters 12-24 of the New Testament Book of Acts.

The *Acts of the Spirit-Filled* series is available in paperback and eBook editions at **www.HisAboundingGrace.org** and **www.crosshousebooks.com**.

50/50 Chance to Live

SECOND EDTION

© 2009; 2012; 350 pages

100+ pictures

From Virginia to Texas to Hawaii and Alaska follow the tracks of one man's trail that slipped through the grips of death five times, while touching the lives of thousands.

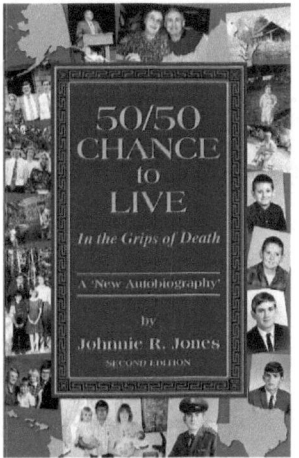

Order online at: www.HisAboundingGrace.org

"Here is the story of a man and his family who have walked through difficulties as severe as anyone can face . . ."
–Dr. Paige Patterson, President,
Southwestern Baptist Theological Seminary

". . . an outstanding journal of one man's triumph over seemingly impossible circumstances. It is a must-read!"
–Dr. Jimmy Draper, President Emeritus,
LifeWay Christian Resources

Transformed!
The Power of God's Presence

Solid, biblically-based principles for spiritual growth!

There's more to a marriage than the wedding day! And there's more to the Christian life than the first day of salvation! Discover the beauty of a transformed life in Jesus Christ. It's called the "new and living way" of reaching your potential through an intimate, maturing relationship with Him.

Children's Guide to Discovering Jesus

Interactive pages filled with puzzles, pictures, and Bible verses that a parent, children's leader, or elementary to middle school children can use to help them discover what it means to become a Christian. Covers baptism and Christian growth as well.

8½ x 11 – 10 activity pages

Diakonos – Deacon
A Word Study and Service Guide for the Deacon Ministry

For individual or group study, seeking the biblical foundation for a servant-based ministry

8½ x 11 – 50 pages

διακονοσ

Diakonos

A Word Study
and
Service Guide
for the
Deacon Ministry

For Individual or Group Study
for Pastors, Deacons, & Anyone
Seeking Biblical Foundations
for Ministry

by
Johnnie R. Jones

One Reader Comments: *"Wow! It is rich with information. I wish every church would make it required reading for all deacons."*

P.E.D.A.L. Plan for
Evangelism & Discipleship

P.E.D.A.L. Plan
for Evangelism
& Discipleship

Using a Simple and Effective Plan
for Personal Witnessing and
Discipleship

Non-Confrontational and
No Memorization Required

Johnnie R. Jones

Be a Powerful Witness . . .
in Personal Prayers.

It's non-confrontational
and no memorization required!

Online Orders: **www.HisAboundingGrace.org**